MW01353100

MEIR (MARCUS) LEHMANN

AKIVA

The Story of Rabbi Akiva and His Times

translated by
PEARLY ZUCKER

FELDHEIM PUBLISHERS
JERUSALEM NEW YORK

Library of Congress Cataloging-in-Publication Data

Lehmann, Marcus, 1831-1890

[Akiba. English]

Akiva : the story of Rabbi Akiva and his times / Meir (Marcus) Lehmann; adapted from the German by Pearl Zucker.

p. cm.

ISBN 1-58330-602-1

1. Akiba ben Joseph, ca. 50-ca. 132—Fiction. I. Zucker, Pearl. II. Title.

PT2623.E324A7 2003

833'.8—dc21 2003048306

First published 2003

ISBN 1-58330-602-1

FELDHEIM PUBLISHERS
POB 35002 / Jerusalem, Israel

208 Airport Executive Park
Nanuet, NY 10954

www.feldheim.com

10 9 8 7 6 5 4 3 2 1

Printed in Israel

A Tribute to the Author

RAV MEIR (MARCUS) LEHMANN *zt"l*, the remarkable, talented, and prolific Rav of nineteenth-century Germany [1831–1890] remains famous for his scholarly works and for his unique adaptation of the secular to serve our Creator. He was the prototype of a new generation of Jewish leaders who stopped the advancing destructive forces of assimilation. Like a military chief-of-staff, he approached his objectives on many fronts.

As a young Rabbi in Mainz, whom the Reformers wanted to "run out of town," he eloquently presented the case of his fledgling Orthodox community to high government commissions, using formal German and Latin to impress the review boards. This led to a historical granting of the right to run their own Orthodox *kehillah*, and the right to secession from the official Jewish community which had been taken over by the Reformers.

Rav Lehmann was instrumental in establishing and guiding a new type of local institution — a boy's and a girl's Yeshiva. In the 1850s, such schools were almost non-existent.

Rav Lehmann's personal guidance was sought by many, who journeyed from near and far to hear his wise advice. For example, a troubled woman from Amsterdam once traveled for several days by horse-drawn carriage and primitive, slow trains to the Rav of Mainz to discuss a serious family problem.

A Torah scholar who had studied at yeshivos in Prague, Halberstadt, and Berlin, Rav Lehmann made available to the public the earliest extant commentary on the Talmud Yerushalmi, written by Moreinu HaRav Shlomo Sirilio, a survivor of the Spanish expulsion of 1492. Hitherto available only in manuscript at the British Museum, Rav Lehmann published R.

מסכת

ברכות

תלמוד ירושלמי

עם פירוש נפלא

מרבנו מוהר״ר שלמה בכר יוסף סיריליאו ממגורשי ספרד

(חי בסוף מאה השלישית מאלף החמישי)

הירושלמי עם הפירוש יחדיו תמים נמצאו בכתובים בעה״ק ירושלם תובב״א

יצא ראשונה לאורות, עם הערות, בשם „מאיר נתיב״ נקראות

מסני

מאיר (דר.) לעהמאנן

שומר משמרת הקדש בעדת בית ישראל פה

מגנצא

הוגה ונדפס על ידי יחיאל בריל

בשנת ה תרל״ה לילירה

פערלאג פאן י. קויפמאנן אין פראנקפורט אם מאין

Druck von J. Bril in Mainz

Sirilio's commentary on *Berachos* in 1875 together with his own scholarly *perush*, called *Meir Nesiv*. Glowing approbations came from many contemporary Torah giants, including Rabbi Shimon Sofer, the Malbim, the Netziv, Rabbi Ezriel Hildesheimer, and others.

Rav Lehmann received Rabbinical ordination from HaRav Shlomo Yehuda Leib Cohen Rappaport, Rav and Rosh Beis Din of Prague, in 1852. He also received a PhD in Philosophy from the University of Berlin. Thus he had attained the perfect prerequisites for authoring the numerous inspiring historical novels which he wrote over a 23-year period. Carefully researched and based on the Talmud, Midrash, and on more recent Jewish sources, records, and archives, they all became bestsellers and were translated into Yiddish, Russian, English, Hebrew, French, and other languages.

Rav Lehmann proved to be as familiar with the details of Jewish life in ancient times and places as he was with contemporary Jewish life in Germany. Replete with historical detail and inspiring Jewish heroes, his wonderful stories featured Rabbi Akiva, Rabbeinu Gershon, the Crusades, the Spanish Inquisition, a Jewish Pope, the Protestant Reformation, the daughter of the Shach, and more. His youngest son Yonah, in an endearing biography, describes his father's underlying motivation for these stories:

> It was not from artistic principles that he embarked; it was not that fascinating material gripped him, nor great characters whom he felt compelled to portray. His art of storytelling had only one professed purpose, namely, to show how a life in accordance with the Torah brings happiness in this world and hope in the World of Souls.

In 1860, Rav Lehmann became the publisher and editor of *Der Israelit*, the first weekly Jewish newspaper in Germany, in which his novels were serialized. His son recalls:

> I can still remember how as a youth I read these stories with burning checks and a beating heart. When they would appear in installments in *Der Israelit*, I could hardly wait to discover the next phase in the plot. Countless thousands of readers felt the same. In our youth, we laughed and wept with his heroes and heroines and chose them as our models. Neither the argumentative editorials that engaged the adversaries and, in a logical manner, sharply refuted their views, nor the simply written but often extremely profound expositions of Jewish learning had as wide and powerful an effect as his stories.

There were subscribers from every place where Orthodox Jews lived — from America, Russia, many European countries, Eretz Yisrael, and North Africa. His newspaper kept observant Jews informed of each other and served as a medium for confronting the problems caused by Reformers and assimilationists. Yonah Lehmann wrote the following on his father's innovative weekly:

> The leading article, written in a simple and intelligible but nevertheless stylistically distinguished manner, dealt with all contemporary questions affecting Judaism. When there was little to dispute or to combat, the learned Rabbi was most content: he would then provide his readers with stimulating discussions and explanations derived from old Jewish texts. Many a Rabbi used these editorials as bases for sermons; indeed, in the small communities without Rabbis of their own, these simplified expositions of learned themes were recited from the *bimah* [in the synagogue] and served as substitutes for discourses. Everywhere he managed to secure contributing correspondents so that he was in a position to inform his readers with the utmost speed about every significant development of interest to Jews.

Today, some one hundred and forty years later, Rav Meir Lehmann's efforts are still bearing fruit. His works remain relevant and very popular. Much credit goes to Feldheim Publishers for continuing his legacy and producing clear, accurate, and enjoyable translations.

Osher Lehmann
[fourth-generation
descendant of the author]

Akiva

AKIVA WAS RAV Meir (Marcus) Lehmann's magnum opus, culminating years of research. The Talmud and Midrashim were his prime sources as he labored on his works in the capacity of sleuth and historian.

He adapted every scrap and piece of relevant information in order to author this magnificent and detailed account of the life of Rabbi Akiva. It is a classic literary tapestry woven with the details of life in Eretz Yisrael after the Destruction of the Second Temple, colorfully portraying his contemporaries from Rome, Greece, and Egypt, and embroidered with poignant *divrei Torah*.

Akiva was originally published in the year 1881, in Mainz, Germany, as part of the author's German language Jewish weekly newsletter, *Der Israelit*. It was serialized and each week another chapter, steeped with the words of our Sages and the glory of our history, was mailed to local and international subscribers.

Following Rabbi Akiva's life as he developed from a humble shepherd into the leader of his generation is inspiring, edifying, and fascinating. Moreover, this book provides the reader with an additional dimension when studying Talmud!

In 1956, this story of Rabbi Akiva's life was first translated into English by Joseph Leftwich, under the sponsorship of the Keren HaTorah Committee of Great Britain.

Feldheim Publishers has now produced a superb new edition of *Akiva*, newly translated and revised. R' Yaakov Feldheim, his talented translator Pearly Zucker, and his professional editorial, design, and production staff in Jerusalem deserve our accolades for making this unique edition available to contemporary English readers.

This project was undertaken through the generosity of fourth-generation descendants of the author.

O.L.
New York
Sivan 5763
June 2003

Translator's Note

TRANSLATING A TEXT means connecting to the core of what the author is saying and then conveying it in another language. With R' Marcus Lehmann's work *Akiva*, this task was challenging and rewarding. It was challenging in the sense that his rich language was difficult at times to capture in English, which is so much more concise than German. It was rewarding, for in his creative, engaging style Rabbi Lehmann draws you into the world he describes, in a very vivid way.

The world of Rabbi Akiva's times is a fascinating world, filled with glory and tragedy. Learning about the overwhelming spiritual accomplishments people achieved in those days is humbling and inspiring. Where else do we find a more powerful manifestation of human potential than in the story of Rabbi Akiva? Dealing with this era and almost living in it for a little while was a wonderful experience. I would like to thank R' Yaakov Feldheim for this unique opportunity.

Many thanks to Mrs. Karen Paritzky for all her help and support.

* * *

I would like to dedicate this book to my father, who in his great ambition and drive is a role model to all of us, and to my mother, who has always assisted and encouraged me in all my endeavors.

Pearly Zucker

Chapter 1

Jerusalem was destroyed and the Holy Temple was burned to ashes. Judea lay in a state of desolation and misery. The earth was covered with the blood of the slain. Thousands of the finest people had been sold as slaves or sent to fight against wild beasts in the arena, providing the bloodthirsty Romans with gruesome spectacles for their entertainment. It seemed as though Judea's very soul might soon expire. At the same time, however, the seed that was to bring future recovery and eternal sustenance had already been planted. And although it was hardly noticeable, it was destined to grow strong roots and to flourish.

Rabban Yochanan ben Zakkai, the great teacher of Israel, had foreseen the destruction of the Holy City. He had warned his fellow Jews and pleaded with them to seek peace with the Romans and to subjugate themselves to their rule, but to no avail. The city's zealous fighting men insisted that they would rather suffer defeat and even death than bear the yoke of oppression under the Romans. Then Rabban Yochanan arranged for a rumor to be spread that he had died. His disciples Rabbi Eliezer ben Hurkanos and Rabbi Yehoshua ben Chananyah placed him on a funeral bier and carried it to the city gates at nighttime. "We would like to bury this dead body outside the city," they told the guards, who let them pass without any questioning.

Rabban Yochanan went straight to the Roman encampment and asked to see the commanding general, Vespasian. "Hail to you, Roman Emperor!" the Sage called out to him.

Vespasian replied, "If the Emperor hears that, he will kill both of us."

"And nevertheless I say that Vespasian is now the Roman Emperor!" Rabban Yochanan stated. "In only a short while you will conquer Jerusalem and the Holy Temple, both of which can come to pass only if the Almighty wills it, as the Prophet Yeshayahu has foretold."

And lo and behold, as the two were speaking, horsemen came riding up at great speed, and called out: "Hail to our Emperor Vespasian! The old Emperor is dead, and our people and the Senate have chosen the glorious General Vespasian to become our new Emperor!"

Now the new Emperor was quite charmed by Rabban Yochanan ben Zakkai, and he told him that he would grant him whatever he wished. Rabban Yochanan asked for permission to build a *beis midrash* in Yavneh, so that he could teach and study Torah in peace. The Emperor granted him his modest request, and amidst all the travails of war, Rabban Yochanan moved to Yavneh with his disciples to initiate his new undertaking.

And there he sat, like the high priest Eli once had, anxiously waiting to see what would happen to the Holy Temple. When he and his disciples heard the tragic news that Jerusalem had fallen and the Temple had been destroyed, they tore their clothing in grief, and sat down on the ground, and wept. They sat mourning and lamenting for a long time, until Rabban Yochanan gathered his strength and began to console the others.

"It is our task," he told them, "to ensure the future of Israel. Although it seems that we have lost everything, our most precious gem still remains with us: our holy Torah. The Torah is the source of our life and our guarantee for better times to come. Let us not be overcome by pain and sorrow. Let us draw strength from our Torah. We must continue to live our lives and pass on to our children the inheritance of our fathers."

And so Rabban Yochanan ben Zakkai and his followers quietly devoted themselves to the worship of God and the study of Torah, thereby creating a fortress for themselves and for their people, so that the scattered and persecuted flock would find refuge and shelter there from the pursuing wolves.

Although Jerusalem and the Temple were destroyed, the curse that was cast upon the land — that the earth no longer give forth its fruit and that long stretches of land lie desolate and barren — had not yet taken effect. "There is a magnificent landscape at the lake of Kinneret," wrote Josephus. "The rich soil is planted with various kinds of fruit trees and the mild climate accommodates all of them beautifully. Walnuts, which take well to cool air, grow here in boundless amounts. So do date plants, which require heat, and figs and olives, which thrive in a milder climate. One is tempted to call it a competition within nature — so wondrous is it that such diversity can coexist in one and the same setting. Not only does the soil nurture all these different fruits so miraculously, but it also maintains them for a long time. Grapes and figs ripen for ten months continuously, whereas the other fruits take turns throughout the year."

It was in this fertile area that a wealthy man by the name of Kalba Savua lived. His splendid mansion was surrounded by vineyards, olive trees, date palms, and many fields. He also owned large flocks of sheep, which his shepherds took all the way down to the meadows along the banks of the Jordan River, for grazing. Kalba Savua had also owned a house in Jerusalem, and during Vespasian's siege of the city he had been one of the three men who supplied the whole city with provisions for years. But then the zealots had burned down the storehouses, in order to provoke the people to wage war against the Romans.

Kalba Savua was in deep mourning over the tragic fate of the Holy City. He had been forced to pay the Romans a large sum of money in order to avoid being outlawed, and then he withdrew to his country home. There he was occupied with running the estate and supervising the cultivation of his fields, orchards, and vineyards. His wife had passed away and he had only one daughter, Rachel, who was to inherit all his wealth. Like Rachel Immenu, she was beautiful in her appearance, but even more beautiful and striking was her keen mind, and more precious than all her father's wealth was the good heart she possessed.

It was at this time that Kalba Savua was looking for a supervisor to oversee the shepherds and take charge of his herds and flocks, as well as other affairs of the estate. It was impossible for him to do all this himself, and as he had no son of his own to stand at his side and assist him, he was forced to look for a stranger. And it was this stranger whom he would entrust with, among everything else, the task of dealing with the disloyalty of his servants, which had been troubling him lately. Several candidates had been suggested to him, but none of them seemed trustworthy enough. Then one day a young man showed up at his door with a recommendation from Kalba Savua's neighbor, Hurkanos.

Kalba Savua invited him in, and after reading the recommendation, he addressed the young man, who stood humbly before him, "My neighbor praises you for being loyal, hard-working, and honest. Also appealing to me is your apparent physical strength, which suggests that you have the power and ability to work efficiently. What is your name?"

"My name is Akiva. My father's name was Yosef and my grandfather's was Yehoshua. We are descendants of a noble heathen family. Sisera, who was the general of King Yavin of Chatzor and was killed by Yael, was our ancestor. My grandfather came to Jerusalem with Queen Helena and the family converted to Judaism. My parents lost all their possessions, and at the time of the destruction of Jerusalem they were killed. Therefore I must earn my livelihood by offering my services to others."

"And what compensation do you ask for your work?"

At that moment Rachel entered the room, and when Akiva saw her, he thought to himself: "Oh, if only I could answer as our forefather Ya'akov once did: *I will work for you for seven years for your daughter Rachel*!"

Rachel wondered who the stranger was, but did not ask. She turned to her father. "I wanted to let you know, Father, that Papus ben Yehudah, the guest you were expecting, has arrived."

"Please show him to his room, my daughter, and see to it that he gets everything he needs for his comfort. Also tell the servants to prepare a sumptuous meal for him. Please give him my warm regards and my apologies that I cannot receive him right now. I will come to his room later to welcome him."

Rachel nodded and left the room.

"Papus is the son of my childhood friend," Kalba Savua explained to his visitor. "I have him in mind for my daughter, assuming of course that the young people take a liking to each other. And now, Akiva, tell me under what conditions you would be willing to work for me."

"Why should I demand conditions from you, my master? I will ask you to pay me according to the value of my labor. I am certain that you will not underpay me."

"I like you!" Kalba Savua replied. "And I am appointing you as supervisor over all my shepherds. You will see to it that they choose the right meadows for grazing, and that they do not steal or misappropriate anything. You will also see to it that the shearing of the sheep takes place at the most opportune time and that the wool is promptly delivered to my storage house. You will also be in charge of selling those animals that are fit for sale and putting aside other animals for household consumption. Are you familiar with the Halachah in these matters?"

"No, my master. All I know about Judaism is what I have heard from others concerning the history of our nation. I was never encouraged to learn. And why should I become involved with it? All those great Sages together were not able to save the Holy City from destruction!"

"Do not speak like that! The Sages were not responsible for the fate of the Holy City. I see that you are not learned. If you were, I would have put you in charge of the slaughtering work as well. But right now that's out of the question. Follow me — I will introduce you to my servants."

Chapter 2

Kalba Savua had arranged a lavish meal in honor of his guest, Papus, whom he hoped would soon become his son-in-law. He invited several friends from the area. Rachel was the hostess. It was not long before the lively table discussion turned to the great national tragedy.

"What will become of Judea," Kalba Savua asked with a sigh, "now that the Holy Temple lies buried in ashes? The best and most distinguished of our people — the priests, the scholars, the leaders — were either killed or sold as slaves. There are heartbreaking reports about the fate of our brothers and sisters who were taken away! I have heard that four hundred noble young men and four hundred noble young women who were being taken to Rome to become slaves of the immoral Romans decided instead to seek death in the waves of the sea. The heroes of our nation are being forced to fight against ferocious animals in Rome, just to provide the savage mob with a bloody spectacle to watch. And those of us who remain in Judea have been left defenseless, at the mercy of the Romans! What will be? When will our suffering come to an end?"

"We ourselves," Papus said, "are to be blamed for all this suffering."

"That's true," agreed Hurkanos, Kalba Savua's neighbor. "God has punished us for our sins."

"That's not what I meant!" exclaimed Papus. "When I say that we are to be blamed for our misfortune, I mean that we are wrong for wanting to be different from the other nations. Perhaps the destruction of the Temple was good for us, if it forces us to give up all our peculiarities. The Jewish State no longer exists. We no longer have a Jewish king or a High Priest. We must therefore try to merge with the Roman Empire."

"Are you saying that we should worship idols?" cried Kalba Savua.

"Of course not! I despise the gods of Edom, and I would rather die than throw a stone in homage to Mercury, as their foolish practice prescribes. But there are other things, thousands of them, that set us apart, which I say we should give up. We must hold on to our belief in One God, but otherwise we must become Romans!"

There was an unpleasant, painful silence. It seemed as though no one quite understood what Papus was trying to say, and therefore no one responded. At that moment Rachel spoke: "Allow me, dear guest and friend of my father, to differ with you. I am but an uneducated girl and it is not befitting for me to speak in the presence of learned men. But since I see that no one is responding to your words, I feel compelled to express my thoughts on the matter.

"You, Papus, demand that the People of Israel give up all our 'peculiarities' and dissolve into the stream of nations surrounding us — Heaven forbid! Neither the destruction of the Temple nor the weakening of national bonds can destroy Israel's future. We have always been, and always will be, God's people, whom He redeemed from Egypt — descendants of Avraham, His devout follower, descendants of Yitzchak, who was willing to sacrifice his life for God, and descendants of Ya'akov, whom God chose over Esav. And although Rome may have taken everything from us, one thing remains: God's Torah, which will always be with us. And now that our Temple lies in ruins and we can no longer bring sacrifices to atone for our sins, we must embrace the Torah even more strongly and with even more devotion.

"Why should we abandon the eternal life that God has planted within us and lose ourselves among the nations around us? How could we exchange the great virtues and teachings God has bestowed upon us for the immorality and weakness of the heathens? And although we are at fault for the loss of our Temple, that does not mean we have lost our special status as God's Chosen Nation! If we remain loyal to our Father in Heaven, He will surely bring us a happier future.

"Was the Temple not destroyed once before? And then things were worse than now! The mighty ruler Nevuchadnetzar violently drove our forefathers away from this land, and the few who were allowed to stay behind had to flee soon after. Judea lay desolate at the time, until once again God, through His great compassion, brought us back here. And who saved Israel at that time? Was it those priests and prophets who had abandoned Judaism? No, it was the loyal guardians of our tradition — Zerubavel, Ezra, Nechemyah, and their companions. We too will live to see our future redemption if only we guard God's Torah carefully and follow its holy guidelines strictly."

Kalba Savua looked at his daughter with great pride as she spoke.

Then Papus spoke up. "I see you are very enthusiastic," he commented, "about a branch of learning from which your gender is excluded!"

"Although I am not allowed to devote myself to the study of the Oral Law," Rachel replied, "it is surely the women who have the vital task of encouraging men in their study and preparing their children for it as well."

"I am afraid," Papus said, "that you are living in a world of fantasy. The Roman Empire is different from that of Nevuchadnetzar. The Romans acquired their cultivation of the arts and the sciences from the Greeks. Their philosophers despise the worship of idols, just as we do. Plato and Aristotle did not believe in the gods of Olympus. Only if one is open to the sophisticated truths of these great thinkers can one find one's way in every situation life may bring. Only then can a person truly be free — when he is able to distinguish between the outer surface of things and their true essence. Therefore I maintain that our people should keep only the nucleus of our faith, which is the belief in One God. Other than that, let everyone do and think whatever suits the circumstances best."

"And do you think," asked Rachel, "that the belief in One God could be maintained and could still preserve us as the people of God, without His laws?"

"Rachel is right," Hurkanos said. "We Jews must remain Jews. And when one generation turns away from God's ways, then invariably the next generation comes back to them with even greater fervor. I can tell you of a strange example. My father of blessed memory, was a God-fearing, holy, and learned man. He was a disciple of the great Hillel. He suffered his greatest distress when he saw that I, his only son, was not dedicating myself to the study of our heritage.

"You see, my father had neglected our properties because he was so preoccupied with studying Torah and fulfilling all the mitzvos scrupulously. I, on the other hand, have a practical turn of mind, and it upset me that our beautiful lands were bringing in so little profit. I got involved with agriculture and spent my days from early in the morning until late at night in the fields.

"My father persisted in trying to kindle my desire for Torah learning, but to no avail. Once when he was overcome with anger, he said to me: 'I'm going to put an end to all of this! All these worldy goods which you are so attached to, will no longer belong to you — I am donating everything I own to the Holy Temple!'

"At that time, a man from Upper Galilee was working for my father. He had worked for him faithfully for three years. On the day before Yom Kippur, he asked for his salary so that he could go back to his family. 'I do not have any money,' my father said. 'So give me grain.' 'I do not have that either.' 'So show me a field that you can give me as payment.' 'I do not have any fields.' 'So give me some of your cattle for what you owe me.' 'I do not have any cattle.' 'So give me furniture or beds.' 'I do not have any,' said my father.

"And the poor man went back to his family empty-handed and distressed. He had worked for three years without any payment! After the Festival of Sukkos had passed, my father took a bag of gold coins and three donkeys laden with food, beverages, and all kinds of fine things, and set out for Galilee to see his former servant. He gave him his salary and all the gifts he had brought. Then he asked him, 'What did you think of me when I told you I did not have the means to pay you your salary?' The man replied, 'I thought that you had lost your money, that your grain was not tithed yet, and that your cattle and your fields were rented out. When you said you could not give me furniture or beds, however, I thought that you must have dedicated all your possessions to the Holy Temple.'

"'Indeed, you were right! By making this vow, I wanted to compel my son to study Torah. But my friends disapproved of what I had done and they brought about the nullification of my vow. May God judge you as mildly and favorably as you have judged me!'

"What has happened to me, however, is the exact opposite of what happened to my father. My fields and properties were my life and soul, and I demanded the same dedication and enthusiasm from my sons. But all that my son Eliezer wanted was — to learn Torah! One day he decided to run away from home, and he became one of the most outstanding disciples of our great Rabban Yochanan ben Zakkai."

"God bless him," Kalba Savua said. "He is the pride and hope of our orphaned nation."

"He wants the world to learn Torah! As you know, your new supervisor used to work for me. When my son came to visit a while ago, he became somewhat acquainted with him. He was impressed with Akiva's sharp mind and his wisdom, and he tried to persuade him to come with him to Yavneh to study there, but the man absolutely refused to go. He hates Torah scholars!"

Rachel was listening carefully.

"Would it be possible for me to influence that Akiva," she wondered, "even though the great Rabbi Eliezer was not able to do so?"

Chapter 3

Rabban Yochanan ben Zakkai was very ill. His pupils Rabbi Eliezer ben Hurkanos, Rabbi Yehoshua ben Chananya, Rabbi Yosei HaKohen, Rabbi Shimon ben Nesanel, Rabbi Elazar ben Arach, and Rabban Gamliel went to visit him. When he saw them, he began to weep.

"Great teacher!" they cried. "Israel's shining light, pillar of Torah study, he whose mind sends forth sparks as when a hammer strikes a rock and shatters it into pieces — why are you weeping?"

"If I were to be brought to trial before a human judge," Rabban Yochanan replied, "would I not be afraid? And now that I am about to face the Almighty, Master of the entire universe, the omniscient Judge Who cannot be bribed with anything, should I not cry? Who knows which path I will be led to — the one to eternal bliss in Gan Eden or the one to the abyss in Gehinom?"

"Our teacher, bless us!" his pupils replied.

"May you always fear God the way you fear people."

"Is that all?" they asked in astonishment.

"If you are always aware of God's Presence," Rabban Yochanan explained, "then you will never permit yourself to sin, just as you would be embarrassed to do something wrong in front of other people."

Our Sages have compared Rabban Yochanan ben Zakkai to Chizkiyahu, king of Judea. At the time of Chizkiyahu's reign, Israel was struck by misfortune. The Assyrians ravaged the land and took the ten tribes into captivity. It was only through the merit of Chizkiyahu's great piety and trust in God that a small part of the Jewish people was saved. After Chizkiyahu had rescued them, he kept their spirit alive by making sure that they dedicated themselves to the study of Torah.

In the same way Rabban Yochanan ben Zakkai saved his people. After Judea's national glory was extinguished and the Holy Temple was destroyed, he devoted all his efforts to maintaining the continuous study of Torah among the Jewish People.

And now he was gone, the great teacher and pillar of strength who had supported the dwindling numbers of Jews. All Israel mourned him and wept as though the Holy Temple had been destroyed all over again.

The tragic news reached to Kalba Savua's home as well. Rachel in particular was deeply affected by it. Young as she was, she could easily have taken lightly what had happened, and not taken it to heart. At that time, right after the destruction of the Temple, the Jews who remained in the Holy Land under the rule of Vespasian and Titus, were not as yet suffering badly from the Romans. Indeed, Rachel could have lived her life in great luxury and happiness. She could have married a wealthy young man, and even moved with him to Rome, or Alexandria, where the wealthy enjoyed the greatest material pleasures, no matter what nation they belonged to.

But Rachel loved her people, her Jewish faith, and her God! Her only concerns were the future of her nation and the increasing study of Torah. She rejected the frivolous pleasures that most other young girls delight in, and she sought only to do her utmost to shape a happier future for her people. Needless to say, she had absolutely refused to marry Papus, and her father did not pressure her on this matter after he had seen how disdainful Papus was.

In the meantime, Akiva had succeeded in making a very favorable impression on his employer. Kalba Savua discovered that he had a wonderful mind and great ability, and he applied them to the fullest in his work. The flocks and herds were thriving under his supervision and the shepherds did not dare neglect their duties. Kalba Savua grew more fond of his servant every day, and he praised him at every opportunity. There was one thing, however, that he did not like about Akiva, and that was the great disdain with which he spoke about the Rabbis and their learning. He considered them removed from the practical world. And while Kalba Savua and all the members of his household mourned the death of Rabban Yochanan, Akiva was the only one who remained indifferent.

As for Rachel, she could not mourn passively. "The great teacher of Israel is gone!" she lamented. "We must now find another, a man of strong character who will dedicate his life to Torah, and one day replace the great teacher we have lost."

She went out to the pastures, where she found Akiva sitting on a hill overlooking the area where the sheep were being sheared. When he saw Rachel approaching, he stood up.

"Good day to you, daughter of my master," he said. "Would you like to watch the shearing of the sheep? This year's good crop should bring a great increase in your father's wealth!"

"I have come to speak with *you*," said Rachel, "not to see the sheep. God has taken away our greatest man. All of Israel is in mourning. Only you seem not to care much about it!"

"Why should I grieve over someone who devoted his whole life to idle studies, and misled the young men of Israel to do the same?" Akiva replied. "Oh, how I detest those Rabbis! They are so arrogant, and they set themselves apart from the rest of us as though they belong to a different breed of men! To them, a Jew who is ignorant of Torah is barely considered a human being. They don't speak to us because they're afraid that we might defile them! They don't eat or drink with us, because they think that our food and drink are impure. Oh, don't talk to me about those Rabbis! *They're* the ones who've created so much conflict among us. *They're* the ones who caused the destruction of our nation!"

"You speak like that only because you don't know God's teachings, because you haven't learned Torah," Rachel replied. "When God gave us the Torah at Mount Sinai, He proclaimed the Ten Commandments in all His glory and majesty, and there was thunder and lightning as God spoke. Then He gave us the Written Law, which Moshe wrote down, so that it would be accessible to all of our people. But it is only through the Oral Law that we can fully explain and interpret the Written Law, and apply it to practical life.

"Moshe taught the Torah to all of our people," Rachel continued. "His greatest disciple was Yehoshua, and then it was transmitted from Yehoshua to the Elders, from the Elders to the Prophets, and from the Prophets to the Rabbis. The Rabbis embody the Torah's essence, you see — they represent the soul of the Jewish People! What would our nation be without God's spirit that rests upon us and without the fulfillment of His holy commandments?"

Rachel paused for a moment and then went on. "You see, God created all the nations and He is a loving Father to all of them, no matter who they are, even if they worship idols and they sin. But it was our Jewish People whom He chose above all the other nations. He endowed us with His spirit and sanctified us through His commandments. And now, although the Jewish State has fallen apart, the Temple is destroyed, and prophecy no longer exists among us, the Torah alone remains and always will remain with us. And it is the Rabbis' task to pass on the Torah, in its complete purity and holiness, to the coming generations. Who knows what the future has in store for us? Who knows the dangers that await us? We must see to it that Torah is not forgotten, that Israel is not stripped of its greatest treasure!

"You know, I remember when I was still a young child, how I would hear some of the great Rabbis conversing in our house. I often heard them discussing the dangers that are threatening us. They said that we must make sure to link our Oral Law —

which has come down to us in an unbroken chain of transmission from Sinai — so closely and tightly with the Written Law, that it would be impossible for that Oral tradition ever to be forgotten.

"Oh, Akiva, if only you would take this task upon *yourself*... yes, upon yourself! — you would bring joy to your people for eternity! God has granted you a keen mind and a strong will. Why don't you leave my father's herds and flocks and become instead the shepherd of our people?"

"You surely think too highly of me," Akiva answered. "How could I possibly begin to learn now, when I have spent all these years in ignorance?"

"You can do whatever you want to do! I have seen how you do things. You are hard-working, your perseverance is unlimited, and your mental abilities are unsurpassed. All you have to do is to activate your will and then, God willing, you will attain what seems entirely impossible to you now. If you take up the challenge of learning Torah, one day you will become one of the greatest men of Israel!"

"If I were to decide to study," Akiva said pensively, "I would have to dedicate my life to it totally. And in that case I would also have to give up my work... what would I do for my livelihood? What is the compensation for all this?"

"The knowledge that you are making a great contribution to our people, honor in this world, and eternal bliss in the next!"

Akiva smiled. "Even with all these beautiful things," he said, "one can still go hungry."

Chapter 4

Although Akiva had appeared to reject the words of his master's daughter, in fact her enthusiasm had not left him indifferent. Her spirited words had penetrated his heart and his mind deeply. Rachel's words had opened new horizons for him. In the following days, he found that all the mundane issues of his daily life and work, which had always been of utmost importance to him, seemed to fade in significance, in the light of Rachel's moving portrayal of Israel and the Torah, of the future of his people. He did not neglect his duties at work, but somehow he was no longer involved with all his heart.

Until now he had lived his life untroubled by serious worries. His main concern had been to work hard and save money so that eventually he could lease some land and become partially independent. But now his strenuous toil for the sake of his material needs seemed futile and unworthy of the abilities which he was becoming more and more aware of. He began to say his daily prayers with greater concentration and fervor and he began to fulfill God's commandments more carefully than ever before. It soon became clear to him that he was not even knowledgeable enough to understand properly what he was saying in his prayers, and for the same reason he was unable to scrupulously fulfill the commandments.

In the past, he had heard it said — to his great annoyance — that the ignorant could not be truly pious. He had viewed that as an arrogant statement, and it had increased his animosity to the Rabbis. Now, however, he began to realize that piety was not simply a matter of emotions or temperament, but of mature thinking as well. Questions arose in his mind which he could not resolve on his own, and he had begun to feel a great yearning to learn more about Judaism.

Behind Kalba Savua's home there was a large garden through which ran one of the many streams that flowed into Lake Kinneret. One summer morning Rachel decided to take a walk through the garden to calm herself, for she had been in inner turmoil since her appeal to Akiva. She had lost her mother at a young age, she had no siblings, and even among the faithful household servants there was no one she could really talk to. The only servant she had been close to was the woman who had raised her, and she had died the year before. Most of her childhood friends had either perished during the war, or been sold as slaves by the Romans. Those that remained were scattered throughout the country. Thus Rachel was often lonely. She could not confide in her father either, for his suffering had left him embittered and withdrawn.

Deep in thought, she wandered alongside the stream, following it to its source up in the hills. As she made her way higher and higher, still following the path of the stream, she looked down at her father's garden far below her. She climbed some more and finally reached her destination: a bench which the servants had built for her in the shade of a grove of olive trees. As she sat gazing at the running water as it splashed against the rocks, she suddenly saw Akiva standing nearby.

"Forgive me, honored daughter of my master," he said. "I am sorry for disturbing your solitude, but I must tell you that since you introduced me to all those ideas, they have been occupying my mind and I have questions which I cannot possibly answer myself. I am hoping that you can help me and answer them, for otherwise they will remain unsolvable riddles to me."

Rachel listened intently. "You spoke about the fate of our people," Akiva went on. "Tell me, then, why is it that of all the nations, Israel has to suffer the most?"

"The greater and more meaningful a person's task is in this world," replied Rachel softly, "the more he has to struggle, and the more pain he has to suffer. You see. Akiva," she went on, "people who are simple and ignorant, who don't worry about anything that doesn't directly concern them, usually live in peace and tranquility! Those who want to act, who are aware, and are interested in contributing to the good of the world, take a heavy burden upon themselves." Rachel's voice grew strong. "God chose Israel over all the other nations, and charged it with a higher purpose. He made the People of Israel like priests among the other nations, and it follows naturally that we are to be at the center of all great conflict. Whenever something great is being fought for, Israel is part of it.

"There are always a few nations that rise above the others and subjugate them. Those individual nations become powerful and they expand — and then they fall! Israel has taken part in the glory of every one of those nations. Of course Israel also suffered pain and misery under their rule. We were often cast to the ground and crushed relentlessly. But God has always raised us up and put us back on our feet again, never allowing other nations to destroy us. He has never punished us the way He punished our pursuers, and although we do suffer far more than all the other nations, God has also granted us the strength we need to endure the pain."

"You speak like a prophetess!" cried Akiva. "It seems as though everything is Divinely revealed to you! And so I will ask you another question which I have been pondering for the last few days. We are taught to believe that God foresees everything — but if God knows all our actions in advance, how can we really choose between good and bad? And how can we be responsible for our actions if they are predestined and are not anchored in our free will?"

"Oh, Akiva, why are you asking me, an ignorant girl, all of these questions?" Rachel answered. "Go and learn, and then you will understand how God governs His world."

"And does the Torah really teach such things?" Akiva asked.

"Look, Akiva!" Rachel replied, pointing down at the stream. "There are huge rocks that block the stream's natural course, but it splashes against them and the water is splattered about in many little droplets — but nevertheless they unite again and the stream continues along its course. Then the stream encounters new obstacles, which it surmounts as well. And so it flows on, continuing steadily towards its destination, Lake Kinneret.

"And now look at the huge rocks! Those weak little droplets of water wore them smooth, carved them and pierced them. This stream can be compared to our People, Akiva, when they follow God's ways. Great enemies may stand in our way, like big rocks in the path of the stream, but we persist in following the way that God has laid out for us, without letting the rocks stop our course. The great rocks, however, are sculpted and worn away by the seemingly feeble droplets of water, as it says in *Tanach*, 'Water wears down rocks.'"

"Is that really written in the Scriptures?"

"Yes — Iyov, the great sufferer, said it."

"How beautiful! And is there such wisdom in the Torah?"

"Yes, in the Torah which you despise and the Torah on which you should be focusing all your energy!"

"Leave that aside for the moment, and tell me one more thing, please," said Akiva. "Why did all tragedy — the fall of the Holy Temple, and the destruction of sovereignty in Eretz Yisrael — have to occur in our times? Why are we the ones who have to bear it all? Why couldn't we have been born in times of happiness? Why must we pay for the sins of our fathers?"

"I can only repeat what I said before," Rachel replied. "Go and learn! The history of our nation shows us that even ignorant people can understand something of the mysteries of Divine Providence. When God made a covenant with Avraham, He told him: 'And your descendants will be strangers in a land that is not theirs, and they shall serve them, and they will be afflicted for four hundred years.' Now think about it: Those Jews who were born into slavery and who grew up as slaves and who died as slaves — what did they do to deserve such a fate? And yet they too were an important link in the chain of events. *Their* children received the Torah at Sinai, *their* grandchildren inherited the Promised Land! Life of those who lived in slavery was surely miserable! But God granted them a great measure of joy in their unfortunate life.

"It was the women — the noble and pious women of Israel — who took it upon themselves to make their suffering husbands happy. Thus they adorned themselves for them and dedicated themselves fully to them. They disdained their Egyptian masters and remained completely loyal to their husbands. And even when Pharaoh decreed that their beloved children would be taken from them and drowned in the river, they never lost their hope, their strength, and their courage. And just as in those times it was the harmony and strength of the Jewish home that kept Israel alive, so is this the case in all times of sorrow and danger for us. In our days, as well, it is this that will guard us and give us the strength to endure all our tribulations."

Akiva sighed. "Ah, if only *I* could find a wife who would stand by my side like that, I would not worry about the mundane needs of life! I would happily dedicate myself to the study of the Torah, even if I had no means to pay for food and clothing! But that wife would have to be someone... someone like *you*, my master's daughter — although I would never dare to approach you with such an idea."

"If I knew that one day you would become a great teacher of Israel," Rachel replied slowly, "I would not turn you down!"

"But that may be an impossible condition to fulfill."

"Then I would not turn you down if you promised me that you would dedicate your life to Torah, regardless of whether you fulfill that condition or not... speak to my father!" she added, and left.

Chapter 5

Akiva was stunned. He had never experienced such joy. Rachel would agree to marry him! The brilliant, devoted, wonderful daughter of his master was descending to him, a poor shepherd — even in his wildest dreams he could never have imagined this!

As he stood gazing at the lovely landscape around him, at all the lands which belonged to Kalba Savua, the thought came to him: Was he to inherit all this one day? But the idea of such wealth paled in comparison to Rachel, who would elevate him to her level of faith, a level he had seen but a glimpse of.

With that thought he felt a sudden sadness: He did not feel worthy of the wealth and honor that he would receive from his future wife.

"If only you were poor, Rachel," he thought to himself, "and *I* could shower all the riches of this world upon *you*, I would feel a lot happier! And I would not have the difficult task of approaching your father, for how can I dare approach him with such a request? He'll think I'm crazy... that I, his poor and ignorant servant, would have the audacity to set my heart on his only child! He will surely chase me away and try to marry off his daughter as quickly as he can — to someone more worthy than I. And yet I must do it. Oh, help me, merciful God, to win his approval, and I will make a holy vow to dedicate my whole life to serving You and to studying Your Torah!"

Akiva did not allow his dreams of a new future to affect his work for his master. He continued to be as conscientious as ever, always seeking to fulfill Kalba Savua's wishes to the utmost. Akiva was everywhere, and nothing escaped his watchful eye. The servants knew this and were on their best behavior.

Since his encounter with Rachel near the stream, they had not spoken. Whenever he saw her in the distance, he was happy. But so far he had not gathered the courage to approach his master with his request.

Then one day Kalba Savua came to him and said, "Akiva, I am very satisfied with your services. You work hard, and my lands and herds are flourishing under your care. You still have not told me how you would like to be paid."

Akiva was trembling. The moment had come for him to speak to his master. He gathered all his courage and spoke. "Oh, master, you asked me this question once before. It was just at that moment that your daughter walked into the room, and when I saw her then, I thought to myself, 'If only I could reply what our forefather Ya'akov said: "I want to serve you for seven years for your daughter Rachel."'

"Now, my master, I would like to make that request in a slightly different manner. Please, release me from my duties so that I can go and study Torah. Your daughter has promised to marry me on the condition that I begin to learn."

Kalba Savua was astonished. He looked at his faithful worker with pity and said, "Akiva, has a demon come to you and placed these fantasies into your head?"

"I am aware," replied Akiva, "that what I am saying seems to you like baseless audacity. But I would not have dared approach you with such a request if your daughter had not asked me to."

Kalba Savua called to a servant to bring in his daughter.

Rachel appeared within a few minutes. She approached her father with confident steps, took his hand, and kissed it. "You called for me, my father."

Kalba Savua nodded. "My dear child, you have always been an obedient and wonderful daughter to me. I never found it necessary to give you any commands or lay down prohibitions, for my wishes were yours also. When Papus came here, neither of us liked him, and I sent him away without even asking you first, because I knew you would never want to marry him."

"I know, my father. You have always been kind and understanding, and it has been my pleasure to obey you."

"And that," Kalba Savua continued, "is why I cannot believe what this man is saying! He claims that *you* told him to ask me for your hand in marriage! Not only is he poor, not only does he come from a pagan family, but he is utterly ignorant as well! And you, who always wanted to marry a Torah scholar, a person whose entire being had been shaped by the wisdom he acquired — can it be that you want to marry this man?"

"Listen to me, Father," Rachel cried. "Akiva has an unusually gifted mind! He has promised me that he is going to spend day and night studying Torah. With his intellectual abilities and his great soul he can become one of the greatest teachers of Israel. I have promised to marry him with the intention of encouraging him in this great task."

"Foolish child! Do you think an adult can ever make up all that he missed in his childhood? And even if that were possible, what makes you think he will keep his promise? 'Three things cause the earth to quake,' Shlomo HaMelech says — and one of them is a servant that has become a ruler! This man wants to marry you for your wealth, and once he is rich he will want to enjoy it."

"You judge me wrongly, my master," Akiva spoke up in a respectful tone. "I want to marry your daughter for herself, and I would consider myself happy if she were as poor as I am."

"And if she were poor," said Kalba Savua, "would you not have to work very hard to support your family? How then would you find time for your Torah study?"

"If I were poor," Rachel answered instead of Akiva, "*I* would make every effort to sustain my family by working, so that my husband could fulfill his holy mission undisturbed!"

"You can only talk like that, my foolish child, because you do not know what it means to be poor. You have never experienced hunger."

"Although I have never experienced it, my father, I am not afraid of it. If I am able to help sustain our endangered people, I will be willing to eat dry bread and sleep on a bare floor! You too, my father, have always loved our holy nation. You sacrificed a great part of your wealth in order to sustain Jerusalem during the siege. I, however, would like to help our people save those riches that no fire can consume, those riches that have preserved and enlightened us for generation after generation. And with this in my mind and my heart, I discovered how gifted your servant is. With his penetrating mind he will surely be able to pierce the depths of Torah and absorb the full scope of its wisdom. He will be a blessing for our people, as were the greatest men of Israel. He will teach them, and it will be like the fulfillment of the prophecy, 'And all your sons will be scholars of the Lord, and peace will reign among all your children.'"

Rachel had spoken like an inspired prophetess, and Akiva was moved by her words of wisdom. Yes, he knew that with her support he would be able to attain what he strove for.

Kalba Savua replied to his daughter, "I don't understand your mad fantasies, Rachel. What makes you so sure, foolish child, that this ignorant man will become a great scholar? I see that it is my duty to think and to decide for you."

He turned to Akiva. "You are to leave my house this very day! And you, Rachel, must completely abandon the idea of marrying him. And I will set out for Yavneh, to choose a son-in-law from among the students of the great Rabban Yochanan ben Zakkai!"

"Oh, father," Rachel implored, "I have given Akiva my word and I will keep it. I will never marry anyone else!"

Kalba Savua knew his daughter well, and he realized that she was telling the truth. He found himself in a rage over her defiance, however. "In that case," he said angrily, "I want you to know that if you do not comply with my request, I no longer consider you my daughter! If you insist on pledging your life to this beggar, then you will learn very well what it means to be poor. Listen carefully to the vow I am about to make: *You will not receive anything, not the slightest thing, from all my possessions. You are not to take a thing from this house with you except the clothing that you are wearing.* Then you can go with this beggar from door to door, asking compassionate people for charity. Now choose between him and me!"

"Father," Rachel said in a voice filled with pain, "God is my witness that it hurts me deeply to have angered you so. Your riches I can part with easily, but I will miss your fatherly love greatly."

"So your mind is made up?"

"Yes."

"Then be gone with this man! You are no longer my daughter. You have depleted my fatherly love. Consider yourself fortunate that I have not put any curses upon you."

Chapter 6

In a small town by the name of Gimzo, close to Lod, lived one of the great Sages of Israel. His name was Nachum of Gimzo, and later he became known as "Nachum Gam Zo," for it was his principle to always see the good in whatever happened to him. He would always say: *"Gam zo l'tovah!"* which means, "This too is for the good!" Nachum steadfastly believed that whatever God sends us, no matter how bad it seems, is meant for the good.

One day he had just finished his lecture at his yeshiva and dismissed his pupils, when a poverty-stricken young woman entered the room.

"Forgive my audacity in coming to you myself, Rabbi," she began, "but my husband is not used to dealing with Torah scholars yet. I would like to ask you to please let him join the group of pupils that you teach."

"You seem familiar to me, my daughter. What is your name?"

"My name is Rachel. My father is Kalba Savua."

Nachum was shocked. "The daughter of Kalba Savua! Has your father lost his wealth?"

"Oh, no! My father still has all his riches, but he has disowned me."

"Disowned you! If you will permit me to inquire — for what reason?"

"I have chosen to marry one of his servants on the condition that he dedicate himself to the study of Torah. My father opposed my decision and drove me from his house. My husband wants to keep his promise to me, and I have therefore come to ask you, please, to show him the path that will lead him into the world of Torah wisdom."

"I see... and what are you going to live on if your husband spends his time learning and your father has cut you off?"

"I have sold the fine clothing and jewelry that I was wearing on the day I left my father's house. With the money we bought ourselves a small hut and a few household items and tools. From now on I intend to support my husband and myself through the labor of my hands."

Nachum listened to this young woman, who had grown up in such affluence, with great admiration. "You are very brave," he said, "and you surely deserve to see your husband become a Torah scholar, a great teacher of Israel one day. Your self-sacrifice will be praised by our people for thousands of years and you will serve as a role model to all the daughters of Israel!

"Bring in your husband now, and I will see what I can do for him."

Rachel left and returned with Akiva.

Nachum of Gimzo greeted him. "And what have you learned in your life so far?" he asked.

"I have learned," Akiva replied, "how to farm the land, how to tend fruit trees, how to look after sheep and cattle, and how to take care of whatever else has to be done on a farm. The Torah, however, is still foreign to me. I don't know how to read or write."

"*Gam zo l'tovah!*" the Rabbi exclaimed. "Naturally, it will be difficult for you to follow my lectures, which are based on our holy books. It is most important that at this stage you learn the alphabet. If you are willing, you can remain here now and I will begin to teach you."

"Thank you, Rabbi!" Rachel said. "I praise God that my husband has found such a good-natured and friendly teacher. I will be on my way now; my work is waiting for me at home."

Rachel left the yeshiva, and as soon as she reached her meager little hut she sat down on her spinning stool so that she could earn whatever she needed for the next day.

When evening fell, she set the table and lit the oil lamp. The door opened and Akiva walked in. She welcomed him happily. They washed their hands and sat down to their modest meal.

"Tell me, my beloved husband," Rachel said, after he had eaten, "have you learned anything today?"

"I learned to read and write the letters of the alphabet. Rabbi Nachum is a teacher who really makes one want to learn! He also taught me the numerical value of each letter, and he answered every one of my questions — even those that were probably quite silly — with the greatest love and eagerness. Once I knew the alphabet, he let me read in the holy Torah. 'My son,' he said, 'when you have questions, be sure to ask without feeling embarrassed. A bashful person will never learn.' So immediately I asked him why the Torah starts with the letter *beis,* whose numerical value is so small. The Torah should have begun with the letter *tav,* I said, since the word *Torah* starts with it and since it has the highest numerical value!

"'That's a good question, my son,' he said. 'Now listen to what the Sages have said about this. The twenty-two letters of the alphabet contain all the wisdom of this world, and the whole Torah is built on them. Originally God created these letters in the form of flames. In the beginning, when God was about to create the world, all the letters surrounded His throne, each of them begging Him to be used first in the Creation of the world and in the Torah. At first the letter *tav* appeared before Him and said, "I deserve to be first, because my numerical value is the greatest and because the word *Torah* starts with me!" But God rejected the *tav*, because He was going to use it in the time of Yechezkel as a symbol imprinted on the foreheads of the sinners who were doomed to death. Then the letter *shin* appeared before Him and was also rejected, since the word *sheker* ("a lie") starts with it. Then the letter *reish* requested to be first, but it too was turned down, because *reish* is the first letter of the word *ra*, which means "bad."

"'And so it was with all the letters. They came and they were all sent away, until the letter *beis* presented itself, saying: "Almighty God, may it be Your will to create the world with me, for I am the first letter of the sentence, *Baruch Hashem le'olam!* [Blessed be God forever]." 'And God said, "Blessed be the one that comes in the name of God!" And He heeded to the request of the letter *beis* and created the world with it, as it is written: "*Bereishis bara Elokim* — In the beginning..."

"'Now the letter *aleph* drew back sadly. It was the only one that had not voiced its request. God called to it and said, "*Aleph*, why are you silent?" And the *aleph* replied, "How dare I speak up when my numerical value is one and all the other letters are worth more than I am?" And God said: "Don't worry! You shall be the first among all of them, and have the priority of a king. You are one, I am One, and the Torah is one, and when I reveal myself to My nation at Mount Sinai, I will begin the Ten Commandments with you, as it says: "*Anochi Hashem Elokecha* — I am Hashem, your God."'"

Rachel had listened to him in amazement. When he finished, she jumped up in great joy and excitement and cried, "Oh, beloved husband of mine, you will indeed fulfill all the great hopes I have for you. One day you will be a great teacher of Israel!"

After this first meeting, Akiva began to make his way to Gimzo daily, to learn with his new teacher. Rabbi Nachum grew very fond of his earnest pupil and he tried to advance his learning in every way possible. Of the large group of students who came to learn from him, Akiva was the oldest among them and the most ignorant.

The youngest one was Yishmael, a descendant of a noble family of Kohanim. He had been a young child when the Holy Temple was destroyed. A boy of extraordinary beauty, the enemy had taken him captive and sent him to Rome to be their slave. There he spent his first days in a Roman prison.

It happened that Rabbi Yehoshua ben Chananyah was in Rome at that time, and he passed by the prison. Through the barred window he saw the beautiful young Jewish boy with sad eyes and dark, shiny curls that framed his face. And Rabbi Yehoshua called out loudly in Hebrew, with words from *Yeshayahu*: "Who has given up Israel to thieves?" Immediately the imprisoned boy called out a reply from the same verse: "Is it not God, Whom we have sinned against? And they did not want to walk in His ways and listen to His teachings."

"Truly," Rabbi Yehoshua said, "this boy will one day grow up to be a great man! I will not rest until I have redeemed him, no matter how much money they demand."

And so he did. Although the Romans asked for a huge sum, for they were very reluctant to release the boy, Rabbi Yehoshua did not allow himself a moment of peace until he had collected all of it from his friends in Rome. He freed the young boy and brought him back to Eretz Yisrael with him, where he entrusted him to Nachum of Gimzo who would raise him and teach him.

By now Yishmael had grown to be a fine young man, the pride and joy of his teacher. Akiva, who was much older, nevertheless sought his friendship and soon they became so close that their bond would last a lifetime.

While Akiva worked zealously, focusing all his energy and concentration on his learning, Rachel did not sit idle either. She was busy making every effort to earn the bare minimum that would provide for their modest needs. Time after time, out of love and respect for her father, she had tried to make peace with Kalba Savua, but to no avail. He remained hard and relentless toward her.

Not only did Rachel have to work very hard (which was unknown to her in her father's house), but she also had to give up various basic things, for at this point it was no longer enough just to make ends meet. Now it was necessary to put away some savings, as they were expecting a happy event in the near future... And with her determination and courage she succeeded in doing so. But just as she had managed to set aside a modest sum, something happened that would cause her to lose it.

Chapter 7

Akiva and Rachel lived in a little village called Korchah. Their hut was small and crude. It consisted of two tiny rooms, one which served mainly as a bedroom, and the other which Rachel used as a kitchen and Akiva used as his study. The couple didn't even own beds; they slept on straw.

When Akiva saw Rachel removing the straw from her hair every morning, it pained him that his wife, who had lived in luxury, was now leading such a deprived existence.

But there were people who were poorer than they. There was a man in Korchah by the name of Eliyahu, who had broken his leg at work and was confined to bed for weeks. Having no source of livelihood, he had just sold his last possessions. Now his wife had just given birth to a baby boy, and so they were both lying in bed and they were both helpless. One day, when Akiva was coming home from Gimzo in the evening after learning Torah with Rabbi Nachum all day, he heard the sound of weeping from Eliyahu's hut. He went in and saw the terrible state of misery they were in, and he came home in great distress.

"Oh, if only I had some money," he told Rachel, "I could make such great use of it now!" And he described to her about the suffering he had just seen.

Rachel immediately brought out a little sack of silver coins and handed it to her husband. "Here," she said. "This is money that I have put aside for the time in the near future when I will not be able to work. Take this money and bring it to poor

Eliyahu and his wife. As for us, God will find other ways to help us."

"What a righteous woman you are!" Akiva said. "Not only have you made the greatest sacrifices to allow me to study Torah; not only do you, the daughter of the wealthy Kalba Savua, willingly deprive yourself of so many things; but now you are even giving your meager savings away to alleviate another's sorrow! Your trust in God is as great as your love for Torah, and your concern for others makes you forget your own worries. Oh, what a wealthy man am I to have such a wife — I don't envy the Roman Emperor for his riches! But if God does bless me with wealth one day, I would like you to be adorned like a princess, and in remembrance of this moment, you will wear a gold crown on your head, engraved with an image of the Holy City of Jerusalem, crafted by the most skillful artisan!"

"You are a dreamer," Rachel answered with a smile. "Now go and bring them the money without delay. They need it so much."

Akiva hurried happily to Eliyahu's house with Rachel's savings. Then he asked one of the neighbors to go and buy some basic provisions for Eliyahu and his family. The people that lived in Korchah were poor and therefore could not donate money or food. But they were very kind, and now that there was money available, they were eager to arrange whatever was required.

It was a pleasure to see how the poor, hungry couple came to life again under the new care they were receiving. They lauded Akiva, calling him their "redeeming angel."

He, however, declined their praises. "It is not to me that you owe thanks, but to the noble woman whom I have the privilege of being married to. She was the one who worked with her own hands to save this money, coin by coin. It's not a lot, but it will suffice to support you for some time, and God will continue to help after that."

One day Akiva came to his teacher with a request. He asked permission to be absent for a few hours each day from their learning schedule. "Until now my wife has supported us," he explained, "so that I was able to learn undisturbed. But now she will be unable to work for a while, so I will have to earn whatever we need. But I will make sure not to neglect my studies — I will just have to make use of a good part of the night to make up for time lost during the day."

"Allow me to help you out," Rabbi Nachum replied. "I am a wealthy man and it will be easy for me to provide for you and your family."

"Thank you," said Akiva, "but I don't want to accept any donations as long as I am strong enough to earn my bread. I would just be stealing from others who are too poor and sick to look after themselves. I must tell you, Rabbi, that in my own village there is a poor man named Eliyahu who has been lying in bed for weeks because he broke his leg. Now his wife has given birth to a son, and they are in desperate circumstances. If you could help to take care of these impoverished people, you will be a redeemer to them in their time of great sorrow. These people need help more urgently than I do!"

"You are a noble person, Akiva," Rabbi Nachum replied, and shook his student's hand. "May God bless you! As long as there are people like you, who dedicate themselves to Torah, Israel will not be orphaned. Go in peace and may you earn yourself a living."

"My dear teacher, your blessing is worth more to me than thousands of silver and gold coins."

Akiva returned home and asked Rachel to stop working and to avoid physical exertion. As she was expecting to give birth soon, she had to be very careful about maintaining her good health. Then Akiva went into the woods, where he cut down branches, made bundles out of them, and brought them to the Gimzo market to sell as firewood. Some of them he kept for himself, however. He was going to use them to make a torch, so that he could remain awake at night and learn.

That night he sat in the kitchen on a stool, holding the Torah scroll in one hand and the torch in the other. By now he had mastered reading, and he began to read aloud:

"*Bereishis*... In the beginning God created the heavens and the earth." And he thought about what he had read. He analyzed every letter, every word, and every expression, trying to understand why the Torah specifically chose to use certain letters and not others. He posed questions and he formulated answers. Then he wondered why the word "the" appears both before "heavens" and before "earth." The verse could just as well have said "In the beginning God created heaven and earth."

Akiva pondered this for a long time and he was so deep in thought that he didn't even notice that his torch had burned down to the bottom and the flame was now burning his hand. When he finished learning, he extinguished the torch and rolled up the Torah scroll.

"Thinking is something I can do in the dark too, and that way I will be able to save the wood for the future," he told himself.

So he sat in the dark, contemplating the problem. But soon he began to feel very cold and he rekindled the torch. "My dear torch," said Akiva, "not only do your branches provide me with food and drink, not only do you cast light for my learning, but you also warm me and keep me from falling asleep, for if I fell asleep your helpful flame would put me in danger." And he continued to think about the question that was taxing his mind. Finally he thought he had found the solution.

"If the Torah had written, 'In the beginning God created heaven and earth,'" he said quietly to himself, "people might have misinterpreted that to mean that heaven and earth were the names of gods, and that they had created the world together with God. But since the Torah added the definite articles, it is clear to all that 'heaven' and 'earth' are not creators, but that they were created."

Happy to have resolved the problem, Akiva went to sleep for a few hours to rest up for the next day's work.

Since he had earned enough money on the first day of work to provide for his and Rachel's needs for a few days, he decided to put off gathering more wood for the time being and to devote himself to full-time learning again. He was also curious to see whether his teacher would agree with the way he had explained the seeming difficulty in that first verse.

When Akiva arrived in Gimzo, he met his friend Yishmael and shared his thoughts on *Bereishis* with him. Yishmael listened and shook his head, though, and said, "Akiva, my friend, you have not tried hard enough. The mistake that you assume people would make, if the Torah had omitted the "the's", would only be possible if the verse said, 'In the beginning God heaven and earth created.' However, your question is justified, and the Torah is indeed trying to teach us something by adding the articles.

"As I understand the explanation, when God created the world, He uttered His command and all of Creation came into existence. During the six days of Creation He only improved upon what already was there! Therefore, the article 'the' before the word 'heaven' suggests that at the same time that God created heaven he also created the sun, the moon, and the stars. In terms of their substance, all of these were created from the beginning, but were only given their proper form and position on the fourth day of Creation. Similarly, the article 'the' before the word 'earth' teaches us that the trees, the plants, and Gan Eden were also created together with the earth, but only started to appear on the third day of Creation.

"I will give you a proof for this," Yishmael went on. "It says in Chapter 2 of *Bereishis*: 'This is the story of the creation of heaven and earth, when they were created, on the day that God made earth and heaven.' At the time of Creation heaven was first, but in terms of the completion of the process — earth was first, for the plants came up on the third day whereas the sun, the moon, and the stars were put into place only on the fourth day."

"Thank you, my brother Yishmael!" Akiva exclaimed. "Next time I will make a greater effort to think things through more carefully."

When Akiva returned home that evening, a son had been born to him. He named him Yehoshua.

Chapter 8

The years passed. Akiva developed a love and thirst for learning that amazed everyone. Whenever Rabbi Nachum of Gimzo quoted the words of Yosei ben Yoezer, "You shall drink the words of the wise with thirst," he would mention Akiva as an example. Akiva used every possible opportunity to learn something new. Whenever he met a doctor, he would ask him to teach him something about medicine. Likewise, he sought after mathematicians, astronomers, linguists, and craftsmen, trying to learn from everyone, as he knew he could make use of all his knowledge for the understanding of Torah.

The passage of time had brought changes in Rome too. Vespasian had died. His oldest son, Titus, who had conquered Jerusalem and destroyed the Holy Temple, had become Emperor of the huge Roman Empire. He reigned for only two years, however, and during this short time Rome was afflicted by one calamity after another. First, there was a great fire in the capital which raged for three days and destroyed a large part of the city. Then there was a plague that swept through the region, causing ten thousand deaths daily. The most frightening of all was the eruption of the volcano Vesuvius, which wiped out entire towns in southern Italy.

The Jews thought that these catastrophes were Rome's punishment for the destruction of the Holy Temple. Titus himself suffered severely throughout the time of his reign. In Judea a strange story was told about the nature of his suffering. It was said that when Titus' war with the Jews had ended and he was crossing the Mediterranean to return to Rome, a terrible storm arose at sea and the Emperor's ship was in great danger. Titus stood on deck and looked at the raging waves with great trepidation.

As the storm became more violent and the mast came crashing down, he called out, "You, God of the Jews, did the same thing to Pharaoh when You drowned him and his army in the sea, as You are doing to me now. It seems that You only have power over the waters, however on land I am the more powerful, for I have destroyed Your city and burned Your Temple!"

That is how the arrogant Emperor spoke, and suddenly the storm quieted down and the ship was able to reach shore. When Titus arrived in Brundisium, however, God sent the smallest of His creatures to punish him. A mosquito flew into one of his nostrils until it reached his brain and settled there. The mosquito grew and grew, constantly irritating Titus' brain, so that the Emperor no longer had a moment of peace. One day Titus passed by a blacksmith's shop and was greeted by the sound of loud hammering. The mosquito, stunned by the noise, stopped its ravages inside Titus' head! When Titus noticed, he arranged for constant hammering in his presence, but after thirty days the insect became accustomed to the sound and it renewed its maddening activity. Titus was tormented by the mosquito for two years, until he finally died at the age of forty. When an autopsy was performed after his death, it was discovered that a large winged insect was resident in his brain.

After Titus' death, his brother Domitian, who was ten years younger, took over as Emperor. The Jews decided to send a delegation to Rome to congratulate him on his new position and to bring him lavish gifts. Throughout Judea they collected money for this purpose and they were able to amass a great sum. The money was used to buy gold and diamonds, which were placed in a beautiful, richly decorated chest. But who would have the honor of presenting the gift? Rabban Gamliel, a descendant of Hillel's noble family, had been elected *Nasi*, but he was considered far too young for such a task. So they chose Rabbi Nachum of Gimzo, the oldest of all the teachers at that time. Rabbi Nachum happily accepted the challenging mission.

When he announced his plans to his students, Akiva was very distressed.

"My dear teacher," he said, "how will I be able to manage without your lessons for months?"

"You can come with me!" replied Rabbi Nachum. "And we can study Torah together on the way."

Akiva accepted his offer in great delight. He said goodbye to his wife and children (during these years they had been blessed with two more children, a son named Shimon and a daughter named Shulamis) and joined the delegation, which was made up of Rabbi Nachum and two other aristocratic Jews, Nikodemos and Avuyah.

They boarded a ship in Jaffa which was to cross the Mediterranean Sea and bring them to the coast of Italy. With his great thirst for knowledge, Akiva made sure to absorb everything around him. It was not long before he knew practically everything about the ship. By watching the crew carefully he had learned how to row and how to steer the helm wheel. And he also prompted his teacher to tell him about the wonders of plant and animal life in the sea.

"Every animal that lives on land exists in a similar form in the sea as well," Rabbi Nachum said. "There is the sea snake, the sea lion, the sea spider, the sea horse, etc. The one animal that is found only on dry land without any counterpart in the sea is the weasel. And therefore the land is called *cheled* in our holy language, from the word *chuldah* — 'weasel.'"

"How interesting! Now I understand the words of the Psalmist, 'Those that go down to the sea in ships, and those that work in boundless waters, they have seen Hashem's work and His wonders in the deep.'"

Suddenly, as though with his words he had conjured up the last part of the psalm, a terrible storm arose. The waves rose high into the air and came crashing down. The passengers were in great despair, staggering like drunkards on the windswept deck, and finally fleeing into the interior of the ship. Only Akiva remained on deck to assist the crew, but they themselves were in such terror that they didn't know what to do first.

"We are going to die!" cried the captain, trembling. The rowers had put down their oars and the helmsman gave up trying to steer. Horror was written on everyone's face. A Roman passenger of the aristocratic class, who had led his wife into the ship's lower room, now came up again. He heard the captain's words and he too was terrified.

At that moment Akiva began to speak, and his voice overcame the roar of the storm: "Brothers, do not despair!" he cried. "Just as the Almighty created the storm, so will He bring it to an end. My teacher, who is a pious and holy man, is with us on this ship. He is on his way to Rome to carry out an important mission for his people. He will not drown in the sea, and we too will be saved through his merit. Let us pray to God that He free us from our tribulations and restore peace to the sea."

Akiva then lifted his hands toward the sky and cried out, "Master of the Universe, Creator of the heavens, the earth, and the seas, compassionate Father, save us!"

And everyone joined him in his prayer — the captain, the helmsman, the rowers, the rest of the crew, and also the Roman aristocrat. And at that moment the storm abated and the waves began to subside. The crew joyfully returned to their duties.

Then the Roman turned to Akiva and said, "Praise be to the God of Israel, Who has answered your prayer! My name is Flavius Clemens; I am closely related to the Emperor. If you ever need a reference or anyone to speak for you while you are in Rome, I will be happy to help you."

A few days later they arrived in Brundisium. The Jewish passengers were still seasick from the journey, and they stayed at an inn, where they hoped to rest and to regain the strength needed for their mission.

Chapter 9

While the members of the Jewish delegation were ill and lying in bed, hardly aware of what was going on around them, the innkeeper's wife was looking through their baggage. To her great surprise she discovered the beautifully crafted chest which contained the gift for the Emperor. She took the chest and brought it to her husband. He opened the lock and stared at all the riches with greedy eyes.

"Now we are rich!" he exclaimed to his wife. "I will take these treasures out and bury them in our garden."

"And the chest? The beautiful chest? Don't we want to keep that also?"

"No, we can't. There are a lot of people who know that this chest came along with the guests. It would give us away. I will fill it with earth, relock it, and put it back."

And so it was. When the travelers felt strong enough to continue their journey, Rabbi Nachum opened the chest and discovered that all the gold and diamonds had disappeared. The entire chest was full of earth. The members of the delegation were shaken, but Rabbi Nachum just said, "This too is for the best!"

Nikodemos, Avuyah, and Akiva wanted to rush over to the Praetor to have the innkeepers arrested.

But Rabbi Nachum said, "How will that help us? They will deny knowing anything about it, and there will be no trace of the treasure because they surely will have hidden it well by then. We are strangers in a foreign country and there is no way that we can demand and secure justice. Let us continue on to Rome without any further stops and hand over the chest with the contents that Divine Providence has arranged for. God is pure goodness, and He will make things turn out for the best."

"Perhaps we should return to Judea and raise money for the gift a second time!" Nikodemos said.

"And who says that our second journey will be more successful than the first?" Rabbi Nachum answered. "Don't we risk the same danger again? God has saved us from the stormy waves of the sea and He will also let us achieve the goal of our journey."

No one cared to argue anymore, and they set out on their route. Within a few days they were approaching the great capital of the world. From afar they could already hear the loud tumult and commotion of Rome.

"Only because Israel has sinned has Edom gained so much power," Rabbi Nachum said to Akiva. "Originally lower Italy was an island in the sea. The day that Shlomo HaMelech brought home the Egyptian king's daughter to become his wife, the angel Michael came down from Heaven and put a tube into the sea. That tube became covered with more and more mud until eventually the firm land that connects upper and lower Italy came into existence.

"When Yeravam set up two golden calves, one in Dan and one in Beit El, and said: 'Here are your gods, Israel, who took you out of Egypt!' the twin brothers Romulus and Remus who established the city of Rome, were born. It is told that their mother died at their birth and a wolf suckled them and raised them. And when Eliyahu was taken from us because of Israel's sins, Rome expanded its power and glory. The more Israel sinned, the greater and more powerful Rome became. On the first of January Rome marked world supremacy by celebrating the holiday of *Kratesis*. Therefore it has been determined that this day is the first day of the year. And now Rome rules over the most parts of the world. Judea has been defeated and our Holy Temple lies in ruins."

The delegation arrived in Rome and was received graciously by Emperor Domitian. Rabbi Nachum wished the Emperor success on his accession to power, and presented him with the gift. The Emperor admired the splendid chest. But when he opened it, he fell back on his throne.

"The Jews want to mock me!" he cried. "They have brought me a box of earth! Take these madmen to their death."

When Rabbi Nachum heard the words of the Emperor, he said: "This too is for the good."

The Emperor's guards immediately rushed in. They seized the Jews and took them away. One of the members of the distinguished assembly surrounding the Emperor on that occasion was Flavius Clemens. He asked permission to address the Emperor, and began to speak:

"Mighty Emperor, divine ruler of the universe, allow me to say a word in favor of the Jews. I traveled together with them and they impressed me as being very reliable, reasonable, and special people. Why would they possibly do something as foolish as to mock you, the ruler of the universe? When we were on the ship together there was a terrible storm at sea. The ship was in danger of sinking beneath the waves. I brought my wife, who was terrified, down into the lowest room of the ship, and when I came back up on deck, I found the captain and all his crew in despair and awaiting death.

"At that moment one of the Jews lifted his hands towards heaven and prayed to his God. And lo and behold — the storm suddenly came to an end, the waves calmed down, and we were saved. Please, I beg of you, my Emperor, allow me to express my thought about this gift of the Jews. Their forefather was Avraham. He and just a few servants of his fought a war against four victorious kings and defeated them. The ancient sources of the Jews say that Avraham threw a handful of earth against his enemies and thereby won his victory. Now perhaps the Jews have found that earth again, and have made you a gift of it that is worth more than gold or precious stones."

The Emperor listened carefully to what his cousin Flavius Clemens was saying. He himself had not yet won any glorious victories in war. His father had never allowed him to take part in battle because it had been foretold that Domitian would die by the sword. So firmly did his father, Vespasian, believe in this prophecy that once when Domitian was young and refused to eat mushrooms, Vespasian had said to him, "Just eat them, my son — you don't have to worry about whether they're poisonous. It is only iron that will bring an end to your life!"

During Titus' short reign, Domitian was given no chance to make his mark on the map. Now he was desperately longing for the honor of being a successful warrior. His greatest dream was to have a triumphal march in Rome just like his father and his brother had done. There had been some troubling news from the Germanic tribes lately. The wild Chatti had entered the Roman province of Moguntiacum (Mainz) and tried to capture the Roman fortress. Domitian had decided to go to war against them, and he was hoping to thereby attain the glory he was seeking. If Clemens was right, and this was the same miraculous earth, he would defeat them with ease and be granted the triumphal march in Rome and the title of "Germanicus."

"Well then," he replied, "I would like to see if this earth really has the powers you are talking about, my Clemens. In the meantime you can look after the Jewish prisoners until I return from the Rhineland. After that we will see what to do with them."

Clemens immediately went to the prisoners and brought them to his house. There he made them promise that they would not leave Rome at this time, and then he granted them complete freedom.

Akiva spent most of the day studying Torah with his teacher Rabbi Nachum, just as he used to do in Gimzo. During the rest of his time he tried to get acquainted with the great metropolis. One sector of the city that interested him greatly was the substantial Jewish community in Rome at the time. Some of its members were outstanding personalities. The great teacher of the Roman Jews, Theodoros, who was a contemporary and friend of Rabban Yochanan ben Zakkai, had died recently. Akiva tried to learn as much as he could from the many disciples of Theodoros. They possessed many writings on the laws concerning Jews living outside of the Holy Land, which Akiva was interested in studying. In his dealings with these disciples he soon learned the Latin language fluently.

A Roman Jew by the name of Apella guided him through the city, pointing out to him the prominent works of architecture. Akiva also took interest in the public bathhouses which provided hot water to as many as three thousand people at a time! Two hundred pillars of marble adorned the main bathhouse, and there were 1600 benches for sitting or reclining. The individual baths were called *balnea* and the attendant was called *balneator* (a term which often appears in the abbreviated form of *balon* in the Talmud). Within these bathhouses, there were cold, lukewarm, and warm baths; steam baths and swimming pools; and spacious areas for gymnastics. Not only did they host activities to promote physical well-being, but they also provided a place for orators, philosophers, poets, and other learned men to hold special gatherings and activities in all kinds of weather. Indeed, the bathhouses tried to please everyone.

Within the grounds of the bathhouse, which was surrounded by massive towering walls, one could take beautiful walks along tree-lined paths. There were extensive training areas for young boys who were preparing to become strong and capable Roman citizens and warriors. For these youngsters there were races, wrestling matches, and discus throwing. Close by were swimming pools. Philosophers, poets, scholars, and artists were found in different parts of the bathhouse grounds. In the shade of the sycamore trees, the air heavy with the fragrance of flowers, and the sound of water splashing from fountains, they withdrew from the day-to-day world and engaged in demanding mental exercises and artistic activities. It was here that scholarly debates and poetry readings took place, which were received by the audience with great admiration. Every now and then a theatrical presentation was held for the audience as well. Those who sought to acquire culture in solitude could visit the library.

Long avenues of sycamore trees led from the scholarly area, which was concentrated in the northern wing, to the sports area, the youth halls, and the lakes in the eastern and western wings. The amphitheater, in the shape of a semicircle, afforded the spectators a good view of the athletic and gymnastic exercises. The thermal baths stood in the middle of this complex.

The main entrance was called *Theatridium*, and the Roman aristocrats would sit on its steps and entertain themselves by watching or chatting with others. These steps, which surrounded the whole building, led to a variety of activity centers. There was also a place where refreshments were served. The whole complex sprawled over acres of land. The innermost rooms of the structure were filled with all the gold that Rome had acquired from its conquests, as well as works of art which had been brought from Greece.

Chapter 10

One day, as Akiva was standing and observing all this splendor, he felt a hand on his shoulder. He turned and saw his friend and guardian, Flavius Clemens.

"Hello, Akiva! What do you say of the wonders of our magnificent Rome, capital of the world?" he asked.

"Rome excites one's interest," Akiva replied thoughtfully, "but its emphasis is entirely on worldly pleasures. All of this grandeur will collapse one day, along with the gods that are worshiped here."

"Be careful, Akiva! Watch your words! The Emperor has appointed me Praetor, the highest judicial official of this city, for as long as he is abroad in battle. I could have you punished for insulting the gods — but don't worry! I know that you are under the protection of a truly Divine entity, as I witnessed when we sailed together. And by the way, I am quite amazed to see how fluently you speak our language already. Come with me to my house — I would like to introduce you to my wife. Domitilla has been wanting to meet you for some time."

Clemens' wife was a granddaughter of the Emperor Vespasian and a niece of the Emperors Titus and Domitian.

As the two entered the house, Clemens said, "I am bringing you our Jewish guest, Domitilla. It was thanks to his prayer that we didn't drown in the sea."

"Welcome to you, my guest. I have been wanting to express my thanks to you for quite a while."

"I must decline the thanks you are giving me, honorable hostess," Akiva replied. "It was not on account of *my* merit that God saved us, but because of my teacher's great merit, for he is a pious and holy man. God has performed many miracles for him in the past. As for me, I am just an insignificant student and a beginner in Judaism."

"You may be just a 'beginner'," said Clemens, "but I am sure you have learned a lot already. I can see you learn quickly. Here in Rome I am amazed at how quickly you have learned our language. Not only do you speak it correctly, but you speak it with the eloquence of Cicero!"

"Who is Cicero?" Akiva asked.

"Cicero was a Roman Senator and the greatest orator of our people. His speeches in the Senate set an example for our youth today. He was also a philosopher, and we are very grateful to him for his contributions in this field as well."

"What is a philosopher?" Akiva asked.

"The word 'philosopher' means 'friend of wisdom.' A philosopher is someone who tries to answer the difficult questions of human existence, using his own reasoning. One of my friends, Artemidorus, is a great thinker and teacher of this wisdom. If you are interested in meeting him, I can introduce you to him."

"I will be grateful to you," Akiva said. "My greatest desire is to learn from learned men."

Clemens was silent for a moment, and then he seemed to recall something else. "You haven't congratulated me yet for my new prestigious position of Praetor, which the Emperor in his benevolence has granted me."

"Being a judge involves a great deal of responsibility," Akiva replied pensively. "Justice is in God's domain, the Torah says. Judges who are truthful and fair become partners in Creation with God. Every time a judge sits in court he is faced with the abyss of hell, because the greatest punishments await him if he is negligent or superficial in his verdict — and all the more so if he accepts a bribe or willingly distorts the truth in any other way. And you want me to congratulate you for such a position? It is a tremendous burden that rests on your shoulders."

"You take this job far more seriously than any Roman ever has," Clemens said with a smile. "To me it's a great — almost royal — honor, and it means having the highest authority in the absence of the Emperor. Everything in Rome revolves around the Emperor. Whatever he wishes becomes the law."

"Allow me, dear master Clemens, to share with you what the teachings of Judaism say about this. A very long time ago people lived in great happiness. Both men and women reached a ripe old age and they never experienced sickness or pain. The earth provided plenty and there was no lack of nourishment."

"The golden age!" Domitilla interjected.

"Indeed, a golden age in terms of nature and its bounty — but people misused the precious gifts that God gave them. They surrendered to all their material desires, which led to terrible moral corruption and violence in the world. The strong oppressed the weak. They stole their wives from them and forced their children into slavery. So God decided to annihilate this sinful generation, except for a man named Noach and his family. Noach found favor in God's eyes since he was righteous and followed God's ways. And God commanded Noach to build an ark — a ship for him, his family, and all the animals that God wanted to save. Then God sent down rain for forty days and forty nights. All the channels in heaven opened up and the wells below the ground also released their waters. There was a huge Flood all over the world, that covered even the highest mountains. All the living creatures drowned except for the fish in the sea and the people and animals in the ark."

"Deucalion!" Domitilla cried out.

"Who is Deucalion?" Akiva asked.

"Deucalion," she explained, "was the father of Helen, the original ancestor of the Greeks. This Deucalion was also the son of Prometheus and the husband of Pyrrha. When Zeus, the father of the gods, decided to destroy the human race with water,

Deucalion, following his father's advice, crafted a wooden vessel for himself and his wife. During the flood, which lasted for nine days, he and his wife floated around in their vessel, until they reached Mount Parnassus, when the water had receded. When Deucalion asked the oracle how he could repopulate the world, he was told that he and his wife should throw the bones of their mothers behind them. They interpreted this mysterious answer to mean that their mothers were the earth and their mothers' bones were the stones. So they did what the oracle had commanded, and the stones that Deucalion threw became men, and the stones that Pyrrha threw became women."

"It's possible," replied Akiva, "that the Greeks have some vague, distorted memories of the Flood. But allow me to continue. After the Flood had subsided and Noach had left the ark, God instituted laws for him and his family. One of these laws demands that justice reign in the world and that the weak should be protected from the strong, so that the world never again become filled with evil and injustice.

"And that, my friend, is the holy task of the judge — to protect the lives and property of his fellowmen from thieves and oppressors. If law is determined by the whim of individuals, then the world will once again become filled with violence, and no one will feel secure about his life and property. Only justice must reign in the world, and justice cannot be defined arbitrarily; it must originate from the highest Source of wisdom. The laws that are meant to regulate our lives have been given to us by God, the Creator of the universe. He revealed Himself in His majesty to His people, Israel, and forbade us to have any other gods or to desecrate His Holy Name. He commanded us to keep the laws of the holy Sabbath, to honor our parents, to respect the lives and property of our fellowmen. He told us to preserve the sanctity of marriage, to speak the truth, and to exercise control over our thoughts so that we won't covet someone else's wife or property."

"What you are saying is completely different from the principles that guided our upbringing," Domitilla said.

One of the servants came in and announced that dinner was ready.

"Will you join us, Akiva?" Domitilla asked.

"Thank you, but I am not allowed to eat at your table. God has given us special laws for food and drink. Many of the animals which you eat are considered impure for us by our faith, and even those that are pure must be slaughtered and prepared in a special manner."

"So where do you eat?" asked Clemens.

"My teacher and I get along quite well with fruit and bread throughout the week, and on the Sabbath we eat with a Jewish friend who lives next to the Tiber River."

"Then I will send you some of the exquisite fruits that grow in my orchards. And I ask you in turn to come and visit us often, so that you can tell us more about the teachings of Judaism."

Chapter 11

The Emperor had proceeded with his army to the Rhine, where the Germanic Chatti tribesmen were occupying Moguntiacum. When the Chatti heard that the Roman Army, led by the Emperor himself, was approaching, they boldly launched an attack against the Romans. At that moment the Emperor commanded that the earth in the Jewish delegation's chest be thrown against them. The Chatti were filled with terror and they fled. The Romans pursued them and took many captives. Then the Chatti sent messengers to the Emperor, promising to surrender. A treaty, favorable to the Romans, was signed between them, and for a long time afterwards peace and tranquility reigned in the region. So decisive was the victory that a few years later Rome was able to take over the whole area and integrate it into its empire.

On the wings of triumph and joy the Emperor rushed back to Rome. The Senate dispatched a delegation to inform him that he was worthy of a Triumphal march when he entered the city. Domitian therefore stayed outside the walls of Rome until preparations for the victorious ceremony had been completed. Then he marched in through the Gate of Triumph, at the head of his troops, wearing all his military insignia. He paraded through all the prominent streets and finally came to the Capitol, where he brought a sacrifice to Jupiter on behalf of the Roman nation.

The Emperor felt deeply gratified by the honors he was receiving. The populace of Rome applauded; the soldiers, who had received a bonus, cheered him as he entered the city, holding their weapons aloft; the poets wrote songs of praise to him; the Senate gave him the title of "Germanicus." In the midst of all his enjoyment, the Emperor had the Jewish delegation brought to him and he thanked them publicly for their wonderful gift and gave them lavish gifts in return.

Rabbi Nachum and the other delegates prepared themselves for their homeward journey. Akiva said goodbye to his kind hosts, Clemens and Domitilla.

"You are leaving us now," Domitilla said, "but the seed you have planted within us will continue to develop. My husband and I have come to feel that Israel's God is the one true God and that there is no other God."

Akiva replied, "Pagans who come to recognize the exclusive dominion of our One and only God can be compared to our Father Avraham. He too lived in the midst of a pagan world. His father, his mother, his siblings, and all of humanity at the time, were idol-worshipers."

"And how did it come about that Avraham came to know the One God?" Clemens asked.

"It is told that Avraham's father, Terach, lived at the court of King Nimrod," said Akiva. "King Nimrod wanted to have Avraham killed as soon as he was born, so Terach hid him in a cave for many years. When Avraham left that cave, he marveled at all the 'ordinary' things in the world that we take for granted. He asked himself how the sun, the moon, the stars, the earth, the mountains, the rivers, the trees, the animals, and human beings came into existence. He couldn't understand how gods made of wood and stone could have created such a beautiful, perfect world. 'They have mouths but they do not speak,' he said to himself. 'They have ears but they do not hear, they have noses but they do not smell, they cannot touch with their hands and they cannot walk with their feet and there is no voice in their throats.' After pondering this question deeply for a very long time, Avraham finally came to the realization that there is

One, omnipotent, and invisible God.

"And then God revealed Himself to him and taught him the highest form of wisdom. Following this, Avraham destroyed his father's idols and Nimrod caught him and had him thrown into a burning furnace. But God saved him from the fire and commanded him to leave the land of his birth, and to go to the Land of Cana'an. There Avraham spread the name of God amongst all people, and he brought up his son Yitzchak, whom God granted him in his old age, in the same faith as well. Yitzchak's son, Ya'akov, became the progenitor of our people. Almighty God gave our ancestors the Land that He had promised to Avraham and his descendants.

"We will try to think about the lofty ideas you have taught us," Clemens said. "My wife and I are unhappy about our nation's belief in a multitude of different gods. Domitian doesn't have any children, and Domitilla and I are his closest relatives. Perhaps he will choose either me or one of my sons as his successor. If that happens, then you will hear from me, Akiva!"

Rabbi Nachum and the rest of the delegation returned to Judea. On their way, when they passed through Brundisium, they met the wicked innkeepers, who were amazed to hear about the miraculous quality of the earth they had put in Nachum's chest. Afterwards they loaded a whole carriage with it and brought it to Rome!

It was at this time that the Dacians on the lower Danube revolted against the Romans. The Emperor appointed Cornelius Fuscus, the Prefect of the Praetorians, as chief commander and sent him with his troops to fight against the Dacians. The Emperor also gave Fuscus the earth that the innkeepers from Brundisium had brought, which was supposed to guarantee his victory — but it had no effect whatsoever. Decebalus, the leader of the Dacians, retreated with his troops from the valleys of Moesia, thereby causing Fuscus to follow him a long way and to cross the Danube, until Decebalus was in an advantageous position to attack. The earth from Brundisium had failed its purpose, and the Romans were defeated. Fuscus was killed and thousands of Romans lay dead on the battlefield. The enemies basked in their glory.

When news of the defeat reached Rome, the Emperor immediately had the innkeepers put to death.

It was a joyous reunion when Akiva came home to his wife and children. The Emperor's gifts, of which he had received a share, allowed him to provide for the modest needs of his family for quite a while. He therefore hoped to resume his Torah study at Gimzo without difficulty.

When he went to see his teacher, however, he found him in a terrible state. Nachum was blind in both eyes, his arms and legs were paralyzed, and his body was covered with boils. When Akiva saw him like this, he began to cry out loud. "Rabbi," he wept, "how did this happen?"

"I have brought this upon myself," replied Rabbi Nachum. "I was on my way to visit my father-in-law, and I had three donkeys loaded with food, drink, and all kinds of other delicacies for him. When I arrived, a poor man stood in my path and he said, 'Rabbi, please give me something to eat, or I will die of hunger!' 'Wait until I unload,' I said. And while I was in the midst of unloading, the poor man died! Then I cried, 'Woe unto me! I am at fault for this man's death!' And I addressed him, saying, 'May my eyes, which didn't look out for you, be blinded; may my legs, which were hesitant to move towards you to help you, become paralyzed; may my arms, which didn't provide food for you at the right time, stiffen; and may my body become covered with boils!'"

"I cannot bear to see you like this!" Akiva cried.

"Fortunate am I for receiving punishment for my sin in this world!" Rabbi Nachum answered.

Although Nachum suffered great pain, this did not stop him from teaching the holy Torah to his students.

In the depths of winter, there was once a heavy snowfall and

Rabbi Nachum's house, which was very flimsy, was threatening to collapse. As the students rushed to carry out their sick teacher while he lay in bed, Rabbi Nachum said, "My children, first remove all my belongings, for I know that as long as I am in this house, it will not fall."

And that is exactly what happened. After the students emptied the house, they carried out Rabbi Nachum's bed. And as soon as they left the house with him, it collapsed.

Rabbi Nachum's illness lasted only a short while — and then all of Israel mourned the death of the great teacher.

Akiva decided to go to Yavneh, which was the greatest center of Torah study at the time. Rabban Gamliel, the *Nasi*, was the head of the yeshiva there. He was a descendant of Hillel, and members of the family had served as *Nasi* for about a hundred years. Hillel had been followed by his son Shimon, who was followed in turn by Shimon's son Gamliel. After Gamliel, leadership passed to his son Rabban Shimon ben Gamliel. He was killed in the war against Vespasian, however, and his son Gamliel was too young at the time to assume the role of *Nasi*. Therefore Rabban Yochanan ben Zakkai was chosen instead of him, and after Rabban Yochanan died, Rabban Gamliel was appointed as the head of the yeshiva. At his side stood the great Rabbis Rabbi Eliezer ben Hurkanos and Rabbi Yehoshua ben Chananyah. There were also many other great men in Yavneh, such as Rabbi Tarfon and Rabbi Yochanan ben Nuri.

Yavneh was a wonderful place for Akiva. It was here that the living wellspring of Torah flowed and Akiva could quench his great thirst for knowledge.

Chapter 12

Akiva had a difficult time in Yavneh at first. Many of the ways of his youth which he still retained fell short of the high standards of holiness and purity there. Rabban Gamliel was very strict, and even the great men that stood at his side did not escape his admonishment. We can only imagine how much greater was his severity towards his students! And Akiva was lacking in quite a few areas, whether out of ignorance or out of old habit. It was Rabbi Yochanan ben Nuri in particular who brought Akiva's failings to the *Nasi*'s attention, causing him to punish Akiva severely. As Rabban Yochanan himself admitted, "I call upon heaven and earth as my witnesses that it was because of me that Akiva suffered punishment many a time. But he loved me all the more, just as it is written, 'Do not reprimand the mocker for he will hate you; punish the wise and he will love you.'"

In terms of scholastic achievement, Akiva also had to struggle very hard. He was afraid to speak up in the midst of this great scholarly assembly, for he still felt too ignorant. So for twelve years he sat at the feet of his teachers like a mute, saying nothing. And Rabbi Eliezer would often make critical comments about him. Rabbi Yehoshua ben Chananyah, however, recognized the great power of Akiva's intellect in spite of his silence.

The Sages tell us that Akiva was at this time like a merchant who carries a big basket on his shoulders and buys a variety of useful things: wheat, barley, flax, etc. He takes it all and puts it into his big basket. When he comes home with his heavy load, he starts sorting the items according to type. This is what Akiva did in yeshiva: everything he learned would be stored away in his memory, and in privacy he would try to arrange and clarify things for himself.

So immense was his thirst for knowledge that at times he would act quite boldly. He would follow his teacher Rabbi Yehoshua wherever he went, in order to observe his behavior. Once his curiosity almost got him into serious trouble. He met one of the greatest men of his time, Rabbi Nechunyah, who was called "the Great" for being so learned. Rabbi Nechunyah had been a contemporary of Rabban Yochanan ben Zakkai, and he was quite old at the time. Akiva approached him and asked, "Rabbi, how did you merit your advanced age?"

Rabbi Nechunyah's servants considered this an insulting question, and they were about to seize Akiva and punish him for his audacity. Akiva fled and climbed a tree. From the top of the tree he continued to question Rabbi Nechunyah: "Rabbi, why do we say '*keves echad* — one sheep' when *keves* alone means 'a sheep' — one sheep?"

"Leave him alone!" Rabbi Nechunyah told his servants. "He is a scholar. It was not mere curiosity that prompted him to ask how I got so old — it was because he wants to learn."

Then Akiva descended from the tree.

The Rabbi said, "I will answer both of your questions. The '*echad*' implies that the best sheep of the flock is to be used for the sacrifice. And how did I merit such a long life? I never accepted gifts, as it says, 'Whoever hates gifts will live.' I also never took revenge for any bad that was done to me, and because I always forgave people for the harm they caused me, God also forgave me for my sins. And I also tried to use all the riches God gave me for the benefit of others. Thus I often lent money to the poor so that they could improve their position and sustain themselves independently."

"Thank you for your guidance, Rabbi," Akiva replied. "I will try to follow your example."

Finally, after twelve years, Akiva felt confident enough to express his own view in front of his teachers. The first instance of this had to do with the religious laws concerning the Pesach sacrifice when *Erev Pesach* falls on Shabbos. Everyone agreed that the sacrifice had to be brought on Shabbos. It was only regarding some of the preparations that Rabbi Eliezer and Rabbi Yehoshua differed. Just as Rabbi Eliezer had seemingly won the dispute, Akiva came up with a proof as clear as daylight that the Torah forbids making any preparations on Shabbos which could have been done before Shabbos. And Akiva's argument prevailed. From then on both teachers and students looked at him in a very different light.

"Look!" Rabbi Yehoshua said to Rabbi Eliezer, quoting the words of the Torah: "This is the people which you have underestimated; now go and fight against them."

It was on that important day that a new sun, so to speak, had risen in Israel and was now climbing above the horizon, casting its light on the whole world. Everyone admired Akiva for his vast knowledge, his deep understanding, and his keen analytical mind. They were also astounded by his phenomenal memory.

Whenever there was an attempt to establish what the tradition was concerning a specific law, and Akiva was not present at the time, they would say, "*Halachah bachutz*!" meaning that Akiva, who was familiar with all the particulars of the law, was not there.

Whenever there was an attempt to establish the correct translation of a word or phrase, and Akiva was not present, they would say, "The Torah has gone out," which implied that Akiva, who had delved so deeply into the wisdom of the Torah, was not there.

Whenever they had a question about mathematics, astronomy, or biology, and Akiva was not there, they would not answer the question until Akiva was brought in. He would then sit down modestly at the feet of Rabbi Eliezer.

From that time it did not take long for the Rabbis to finally recognize that their student Akiva was a great Rabbi himself. Many of the young boys, eager to learn, began to crowd around him.

For twelve long years Akiva had not seen his wife and children. Only once during that time had he come to the village with the intention of visiting them. As he had stood at the entrance of his house, he heard the loud, strident voice of a neighbor criticizing Rachel harshly for her extreme loyalty to her husband, who had been away for so long, and had surely forgotten her!

"Rachel, why do you cause your father to hate you, because of this man? Why don't you just turn your back on your ungrateful husband and return to your father? He will surely be happy to take you and your children in."

"Do not speak negatively about my husband for being away for so long, for it is with my consent and encouragement that he is doing so. Oh, if he becomes a great teacher of Israel, I would accept his absence for even longer!"

Akiva heard the words of his noble wife and he immediately returned to Yavneh, without even having seen Rachel and the children.

Rachel's dream had been fulfilled, and Rabbi Akiva was rushing to go home. Thousands of his disciples were accompanying him.

People streamed from all directions to see the renowned scholar who was now journeying with crowds of pupils following him. Rachel also heard about this, and her heart was filled with both joy and trepidation as she set out to welcome her beloved husband. Then she saw him, surrounded by pupils, and she was about to rush towards him when the pupils blocked her way.

But Rabbi Akiva had seen her. "Rachel!" he cried. "My beloved wife, Rachel! Leave her alone! If not for her, I would have remained an ignorant shepherd. All my Torah and all your Torah are hers!"

During all these years, since the beginning of our story, Kalba Savua's life had been overshadowed with grief. Despite his sorrow, he had remained firm in his resolve. He had declined all attempts by his daughter and son-in-law to appease him. Now he was old and lonely. He felt that his end was near, and his final wish was to use his wealth for charitable causes and *chesed*. When he heard that a great Rabbi had taken up residence nearby, he decided to go and see him, to consult with him about how to distribute his wealth.

As he stood in front of Rabbi Akiva, he did not recognize his former servant.

"Rabbi, I would like your advice," he began. "I must make some decisions about the distribution of my property and assets after my death."

"Do you have any children to inherit the estate?"

"I have one daughter, but she married a poor, ignorant shepherd against my will, and I vowed to disown her, which I did."

"And if that poor shepherd had become a Torah scholar, and if you had known at the time that he would, would you have still made that vow?"

"It wasn't his poverty that angered me so much, but his ignorance. He didn't even know how to read or write."

"And if he had become a man whom everyone recognized for his knowledge and scholarship — if he had become someone like me, for example?"

"Oh, how fortunate I would have considered myself if my daughter had chosen someone like you!"

"My dear father, I am Akiva ben Yosef!" Akiva cried out. "I was the shepherd who served you, and your daughter Rachel is my beloved wife!"

Then Kalba Savua began to weep. "Can you forgive me, Rabbi?" he sobbed.

"There is nothing to forgive you for," said Rabbi Akiva. "What you did was justified. But now I will nullify your vow for you. I am uprooting it entirely, as if it never existed, for if you had been able to foresee what would happen later on, you would never have taken that vow."

"God bless you, Rabbi! Come and move into my house with me. I will give you half of my wealth immediately and the other half will become yours in the near future."

Rabbi Akiva called Rachel. When she entered the room and saw her father, she fell to the floor and embraced his knees.

Kalba Savua lifted her up, and hugged and kissed her. "My daughter, you were able to foresee the future better than I was! Forgive me for having caused you so much anguish and pain all these years."

"Oh, no, my father! How could I have suffered anguish or pain when I am married to the wisest and most noble man on earth? How could I have been unhappy when my children too are following in his footsteps, and one day they will become the pride and joy of Israel as well? I am as fortunate and happy as a woman could ever be. All I was missing, of course, was your fatherly love. And now that you have made peace with me again, my happiness is complete."

"God bless you, my daughter! Now that I have my grandchildren, I will no longer spend my old age in loneliness. Oh, bring them into my house, please, so that they can bring joy into my life."

It was a glorious sight to behold when Rabbi Akiva moved into his father-in-law's house with his wife and children, while all his disciples looked on.

Rabbi Akiva was now a wealthy man. One of the first things he did was to order a golden crown with a beautifully crafted image of Jerusalem engraved on it. This was for his beloved Rachel, for he had promised it to her in the days of their greatest poverty, when she had helped those that were even poorer than they. And Rachel, the modest and pious Rachel, wore the crown with great joy. It was not out of pride that she wore it, but rather to show the daughters of Israel through her example what great things can be accomplished through a woman's self-sacrifice for the sake of the holy Torah.

Chapter 13

Rabbi Akiva's daughter Shulamis had grown to be a lovely young woman. Her parents were thinking about marriage for her, and Rabbi Akiva had chosen one of his talented young students as his future son-in-law.

Shulamis' response was not what Rabbi Akiva expected, however. "I hope you won't be angry with me, Father," she began, "but I have a confession to make to you. There was a boy in our neighborhood who stood out among all the others for his exceptional mind. Once, when we were children, we were playing, and he asked me to promise that I would marry him one day. So I said, 'Go and learn, and become someone great among our people, and then I will marry you.'"

Akiva listened to his daughter's story with a smile. "Don't worry," he said, "I won't keep you from carrying out your promise. You are just confirming that you are your mother's daughter! And now tell me, who is this young man you have chosen?"

"His name is Shimon ben Azzai."

"Ah, my friend and student Ben Azzai! That's certainly not a bad choice, my daughter!"

Our Sages tell us that Ben Azzai could "uproot mountains" like no one before him or after him. This expression is used in the Talmud to describe the pinnacle of intellectual acuity. Shimon ben Azzai was so extraordinary in his mental capabilities, and his penetrating mind was so impressive, that all the other Torah scholars paled in comparison. He himself was aware of this as well. Indeed, the only scholar whom he considered superior to himself was Rabbi Akiva.

There was only one attribute that Ben Azzai had which exceeded his intellect: this was his boundless love for Torah. He was constantly studying the Torah, and it had been his only true love throughout his life. Thus Ben Azzai had mixed feelings when Rabbi Akiva offered his daughter to him in marriage.

The fact is that Ben Azzai was afraid of getting married and establishing a family because he feared that this would distract him from his learning. Although he was still very young, he had already taught many students, and once, when he had spoken to them about the Torah's first commandment — to marry and procreate in order to populate the world — one of his students had asked him, "Our revered teacher, why are you yourself not fulfilling this obligation, which you consider so important and which you have told us so much about?"

Ben Azzai had replied, "What can I do? My soul is bound up with the Torah in indescribable love. Let others maintain the human race!"

Nonetheless, Ben Azzai felt compelled to honor the proposal he had made to his childhood companion, and he accepted the offer of his teacher and friend Rabbi Akiva.

Kalba Savua wanted his granddaughter's wedding to be an elaborate celebration, and so it was. A large number of guests had been invited, among them the greatest and most famous men in Israel. Kalba Savua's mansion thronged with people, packed to its full capacity. Entire herds were slaughtered to feed the guests, and there were teams of cooks and bakers using all the ovens and stoves in the house. In the evening an immense table was set up in the garden. All the servants had their hands full serving the long rows of guests on either side of the table.

It was at that moment that a poor man dressed in dirty, torn clothing appeared on the scene. The servants brushed him aside and told him to leave. Rabbi Akiva and Rachel, who were looking after their guests and making sure they were well-served, did not notice the stranger.

But the bride noticed, and she picked herself up from her seat of honor at the head table and rushed toward the poor man. She greeted him graciously, offered him something to eat and drink, and told him to enjoy the wedding. Once he had eaten, she instructed the servants to provide him with the finest clothing to wear, so that he could participate in the following days of celebration without feeling ashamed.

It was on the next day that the actual betrothal ceremony took place. Just as the traditional *tallis* was placed over the young couple, Shulamis felt bothered by a golden pin in her head-covering. She pulled it out and stuck it into the wall behind her, without turning around.

The ceremony was over and the newlyweds and the parents were receiving their guests' congratulations inside the house. Shulamis suddenly remembered the golden pin which she had left in the garden wall, and she asked a servant to go and bring it to her. When the servant went to get it, he discovered to his great amazement that the pin had pierced the head of a poisonous snake and had riveted it to the wall until it died. He brought the pin, with the snake's head still attached to it, into the house, and everyone reacted with shock and amazement. It was clear that if Shulamis had not stuck her pin through the snake's head, it might easily have killed her with its venomous bite!

"My daughter," Rabbi Akiva cried, "God has saved you in a miraculous way! Tell me, how did you earn this special merit?"

"Father, I was undeserving of the Almighty's compassion."

"No, that isn't true!" her bridegroom interjected. "It is because of your noble character that you were saved, Shulamis. Indeed," he continued, "you have taught me the proper understanding of one of the sayings of the wise Shlomo HaMelech in *Mishlei*: 'Doing acts of charity saves a person from death.' Until now I had always believed that these words refer to the World-to-Come, but now I see, from what happened to you today, that it is also fulfilled in this world. Doing acts of charity and kindness saves a person from death in the literal, earthly sense, although true reward is reserved for the World-to-Come."

The seven days of the wedding feast were celebrated in great joy, and afterwards the guests returned to their homes. Shulamis was happily married to the husband she had selected in her childhood. But Ben Azzai was not a partner to her joy. There was a solemn expression on his face all the time.

"My husband, it hurts me to see you unhappy," Shulamis said to him one day. "Please, tell me what is troubling you."

"I cannot tell you, Shulamis. I am afraid it would upset you too much."

But after Shulamis implored him repeatedly, he decided to open his heart to her and tell her what was causing him such pain.

"A long time ago, you, Shulamis, were the one who caused me to dedicate my life to Torah," he began. "Since then, my love for Torah has grown so great that there is no room for any other love in my heart! Every minute that I have to take away from Torah study fills me with anguish and distress. And that is what is robbing me of my peace of mind."

"Oh, my beloved husband, you needn't worry! I won't hinder you from dedicating yourself entirely to Torah. On the contrary — the more attentively you learn, the more I will honor you and appreciate you!"

Ben Azzai shook his head. "But you see, Shulamis, the very thought of my duties as a husband and, in the future, as a father, disturbs me terribly. I did not want to go back on the proposal I made to you when we were children. And I know that to be married to you, such a noble, pious, and kind woman, who is also the daughter of the greatest man of Israel, would be considered by any other man to be the most desirable goal. To me, however, whose sole desire it is to learn and acquire the truth, it is a crushing burden to have any other responsibilities."

Shulamis began to cry. “It is true, my husband,” she said through her tears, “that what you have just told me upsets me greatly. But not because of me — because of *you*. It would truly be a great loss for Israel if you were to be hindered from reaching the great heights that you are capable of reaching. As for me, I will always love you and I will never marry anyone else. I will ask you nonetheless to give me a divorce, so that you will be freed from the ties that marriage creates.”

It was with a heavy heart that Ben Azzai decided to accede to his wife’s request. He felt that he could not do otherwise.

When the divorce had been carried out, Rachel hugged her weeping daughter. “What you have done, Shulamis, is far greater than what I did,” she said. “Everyone praises me for having sacrificed the material pleasures and luxuries of life for the sake of Torah. But *your* sacrifice is greater — you have released the man who is dearest to you in order to not hinder him in his great spiritual pursuits. God bless you, my child!”

Chapter 14

Rabbi Akiva had moved to the yeshiva in Yavneh with his family, where he was soon offered a very important position. Rabbi Yehoshua ben Ilem, who had been head of the administration of charity in Israel, had died, and Rabbi Akiva had been nominated as his successor. It was fitting that Rabbi Akiva replace the man who had been held in the highest esteem by the entire nation. There was a remarkable story told about Rabbi Yehoshua ben Ilem that merits repeating.

One night, when Rabbi Yehoshua ben Ilem was in a deep sleep, he heard a voice calling out to him, "How fortunate you are, Yehoshua! In Gan Eden your permanent place will be next to the butcher Nannes!" Rabbi Yehoshua ben Ilem had devoted his whole life to serving God, and he had eighty disciples who admired him greatly. He always fulfilled his duties as head of the charity administration with the greatest devotion. Now he greatly wished to meet the simple butcher who was to be his distinguished neighbor in the World-to-Come.

Rabbi Yehoshua ben Ilem set out to find him. He traveled from town to town with his students, until he finally found the butcher Nannes. Nannes was an ordinary man who followed the Torah's ways in a simple and straightforward manner. He had elderly parents who were sick and weak. He treated them with the greatest care and respect, for there was nothing in the world that he considered more important than serving them. He dressed them himself, brought them food, and fulfilled all of their requests willingly and kindly. Everything he could possibly do for them he would do himself, without involving servants.

When Rabbi Yehoshua ben Ilem heard this, he kissed the man and embraced him, exclaiming, "May God bless you in everything you do. I consider myself honored to have been assigned such a neighbor in Gan Eden!"

Now Rabbi Yehoshua ben Ilem had died and had found the place promised to him. Rabbi Akiva was chosen to become his successor. But Rabbi Akiva said, "I cannot accept this position until I have asked my wife for her consent, for I have promised her to devote all my time to studying Torah. She therefore has the right to decide whether, temporarily, this takes precedence over my learning."

Rachel had no objections, and thus Rabbi Akiva, the former shepherd, become head of the administration of Jewish charity throughout Eretz Yisrael. He fulfilled this task with the same energy that he applied to everything else. Soon he became known as "father to all the poor," and they showered him with their blessings. The following anecdote illustrates how ingenious he was when it came to raising the necessary funds:

Rabbi Tarfon, a former teacher and now a friend of Rabbi Akiva, was a wealthy man. One day Rabbi Akiva came to him and said, "My friend and teacher, I have just heard in the market an offer of a wonderful opportunity to buy some commodities. If you have a large sum of money available, I would be happy to carry out the purchases for you."

Rabbi Tarfon gave him four thousand gold coins, which Rabbi Akiva distributed to the poor. In the evening he returned to his friend. "I have brought you the receipt of the purchases I made with your money," he told him, and showed him the ninth verse of Psalm 112: "He distributes and gives to the poor; the most wonderful reward will be his in eternity."

Rabbi Tarfon kissed his friend and gave him even greater sums of money for further purchases of that kind.

One day, when Rabbi Akiva was about to enter the *beis midrash*, he found that it was locked. The guard at the door informed him that he had been instructed to tell him to go to Rabban Gamliel's home. Rabbi Akiva went there immediately, and as he entered the *Nasi*'s house, he saw his teacher Rabbi Yehoshua ben Chananyah, and Rabbi Elazar ben Azaryah, who was very young but very learned. With them, he saw a stranger there whom he soon recognized as his old friend Tadaeus from Rome. Rabbi Akiva greeted him warmly, but Tadaeus seemed to be very troubled.

"Let us not waste any time, great teachers of Israel," said Tadaeus. "Please sit down and allow me to deliver my message to you. Our brothers in Rome have sent me here to ask you to come to Rome. The Jewish people are in great danger. It will take some time for me to explain, so please bear with me."

The Sages sat down and listened to Tadaeus carefully, as he continued to speak:

"Our Emperor, Domitian, the brother of Titus who destroyed our Holy Temple, is a man of strange character. He is full of contradictions. I am telling you this so you will be able to understand the kind of danger that threatens us. The Flavian dynasty comes from undistinguished origins. Vespasian, who was Domitian's father, was from the Sabine hills near Reate. He was tyrannical and narrow-minded, and he has managed to endow his son with the same traits.

"Domitian's ideal is to recreate the old Republican customs in religion and ethics (although he himself despises them and transgresses them daily). He has proclaimed himself a god, and whenever he hears anything critical said about himself he calls it blasphemy and decrees harsh punishment for it. He also severely punishes those who don't worship the old gods. At the same time, he encourages his flatterers to make fun of his predecessors, including his own father and brother, although they too had been proclaimed as gods.

"As for moral conduct, he refused to marry Titus' only daughter Julia, citing an old Roman law that forbids a person to marry the daughter of his brother. But actually this law had been nullified under Claudius' reign. And what is stranger still is that when Titus died and Domitian became Emperor, he arranged the murder of Julia's husband because he had then taken a liking to her! And all this doesn't stop Domitian from punishing his people cruelly when they are only suspected of transgressing the moral laws.

"You know, my teachers, that the majority of the Romans have rejected the old Roman gods. Many of them have turned to Egyptian cults instead. There are also many noblemen who have discovered and accepted the truth of Judaism, although our faith is an absolute abomination in the Emperor's eyes. Whenever anyone is accused of taking an interest in Judaism, the Emperor immediately sentences that person to death or sends him into exile. Nonetheless, he has not succeeded in controlling the religious beliefs of his subjects.

"Despite all the executions, there are nevertheless more and more aristocratic Romans who are converting to Judaism! Flavius Clemens is their leader. He is the son of Sabinus, who is Vespasian's only brother, and his wife Domitilla is the daughter of Titus' and Domitian's sister. Recently Clemens called in the heads of our community and told them that Domitian had decided to kill Jews throughout the empire in order to bring an end to the spread of Judaism."

When the Sages heard the terrible words, they tore their clothing like mourners and cried. Tadaeus wept with them. Then he wiped his tears and continued to speak:

"Since the days of Haman, our people have never been in as much danger as now! Clemens has tried again and again to influence the Emperor. He pointed out to him how much profit Rome makes on us since we pay twice the amount of taxes that other subjugated nations pay. But the Emperor's desire to defend the authority of the old gods outweighs even his greed.

"Clemens told us: Send people to Judea to tell the Sages to institute fast days and organize prayers to be said in the synagogues, and tell them to come to Rome to consult with me and my friends about how to deal with this situation! Know that we do have influential allies in the city, because some of the most prestigious Roman citizens and some of the senators are in fear for their lives. The tyrant is in a rage even against the philosophers and the greatest thinkers of the nation — he threatens to kill them or send them into exile.

"That is why the heads of the Jewish community of Rome have sent me here — to deliver Clemens' message. I have fulfilled my task — now tell us by the power of God's spirit which rests upon you, what should be done."

"Very well," Rabban Gamliel said. "First of all, we will do as Clemens has advised us to do: everyone will fast on the second and fifth day of the week, and the synagogues will be open all day long for prayer. And I will go to Rome." He turned to the Sages. "Would you like to accompany me, my friends?"

"I will go with you," Rabbi Yehoshua replied.

"So will I," said Rabbi Elazar ben Azaryah.

"And you, Akiva — why do you remain silent?" Rabban Gamliel asked.

"There are Sages," replied Rabbi Akiva, "who are far more worthy of the great honor of accompanying you than I am: Rabbi Eliezer, Rabbi Tarfon, Rabbi Yishmael, Rabbi Yehudah ben Bava, and many others. If one of them were left behind because I went, he might feel hurt."

"Your humility does you honor, Akiva," Rabban Gamliel replied. "But Tadaeus has already told us that Clemens especially requested that you accompany us to Rome. That is why we called you and not all the others to this consultation. Would you like to discuss it with your wife first, Akiva?"

"That won't be not necessary," Rabbi Akiva answered with a smile. "Wherever you are, and wherever Rabbi Yehoshua and Rabbi Elazar are, is where the Torah is too. And every moment I spend in your company increases my knowledge. That I will be of learning from the shining lights of Israel will certainly make my wife very happy."

Chapter 15

Rabban Gamliel had arranged for prayers to be said in all the synagogues throughout Judea, and he designated every second and fifth day of the week as fast days. Then he and his friends who were to accompany him to Rome went to visit the ruins of the Holy Temple so that they could pray at the Western Wall for a successful journey and mission. As they reached the crest of the hills and looked upon the ruins of Jerusalem before them, they burst into tears and tore their clothing as a sign of mourning. "Zion has become like a desert!" they wept. "Our holy, glorious Temple, in which our forefathers used to praise the Almighty, blessed be He, has become a heap of rubble, and all our joy has been taken from us!"

Then Rabban Gamliel cried out in a loud voice:

"Oh, God, the nations invaded Your abode, and caused the Holy Temple to become impure! They turned Jerusalem into a heap of rubble, and left Your servants' dead bodies for the birds to eat. They gave the flesh of Your pious ones to the wild animals, and shed their blood as though it were water, all around Jerusalem, and there was no one to bury them. We have become a mockery to the people around us; we are despised and ridiculed by all our neighbors. How much longer, O God? Will You be angry with us forever? Will You continue to rage like a blazing fire? Pour out Your anger on those nations who don't want to know You, and on those kingdoms who do not call on You, because they have devoured Ya'akov and have laid waste to his habitation. Don't make us accountable for our sins of the past any longer! Treat us with compassion, for we are so impoverished! Help us, God, our Redeemer, for the sake of Your Name's honor. Forgive us for the sake of Your Name. Why should the nations say, 'Where is their God?' Let it become known among those nations — and before our eyes — that the spilled blood of Your servants is being avenged. Let the groaning of the prisoner penetrate Your mercy! Rescue those people of Yours who are doomed to death, with Your mighty arm! Revenge our neighbors' blasphemy and evil seven times as much as they have heaped upon You. And we, Your people and Your flock, will know and glorify You forever."

The others had listened to him in silence. Now they began to moan and tear their clothing again, and they cried out in loud voices: "Praise to You, our God, King of the universe, the true Judge! God is a rock; His deeds are deeds of perfection, for all His ways are just. God is the fount of truth; there is no injustice in Him. He is benevolent and compassionate."

Then they went down the hill until they reached the Western Wall of the Holy Temple, the remaining remnant. They removed their shoes and prayed with great fervor. Suddenly a fox came running out of the place where the Holy of Holies had been. When the Sages saw this, they began to cry bitterly. Only Akiva remained silent — and he smiled.

"Why are you smiling, Akiva?" the Sages asked him.

And he, in turn, asked them, "And you, my teachers, why are you crying?"

"The Holy of Holies is the place that was entered only once a year by the Kohen haGadol, and he was permitted there only if he came in a state of utmost purity and holiness. It was the place about which it is said, 'And any stranger that will enter it shall be killed.' And now that we see that foxes run in and out of that very place, how can we not cry?"

"My teachers, that's exactly why I am rejoicing!" declared Rabbi Akiva. "It says in *Yeshayahu*: 'And I will get myself loyal witnesses — Uriah the Kohen and Zecharyah ben Yeverechyahu.' How do these two come together? Didn't Uriah live in the time of the First Temple and Zecharyah in the time of the Second? But Scripture is creating a link between Zecharyah's prophesy and Uriah's.

"In Uriah's prophesy it says: 'Indeed, because of you Zion will be plowed like a field, Jerusalem will become heaps of rubble, and the Temple Mount will be like a forest in the high places. In Zecharyah's it says: 'Thus God spoke: I am returning to Zion and I will dwell in the midst of Jerusalem; then Jerusalem will be called the City of Truth... Once again there will be old men and women in the streets of Jerusalem, walking with canes because of their old age, and the city will be filled with boys and girls playing in its streets.'

"Now, as long as Uriah's prophesy remained unfulfilled, I had good reason to fear that Zecharyah's prophesy would not be fulfilled either. But look! Now that the Temple's grounds have become 'like a forest' — a place for foxes to live in! — just like God foretold through Uriah, we can be certain that God will rebuild His Holy Temple, just as He promised us through Zecharyah."

"You have consoled us, Akiva," the Sages said to him. "You have consoled us."

Full of new confidence they set out on their journey. They boarded the ship in Jaffa and eventually arrived safely in Brundisium.

They found that the Emperor Domitian was terrorizing and persecuting all upper-class Roman citizens. By leisurely executing them, one by one, he was able to put fear in the hearts of all. At the same time he tried to flatter the common people and the army as much as possible. He gave the soldiers double pay and arranged all sorts of entertainments for those who were loyal to him. He used the riches confiscated from the executed senators to pay for all this.

The whole city was filled with statues in his image, and the

Capitol was also decorated with many portraits of him in bronze. The most splendid statue of all was the figure of a horseman in gilded bronze that stood in the middle of the Forum and in front of the Flavian family's temple. It was set on a high pedestal, and it seemed as though Domitian's head was lodged in the sky and was looking down at all the roofs of the halls and temples of the city. His right hand was outstretched, as though he was giving a command, and his left hand held the figure of Minerva. His sword was resting peacefully in its scabbard, while his horse was stepping on the chained head of the captured Rhine.

Grand theatrical productions and lavish banquets were arranged in honor of the dedication of this statue. All of Rome was out in the streets, celebrating and indulging in feasts and spectacles. It was at this time that the Sages approached the city. From afar they could already hear the roar of the cheering mob. They stood still and broke into tears. Only Akiva didn't cry, and there was a smile of contentment on his face.

Seeing this, the Sages asked him: "Why are you smiling, Akiva?"

And Akiva asked in turn, "And you, my friends — why are you crying?"

They replied, "These pagans, who bow down in front of images and offer incense to their idols, who surrender to all their evil desires and weaknesses, and who know nothing about the higher purpose of life, live in security and happiness. We, on the other hand, have recently witnessed the destruction of our Temple, lost our national independence, and are being persecuted by our enemies. We fear for our lives daily! How can we not cry?"

"Ah, but that is precisely why I am happy," said Rabbi Akiva. "If God grants so much pleasure to those who transgress His will daily and at every hour, then just think how much more He has in store for His true servants, whose sole ambition is to live their lives according to His command!"

"You have consoled us, Akiva," the Sages said. "You have consoled us."

While the people of Rome were feasting and celebrating in the streets, the Emperor put fear into the hearts of his close friends and relatives. He arranged a "special" dinner for a select few of the highest rung of the aristocracy. He had decorated an entire room in black: the ceiling was black, the floor was black, and there was a black cloth spread on all the stone seats. The guests who were invited for the evening were asked to come without their servants. Next to their individual seats every one of them found a sculpture of the kind used for burial, with their individual names imprinted on it. There were also three-legged burial lamps hanging above them.

As soon as the guests had taken their seats, a group of young boys in black came in and performed a ghastly dance for them. Then they offered the guests leftover food as their meal, reminding them of the Roman custom of bringing leftovers for the dead. The guests were so horror-stricken that they could hardly move. They were expecting to be killed any minute.

It was at that moment that the Emperor entered the room, proceeding slowly and elegantly. He sat down, and was served some of the leftovers.

"Yes," he began, "those people that have left the ranks of the living have to be content with leftovers. Leftovers are considered a wonderful meal for the condemned souls that go down to Hades. And let me remind you that it is always within my power to send you down the path that leads to Hades! And I will use that power against anyone who dares to question my divine authority. My power is like that of Jupiter, and anyone who tries to rebel against me will leave this world as though he was struck by lightning!"

The Emperor rose, and to the great surprise (and relief) of the guests, they were allowed to leave. The next day each of the young slaves who had served the guests appeared at the door of that guest, clean and well-groomed, and offered their services.

Each one also brought with him the silver plate and cup which had been used at the meal, as a gift from the Emperor to those who had been his guests. By sending them slaves and gifts, Domitian was trying to compensate them for the terror he had subjected them to.

Chapter 16

When the Sages arrived in Rome in the midst of festivities, Domitian had just instituted the Capitolinian contests, in which poems were recited in honor of the gods to whom these festivities were dedicated. Domitian, however, had made himself the subject of these poems. The best poets of the time — Martial, Statius, and Quintilian — were all competing in their effusive songs of praise to the Emperor. And the Emperor presided over all, dressed in royal purple and wearing a golden crown, surrounded by lavishly dressed priests. He distributed garlands of gilded oak leaves as prizes.

While the common people and the soldiers were taking part in all the celebrations in honor of the Emperor, the senators and the noble Roman families continued to live in fear for their lives. The most distinguished Roman citizens were accused of the most insignificant charges and then put to death. The most outstanding victims of Domitian's cruelty were three famous and virtuous men by the names of Herennius Lenecio, Arulenus Rusticus, and Helvidius Priscus. The first two were accused of having written poems in praise of men whom the Emperor disapproved of, and the third was accused of having written a satire which suggested that the Emperor was planning to separate from his wife. (The Emperor took great pleasure in watching their execution. The Empress had been found guilty of disloyalty to her husband and was sent into exile. However, Domitian couldn't bear being separated from her, and he changed his decree, allowing her to come back to him. The

Romans found the story to be quite amusing, and there was a satire written about it; and Helvidius Priscus was accused of being the author.)

The three men were sentenced to death and were killed in the presence of the Emperor and all the senators.

Now the blows fell one after another. The more friendly and kind the Emperor would be towards one of the important men of the city, the more certain that man could be of his impending death. Thus the Emperor showered praises on the Consular Arretinus Clemens, but once while he and Arretinus were together, the Emperor stopped one of his agents who was passing by and assigned him the job of coming up with an incriminating accusation against the man who was next to him. The next day Arretinus was sentenced to death and executed!

Domitian's deeply superstitious nature caused many innocent deaths. As soon as he heard from any of the fortune-tellers in Rome that a certain man was going to become Emperor, he would have that man executed. One of Domitian's cousins, Flavius Sabinus, was appointed consul. The herald who announced the ceremony mistakenly said the word "Emperor" instead of "consul," this cost Sabinus his life.

Such were the troubled circumstances in Rome when the four Sages arrived there.

"Shouldn't we first visit our friend, the philosopher Artemidorus?" Rabbi Yehoshua asked. "So many philosophers have either been executed or sent into exile. They must naturally feel a certain kinship to us!"

"No," replied Rabban Gamliel. "We should first go to the person who asked us to come here. Show us the way to the home of Flavius Clemens, Akiva."

Flavius Clemens and his wife Domitilla received Rabbi Akiva and his colleagues in the warmest manner.

"My dearest friends!" Rabbi Akiva said. "This is Israel's leader, Rabban Gamliel, teacher and beacon of our nation! And this is my honored teacher, Rabbi Yehoshua, whose light shines like the sun. And this is my young friend and colleague, Elazar, the pride and hope of our people. You sent Tadaeus to us and we have heeded your call. We are here to consult with you as to how, with God's help, we can avert the terrible danger that is threatening the Jews."

"Welcome to you, my friends and teachers," Clemens said. "I address you like that because Domitilla and I have decided to convert to Judaism, though Domitian punishes such decisions with a death sentence. We gave up the Roman idols a long time ago."

"Think about your decision very carefully, sir!" Rabban Gamliel said. "Pious people will have a share in the World-to-Come no matter what nation they are from. As long as you give up idol-worship; refrain from murder, adultery, and eating meat taken from a living animal; you do not blaspheme God's Name; you avoid theft and the like, and set up a just judicial system, you will have your share of eternal bliss. You don't have to convert to attain that!"

While Rabban Gamliel was speaking, Domitilla brought in grapes and other fruits, which she put out on the table for the Sages. "I'm sorry that I am not serving you anything else," she said. "Although we have already made our household kosher, I am afraid you won't want to eat anything other than fruit, because we have not actually converted yet."

The Sages sat down and ate some of the fruit which Domitilla had offered them. Then Clemens asked Rabbi Akiva to tell them everything that had happened since the last time they had seen each other. When Rabbi Akiva told them about the death of his teacher Nachum, Domitilla cried bitterly.

"We too have suffered," she said. "Both of our sons..." Her voice broke.

"Both of our promising sons," Clemens continued, "died in the flower of their youth. They had a glorious future awaiting them. Domitian loved them, especially the older one, who was named after his father."

"I won't cry over their fate," Domitilla said, after she had wiped away her tears. "It's better to die young than to be Emperor of this vast empire. My uncle Domitian was once one of the most good-natured people. When he became Emperor it was his greatest ambition to satisfy his people by being a strong, good ruler, and by instituting wise and reasonable laws. But what a change has come over him!

"During his early days as Emperor of Rome he said, 'Whoever fails to show disgust towards the informers encourages them.' And in the beginning he acted upon this principle, but soon it became clear that he couldn't do without these despicable agents. Since the rebellion of Sartorius Antonius, the general, he suspects conspiracy everywhere.

"The thought that every Roman citizen has the right to yearn for the Emperor's crown leaves him no peace. He feels compelled to win the people's love by providing them with luxurious entertainment and to secure their loyalty to him by paying them generously. Thus the funds of the state treasury are constantly running out, and in order to replenish them Domitian plunders the subjugated provinces and kills in order to confiscate their wealth. That is why I consider my sons fortunate for not having been put to the test of contending with these horrible temptations."

"You have a noble way of looking at things and I respect you for it," said Rabbi Akiva. "You deserve to be taken under angels' wings and to become a daughter of Israel."

Rabban Gamliel then said, "Let us talk about the purpose of our trip, and about what we can do to dampen the Emperor's rage."

"To change Domitian's attitude towards the Jews would be impossible," Clemens said. "He hates the Jews for the same reason that he hates the philosophers — because they are against his gods. There is only one thing I know of that will save the Jews — and that is, the Emperor's death."

Clemens had spoken in a very grave and frank manner, and

his listeners were shocked.

"If God punishes the Emperor," said Rabbi Akiva, "we will welcome his death as our salvation — but we cannot have a hand in his death. Our holy Torah forbids us to kill even the most abominable ruler."

"The circumstances are such that we are at a great advantage," Clemens went on. "The finest Roman citizens long for his death more than anything else. If the Jewish community armed themselves and rose up against him, then all the noblemen would come to their aid, and Domitian's power would soon come to an end."

"We cannot have anything to do with these ideas of yours," Rabbi Elazar ben Azaryah said. "We are forbidden to take part in anything that would give our persecutors a pretext or a reason to destroy us. We may only do what God's law permits us, whether this relates to saving our people or any other matter."

"I am afraid," Clemens said, "that there are no lawful means whereby one might persuade a Roman Emperor to retract his own decision. And now that all of Israel is in danger, will you really be able to restrain yourselves from responding to violence with armed resistance?"

"God will not forsake us," Rabbi Akiva said. "It says in Scripture, 'I have spread you abroad like the four winds.' As the world can't do without the winds, it likewise can't exist without Israel. God will show us how to overcome the danger in a more peaceful manner."

Clemens weighed his own reply, and said, "So far there has not been any definite decree. We can therefore wait a little. Where are you staying?"

"We came to you first," Rabban Gamliel said.

"I advise you not to stay with anyone who is Jewish, so that you don't attract the attention of Domitian's spies. I will have one of the supervisors of my estate bring you to a Roman citizen by the name of Cocceius Nerva. He's not suspected of anything and he will gladly let you stay in one of his houses."

He knocked on his wall three times — and his property manager appeared a few minutes later. "Stephanus, bring these men to the house of my friend Cocceius Nerva and ask him in my name to please allow them to stay in his house for the duration of their visit to Rome."

Chapter 17

Marcus Cocceius Nerva welcomed the group of visitors from Judea in friendship and warmth, and he lodged them in one of the apartments in his palace. Nerva was one of the most prominent senators, and he had been Consul twice. He was now 64 years old and was one of the Emperor's closest advisors.

The following night Nerva was awakened by a messenger from the Emperor and told to appear before the Emperor immediately. The elderly man began to tremble with fear. Was this summons in the middle of the night connected to the fact that he had taken the strangers into his house?

In the antechamber outside the Emperor's private quarters, Nerva sat and waited. Soon he was joined by Flavius Clemens, which seemed to confirm his fears that his present predicament had to do with the Jewish guests sent by Clemens.

"My dear Clemens," said Nerva, "what have I done to you that you have sent me people who may cause us harm?"

He had barely finished his question when Catulus came rushing in.

"What has happened? Have the Chatti or the Sicambri gone to war with us? Have the Britons or the Dacians started a rebellion?"

It was not long before Junius Maricius, whom Domitian hated, joined the men in the antechamber. He was the brother of Arulenus Rusticus, who had been executed. "What's going on?" he asked. "Why have we all been summoned in the middle of the night? Are we all going to be dispatched to our death?"

And so one senator after another appeared, until there were eleven of them, all members of the Emperor's secret Council. They were all deathly pale and trembling with fear, and they were kept waiting in terror for a long time.

At one point the Emperor's servants appeared, carrying an enormous fish into their Master's chamber. Half an hour passed, and the senators sank deeper into despair.

Finally the Emperor's chamber was opened, and they were granted entry. Now they would learn what fate had in store for them.

The Emperor received them in a very solemn manner. "I have called you together to help me decide on an important matter," he proclaimed to them, "for you are the vital supporters of my throne, and you excel in wisdom and virtue. Forgive me for having disturbed your sleep, but the matter at hand could not wait.

"Look at this huge fish! A poor fisherman caught him off the coast of Ancona, and he carried him across the mountains out of his love and loyalty to me, so that it might enhance my table. But I don't have a platter that is large enough to hold this king of all fish!

"The question which I would like you to discuss with each other is the following: Should the fish be cut into small pieces and served on several ordinary platters or should I have a new platter made, which will be able to contain the whole of this wonderful fish on it?"

The senators couldn't believe their ears. They looked back and forth from the fish to the Emperor in great bewilderment. When they finally grasped what their middle-of-the-night summons had been for, they were greatly relieved. They had escaped what they were sure was a close brush with death. But on second thought, they began to feel outraged for having been treated like that. Here they were, the most distinguished senators of the world's capital city, Rome, and the Emperor was abusing them and playing games with them! And yet they knew very well that they should hide their feelings. Therefore they studied the issue very carefully, weighing the pros and cons as though they were dealing with a matter of life and death. Finally the majority voted that the fish should not be cut up, but that a special platter be made for it.

The visiting leaders of the Jewish people were also affected by this strange incident. The very next day Nerva asked them to leave, since he had suffered too much anxiety because of them. Actually, they were quite pleased with the idea of lodging with a fellow Jew instead. It was only out of consideration for Clemens' request that they had gone to a pagan's house.

They went to the home of their friend Tadaeus, who was happy to host them. Now Rabbi Yehoshua repeated his question: "Shouldn't we visit our friend Artemidorus, the philosopher?"

This time Rabban Gamliel had nothing to say against the idea, and the Sages set out for Artemidorus' home, which was on an estate outside the city.

The Emperor had driven the philosophers out of Rome seven years earlier. Recently he had renewed his measures against them, before many of them had defied their banishment and had returned to Rome. The philosophers at the time were for the most part Stoics. Domitian feared all the Stoics — just as he feared the politicians of the senate. To his mind, they all used the same language and the same logic; they all based their ideas on the same principles and came up with the same solutions.

He was as suspicious of those who voiced their beliefs openly as he was of those who avoided the public and aired their bitterness in the privacy of their homes. While in the former case he felt threatened by the expressed hostility, in the latter he was worried about covert plots. The politicians, however, were punished far more severely. They often suffered gruesome deaths, whereas in the case of the philosophers their banishment was enough to make Domitian feel secure. Some of them were sent to the most remote and deserted corners of the empire, such as the shores of Gaul, the desert of Lybia, or the steppes of Scythia. In the case of Artemidorus, who was more of a geographer than a philosopher, Domitian only demanded that he leave the city and reside at his estate outside of Rome.

Artemidorus was famous for his explorations in the Mediterranean Sea, the Red Sea, and the Atlantic Ocean. On his travels he had also visited Eretz Yisrael, where he became friendly with the Jewish leaders.

When the four Sages reached the home of Artemidorus, Rabbi Yehoshua knocked on the door, which was not locked. Artemidorus heard the knocking and said to himself, "Those must be the wise men from Judea. They never enter a house (not even their own) without knocking beforehand." He threw off his housecoat and quickly put on the clothing he reserved for receiving distinguished visitors. In the meantime Rabbi Yehoshua knocked again. "Such are the wise men from Judea," Artimedorus thought to himself. "They will not enter before I have opened the door for them. No one in the world is as well-behaved as they."

When he was properly dressed — after Rabbi Yehoshua had knocked for the third time — he ran to the door and opened it wide. Then he saw the Sages of Israel. Rabban Gamliel stood in the middle of the group, with Rabbi Yehoshua and Rabbi Elazar ben Azaryah on his right side and Rabbi Akiva on his left.

Artemidorus called out to them, "Welcome to you, wise men of Israel, with Rabban Gamliel as your leader!"

As he led them into his house, he said, "Blessed be the God of Israel for having granted me the opportunity to see my friends again!"

After they sat down, Rabban Gamliel explained the purpose of their visit. "We too," he said, "are happy to renew our friendship with you. But unfortunately it is not a joyous occasion that has brought us to Rome. Our people, the Jews, are in great danger. The Emperor feels even more threatened by the Jews than by the philosophers. He is worried about the fact that so many respectable Roman citizens are converting to Judaism, so in order to protect the cult of the old Roman gods, he has decided to destroy all the Jews. Now we have come to you for advice. What can we do to prevent this terrible tragedy?"

Artemidorus was silent for quite a while, and the Sages awaited his reply expectantly. "My friends," he finally said, "it is difficult to give you advice in this situation. Domitian has no compassion. If you go down on your knees to plead with him, he will receive you lovingly and will promise to treat you with mercy and kindness, but afterwards he will surely try to destroy you. Our only hope for salvation lies in the fact that his cup of transgressions is filled to the brim, and that his horrible tyranny won't last too much longer. Believe me, he will soon be overthrown, and then he will die a humiliating death!"

"Our friend Artemidorus," said Rabbi Yehoshua, "if Domitian's plans to destroy us (Heaven forbid) are carried out before his appointment with death, what help does that bring us?"

"Then the only thing you can do is to try to get the decree postponed or nullified," Artemidorus said. "I can direct you to someone who would make a good ally. I'll tell you a secret, which I found out from my father-in-law, Musonius. One of the informers told him that the Emperor has put Marcus Cocceius Nerva, one of our most prominent senators, on his list of those scheduled for execution. If this man is going to be killed by Domitian, then there isn't a senator left who can feel safe anymore. Tell Nerva this secret, and he will make every effort to hasten the death of the Emperor!"

Chapter 18

After the Sages had left the home of Artemidorus, they decided that it would not be a good idea for all of them to go to Nerva together, seeing that he had asked them to leave his home for political reasons. Rabbi Akiva thus took it upon himself to go and tell Nerva about the impending danger, and he arranged for a private meeting with the senator.

The two men greeted one another and Rabbi Akiva came quickly to the point. "Sir, you told us to leave your house because you were afraid of making an unfavorable impression on the Emperor. This precaution was apparently unnecessary. Domitian had put your name on his list of those doomed to be executed before we even arrived in Rome!"

Nerva was shaken. "Are you a prophet, who is able to penetrate the Emperor's secret plans?"

"I am neither a prophet nor the son of a prophet," replied Rabbi Akiva. "I found this out from a friend. Musonius, the father-in-law of Artemidorus, heard it from one of the informers."

When Nerva heard this, he began to tremble. He became so unsteady on his feet that Rabbi Akiva rushed to him to support him, brought him to a sofa, and helped him sit down. Nerva gathered all his will power to surmount his overwhelming fear. Then he spoke.

"You have brought this news from a reliable source, and I have no doubt that what you say is true. A violent death awaits me! But tell me, stranger, what causes you to come to me?

Surely I haven't done anything to deserve your concern for me."

"I am a Jew, sir," explained Rabbi Akiva, "and the Jews are descendants of Avraham, of whom it is written, 'And all the nations of this world shall be blessed through him.' I therefore consider it my duty to be concerned with the well-being of all my fellowmen. But today I have an additional reason for helping you to protect yourself from the Emperor. Domitian has murderous plans against the Jews, and that is why his enemies are our allies."

"And how do you think I can protect myself?"

"You must know that better than I do, sir. You have a lot of friends, and the same fate that awaits you today might easily devour them tomorrow."

"You are right, Rabbi Akiva. I will discuss with my friends what we can do. I was planning to spend my few remaining days in peace! I am an old and lonely man, and the astrologers foretold that although I only have a short while to live, I would die peacefully in my bed."

"If that is what they have prophesied," said Rabbi Akiva excitedly, "and you still have the horoscope, it could save your life! Domitian is very superstitious, and he believes in everything the astrologers say. You just have to arrange things so that he learns about the horoscope, and then he will no longer want to kill you. He will certainly prefer to have you die without him being the culprit — then he won't have to worry about all your friends hating him and wanting to avenge your death."

"Oh, you do indeed have divine insight! Your advice is truly of great value and of course I will follow it. If I am able to save my life, I will find a way to express my gratitude towards you."

"Nerva, my life is just as endangered as yours is! If you can help me to save our people, then you will surely have paid me back handsomely."

"But how can someone who is doomed to death be of help to you?"

"God's Providence rules over everything. The Almighty can

overthrow the tyrant in a minute and raise up all those that seemed weak and defeated."

"May your God perform this miracle, Rabbi Akiva, and I will do whatever I can for your people."

That same day the members of the secret Council were called to the Emperor. In accordance with his usual habit of treating his next victim in the most amiable manner, Domitian showed great warmth to Cocceius Nerva. He sought him out and hugged and kissed him. "My dear Nerva," said the Emperor, "why do you look so troubled and unhappy? Has anything unpleasant happened to the dearest of my friends whom I consider closest to my heart?"

"How can I not be sad when the stars predict my approaching death!" replied Nerva.

"Your words sadden me," said Domitian. "Let us hope that the stars are not telling the truth this time, even though they are usually so accurate in predicting one's fate. Tell me — did they foretell the manner of your death?"

Nerva pulled out a plaque and showed it to the Emperor. "Here is the horoscope which they reckoned on my last birthday, based on the exact hour of my birth."

Domitian took the plaque from him, and studied it very carefully. "Indeed," he said, "the stars are proclaiming that your end is near. But your star will go down in a beautiful way, without losing its brightness. You are right: they say you will die in your bed, without suffering any pain."

Nerva sighed in relief. He knew the Emperor well, and he could tell from what he was saying that he had given up his plan of killing him.

In the meantime the secret Council had assembled. Domitian sat on his throne, and the senators sat at his feet on small cushions. "My friends," he said to them, "what should one do if he has a painful abscess on his foot? Should he leave it alone, allowing it to grow and spread over the whole body until he dies from it, or should he use a sharp knife to cut it out, in order to save his life?"

"You must be asking this as an introduction to something else," Junius Maricius answered, "for it is self-evident that one would have to perform the operation, no matter how painful it would be, in order to save the rest of the body."

"You understood my words well, dear Junius!" exclaimed the Emperor. "All of you know that our ancestors' religion is in great danger. The Romans are beginning to have their doubts about the omnipotence of Jupiter, and Minerva, my dearest patron, is not receiving the honor she deserves. I have expelled the philosophers because they poison the hearts of our youth with their false teachings. But a powerful enemy of our gods still lives in our midst, protected by our toleration. That enemy — that godless enemy — is the Jewish people.

"You know that the Jews differ from all the other nations of this world — they don't worship any gods. The Egyptians, the Chaldeans, the Gauls, the Germans, and all the other nations worship gods like ours. They just have different names. But the Jews don't have any gods at all! They don't even have a godly image in their religious rites. And furthermore, they were always enemies of the Roman Empire. My father, the divine Vespasian, subjugated them. My brother, the divine Titus, destroyed their Temple, in which they devoted themselves to an unknown, invisible being. Yet despite this, they have remained a threat to us. They mislead my people, convincing them to become godless too. Many aristocratic Romans have already been punished with death because of their interest in Judaism. But the Jews continue to mislead people, with even greater energy.

"As long as we tolerate the Jews within the Roman Empire, their godlessness will spread like a contagious disease. I therefore consider it my duty to complete the work which my father and brother began. For what they did was not effective — they destroyed the Jewish state and the Jewish Temple, but they left the Jews alive. I will wipe out the entire nation! And thus we will prevent the downfall of the gods of Olympus. Not one member of this sinful, godless race should be left alive. Men, women, and children alike are to be killed! In thirty days from now the senate will decide that they should all be executed — all of them — throughout the whole Roman Empire, wherever they live, in Rome and all of Italy, in Judea, and in Syria, Egypt, Africa, and everywhere else. I expect all of you to agree with me and to make my decision your decision as well."

Flavius Clemens stood up. "Caesar, allow me..."

"Be quiet, Clemens," the tyrant cut him off, "You should not be the one to speak concerning this issue. I have been told that you too take an interest in Judaism, that you have dealings with Jews, and that you refuse to give the gods the respect they deserve. By the name of Hercules, if you were not my closest relative, and if it were not for the fact that I want to spare my niece Domitilla, I would have long ago made you account for your godless behavior! Do not you dare say another word in favor of the Jews, or — I swear by Minerva, my exalted protector — you will be brought to trial for godlessness!"

Flavius Clemens was silent. The other members of the secret Council were aghast.

"So, do we all agree?" asked the Emperor.

"Great and powerful Emperor! What you have said is true indeed, but..."

"My dear Nerva," Domitian interrupted him, "I thought you wanted to live the few days you have left in peace and quiet. So please refrain from defending the Jews."

No one dared to argue anymore, and thus the Emperor's execution plan was sealed.

Before Domitian dismissed the members of the Council, he said, "Keep in mind that you are my secret council! Whoever divulges any information about this decision will be sentenced to death. You must keep this secret even from your wives."

At that point he cast a sharp look at his cousin Clemens. It was for him that this warning was intended.

Chapter 19

In spite of the Emperor's explicit warning, Flavius Clemens hurried to the Sages to tell them about the dreadful plan which was to be brought before the Senate thirty days later. There wasn't even the slightest chance that the Senate would oppose the Emperor, for the senators were quaking with fear for their own lives. Each of them tried to outdo the others in pleasing the vain and power-hungry Emperor. At every opportunity they would arrange flattering ceremonies for him, which suited his nature well. (Just a few days before, the Senate had offered to provide him with a troop of elite horsemen as bodyguards.) It was therefore to be expected that the Senate would meekly sanction his plan to kill the Jews.

The leaders of the Jewish people were in despair. Flavius Clemens consoled them: "Do not fear, God will not forsake you! He will send you salvation. If the merit of only one single Jew was capable of foiling Haman's decree, then surely now, when there are so many pious Jews in Judea, God will have compassion!"

One of the Sages spoke for the group: "If only we knew what to do to assist our people. We stand here so helpless! All we can do right now is to pray to our Father in Heaven and repent. We must return to God wholeheartedly, from the depths of our souls, as it is written, 'When you are persecuted and all these things befall you, you will then return to Hashem your God and heed His voice. For Hashem your God is a merciful God; He will not let you slip [from his grasp] nor harm you, and He will not forget the covenant of your forefathers that He swore to them.'"

Flavius Clemens had not yet told his wife about the Emperor's evil plans. But since she could sense his sorrow and distress, Domitilla begged him to tell her what was bothering him. He finally revealed the secret to her. She too was a Jew; both of them had converted, and Flavius Clemens had performed his circumcision himself.

Twenty-five of the thirty days had already passed when Domitilla turned to her husband and said, "You must save the Jews, dear Clemens, before it's too late! In only five more days the Senate will confirm the Emperor's plan, and then there will be terrible suffering among God's people!"

"What should I do, my dear wife? I am at a loss!"

"It's in your power, my husband, to at least ask for a postponement. Look, what is this life worth, this life full of fear, sorrow, and pain? In the World-to-Come, God the Almighty has prepared bliss and happiness for His pious ones. After the Emperor, you hold the highest position in the empire. The Romans have chosen you as their Consul... *If you were to die*, the Romans would first have to appoint a new Consul in order for the Senate to make a valid decision. As you know, choosing a new consul is a lengthy process. During that time a lot of things can happen, and the Jewish people can be saved. I am therefore appealing you: Please, go to the Emperor and admit that you have converted to Judaism! He will sentence you to death and have you executed, and then your blood will be the source of redemption for the Jewish people."

"Domitilla, what are you asking of me? That I sacrifice my life so that the decree be postponed?"

"Oh, Clemens, if only it were in *my* power I would be more than willing to give up my life for such a cause! What does life have to offer us other than pain and anguish now that our beloved sons have died and my uncle Domitian has become a monster? Clemens, consider yourself privileged and fortunate for being granted the opportunity of achieving eternal life by sacrificing yourself!"

"And how shall I bear the degradation of execution?" replied Clemens.

"Take this ring from me! Hidden inside it are a few drops of deadly poison. They take effect immediately after you swallow them. Then you will be able to avoid a disgraceful death."

The next day Clemens asked for an audience with the Emperor. Domitian had lately taken the strictest precautionary measures in order to protect himself. Even his most trustworthy friends were examined to make sure they weren't carrying weapons, before they were allowed to approach the ruler.

"Great and most powerful Emperor, I have come to plead with you to have compassion on the Jews," stated Flavius Clemens.

"Hold your tongue," Domitian cried out, "or you will die!"

"I have no fear of death," Clemens replied, "and I will continue to speak, even if I risk your forgetting that I am your closest relative, and that I am married to your niece. You will never succeed in destroying the Jews! You may be able to kill some of them, and to cause them suffering and sorrow, but you can never annihilate the entire nation. God the Almighty, Creator of heaven and earth, protects them, and He will not permit anyone to destroy them, for they are His people, whom He looks after with great love and care, like a shepherd who watches over his flock. Not only will your plan fail, but you will bring your own downfall upon yourself."

"What could those miserable Jews do to me?" thundered the Emperor. "They are a defeated, downtrodden people, and I am the ruler of the world!"

"It's not the Jews that pose the danger," said Clemens. "It's their God, Creator and Ruler of the world, Who will judge you and punish you, if you undertake anything against them. For they are the nation He has chosen among all the other nations of the world."

"And do you believe in this deity, Clemens?"

"Of course I believe in Him — He is the Master of the Universe."

"You sadden me, my dear Clemens. I don't want your blood to be shed like that of a criminal. Take back your words — or you must die!"

"Will you cancel your plans to kill the Jews?"

"No, no — absolutely not!"

"Then have me killed too, and thus you will grant me the privilege of sacrificing my life for the sanctification of God's Name."

"You are mad, Clemens! You are losing your mind! Just take back your words and I will give you more power and honor than you ever dreamed of! At the present time you have already reached the highest position a Roman citizen ever attained. You have the same judicial authority as I do: you are a Consul. And yet I can elevate you even more. You are my closest male relative, and Domitilla is my closest female relative. There is no one I am as close to as you and your wife, now that my only son has died and I no longer have any direct heirs. I therefore intend to adopt you as my son, and to appoint you Co-Emperor. Take back your words, my dear Clemens, and you will become a god on earth!"

"This golden future which you are offering me does not tempt me in the least," replied Clemens. "At one time I relished the thought of such opportunities. Such were the dreams that I lived for. But since you have shown the world how much evil a ruler can do, I have decided that worldly prestige and honor are not worth anything. And apart from that I am determined to remain loyal to my religion.

"For as long as I live I will never again bow down to the Roman gods. And for as long as I live I will never bring any sacrifices to them! And if you were to die today, and the Roman people were to appoint me as your successor, I would turn down the crown! Yes, I would! I strive only for eternal bliss; mundane goods and worldly prestige mean nothing to me now."

"And Domitilla?"

"She shares my views. She herself has encouraged me to come to you and admit that we have both converted to Judaism."

"You must die!"

"I know," said Clemens.

"I am obligated to present the accusation against you to the Senate, and they will sentence you to a humiliating death."

"Caesar, look at this. Domitilla gave me this ring. All I would have to do to avoid a humiliating death is to swallow the few drops that are contained within. And in fact I had decided today to end my life in your presence by taking this poison. But I have changed my mind. I want to sanctify God's Name in front of the whole world. Future generations will be able to take an example from my behavior and learn how powerful is the truth of my belief."

"You have lost your mind, Clemens," said Domitian. "One last time I will plead with you: Retract your foolish confession! We are alone. No one else but me has heard your mad words — and I am willing to forget them!"

"I will affirm my beliefs in the marketplace and in front of the Senate. I will shout so that the whole world will be able to hear that I have become a Jew, that I devote myself to the One and Only God, Creator of the universe, and that I totally reject the Roman gods and the gods of all other nations as well!"

Domitian opened the door and called out to the guards in the corridor: "Seize this man and have him watched carefully! He is a dangerous criminal!"

That same day Domitian came to the Senate to formally accuse the Consul Flavius Clemens of having adopted Judaism. Clemens did not deny the charge, and he was unanimously sentenced to death. When the people heard this, they were dismayed. They were terribly frightened that the Emperor had engineered the public execution of his closest relative and his most probable heir to the throne. The aristocrats and noblemen trembled with fear. But the ones who were the most affected by this development were the Jews. Their sorrow and despair were overwhelming. They had no idea that Clemens had sacrificed his life in order to save them.

Chapter 20

When the Sages from Judea found out about the death of Flavius Clemens, they tore their clothing in the traditional gesture of mourning, sat down on the ground, and wept. After they had sat in silence for a while, Rabbi Akiva said: "My teachers, this is not the time to sit passively and mourn. Let us go and visit Clemens' wife. Perhaps we will find out something that could be helpful to us and to our nation."

"Visiting Domitilla under the present circumstances would be very dangerous," Rabbi Yehoshua replied. "The house is probably surrounded by the Emperor's spies, who report to him on anyone who approaches."

"There are dangers — but our obligations are greater. It is our duty to visit the wife of the man who sacrificed his life for the sanctification of God's Name. We must try to console and encourage her in her great sorrow," Rabban Gamliel said.

When the Sages went to visit Clemens' wife, they found her strong and calm.

"My friends," said Domitilla, "you are still unaware of what Clemens has done for you. In five days' time the campaign to wipe out the Jewish people was scheduled to begin. By giving up his life, Clemens has caused the evil decree to be postponed for an indeterminate period of time. And in the meantime God will send His people their salvation. After my dear husband had circumcised himself, he went to the Emperor and admitted that he had converted to Judaism. He knew that if he were killed, a new Consul would have to be elected before the Senate could confirm the decree. He asked me to tell you that he had given himself the name *Shalom*, with the addition of the name *Ketiah* [from the verb 'to cut off'] because he had performed the rite of circumcision on himself."

"May Shalom Ketiah's memory be blessed forever!" Rabban Gamliel declared, and he went on to quote from Scripture. "It says in the last verse of Psalm 47: 'The princes of the nations have all come together within the nation of Avraham; for the shields of this world are God's; He is greatly exalted.' And in the Torah, God says to Avraham: 'I will make you into a great nation, I will bless you, and I will make your name great... and I will bless those that bless you and I will curse those that curse you, and all the peoples of the earth shall be blessed through you.' Only after all these promises did God command Avraham to perform the covenant of circumcision on himself, and He said to him: 'Have no fear, I will be a shield for you.'

"Shalom Ketiah, however, had none of those promises from God, and yet he entered the covenant of Avraham and sacrificed his life for the Jewish nation — therefore he is greater than Avraham, and the promise 'for the shields of this world are God's; He is greatly exalted' is referring to *him*, for he is more exalted and greater than our great forefather Avraham."

Just as Rabban Gamliel paused for a moment, Stephanus, the former slave who was the administrator of Domitilla's household, came running into the room, crying out a warning: "You must escape from here quickly! The Emperor's men are approaching! Follow me, and I will show you a different exit."

"Go!" Domitilla said. "And pray for me and my beloved husband."

"For Shalom Ketiah we don't have to pray. He has achieved the highest level that a human being is capable of on this earth. He will be granted eternal bliss, and you too will join the fortunate ones one day."

"Hurry!" Stephanus called out. "Don't let the envoys of the Emperor find you here!"

The Sages followed Stephanus.

Shortly afterwards, the delegation of the Emperor arrived at Domitilla's house. They brought a message from the Emperor that although it was his duty to have her brought to court and sentenced to death as well, he nevertheless was going to take advantage of his royal authority to spare her life. She would, however, be sent into exile on the island of Pandataria.

The senators suffered a great shock once again when one of the greatest and most noble men among them, Acilius Glabrio, the Consul, was sentenced to death, and killed soon after that. He had been accused of having once fought with wild animals in the amphitheater. The Emperor's informers were all over Rome. They knew how to gain entry everywhere, using all kinds of disguises. They would glibly complain about the Emperor and his cruelty for as long as it would take to get their targeted victim to join them in talk against the Emperor. Then they would inform against him, and he would be accused of trumped-up charges and sentenced to death.

It was because of all that cruelty and the dreadful executions that several senators finally came together in the house of Cocceius Nerva to work out a plan to kill the Emperor. They were willing to face the dangers involved since they already feared for their lives. And the risks were great indeed. Even if they were to succeed in killing the Emperor, the common folk and the soldiers, whom Domitian had always flattered and treated well, might very well want to avenge his death. That is why no one was willing to become the next Emperor, because it was expected that Domitian's successor would be the target of everyone's revenge. After all the men had refused to step forward, Cocceius Nerva said: "I am an old man, and I was hoping that the responsibility and the burden of leading our nation would fall on younger and stronger shoulders. But since I see that no one wants to face the risks of being the Emperor, I am willing to dedicate the last few days of my life to the service of my homeland."

The senators congratulated Nerva and thanked him for his heroic decision. Now they could focus on the assassination plan. They decided that the tyrant would be stabbed to death in the middle of a Senate meeting, just like Julius Caesar had met his end.

But things were meant to happen differently...

Domitian no longer trusted his own servants. He had the overseer of the palace and the bodyguards arrested, and he executed some of the informers whom he did not trust. Everyone in the Emperor's surroundings was filled with fear and trepidation. Then one day it happened that a young servant by the name of Ganymede found a list which the tyrant had hidden underneath his pillow. On that list he had once again marked down some of his new victims. Two of the people whose names were inscribed there were Domitia, the Emperor's own wife, and Parthenius, the servant he had trusted most. Ganymede showed his discovery to the Empress. Domitia then called in Parthenius and all the other people on the list, and showed them what the Emperor had recorded in his own handwriting.

"We must act quickly — to beat him at his own game," Parthenius exclaimed.

"Yes, indeed," the Empress said. "But whom can we trust to carry it out?"

"Leave that to me, my Empress!" Parthenius said. "I know a very strong man who would consider himself fortunate to be the one to stab the Emperor to death. Since Domitian is quite strong, and he allows only one servant at a time to be with him in his chambers, only someone who can compete with him in strength has a chance of succeeding."

Not too long after that, Parthenius went to the vacant house of Flavius Clemens and asked to see the administrator of the household, Stephanus. Since the overseer was not there at the time, Parthenius decided to wait for his return.

Stephanus had gone to the lodging of the Sages. "Dear friends," he said to them, "I have brought you my master's last will. Before Clemens went to the Emperor he gave me this package, and said, 'My faithful Stephanus, you have always been a loyal servant to me. I will now ask you to fulfill what is probably my last wish: if this indeed is our final meeting, then bring this package to the wise men of Judea and tell them it is for Rabbi Akiva and his companions.'"

Stephanus left without awaiting their reply. Rabbi Akiva opened the package and discovered that it contained pearls and gems of enormous value.

When Stephanus came back to the house of his master and saw Parthenius waiting for him, he called out to him,

"Parthenius, what message do you have? Did you come here to lead me to my death, as happened to the master of this house?"

"No — on the contrary. I have come to offer you the opportunity to avenge the death of your master."

"I don't want to avenge the death of my master," said Stephanus. "He received the punishment he deserved, and his wife Domitilla was spared because the Emperor was compassionate. I revere the Emperor Domitian, and I bring sacrifices to Minerva daily so that she will kindly protect him from all harm."

"You are very clever," said Parthenius, "and your cautiousness is praiseworthy. But please read what the Emperor wrote with his own hand on this slate. You recognize his handwriting, I am sure."

Stephanus took the slate and read it.

As he read the list of the doomed, which included the names of Parthenius and the Empress, his hand trembled. Turning to Parthenius, Stephanus said, "This changes the situation considerably; now we are allies."

"Very well, then," Parthenius replied, clasping Stephanus' hand. "I am holding this hand and dedicating it to the noblest task any Roman has ever fulfilled in history. This hand is going to stop the raging tyrant from shedding more innocent blood, and from killing the best of our people."

"But why have you chosen me, Parthenius?"

"Because Domitian is a very strong man, and you are the only one among those that I can trust whose strength is greater than his."

"What is your plan?" inquired Stephanus.

Pathenius explained how it would be done. "You must apply to the Emperor, offering your services. He knows you and likes you. He won't have any ill-feeling towards you or suspect you of wanting to take revenge, since he doesn't believe in loyalty. On the day that we are ready to act, I will remove all the weapons from his chamber before you go in. You, however, will carry a dagger, hidden underneath your clothing, and you will stab the Emperor with it in his evil heart. Jupiter will strengthen your arm and grant you success in this deed. All the gods have turned away from the tyrant. This past night he had a dream that Jupiter, the protector of the Roman Empire, forbade his daughter Minerva to watch over Domitian any longer, because he is destroying the empire. All the signs are favorable. Just make sure that you take advantage of them soon!"

"There is no need for you to say anything more! My beloved master, Flavius Clemens, shall have his revenge!" cried Stephanus.

Chapter 21

Time was passing far too quickly for the frightened Jews. In the days preceding Rosh Hashanah they had all prayed more intently than ever, and the sound of the shofar on Rosh Hashanah had pierced their hearts. On September 18 the new Consul, who was to replace Clemens, was due to be elected. On that same day the deadly decree against the Jews would once again be presented to the Senate for confirmation. The Christians were included in the decree as well, because at that time they were still regarded as a Jewish sect. They too were all doomed to death, without exception. The 18th of September fell on Yom Kippur that year. One can only imagine how fervently the Jews of Rome prayed to their Father on High, and how deeply they regretted their sins. Our Sages tell us in the Midrash that in those days the promise written in the Torah — "when you are persecuted and all these things befall you, you will then return to Hashem your God and heed His voice" — was fulfilled.

In one of the towns of Germany (today's Cologne) there was a fortune-teller by the name of Mardonius who proclaimed that the Emperor Domitian was going to be killed on September 18 at noontime. Mardonius was brought to Rome in chains. There he was interrogated and sentenced to death. But Mardonius just laughed, and said, "You may sentence me to death as you wish, but my fate has something else in store for me. I am destined to be torn apart by dogs, and that's that!" To punish him for his arrogance, the Emperor commanded that a large fire be lit, and then he threw Mardonius into it.

The Emperor's command had been carried out immediately. Domitian himself was there to witness the punishment. There was a smile of contentment on his face when they threw poor Mardonius into the roaring flames. But at that moment a violent storm broke out, and the rain extinguished the fire. Mardonius, who had almost been burned to death, managed to survive. As he was trying to make his way out of the area where the fire had raged, though, he collapsed on the ground, unable to move any further. And just then a pack of dogs came running towards him and tore him to pieces. When Domitian saw that, he began to tremble with fear.

"My fate is sealed!" cried the Emperor. "If this awful man's prophecy concerning his own end was accurate, than his predictions about my destiny will come true as well."

The Emperor spent the following days and nights in the greatest anxiety. Finally the 18th of September arrived.

"Today something is going to happen which the whole world will be talking about!" said Domitian. He had a ruptured vein on his forehead, and he wiped off a drop of blood. "If only this was all that I had to worry about," he sighed.

Noontime came, and still nothing had happened. The Emperor was overjoyed. He decided to have his bath, and to get dressed for midday dinner. Just as he left his dressing chamber, Stephanus came into his room.

"What can I do for you, my Stephanus?" he asked him.

"I have hardly entered your services, my master, and I am already approaching you with a request!"

"As long as it has nothing to do with Domitilla," said the Emperor.

"Oh, no!" Stephanus answered. "It concerns the Emperor of Rome, the chosen of all men, and the one whom all the gods favor!"

With those words he handed the Emperor a note, which he started to read. At that moment Stephanus pulled out a dagger and stabbed Domitian with all his might. He wounded him but failed to kill him, and Domitian was about to retaliate with his own sword when he discovered that it was missing. He then tried to grab the dagger away from his adversary, and in this attempt he cut his hands deeply. With bloody fingers he began to hit Stephanus's head with a heavy golden cup, screaming for help all along. It was a gruesome battle, and in spite of his enormous strength Stephanus would have lost if Parthenius, Maximus, and all the other conspirators had not come to the rescue. They all went after Domitian with their swords, and soon they had him on the floor. Their intervention was decisive. Domitian was barely alive when his loyal troops came running in with their swords drawn, having heard the Emperor's desperate cries for help.

To their great horror they found their master on the floor, bleeding to death. "Who has done this?" one of them cried.

The Emperor gathered all his strength, and choked out his last word: "Stephanus!"

The soldiers then started to attack Stephanus with their swords, while all the other conspirators ran out. Stephanus was cut to pieces, and thus both the Emperor and his murderer suffered the same fate.

The news of the Emperor's death spread rapidly. The senators, who were assembled in the Senate hall, gave vent to their joy. The leaders of the Roman people were finally free to express all their hatred and contempt for Domitian, and they took full advantage of the opportunity. Without delay they tore down and destroyed all the images and sculptures throughout the city that represented Domitian. The grand sculptures made of marble were pulverized, and those made of gold, silver, or bronze were melted down, including even the glorious one at the Forum. All the Arches of Triumph which Domitian had erected in the streets, were removed, and his name was blotted out from all remaining monuments.

As soon as the initial excitement had subsided, the senator

Marcus Cocceius Nerva was acclaimed as the new Emperor.

It was towards the end of Yom Kippur and the Jews were still in the synagogue when they heard the news. Rabban Gamliel raised his hands towards Heaven and called out, "God is Eternal, God is Eternal!"

And all the Jews followed his example. Rescued at last from the great danger that threatened them, they cried out in such joy and fervor that the walls of the synagogue shook.

Rome was also elated after the recent events. Not one person was interested in laying the murdered Emperor to rest — not his wife, Domitio, not any of the informers whom Domitian had showered with wealth and honor, and not any of the flatterers who had worshiped him in his lifetime. Finally his old nursemaid, Phyllis, took care of the disposal of his remains. His body was cremated and the ashes deposited in the Flavian Temple. Thus Phyllis was the only one to remain loyal to Domitian after his death.

The new Emperor was also having his troubles. The Praetorion Guards were bloodthirsty; they killed Parthenius and Maximus. Calpurnius Crassus, a descendant of the famous Marcus Crassus, demanded the imperial crown for himself. It was only with great effort that the revolt was put down.

Things finally quieted down, however, and Rome entered a new era of peace under Nerva's temperate leadership. Domitian's oppressive laws were abolished, and the people who had been sent into exile were allowed to return to Rome. For Domitilla, however, this heartening news came too late. The sorrow and grief she suffered over her husband's death overcame her and she died shortly afterwards.

The new Emperor summoned the visiting Sages of Judea, and he received them lavishly. "I am now in a position to pay you back for all that you did for me," said Nerva. "I will always be a benevolent ruler towards the Jews."

With these words he handed them a new coin. On one side of the coin there was an image of the new Emperor, and on the other side the imprint of a palm tree, symbolizing Judaism. Beneath it were the Latin words *Fisci judaici columnia sublata*: "The accusations against the Jews are cancelled."

The Sages thanked the Emperor, and Rabban Gamliel gave him some writings about the Jews, in which all the false accusations against them were refuted. Then the Sages blessed Nerva and bid him farewell.

Although winter was approaching and the sea could be stormy, the Sages didn't want to wait for milder weather for their journey home. They missed their homeland, their families, and their regular learning and teaching schedules too much. They set out overland to Brundisium and there they boarded a ship which would take them to Eretz Yisrael.

The voyage was indeed stormy, and the ship was often driven off its course, causing them great delay. The provisions that the Sages had brought with them were barely sufficient for the lengthened journey. In addition, they would have to set aside tithes from their food, the Levite's tenth and the tenth for the poor, as it was the third year of the *shemittah* cycle.

How did the Sages overcome this problem? Rabban Gamliel said, "I am going to separate the Levite's tenth for this grain from the stack of grain I have at home, and I am hereby transferring the separated portion to your ownership, Rabbi Yehoshua, since you are a Levite. I am also renting out to you the area which contains the grain. And I will do the same with the tenth for the poor. The tenth, which I will set aside in my home, shall be yours as of this moment, Akiva, since you direct the distribution of the charity in Eretz Yisrael, and I am renting out to you the area which it is in."

In a similar manner Rabbi Yehoshua transferred the Kohen's tenth, which he had to set aside from his Levite's tenth, to Rabbi Elazar ben Azaryah, who was a Kohen. Thus the Sages were able to enjoy all the food they had with them, and it lasted them until the end of their voyage.

It was on a Friday, towards evening, when their ship approached the shore of Jaffa. "We won't reach the shore before Shabbos, so we won't be able to leave the ship!" Rabbi Elazar ben Azaryah told his companions.

"I don't agree with you," Rabban Gamliel replied. "It is still considered day now and we are already within the Shabbos boundaries — we are less than 2000 cubits away from the shoreline. Even if the ship docks after night has fallen, we are still allowed to go ashore. But now, my friends, please come and follow me down to the lower part of the ship."

Rabban Gamliel and Rabbi Yehoshua had already gone below, but Rabbi Elazar lingered. "Why don't we stay on deck?" Rabbi Elazar asked. "The view of the Holy Land is a delight to my eyes!"

"My brother Elazar," Rabbi Akiva replied, "if we want to leave the ship today, then we are not allowed to remain up here now. You see, as soon as the ship docks, it will be Shabbos already, and the crew will put down a gangway so that we can get from the ship to the shore. Had the gangway been prepared especially for us, then we wouldn't be allowed to use it on Shabbos. But if the crew puts it in place for themselves, then we are allowed to use it as well."

"But why must we leave the deck?" Rabbi Elazar asked.

"This is the reason," said Rabbi Akiva. "If the gangway was set up in our presence, then it would seem as though it were intended for us. If we keep away from the deck, however, then it looks as though we are in no rush to leave the boat and the gangway is being put into place solely for the use of the crew and the other passengers. Then there is no problem if we wish to take advantage of it as well."

As they spoke, they went down to the lower part of the ship, and Rabban Gamliel overheard the end of their conversation. "That's exactly what I meant, Akiva," he said.

And so it came about that Rabban Gamliel and his companions arrived happily in Eretz Yisrael just as the Holy Shabbos was settling in.

Chapter 22

All of Israel was filled with excitement and joy when the Jews found out about the death of the tyrant Domitian and about the new Emperor, Nerva, who was a friend of the Jews. The Sages resumed their teaching with great enthusiasm. Now that there was peace and quiet, they were determined to take full advantage of these circumstances in order to clarify and resolve a number of difficult matters regarding the Oral Law.

At this point we must explain to our readers a little about how these difficulties had arisen.

When the Almighty revealed Himself to His people on Mount Sinai, He gave Moshe Rabbeinu the entire Torah — 613 commandments — 248 of which are precepts directing us to perform an action and 365 of which are precepts prohibiting an action. Along with each and every one of these precepts, God also gave Moshe the interpretations of the Law, the Oral Law. Moshe later transmitted these to Yehoshua, who passed them on to the Elders. The Elders handed them to the Prophets, the Prophets deposited them with the Men of the Great Assembly, and the Men of the Great Assembly passed them on to the "Zugos" (pairs of sages who together led their generation).

The last of these pairs were Hillel and Shammai. Both of them had created schools of thought that were in opposition to each other in many spheres of learning. How did it happen that they had such differing opinions? Our Sages tell us that during the thirty days of mourning over Moshe's death there were already a number of teachings that had been forgotten. With his outstanding mind, Osniel ben Kenaz, who was to become the first of the Judges later on, was able to retrieve these teachings for us. Thus the Oral Law was continuously passed on, side by side with the other branches of Torah learning. Whenever any doubts arose about how to interpret any of the teachings, the Sages would not rest until they had clarified the matter and settled the halachic issues.

In the times of the Judges, for example, there was some disagreement as to whether the exclusion of the Ammonites and Moabites from our nation applies to both men and women or only to men. That is why Boaz's relative refused to marry Ruth, who was a Moabite and had converted to Judaism, whereas Boaz himself did not hesitate. Even Yishai, Ruth's grandson, who was to become the father of King David, suffered because of his doubts about the legitimacy of his lineage. Only the Prophet Shmuel was able to fully establish that the exclusion applied only to the male members of those nations.

One of the sharpest disagreements that could possibly exist, however, was the one that divided the schools of Hillel and Shammai. The debate was centered on one aspect of a crucial area of Jewish life: the laws of marriage and the family. When a man (we will call him Reuven) dies childless, then his brother (we will call him Shimon) is obligated either to marry the widow of Reuven or to undergo a procedure called *chalitzah*. But if the widow is a close relative of her brother-in-law (Shimon) — for example, if Shimon's wife is the widow's sister — then neither marriage nor *chalitzah* takes place.

When polygamy was practiced, this law applied to the co-wives of the deceased relative as well. But in the case of the daughter's co-wives, Shammai ruled it was permitted to marry the brother-in-law, whereas Hillel ruled that it was prohibited.

The Halachah had followed Hillel's ruling for a long time, when suddenly there was a rumor that Rabbi Dosa ben Harkinas, one of the oldest and most revered teachers, had based one of his halachic decisions on the position of Shammai's ruling. Rabbi Dosa was very old at the time, and he was also blind, so that it was impossible to call him to Yavneh to clarify the matter.

On the other hand, he was a highly respected authority, and his opinion could not be ignored. Rabban Gamliel therefore decided to send a delegation to him. Although it was a difficult task, Rabbi Yehoshua, Rabbi Elazar ben Azaryah, and Rabbi Akiva offered to go. But Rabbi Akiva and Rabbi Elazar ben Azaryah were quite worried about their sensitive mission. How would they be able to convince this revered Sage to give up his opinion?

"Have no fear," Rabbi Yehoshua consoled them. "It will be easier than you think. I once faced a far more difficult task, and I was on my own. Back in those days, when my great teacher Rabban Yochanan ben Zakkai was still alive, there was a rumor about some very strange happenings in Antipras. There was a wealthy, learned, and distinguished man by the name of Shimon who lived there. His house was open to travelers and guests at all times, and people compared him to Avraham Avinu. He served every one of his guests in the most lavish manner, and invited them to stay with him as long as they wished. However, just as a guest was about to leave, as he was profusely thanking his host for his hospitality, Shimon passed a signal to his servants. The servants would then grab the guest, tie him up, and beat him mercilessly. That's the story that was spread by the rumor.

"When my teacher Rabban Yochanan ben Zakkai heard about these things, he said to me, 'Yehoshua, my son, I cannot tolerate such behavior. Go to Antipras and see whether there is any truth to what people are saying.'

"Now that was a frightening task — I was in danger of being beaten up by Shimon's servants! When I arrived in Antipras, I asked where Shimon's house was, and I was directed to a building which resembled a palace. The host came to the door right away and greeted me in the friendliest manner. I stayed in a beautiful room, and was served a lavish meal, during which I was granted the honor of sitting near the host. I was hungry, and I greatly enjoyed the delicious food and fine wines. After the meal I spoke to the host for quite a while. We discussed Torah matters, and I discovered that he was a pious and learned man, and he had a keen and refined way of thinking. Nevertheless, I didn't dare mention to him why I had come to his home, for in his face there was a hint of concealed power which intimidated me. I was afraid that I would awaken some wild, hidden nature within him.

"That night I had the most terrible nightmares in which I was being beaten up by Shimon's servants. The next morning I went to the synagogue with my host, and after that we ate breakfast together. The time had come to say good-bye to him, and I was trembling at the thought of what awaited me. But nothing of that sort happened, thank God. I praised Shimon for his hospitality, but he modestly declined my compliments, and he offered to walk with me a bit on my way out. 'Let's walk through my garden,' he said. 'It's shorter that way.' It was a beautiful garden. It looked like a carefully tended park. 'So that's how it's done!' I thought to myself. 'At the end of the garden, in the shadows of the forest, is the place where the servants are hiding, waiting to beat me up!'

"I left the garden safely, however, and Shimon continued to accompany me along the main road. 'Thank you again,' I said. 'I don't want to burden you.' 'Thank you for your visit,' said Shimon. 'I truly enjoyed it!' Then he embraced me and kissed me, and we parted from each other. As I continued down the road, however, I suddenly realized that I hadn't fulfilled my mission! Perhaps Shimon had decided to spare me only because he respected me for being a learned rabbi. So I turned around and called out, 'Rabbi, Rabbi!' Shimon turned in my direction and I ran towards him. 'Rabbi, there was a specific reason for my visit to your house. I was sent by Rabban Yochanan ben Zakkai in order to find out whether it's true that you beat your guests at the end of their visit.' 'Yes,' said Shimon, 'I have done that quite often.' 'And why have you spared me?' I asked. 'My learned guest, you ate and drank heartily, but as soon as you were satisfied you refused any further nourishment, even though I offered more. Some of the foolish people who have stayed in my home behaved quite differently. At first they refused to eat or drink anything, and when I tried to persuade them, they swore on oath that the idea of eating, etc. was out of the question. But in the end they ate and drank in spite of the oath they took. That is why I beat them before they left — in order to punish them for the great transgression of swearing falsely.'

"'You have done the right thing,' I said to him. 'And if you meet more people like that, I hope you will beat them twice — once for the atonement of their sin and once for having caused me to experience such fear!'"

The Sages had arrived at Rabbi Dosa's home. His maidservant greeted them and asked them to enter. Rabbi Dosa told the servant to give Rabbi Yehoshua a chair. Rabbi Yehoshua sat down, and said to the blind Sage, "Rabbi, please allow another of your students to take a seat as well."

"Who is it?" asked Rabbi Dosa.

"It is Elazar, the son of Azaryah."

"Oh, so my old friend Azaryah left a son who is also great in Torah? Once again we see the fulfillment of King David's words: 'I was young and I grew old, and I never saw a righteous man forsaken, nor his descendants ask for bread.'"

"Rabbi, please allow another one of your students to take a seat as well," said Rabbi Yehoshua.

"Who is it?" asked Rabbi Dosa.

"It's Akiva ben Yosef," replied Rabbi Yehoshua.

"Oh!" Rabbi Dosa called out joyously. "You are the one, Akiva, whose fame has spread from one end of the world to the other. Have a seat, my son. May there be many like you among Israel!"

The Sages bagan to discuss Torah matters with Rabbi Dosa, and it was not long before they introduced the topic of *tzaras ha-bas* (the marriage between a man and his brother's widow, who was the co-wife of his daughter). Rabbi Dosa commented that the Schools of Shammai and Hillel were divided over the issue.

"And by whom do we abide?" asked one of the visitors.

"We abide by Hillel," said Rabbi Dosa firmly.

The visiting Sages were quite surprised. "But we were told that you based one of your halachic rulings on Shammai's view," one of them said.

"Did you hear that Dosa made that decision, or Ben Harkinas?" asked Rabbi Dosa.

"We aren't certain about that."

"Well, here's a fact you ought to keep in mind," said Rabbi Dosa. "I have a younger brother by the name of Yonatan. He is a very talented man, and he belongs to the School of Shammai. He teaches that one *is* permitted to marry the widowed co-wife of one's daughter. But I call upon Heaven and earth as my witnesses that Chaggai the Prophet examined this problem inside and out and taught that such a marriage is forbidden. Now go back and teach people this law! Make sure, however, that you don't meet my brother! For with his keen mind, he might succeed in putting the law into question once again."

The Sages left through three different doors. Rabbi Yehoshua and Rabbi Elazar ben Azaryah got away without incident, but Rabbi Akiva encountered Yonatan, the younger brother of Rabbi Dosa. Naturally, a heated discussion erupted, but at the end of it neither side had changed his views.

"Are you the Akiva," asked Yonatan, "whose fame has spread from one end of the earth to the other? You are fortunate to be so famous — you don't deserve it! With a mind like yours, you can't even compete with a cattle herdsman!"

"Nor even with shepherds!" Rabbi Akiva replied modestly.

Chapter 23

The greatest teacher in Israel at that time was Rabbi Eliezer ben Hurkanos, whom we have mentioned several times. Once Rabbi Yehoshua came to the yeshiva in Lod, which is where Rabbi Eliezer taught. When he saw the stone which Rabbi Eliezer used to sit on, he kissed it, saying, "This stone is like Mount Sinai, and the one that sat on it is like the Holy Ark."

One can only imagine how much turmoil there was when the Romans suddenly took Rabbi Eliezer captive, accusing him of being a secret follower of Christianity! In order to understand this strange accusation, we must take a look at what was happening in the world at that time.

The Roman Emperor Nerva, who was very friendly to the Jews and treated them kindly, had no children of his own. He therefore adopted the general Marcus Ulpius Trajan as his son and made him co-Emperor. Nerva died soon after that, and Trajan succeeded him as Emperor.

Trajan was originally from Spain. His father had gained fame in the war against the Jews in the time of Vespasian, for he had succeeded in conquering the strongest Jewish fortress, Jaffa. Jaffa was not only well-protected because of its natural position, but also because the Jews put a lot of thought and effort into the way they built the fortress. Vespasian equipped Trajan's father with 2000 foot soldiers and 1000 horsemen for this campaign. Many of Jaffa's inhabitants had taken up positions outside the city, in the hope of halting the Roman advance there, but the Romans outfought them and the survivors were forced to flee.

As they tried to enter the city's outer gates, however, they were unable to stop the Romans from following them, and at that point the remaining inhabitants of Jaffa closed the inner gates of the city. What followed was a horrendous massacre in the area between the two gates, in which 2000 Jews — the entire force that had gone to challenge the Romans outside the city — were killed. In their desperate attempts to defend themselves, the Jews had killed an even greater number of Romans, so that there were several thousand dead lying on the ground between the two walls.

Trajan's father called for reinforcements, and Vespasian sent him his son Titus with 500 horsemen and 1000 foot soldiers. The Romans brought in large scaling ladders to drive the Jewish defenders away from the walls, and Titus and his men jumped down from one of them into the city. In the narrow streets of Jaffa the Romans fought the Jews at close quarters, and once again it was a raging, bloody battle. The women stood on the rooftops and hurled down on the enemy whatever they could find. The struggle continued until late afternoon, and by then the Jews had no choice but to surrender. Despite their surrender, the Romans proceeded to murder all remaining males, searching for them in public squares and in private houses. The women and children were led into slavery. Altogether, thousands of Jews were killed and captured.

Marcus Ulpius Trajan had witnessed this gruesome war at the age of 16. He had experienced the bravery and resilience of the Jews, and these certainly left their mark on him. Even at the age of 45, when he ascended the Emperor's throne, his bad memories had not faded. And although Roman writers praised him as being the best Emperor of all times, he was to bring great suffering upon the Jews.

His views on Christianity were not favorable either. The Christians at that time were a persecuted group. The ruling Roman establishment didn't know or want to know anything about the Christians' goals or interests, and their community was not publicly recognized. Thus, all Christian activities were conducted in secret, and anyone who openly professed to belong to the religion was sentenced to death.

These were the early years of Christianity and the majority of Christians at the time were Jews who had converted to Christianity. They (unlike the later Christians of heathen origin) remained faithful to Jewish practices — they observed the Sabbath and the holidays, they kept the dietary laws, they circumcised their sons, etc. The leader and founder of this sect was someone named Jacobus. He was from the village of Seconia, in Galilee.

Let us now return to Rabbi Eliezer and the accusation against him. He was taken to the prison and confined with those who were charged with capital crimes. When he was brought before the judge, the judge said to him, "How does a wise man like you take an interest in this?"

Rabbi Eliezer replied, "I praise the truthful Judge!"

Although Rabbi Eliezer had meant God, the Roman judge thought the Sage was talking about him, and he said, "Because you have acknowledged me as a truthful judge, I will set you free!"

When Rabbi Eliezer came home, he was inconsolable about what had happened to him. He was deeply disturbed that anyone could accuse him of being a Christian. His disciples gathered around him, trying to comfort him, but to no avail.

"What could I have done to deserve this accusation?" cried Rabbi Eliezer.

"My teacher," Rabbi Akiva said, "allow me to mention something you have taught me."

"Speak, Akiva."

"Perhaps one of the leaders of their religion once told you something that you found interesting, and because of this you were suspected of belonging to them."

"Akiva, you have indeed awakened my memory," replied Rabbi Eliezer. "When I was walking through the marketplace of Tzippori once, I met a pupil of Jacobus from Seconia, the founder of this sect. He repeated his teacher's explanation of a certain halachah to me, and I found his presentation appealing. It was at that moment that I transgressed the commandment in the Torah, 'You must keep your path far away from it,' which is interpreted by the Sages to mean that you must stay away from anything that deviates from Judaism. That is why this happened to me!"

When we take a closer look at the relationship between the Jews and the "Jewish Christians" at that time, it becomes clear how characteristic the aforementioned incident was. Essentially, the only difference between these followers of Christianity and the Jews was in the realm of belief. Thus the Jewish Christians had contact with the Jews, they proclaimed halachic interpretations in the name of their master, and they would visit the synagogue, where their local leader would speak. Under these circumstances it was almost inevitable that some Jews were misled; even some of the most distinguished Jews adopted Christianity.

We are told in the Midrash on *Koheles* that Chanina, who was Rabbi Yehoshua ben Chananyah's nephew, might have become an apostate if his uncle had not saved him just in time. And Chanina was one of the most outstanding men of his time — it was said that when he left Eretz Yisrael for Babylonia, there was no one left in the Holy Land who could compare to him. The Midrash on *Koheles* mentions quite a number of other examples as well, that show us how dangerous this close contact was. That is why it was so crucial for Rabbi Eliezer to openly declare in front of his students that he had committed a sin by discussing Halachah with someone who was a Christian.

As Rabbi Eliezer was speaking to his students, a pleasant-looking young Roman entered the room.

"Excuse me, Rabbi, for coming to see you here without invitation. I saw you today at the residence of the Proconsul, and I decided that I would like to become your pupil. My name is Aquila. I am a close relative of the Emperor. When I was growing up, I had a Jewish teacher, a man whom the Emperor's father had brought to Rome from the war with the Jews. I learned Hebrew with him, and since then I have studied your Torah quite a bit.

Rabbi Eliezer listened as the young man continued. "I have read that there is only one God, that He created the world, and that He chose the Jews as His people. I would like to join your nation, Rabbi, but I have one question. It says in *Devarim*, Chapter 10, verses 17 and 18: 'For it is Hashem, your God, who is the God of [all] powers and the Lord [over all] lords; the great, mighty and fearful God, Who shows no favoritism and accepts no bribes; Who carries out judgement for orphans and widows, and loves the proselyte by giving him bread and clothing.' Now tell me, Rabbi, is that the kind of love God has for the stranger, that He gives him only bread and clothing? Truly now, when I want to reward my slaves, I offer them pheasants and peacocks!"

Rabbi Eliezer became very angry with Aquila. "We do not seek converts," he said, "and certainly not those who are dissatisfied with the very things that our forefather Ya'akov asked God for when he left his parents' home: 'bread to eat and clothing to wear.'"

Aquila left in great distress, but Rabbi Akiva followed him outside. "Would you perhaps like to present your question to one of our other scholars?" he asked.

"Yes, I would," said the young man. "Lead me and I will follow."

Rabbi Akiva brought him to Rabbi Yehoshua ben Chananyah, and Aquila repeated his question.

"My son," Rabbi Yehoshua said, "when a non-Jew converts to Judaism out of pure conviction and with sincere intentions, he can become great in Torah, which is signified here by the 'bread' that God feeds him; and furthermore he will one day envelop himself with the 'garments of bliss' which God will present us with in the World-to-Come. He can also marry off his daughter (who will be born Jewish) to a Kohen, and his grandson can become a Kohen haGadol, who will be able to bring offerings on the altar of the Holy Temple — which are considered 'God's bread.'"

Aquila was very grateful for this answer. "Thank you, Rabbi, for your explanation! Please allow me to learn the teachings of God the Almighty under your guidance."

And Rabbi Akiva said to Rabbi Yehoshua, "The words of King David have fulfilled themselves in you: 'Better to be soft and patient than strong and powerful.' If not for you, Aquila would have turned away from Judaism."

Chapter 24

It says in Koheles, "The words of the wise are like goads, the gatherers' talks are like nails that are sunk into the ground; they all come from one shepherd."

The Sages explain this saying in the following manner:

The "gatherers" are the teachers of Israel, who gather the religious precepts of the Oral Law. At times it will happen that some of them consider something to be pure while the others say that it isn't, or some of them will permit something while the others forbid it. Likewise, some of them may define something as useless while the others will decide that it has a use. All this, however, shouldn't mislead us, for even the contradictory arguments all stem from God. It was the One and Only God that gave them to us, and it was one leader that announced them. And that leader had heard them directly from God's mouth, from the Master of all creatures in this world, as it says, "God said all these words." And now the task is ours to work on broadening our understanding, so that we are able to conceive of the possibility that two things may contradict each other yet both may be true.

When Moshe was about to die, and he bid farewell to Yehoshua, his loyal pupil, he said, "My son, Yehoshua, the time has come for me to leave you. If you have any questions, ask me now."

"Moshe, my master, I have never left the tent of Torah for even one moment. And you have taught me the entire Torah in such a way that nothing is unclear to me."

After Moshe died, all of Israel mourned him for thirty days. But in their deep sorrow and pain the Jewish people neglected the study of the Torah, and so it happened that they forgot a number of religious precepts. But although Yehoshua, the new leader of Israel, could not recall some of the details of these halachos, he did remember the general principles. And thus Osniel ben Kenaz, with his keen mind, was able to reconstruct the missing parts of the Halachah through logical reasoning. That has been the situation in Israel for centuries. It is through logical reasoning that the great minds of every generation arrive at their specific conclusions from the general principles at hand.

It is inevitable, however, that there will be some disagreement concerning various complex circumstances. For individual halachic authorities will choose to focus on different points as determining factors. And thus it was that even in ancient times certain halachos were the subject of debates which remained unresolved for a while, until finally one of the authorities would establish the law in conformity with majority rule.

An example of this is the halachah we mentioned above, that Ammonites and Moabites are not permitted to us as marriage partners. Whether this halachah also applies to the women of these nations was not clear at first. It was Shmuel the Prophet who finally established the Halachah, in conjunction with the Sanhedrin. Whenever such decisions had to be made, the Sages would take a vote according to the principle of majority rule. But not all cases of this kind were resolved in harmony — as we shall now see.

The greatest man at the time of our story was undoubtedly Rabbi Eliezer ben Hurkanos. His contemporaries called him "Rabbi Eliezer the Great" for that reason. His knowledge of the Torah was immeasurable. His teacher, Rabban Yochanan ben Zakkai, compared him to an impermeable water cistern which doesn't lose even a drop of its water. Once, when Rabbi Eliezer visited him on Rosh Chodesh, Rabban Yochanan said to him,

"You, who are like a fountain which contains only pure water, why do you find it necessary to visit Yochanan the son of Zakkai?"

Rabbi Eliezer answered, "After all, I have an obligation to greet my teacher!"

The Sages say that Rabbi Eliezer was qualified for the gift of prophecy, but his generation was not worthy of this. Long before, Moshe was told that one day there would be a great man by the name of Eliezer, who would be a teacher of Israel; that is why Moshe named one of his sons Eliezer.

Rabbi Eliezer's teacher, Rabban Yochanan ben Zakkai, had belonged to the School of Hillel. He admired him as a great Torah leader, but nevertheless he also learned from some of the Rabbis who belonged to the School of Shammai. This is the background to a famous dispute between Rabbi Eliezer and his contemporaries in Yavneh.

There was a certain oven — called Achnai's oven — that these Sages differed about. Rabbi Eliezer considered that oven to be like a building, and held the halachic opinion that it was not susceptible to impurity. His colleagues however, considered it to be like an earthenware vessel, and thus they believed that it could become impure. It was a heated discussion, and although Rabbi Eliezer supported his view with a wealth of arguments and proofs, the other Rabbis refused to change their minds. At this point Rabbi Eliezer said, "If my authority is not enough for you, then let 'the Charuv' ('the Carob Tree') decide!"

"The Charuv" was a name which people used for Rabbi Chanina ben Dosa, who was one of the most renowned men of his time. He was so poor that he lived solely off the fruit of his carob tree (carob trees were quite common in Eretz Yisrael). He too had been a disciple of Rabban Yochanan ben Zakkai. He was a great *tzaddik*, and God had often answered his prayers in a miraculous manner. So highly esteemed was he that even his teacher, Rabban Yochanan ben Zakkai, once asked him to pray for his son, who was very ill at the time. And God answered his prayer, and Rabban Yochanan ben Zakkai's son recovered.

Now Rabbi Eliezer called for him, so that he should voice his opinion on the disputed matter. And the result was that the great and celebrated Rabbi Chanina ben Dosa agreed with Rabbi Eliezer! But Rabbi Eliezer's colleagues still held firmly to their view.

So Rabbi Eliezer said, "If our authority is insufficient, then let 'the Brook' decide!"

"The Brook" was the nickname of Rabbi Elazar ben Arach, one of the most distinguished Sages of his time. His teacher, Rabban Yochanan ben Zakkai, had compared him to a powerful spring that gathers force and turns into a strong, flowing brook. He favored his sayings over those of all his other students. He also said of him, "If all of Israel's Sages were measured in greatness against Elazar ben Arach (even if Rabbi Eliezer ben Hurkanos would be counted among them), he would take first place over all of them."

When Rabban Yochanan ben Zakkai died, Rabbi Elazar had moved to Emmaus. He expected all his companions to follow him there, but they did not. Then he thought of moving to Yavneh, but his wife, who was very proud of him, felt that it was beneath his dignity to do so if the other scholars had not followed him to Emmaus. Because they remained in Emmaus, Rabbi Elazar hadn't participated in the study sessions in Yavneh for many years. Now Rabbi Eliezer called for him, and he too decided like Rabbi Eliezer. But the Sages still refused to accept Rabbi Eliezer's decision.

Rabbi Eliezer then proposed the following challenge: "If you really insist on the rule of the majority, then let 'the walls of the *beis midrash*' decide!"

Who are "the walls of the *beis midrash*"? They are the pupils (the future teachers), who lend purpose and structure to the house of learning. So the pupils who were present stood up and they too confirmed Rabbi Eliezer's view. In reaction to this, Rabbi Yehoshua told them sharply, "My dear pupils, you are still too young and immature to join this debate!" So they remained silent. They no longer dared to take part in their elders' controversy.

Rabbi Eliezer now stood up and said, "So let it be decided from Above!"

And God accepted his appeal. Without delay He sent the Prophet Eliyahu, who said to the Sages: "Why are you fighting against Rabbi Eliezer? He is always right in his rulings!"

Rabbi Yehoshua stood up and replied, "It says in the Torah: 'The Torah is not in Heaven.' The Torah was given to us by God at Mount Sinai, and in it we find the precept that decisions shall be made according to majority rule!"

Rabbi Eliezer, however, would not budge from his view. So they brought out all the vessels that he had declared pure and burned them, and then they placed a ban on him. Someone would have to inform him of that ban — but no one dared to do it. Then Rabbi Akiva said, "I will tell him. It is better if he hears it from me than from the wrong person, lest he be hurt even more."

Rabbi Akiva dressed himself in black garments and went to Rabbi Eliezer. He sat down on the ground at a distance from him, without greeting him.

After a few moments, Rabbi Eliezer broke the silence. "Akiva," he said, "what is this supposed to mean?"

"It seems to me, my teacher," Rabbi Akiva replied, "that your colleagues have cut themselves off from you."

When Rabbi Eliezer heard this, he tore his clothing like a mourner, and took off his shoes. He sat down on the ground and wept bitterly.

It was at this time that Rabban Gamliel the *Nasi* undertook a journey aboard a ship on the high seas. Although he was Rabbi Eliezer's brother-in-law, this had not deterred him from placing the ban on him. Now, on his voyage, a sudden storm came up, which threatened to hurl the entire ship into the depths of the sea. Rabban Gamliel turned to Heaven and said,

"I know that I am being subjected to this danger on account of Rabbi Eliezer ben Hurkanos! Master of the World, may it be clear to You that I did not ban him in order to show that I can exert my power even over the greatest of men! I did it only for the sake of Your honor, to restrict the disputes among Torah authorities, and so that individuals will always know they must yield to the majority, no matter how great they are themselves."

The storm quieted down, and Rabban Gamliel was saved.

Chapter 25

During all this time Rabbi Yehoshua ben Chananyah had stood loyally at Rabban Gamliel's side. But afterwards there were a few incidents which were to change their relationship.

There was a new firstborn among Rabbi Tzadok's cattle. In previous times firstborns were brought to the Temple to be sacrificed. Now that the Temple no longer stood, one wasn't allowed to use these firstborns for anything until they died or acquired some sort of physical blemish on their bodies. Because of this law, many people were tempted to create such a blemish on purpose. Thus, they would put an obstacle before the animal in order to make it stumble and break a leg, or they would send a dog to attack it, to cause it injury. As a result of this development, a halachic decree was issued that blemished animals could not be slaughtered, even if the owner insisted that the blemish was not his doing.

In Rabbi Tzadok's case, the animal had injured its lip while eating some barley. Rabbi Tzadok thought that the halachic decree applied only to people who could be suspected of trying to circumvent the law, namely, the unlearned — but not the Torah scholars. He raised this issue with Rabbi Yehoshua, who confirmed his view. Then he asked Rabban Gamliel for his opinion, and he disagreed; he believed that no such differentiation was applicable in this case. When Rabbi Tzadok mentioned that Rabbi Yehoshua had said otherwise, Rabban Gamliel demanded that Rabbi Tzadok repeat the question in the presence of all the scholars in the *beis midrash*. And there and then

Rabban Gamliel handed down the same ruling he had given before, and Rabbi Yehoshua didn't dare argue with him. At that point, Rabban Gamliel confronted Rabbi Yehoshua over the fact that he had given Rabbi Tzadok a different answer, and made him stand during his lecture, as though Rabbi Yehoshua were one of the pupils. The other scholars were so outraged at this harsh behavior, however, that they compelled Rabbi Chutzpis, who was in charge of interpreting Rabban Gamliel's teachings, to stop the lecture.

It was not too long before Rabbi Yehoshua once again had to submit to Rabban Gamliel's authority.

The Jewish calendar is calculated in accordance with the moon's orbit around the earth. It takes the moon approximately 29½ days to complete its circuit around the earth. This time period amounts to an astronomical month. In ancient times, the calendar was not the decisive factor; it was also necessary that someone see the new moon. Whoever had seen the moon in its earlier phase had to go to Rabban Gamliel, the *Nasi*, to give testimony, and then Rabban Gamliel would announce the blessing of the moon. Fires were then lit on the mountaintops in order to inform all the Jews in Eretz Yisrael that the new month had begun.

This practice was later abolished, because of the Sadducees (the Tzadokim), a faction which tried to mislead other Jews by setting fires at the wrong times. The Sadducees were a sect that opposed the Oral Law, insisting on abiding only by the literal meaning of the Written Law. Thus they maintained that according to the Torah (*Vayikra* 23:15-16), Shavuos should fall only on the first day of the week. When they saw that they were not succeeding in gaining the recognition of the public, they tried to use all kinds of trickery to create confusion in the workings of the calendar. Thus, for example, they hired false witnesses.

Once there was a pair of witnesses that came before the *Nasi* and the Sanhedrin, and after one of them had testified, the other one said, "I climbed to the top of Mount Edom and saw the moon resting between two rocks; its head resembled that of a calf, its ears were like those of a sheep, its horns looked like deer's antlers, and it had a tail. I looked at it, and I fell back in shock! If you don't believe me, then look here and you can see the gold coins which were given to me for this testimony!"

Apparently this sincere man had offered his services to the Sadducees, to prevent them from deceiving the Sanhedrin through someone else.

Once there were two witnesses who appeared before Rabban Gamliel and his Sanhedrin, who claimed to have seen the moon that day. The following night, however, the moon was not in sight, even though the sky was not cloudy. The Sages, among them Rabbi Yehoshua, were therefore of the opinion that the witnesses had lied. But Rabban Gamliel accepted their testimony, since it matched his calculations.

Soon after that Rabban Gamliel found out that Rabbi Yehoshua was intending to observe the holidays of the coming month in accordance with his own calculations. That was something Rabban Gamliel could not tolerate. Such discrepancy among the leading Rabbis would cause enormous confusion and turmoil in Israel. So he sent the following message to Rabbi Yehoshua: "I command you to come to me with your money and staff on the very day on which — according to your calculations — Yom Kippur falls!"

Rabbi Yehoshua was deeply distressed. When Rabbi Akiva, his former pupil, saw this, he asked him, "Rabbi Yehoshua, why are you so upset?"

"Akiva," he answered, "I would rather be ill and bedridden for an entire year than to have to comply with the *Nasi*'s orders."

"Allow me to share something with you," said Rabbi Akiva, "which you yourself once taught me."

"Speak!" Rabbi Yehoshua said.

And Rabbi Akiva explained: "When referring to the arrangement of the calendar, which determines the days on which the holidays fall, the Torah speaks about the holidays as *otam* — 'them.' But the word *otam* is written there three times without the letter *vav*, so that it can be read as *atem* — 'you,' as well. This is meant to imply that *you*, the leaders of Israel, are the ones to decide on which day Rosh Chodesh falls. And this holds true even when you err, or even when false witnesses mislead you. The only day that is considered the valid Rosh Chodesh is the one that you decide upon."

"You have consoled me, Akiva," Rabbi Yehoshua replied. "You have consoled me."

Nevertheless, Rabbi Yehoshua went to see his friend Rabbi Dosa ben Harkinas to ask him for his opinion on the matter.

"You must submit to Rabban Gamliel's authority, my friend," said Rabbi Dosa. "It is for this reason that the Torah did not mention the names of the seventy Elders who stood by Moshe's side. The Torah wanted to prevent us from comparing our teachers to them, for then we might, God forbid, come to belittle our teachers, saying that they do not measure up to the Sages of the past. Thus, since we don't know who they were, we can assume that our leaders are equal to them or perhaps even superior to them.

"In a similar way, we find that the Torah draws a parallel between three of the greatest men in our history — Moshe, Aharon, and Shmuel — and three men of lesser rank — Gidon, Shimshon, and Yiftach. This is to teach us that Gidon in his time was just as entitled to his authority as was Moshe in his time, Shimshon was just as entitled as was Aharon, and likewise Yiftach was just as entitled as was Shmuel. And furthermore it says, 'And you will come to the judge who will be there in your time.' Now, could a man possibly go to a judge who was not alive in his time? What are we to understand from this? The Torah is teaching us here that we must obey and respect all our judges in the same manner as Israel did in Moshe's time."

Rabbi Yehoshua decided to obey Rabban Gamliel's command. On the day that he had reckoned to be Yom Kippur, he took his purse and his staff with him and went to Rabban Gamliel in Yavneh. When Rabban Gamliel saw him, he rose to his feet, went towards him, and embraced him and kissed him.

"Welcome to you, my teacher and pupil! Yehoshua, in your wisdom you are my teacher, but since you listened to me you are my pupil! Blessed is the nation whose great men listen to those beneath them!"

Rabbi Yehoshua's conduct becomes even more worthy of esteem, when we take into account that he was a towering scholar of astronomy at the time. And not only was there no one comparable to him during his time, but his knowledge has not ceased to impress us even today, when science has taken such great strides forward. Rabban Gamliel was also well aware of Rabbi Yehoshua's expertise in this field, as we shall see in the following account.

Rabban Gamliel and Rabbi Yehoshua once journeyed together by sea. Rabban Gamliel had taken bread along with him, but Rabbi Yehoshua had brought bread and flour. After a while Rabban Gamliel had used up his provisions, and he had to ask Rabbi Yehoshua to share his with him.

"My bread has become moldy and inedible." said Rabban Gamliel. "Therefore I would like to ask you to please give me some of the flour you brought with you."

"With pleasure! Consider it to be yours!" Rabbi Yehoshua answered.

"How were you able to know that our trip would take such a long time?" Rabban Gamliel asked.

Rabbi Yehoshua explained: "Every seventy years a certain star becomes visible in the sky and misleads the ships on their course. Since now is the time that this star usually appears, I was afraid that it would be seen during our trip, and I therefore brought food that is less perishable. And exactly what I had feared happened in the end!"

When Rabban Gamliel complimented Rabbi Yehoshua on

his wisdom, Rabbi Yehoshua said, "There are two great scholars of this science in our homeland — Rabbi Elazar Chisma and Rabbi Yochanan ben Gudgada. But despite their achievements they don't even have enough clothing to wear or bread to eat."

After they had arrived safely at their destination, Rabban Gamliel offered employment to these two scientifically inclined Sages, to help them overcome their poverty, but they declined. Rabban Gamliel said to them, "What I am offering you is neither power nor glory, but rather a burden and even hardship. The higher a person's position is, the greater is his dependence and servitude."

One of the most renowned astronomers of recent times [1656-1742] was a man by the name of Edmund Halley. He discovered a comet which appears regularly after long intervals of time. The comet was named after him: Halley's Comet. The former Chief Rabbi of Prague, Rabbi Rappaport [1790-1867], who was a scholar, has proven that Halley's Comet is that same star which Rabbi Yehoshua had been referring to in those ancient times.

Chapter 26

It seems that Rabban Gamliel, in spite of the firm principle of majority rule, demanded more authority for himself. Once, when he, Rabbi Akiva and two other Sages were staying in Rome, they were sitting together next to a lamp on one of the *Yom Tov* evenings. The lamp fell down, and Rabbi Akiva jumped up and restored it to its place. Then the Sages debated whether or not it had been halachically permissible to do so. Rabban Gamliel was the only one who believed that it was forbidden; all the others considered it permissible. And then the *Nasi*, filled with indignation, cried out: "Akiva, how dare you go so far in your conclusions?"

And Rabbi Akiva answered: "Our teacher, have you not taught us that the majority rules?"

Rabban Gamliel complained about Rabbi Akiva on another occasion. There had been a difference of opinion concerning the blessings to recite at the table, in which the viewpoint of the Sages differed from that of Rabban Gamliel. When Rabbi Akiva officially announced the consensus in Rabban Gamliel's presence, the latter once again objected, and Rabbi Akiva, again, responded with the same principle of majority rule.

After Rabbi Eliezer retired from public life, Rabbi Yehoshua was considered Israel's greatest teacher. He found it difficult to subordinate himself to Rabban Gamliel. The *Nasi* had managed to prevail over him twice, but their third confrontation had serious consequences for Rabban Gamliel.

There was a dispute among the Sages over whether the

Shemoneh Esreh prayer of the *Ma'ariv* service is voluntary or obligatory. Rabbi Yehoshua said it was voluntary, whereas Rabban Gamliel held that it was obligatory. Once a student came to Rabbi Yehoshua and asked him about this, and he taught him in accordance with what his view was. Then that same student went to Rabban Gamliel, who instructed him differently. The student responded, "But Rabbi Yehoshua told me the opposite!"

"Come to the *beis midrash* tomorrow," Rabban Gamliel said, "and repeat your question!"

The student did as he was told. Rabban Gamliel then answered the question according to his viewpoint, and Rabbi Yehoshua didn't dare to contradict him. Now, Rabban Gamliel confronted Rabbi Yehoshua on the matter, and Rabbi Yehoshua admitted to having voiced a differing view on the subject. Rabban Gamliel thereupon commanded him to rise to his feet and listen to the ensuing discussion while standing, just like an ordinary student.

Rabban Gamliel went ahead with his teaching while Rabbi Yehoshua was forced to stand. But the other Sages present were strongly offended by this behavior, and they made Rabbi Chutzpis, who would announce Rabban Gamliel's halachic rulings, stop the lesson. Then all the Sages who were present — seventy-two of them — stood up together and called out to the *chazan* Rabbi Shimon (who was in charge of maintaining order): "Speak!" And they made him read the verse, "For who did not feel your continual condemnation!" (*Nachum* 3:19).

While reciting the verse, the *chazan* addressed Rabban Gamliel, and all who were there stood listening, and then they said to one another: "For how long must we tolerate Rabban Gamliel's affronts to Rabbi Yehoshua? First he insulted him regarding Rabbi Tzadok's cattle, then concerning the calendar, and now again. We must strip him of his title and his position!"

They held a meeting, and they decided to depose Rabban Gamliel. But who was to take his place? Rabbi Yehoshua, who certainly was the most suited of all of them? No, absolutely not! Such a substitution would have looked as if the Sages had acted out of pure personal interest, as if they preferred Rabbi Yehoshua to Rabban Gamliel! But what about Rabbi Akiva? He was the greatest man in Israel, after Rabbi Yehoshua, but they were hesitant about nominating him because of his heathen lineage. Finally, they chose the young Rabbi Elazar ben Azaryah.

Rabbi Elazar ben Azaryah came from a very noble family. He was a tenth-generation descendant of Ezra, who had led Israel back from the Babylonian exile. In spite of his tender age he was very learned and he was capable of dealing with questions in all areas of life. He was also very wealthy, and he could therefore be expected to contribute, if need be, to the welfare of the community. When they offered him the position of *Nasi*, he said, "I must first consult with my wife."

Rabbi Elazar's wife was not very ambitious. Moreover, she was afraid that her husband might also be deposed one day, and that he was too young to evoke the proper reverence a *Nasi* was worthy of. So she tried to dissuade him.

But then a miracle occurred: The young sage's hair and beard turned white as snow all of a sudden! Now Rabbi Elazar no longer hesitated to accept the position. (Rabbi Elazar ben Azaryah's famous words, "I am indeed like a seventy-year-old!" refer to the fact that although he was still young, he looked like a man of seventy.) Rabbi Elazar went to the *beis midrash*, took his new seat of honor, and started to lead the discussions.

Rabban Gamliel had kept the doors of the *beis midrash* locked at all times, for he allowed entry only to those people whom he regarded as pure in heart and devoted seekers of the knowledge of Torah. Now the doors were opened wide and everyone was allowed to enter. People came streaming in from all sides, wise men and students alike. And if in the past eight benches had been sufficient, now hundreds of benches were needed!

The rows of men engaged in study were compared to rows of

grapevines in a vineyard — that was the famous *Kerem d'Yavneh* — "the Vineyard of Yavneh."

On that day the Sages resolved countless questions and doubts. On the same day the halachic views and rulings of former generations were validated according to the testimonies they had from the past. And on that day the tractate *Eduyos* took form. Whenever the Talmud says, "on that day," it is referring to that very day that Rabbi Elazar ben Azaryah was appointed *Nasi*.

And likewise, that day also marks forever Rabban Gamliel's strength of character — for he did not seek revenge for having been deposed, nor did he bear resentment or withdraw in bitter silence. Instead, he remained in the *beis midrash* and participated in the learned discussions as though nothing had happened. Many a time he would voice his opinion on questions that were raised and find himself overruled, and he quietly accepted this. Thus it was decided that day that Israel was allowed to accept converts from the peoples that were living in the lands of Ammon and Moav, since they were no longer thought to be part of the original nations whom God had excluded.

Rabbi Akiva was also affected by all these developments — for with regard to his knowledge and accomplishments he would have been the most suitable candidate for the office of *Nasi*, and yet someone else had been chosen instead. He would have been very pleased to take the position, not because he was driven by ambition, but because of his pure desire to give of himself to his people.

"It was not because Rabbi Elazar is a greater scholar than I am that they chose him over me," said Rabbi Akiva, "but because he comes from great ancestors. Fortunate is the man who can lean back on the accomplishments of his forefathers."

The next day Rabban Gamliel decided to go to Rabbi Yehoshua's home and make peace with him. The walls of Rabbi Yehoshua's house were black, since he earned his living as a needle-maker. When Rabban Gamliel saw this, he said, "I can see from the walls of your house that you are a needle-maker."

"You did not know this until now?" asked Rabbi Yehoshua. "That's the tragedy — that you didn't know how hard we have to work in order to make a living. Otherwise you would never have dared to treat us in such a condescending manner."

"I was wrong," replied Rabban Gamliel. "Please forgive me!"

"I cannot forgive you after you hurt me so deeply three times," Rabbi Yehoshua replied.

"If you don't want to forgive me for my own merit," Rabban Gamliel pleaded, "then forgive me on account of the merit of my father! You knew him, and you loved and admired him. He was a great teacher of Israel, and he died as a martyr for the sanctification of God's Name."

And Rabbi Yehoshua forgave him.

Now that Rabbi Yehoshua and Rabban Gamliel had made peace with each other, Rabbi Yehoshua decided to ask the Sages to reappoint Rabban Gamliel as *Nasi*. There was a laundryman who offered to take Rabbi Yehoshua's message to the Sages in the *beis midrash*. When he arrived and gave the Sages Rabbi Yehoshua's message, however, Rabbi Akiva warned his colleagues, "Lock the doors, otherwise Rabban Gamliel's servants will come and do violence to us!"

When the laundryman returned to Rabbi Yehoshua and told him what had taken place, Rabbi Yehoshua said, "In order to clear this up I must go and tell the Sages myself."

And so he did. Rabbi Akiva told him, "If you have reconciled your differences with Rabban Gamliel and have forgiven him, then there is no reason for us to be angry with him any longer." The Rabbis decided to appoint Rabban Gamliel as *Nasi* once again, but they also allowed Rabbi Elazar ben Azaryah to retain some of his authority. Thus, Rabban Gamliel would lead the Torah discussions in the *beis midrash* for two weeks, and then Rabbi Elazar ben Azaryah would take over for the third week.

That is why we often find that the Talmud asks the question, "Whose week was it?" and then answers, "It was Rabbi Elazar ben Azaryah's week." (The student who first posed the question to Rabban Gamliel and then to Rabbi Yehoshua was to become the revered Rabbi Shimon bar Yochai.)

Chapter 27

Our Sages tell us in the Talmudic tractate *Chagigah* that four entered the "orchard" — Ben Azzai, Ben Zoma, "Acher", and Rabbi Akiva. And Rabbi Akiva said to them, "When you reach the stones of pure marble, do not say, 'Water, water!' because Scripture warns us, 'Whoever lies will not last before me.'" Ben Azzai looked, and he passed away. Concerning him, it is written: "The death of the pious is dear in God's eyes."

Ben Zoma looked and went mad. It says about him: "If you find honey, enjoy it slowly, for otherwise you might become overly full and vomit." Acher occupied himself with the plants. Rabbi Akiva, however, entered in peace and came out in peace. Concerning him, it says: "Pull me, and we will run after you!"

This mysterious account has challenged the great minds of our people for centuries. Nearly all of them have agreed that the word "orchard" in this context does not refer to Gan Eden, but rather to the deep and hidden wisdom of mysticism, which Rabbi Akiva and his colleagues were exploring.

The first one, Ben Azzai, was married to Rabbi Akiva's daughter for a short while until he divorced her in order to devote all his energies to Torah study. It was that very special kind of Torah study which caused him to die early, for his mind became too powerful to be contained within his body. He looked — and he died. His soul, absorbed in the contemplation of the highest wisdom, left behind its mortal shell.

Not nearly as outstanding was Ben Zoma, Ben Azzai's fellow student and friend. Although everyone praised him for his wisdom and for his understanding of the Torah, the depth and power of the "orchard" was too much for him. He looked — and his thinking was overwhelmed. He had "eaten too much of the honey," and his mind became impaired.

Acher's fate was far worse. His real name was Elisha ben Avuyah. His father was a well-known and respected man. When Elisha was born, he arranged for a huge celebration of the *bris*, and he invited all the teachers of Israel and all of the most prominent people. While the guests were enjoying themselves with food and drink and music and song, Rabbi Eliezer said to Rabbi Yehoshua, "Let them enjoy themselves! We can learn in the meantime!"

And so they did. Soon the two became so engrossed in lofty and learned conversation that all the guests surrounding them became silent and listened to these two famous sages in great awe. It seemed as though the Torah were emanating from them as on the day of the revelation at Mount Sinai.

When Avuyah noticed how greatly the people respected and admired the pair, he said, "I want my son to become like them! I will see to it that he devotes his life to Torah."

And Avuyah kept his word, but since his undertaking was based on impure motives, it ended badly. Although the young Elisha grew up to be a prominent and learned man, his knowledge lacked roots, for he was deficient in his fear of God. Even as a student, his mind was often not on his Torah study, and many a time books of Greek poetry fell out of his lap in class.

Then he took an interest in "the secrets of paradise" which even the great Ben Azzai and Ben Zoma couldn't master. And when he too failed to penetrate the deeply hidden truths, he began to doubt.

One day as he reclined in the shade of a tree, studying, a man and his son passed by. They noticed a bird's nest in a tree. "Look!" the father said to his son. "There's a nest in that tree! Climb up and take it down for me but let the mother-bird fly away, as it says in the Torah, 'When you will chance upon a bird's nest on the way, on any kind of tree or on the ground, and it has chicks or eggs, and the mother is roosting on them... You must send away the mother-bird and then you may take the young for yourself, so that it be well with you and that you live a long time.'"

The young boy obediently climbed up the tree, chased away the mother-bird and took the nest with the chicks in it. All of a sudden the branch he was sitting on cracked, and he fell to the ground. Alarmed, his father ran to him, only to discover that the boy had broken his neck and died. Crying and lamenting, the grief-stricken man picked up his son's body and left.

Elisha witnessed all this, and when the bereaved father had gone, he flung down his book, and cried, "Is that Torah, and is that its reward? This young boy fulfilled two commandments, both of which were given to us with the promise of happiness and long life as the reward! He obeyed his father, as we are commanded, 'Honor your father and your mother, so that you may live long and that it be well with you.' And he sent the mother-bird away, as it says, 'You must send away the mother-bird and then you may take the young for yourself, so that it be well with you and that you live a long time.' This young boy did exactly what the Torah requires, and he died!"

At that moment Elisha gave up his Jewish heritage completely and became an apostate. On the following day, which was Shabbos, he went out for a walk and met a young woman, with whom he struck up a frivolous conversation. She asked him in great astonishment, "Aren't you Elisha ben Avuyah, the great teacher of Israel?"

They were standing in a turnip field at the time. Instead of answering her, he bent down and pulled a turnip out of the ground and began to eat it. The young woman said, "You must be *someone else*, because the person I was thinking of would never have desecrated the Shabbos."

From that day on Elisha was no longer called by his name. Instead, he was known as *Acher*, "someone else."

The Sages teach us that Elisha would not have become an apostate had he known how, many years later, his grandson Rabbi Ya'akov (his daughter's son), explained the Torah verse that had troubled him.

Rabbi Ya'akov taught, "'So that it be well with you' — but who on this earth is ever happy? For isn't man born to toil in this world? And even those whom the world considers happy, experience more pain than happiness! Almost daily we suffer physical discomfort, disappointments, or other kinds of sorrow. That is why the promise 'so that it be well with you' must be referring to the World-to-Come, which will bring pure, eternal joy to the pious. And regarding '[so] that you live a long time' — is there such thing as long life here on earth? When man becomes 80, 90, or 100 years old, does his life not vanish as though it had been only a fleeting dream, like the shadow of a bird flying swiftly by? That is why the promise of long life must also be referring to the World-to-Come, for there the span of life is eternal."

Rabbi Akiva was the only one of these four colleagues who reached the desired goal. We read that he "entered in peace and he came out in peace," and that concerning him it says, "Pull me, and we will run after you!" — this means that Rabbi Akiva was wise enough to content himself with the human dimensions of mysticism, and he did not attempt to go beyond them. Indeed, he achieved the highest level of understanding that a human being in this world is capable of. There was in fact nothing in the world worth knowing that remained unrevealed to him, including the sciences. He and his friend Rabbi Yishmael traveled all over the Holy Land to treat sick people. Wherever they arrived, people would come running to them for help. They treated external injuries as well as internal diseases, prescribing medication that proved to be very successful.

One of the villages they came to was Bartota. Their reputation had already reached there, and all the sick people came streaming in to see the great teachers and healers of Israel.

While they were distributing medication to those in need, a man with a shovel in his hand approached them, saying, "What kind of Rabbis are you? Who gave you permission to interfere with God's will? God made these people sick, and you are undoing His work by making them healthy!"

"What do you do for a living?" Rabbi Akiva asked him.

"I am a gardener, and this is the shovel I use for my work."

"My son," Rabbi Akiva said, "who gave you permission to interfere with God's will? God created the earth and gave it the form he wanted — and you are mangling it with your shovel? God commanded that whoever injures his fellow must pay the medical expenses involved. In so doing, God granted us permission to cure the injured."

Ashamed — but wiser — the gardener departed.

Then one of the many students that had accompanied the Sages asked, "Rabbi, allow me to put a question to you."

"Speak, my son!" Rabbi Akiva answered.

"You have taught us that King Chizkiyahu did six things, and three of them were approved by the Sages of his time. One of these was that he hid away the book of medical treatments and medicines, a book in which all the diseases and their remedies were written down. Illness had lost its underlying purpose — namely, to inspire people to repent and better their ways, and that is why King Chizkiyahu saw to it that the book was concealed. If that is so, then the gardener seems to be right, and the Torah's permission to cure maladies should really apply only to external injuries such as wounds and fractures."

"Your argument would be correct," replied Rabbi Akiva, "if we did not know the true reason for King Chizkiyahu's move. You see, my son, man's nature and circumstances change over the course of time, and the medication which may have worked well once could be ineffective or even dangerous centuries later. That is why there was a great danger involved in using the book of remedies, especially if the patient was ignorant and tried to treat himself without consulting a doctor. And it is for this reason that King Chizkiyahu hid the book away. As far as repentance goes, however, there are so many illnesses that are beyond treatment, and so many others that linger for long periods of time in spite of medical treatment, that one would have to be thick-headed indeed to pass up teshuvah when sickness strikes."

Chapter 28

After Domitian's tyranny and Nerva's weak rule, the Romans praised the Emperor Trajan enormously. He promised that senators would never be executed, and he kept this promise loyally. There were times during his reign when senators committed crimes and had to be punished, but even then he let the Senate decide the verdict. That alone made him so popular among the senators and the intellectuals of the time that they couldn't praise him enough. The Senate bestowed on him the honorary name "Optimus," which means "the best." Trajan indeed was endowed with many outstanding qualities, and he became a great and beloved Emperor.

Once, when he ceremoniously presented the sword of office to the Prefect of the Praetorions, Trajan said to him: "Use this for me when I am good, and against me when I am bad!"

Trajan was also victorious in his military campaigns. It was his ambition to equal or surpass Alexander the Great in fame, and he loved it when people compared the two of them. In fact, a lot of his contemporaries as well as many people in later generations referred to him as a second Alexander.

He built magnificent works of architecture in Rome and in other places. The provinces he conquered had to provide the funds for these projects. When the Emperor conquered Dacia, he built a Forum in Rome, which in its dimensions and splendor by far exceeded any of the monuments the other Roman Emperors had built. There were countless individual statues decorating the square, many of which represented Trajan. In addition, there were also groups of statues in marble and bronze showing some of his most celebrated deeds. The balustrades of the various buildings glittered with gold-plated horses and armor. This is where his famous "horseman" statue stood.

His Arch of Triumph, lavishly ornamented with impressive sculptures, was there as well. The middle of the Forum was dominated by the towering "Trajan's Column," which was decorated from bottom to top with scenes from the victory over Dacia. A huge statue of the Emperor crowned this column. Attached to the Forum were two libraries, one for works in Greek and the other for Latin writings. On the western side of the Forum there was a basilica of enormous dimensions with various halls and rooms in it for the use of the public. Magnificent hallways with rows of columns connected the chambers to each other.

Aside from the Forum, which was his most important work, Trajan built many other great buildings: theaters, public baths, halls, and arcades. Other parts of Italy, as well as the provinces, benefited from his love of architecture as well. Thus he built a port in Ancona, and the harbor construction he initiated in the port of Civita Vecchia continues to serve its purpose to this day. In Spain he had a bridge erected over the Tagus River in Alcantara, and he did the same at Mainz, on the Rhine. When the water level of the Danube at Tur Severin, Rumania, is low enough, one can still see sections of the mighty bridge that Apollodorus constructed there on behalf of Trajan. The Emperor also had roads built to connect all the provinces of the vast Empire with the capital at Rome, so that the subjects of the Empire could deliver their grain there.

The writers of the time praised Trajan for being just, modest, and hard-working. They also spoke admiringly of his majestic manner, his bravery in war, and his talent for dealing with people. They tried to conceal his weaknesses as much as possible, but nevertheless even they had to admit that he was unbridled in his eating and drinking, and that he was not a particularly moral person. Jewish sources do not have many positive things to say about him, for he was the cause of endless sorrow and pain to our ancestors.

Although Plotina, the Emperor's wife, was praised generously by the writers, some people said that she was the one who encouraged Trajan in his cruelties towards the Jews. Trajan and his wife had a son and a daughter, and both children died at a young age. It happened that the day of their son's birth was Tishah b'Av; while all of the Roman Empire rejoiced, the Jews were fasting and mourning. The day of their daughter's death happened to fall during Chanukah, and the Jews were lighting candles and singing happily. Plotina said to her husband, "Isn't it obvious that the Jews hate you? When our son was born, they sat on the ground crying and fasting, and now that our daughter has died they are celebrating!"

Trajan certainly hated the Jews for political reasons as well. In his war against the Parthians, the numerous Jews who lived along at the banks of the Euphrates and Tigris rivers resisted him stubbornly. And just at the time that the Emperor was celebrating his triumph in Rome, the Jews started to rebel again in the newly conquered provinces of Egypt, Cyrenaica, and Cyprus. They longed to rid themselves of the heavy Roman yoke, for they were suffering greatly. They were at the mercy of the Roman governors, and they were expected to worship the statues of the Roman Emperors. Women and young girls were pursued by the Roman soldiers. Many men and women gave up their lives for the sanctification of God's Name, choosing to die rather than to transgress God's holy commandments. But they were now calling for revenge. The Roman administration also imposed unbearably heavy taxation, which further contributed to the hardship of daily life.

The Jews were dispersed throughout the entire Empire, however, and they couldn't unite as one force against the Romans. To stand a chance against Roman might, they would have needed the help of other subjugated nations in the Empire. In the view of the Sages, no revolt could succeed unless God redeemed them and brought the Mashiach. It was for this reason that Rabbi Akiva decided to travel to faraway places, to warn the Jews everywhere against rebelling.

Cornelius Palma, Syria's governor, had conquered a great part of Arabia on behalf of Trajan. Jews had lived there since antiquity, even before the Babylonian exile. They too were suffering greatly under Roman rule, and were contemplating rebellion. This was Rabbi Akiva's first destination. His name was well-known even here, and everyone, Jews and non-Jews alike, treated him with the greatest respect. Kings seeking advice came to see him, and they followed whatever he said. Thus, he succeeded in dissuading Arabia's Jews from rebelling.

Rabbi Akiva's itinerary stretched as far as North Africa and Egypt. There were a great many Jews in Egypt. Following the murder of Gedalyah ben Achikam, the Jews whom Nevuchadnetzar had left behind in Jerusalem (after his destruction of the Temple) came to take refuge there. Judea had been an Egyptian province for over a hundred years under the Ptolemies. The two lands had established very close ties at the time, and as a result the Jewish community in Egypt grew considerably. The Jews even built a temple there and offered sacrifices. This of course was halachically unacceptable, but it indicates how large and entrenched the community was there. The major city of Egypt at the time was Alexandria, which had been built by Alexander the Great and was named after him. Many wealthy, aristocratic, and learned Jews lived there. Philo, who is considered to have been one of the most prominent philosophers of the Neoplatonic School, was one of these. His fellow Jews had once sent him to Rome to ask the Emperor Caligula to free them of their obligation to worship his image. He died shortly before Rabbi Akiva's time.

Alexandrian Judaism at the time seems to have been focused on the rejection of idol-worship. The Great Synagogue of Alexandria still stood there, bearing witness to the religiosity and devotion of earlier generations. In form it was a basilica, which means that it was built like a royal hall. There were massive pillars supporting the roof, and the gigantic hall was able to hold thousands of people. At the front were seventy golden chairs for the community's elders. The synagogue was so vast that the cantor's voice could not be heard everywhere, and the *gabbai* therefore had to stand on the *bimah* with a flag, which he would wave whenever the *chazan* had concluded his blessings! Thousands of voices would then respond "Amen."

The congregants would group themselves in the synagogue according to their occupation: the weavers would sit in one area, the carpenters in another, and so forth. Thus when a traveler came to Alexandria, he found that the Great Synagogue was an ideal place to get to know his fellow craftsmen. After these initial contacts, assistance or job opportunities often followed.

Chapter 29

When Rabbi Akiva arrived in Alexandria, he went to visit Theogonos, the head of the Jewish community. This man's house was the nicest and most impressive building on the main street of the city. It was furnished in a lavish, regal style, and one would have thought that it was built for a Greek official rather than for a Jew. Many Greek paintings adorned the walls, and busts of philosophers, including one of Plato, were also part of the decor. Marble columns supported the partly open ceiling.

An abundance of comfortable cushions filled the floor of the main room, and when Rabbi Akiva arrived, Theogonos was reclining on one of them, reading a Greek book. He was about fifty years old and he looked fit and healthy. Like most of the aristocratic Alexandrian Jews, he had received a Greek education, and he was essentially a Greek in his way of thinking and in his general conduct. A contemporary writer commented that if more of Alexandria's Jews had been faithful to their religion, the price of pork would have been lower! These upper-class Jews owned the most beautiful horses, and they won a lot of the horse races. In the gymnasium they were the best wrestlers. The only difference between them and the Greeks or the Hellenists was the fact that they despised the Greek gods, which was something they openly admitted. In fact, that was one of the main causes of friction between Greeks and Jews, although anti-Semitism was involved as well.

Theogonos' servant interrupted his master to tell him that Rabbi Akiva had come to see him. When he heard Rabbi Akiva's name announced, Theogonos stood up and hurried towards him. "Great teacher of Israel, welcome!" he said. "Your name has spread to all corners of the earth." Then he invited him to recline on one of the cushions, and he commanded one of his servants to bring some food and drink.

"That's not necessary," Rabbi Akiva told him. "Unfortunately I cannot eat in your house. But that is not all — what my eyes have been forced to see since I arrived in Alexandria has caused me great pain and distress. The Jews here have forgotten God and His holy commandments! You indulge in the worthless pleasures of this world just like the heathens who surround you! Alexandria's sin is greater than that of Jerusalem's before its downfall!"

Theogonos could not believe his ears. "Stranger, have you come to insult me in my own house?"

"No, certainly not," said Rabbi Akiva. "I have been sent by the teachers of Israel to restrain our brothers in Arabia, Libya, Egypt, and the other countries from rebelling against the Romans. Only when God sends us the Redeemer will we regain our freedom and independence. Until then we must bear the heavy yoke patiently. Any attempt to attack the Romans will not only end in certain failure, but will also lead to more pain and suffering for our troubled nation!

"It is my mission to impress this upon my brothers. In Arabia I succeeded in doing so, but here I am confronted with the additional responsibility of admonishing them. I must make them aware of the terrible sins and transgressions they are committing. You don't observe the holy Sabbath or any of the holidays, your food and drinks are not kosher, your whole way of life is not Jewish!"

"Allow me, dear stranger, to appease your noble anger," replied Theogonos. "We Alexandrian Jews are different from the Jews in Eretz Yisrael. We were brought up with Greek wisdom. We believe in the One and Only God, but to us the commandments are more symbolic in nature. How can we build sukkos, for example, in the midst of the Greek population? They would destroy them, and there would be serious unrest in the city. That can be done in Eretz Yisrael, but not here. But quite apart from that, our wise men, who explain the laws to us, teach us that it is enough to pay homage to the spirit of the laws. All else is insignificant. We believe in the One and Only God and we hate and despise the Greek gods. That is our Judaism. We treasure and keep the kernel, but we throw away the outer shell."

"Do you think that the fruit can grow without its shell?" asked Rabbi Akiva. "All the laws which God gave us are of immeasurable value, and we must observe them exactly as He commanded. Your philosophers are misleading you, and you and your followers believe them only because it suits your desires. But God will not permit you to act in this way; He demands from us that we observe the mitzvos no matter where we live! Are you not afraid of angering the Master of the universe? You, the leader of this community, are responsible for the evil that flourishes here! How will you be able to stand before God one day and justify yourself? God is sending out a warning call through me to you and all your people. Turn away from your sinful ways, so that you don't bring ruin upon yourself!"

Theogonos was stunned. No one had ever spoken to him like that before. And this Akiva spoke such a fluent Greek! And he was as powerful an orator as Demosthenes! "Stranger," he said, "I am sure that you are acquainted with the classic Greek writings, judging by your command of our language. Therefore you must be familiar with the teaching of Plato and Aristotle that man's highest goal is to acquire wisdom. And in light of that, what do we need these externals and customs for, if they do not promote wisdom in any way?"

"Neither Plato nor Aristotle ever penetrated to the truth," replied Rabbi Akiva. "The truth was conveyed to us by God, Creator of the universe, at Mount Sinai. Acquiring wisdom cannot possibly be a man's highest goal, because God Himself set limitations to that wisdom, as it says, 'For man can not see Me, for as long as he lives.' Man's goal in life is to fulfill God's commandments, as *Koheles* says: 'The goal of all goals, which encompasses everything: Fear God and keep His commandments, for that is the essence of all of humanity.'"

"Your views are very different from mine," exclaimed Theogonos.

"It is forbidden to have differences of opinion concerning what I have just said."

"But Rabbi Akiva, you yourselves — the Sages of Israel — differ greatly among yourselves in your teachings."

"The fact that God's commandments are binding for all Jews is undisputed. It is only regarding the observance of the individual commandments in particular that there are different views on how to interpret the Torah's instructions. The Torah itself, however, prescribes the rules for resolving halachic issues."

"I am a layman in this field, so I cannot argue with you. Why don't you tell me, instead: What is it that you want me to do?"

"I would like you to gather the whole community in the synagogue and allow me to speak to them."

"In the Synagogue?"

"Yes. The Great Synagogue of your city is the pride and joy of Alexandrian Jewry. Send your messenger around to all of the Jews in the city, and let him tell them that a representative of the Sages of Israel is here and would like to talk to them."

"I will do as you wish," Theogonos replied. "On the Sabbath, after the prayer services, you may give your speech."

Rabbi Akiva left, and when he reached the street, he found a great commotion going on there. The Romans were celebrating the Dionysian Festivities. One could hear the sounds of the drum and the flute, and loud cheering everywhere. A young boy with a staff in his hand and a wreath of ivy on his head came dancing by, leading a long procession of men and women. All of them were cheering and singing, and dancing. Decorative wreaths of leaves crowned people's heads, and the furs of panther and deer that hung from their shoulders flew about in the air from their wild dancing. If the revelers met anyone on the way, they draw him into their procession. Rich and the poor, workers, slaves, soldiers, sailors, officers, musicians, craftsmen — everyone joined in. A few women were dragging a goat along with them to be sacrificed to Dionysus.

No bystander could resist the temptation to follow the happy crowd. The music of flutes and drums could be heard everywhere, and the air was filled with the smoke of torches which young men in costume were waving. A young man who had fastened an oxtail to his back danced around while holding the long tail carefully under his arm and playing a herdsman's flute. The wild laughter, singing, and music grew louder and drew everyone in its wake.

Rabbi Akiva found refuge standing next to the walls of the houses, and turned his eyes away in disgust. Then he said to himself the words of Aleinu: "'It is our duty to praise the Master of the universe and to ascribe greatness to the Creator, because He did not make us like the other nations of the world. He did not give us our portion like He gave them theirs, nor did He give us the lot of all of their multitudes; for they bow down to vanity and nothingness and pray to a deity that can not redeem them...' All of their worship is despicable, and their celebrations blasphemy."

Chapter 30

The Great Synagogue of Alexandria was filled to capacity. There must have been about 100,000 people in its great halls. All of them had come streaming in to hear the world-famous teacher from Eretz Yisrael. The people were concerned — would his voice be strong enough to carry at least throughout the main hall? They had no reason to worry however, for Rabbi Akiva's words echoed all over the synagogue like bolts of thunder.

"My brothers, my friends!" Rabbi Akiva began. "In the olden days there was once a large, wealthy, and powerful city by the name of Ninveh. But the wealth and the luxury caused Ninveh's people to become uncaring and corrupt. They stole from each other, they forged their purchase and rental documents, and they led an extremely immoral existence. Then God sent His Prophet Yonah, the son of Amitai, to warn Ninveh's people about the consequences of their wicked behavior. 'In forty days' time,' said the prophet, 'Ninveh will be destroyed!'

"My brothers, my friends! I have been sent on a similar mission — to warn you! The majority of this populous and wealthy community has turned away from God's ways! You have forgotten about the Sabbath and the Festivals, and instead you celebrate the heathens' ceremonies together with them and you rejoice on the holidays that honor their false gods! Is it not a form of idol worship when you adorn your houses in honor of the Greek gods, and you and your children dress up in special costumes and participate in their pagan processions, and you join in all their cheering, which is dedicated to their gods?

"My brothers, my friends! Our forefathers were once slaves in this country, and God led them out with a strong hand and an outstretched arm. And God elevated us to become His nation. He brought us to Mount Sinai and he said to us: 'I am Your God, the Eternal One; You shall not have other gods before me. And you shall be careful about everything that I say, and you shall not mention the name of the foreign gods; it shall not be heard from your mouths.'

"But you, my brothers, you can't even say three words without calling upon the Greek gods and goddesses or swearing by their names! And you even give your children names which remind you of these gods! For don't many of you have names which mean such things as 'gift from the god of the sun,' or 'offspring of the father of the gods,' etc.? I know you don't intend to be doing anything wrong, and that it's just a habit which you have picked up from your environment. But it is habits like these which have alienated you completely from Judaism!

"The One and Only God Almighty, Creator of heaven and earth, has chosen us as His people, so that we should make ourselves holy and be holy. That is why He has given us laws concerning food and drink that distinguish us from all the other nations of this world. You, however, have forgotten these laws! You devour the meat of impure animals, and you have become like all the heathens around you.

"When Yonah the Prophet proclaimed his message in Ninveh, the people in Ninveh listened to him and repented from all their bad deeds. They wore sackcloth and sat upon ashes, they repented, and they prayed to God. And God saw their deeds and their sincere regret and He forgave them. He didn't carry out the terrible punishment that was looming over their heads, because He was compassionate.

"Dear brothers and friends, you too can return from your evil ways! Why do you want to die?

"Look, this world is like an inn with many shops and stores

attached to it, in which everyone can enjoy himself as much as he pleases. But you mustn't think that you won't have to pay the bills for it. Everything is given on credit, and everything is paid back. The shops are open and the owner gives you his things freely, but a ledger of debts is open too, and a Hand is busy writing everything down. Whoever wants to come and take something is welcome, but the staff is constantly vigilant, making sure they receive their payment, whether the people are aware of it or not.

"Brothers and friends! You live comfortable, pleasant lives. You are satisfied and happy, and even the poorest among you receives so much from his wealthy brothers that he doesn't have to worry about where his daily bread will come from. But is that the goal and purpose of life? My fellow Jews, God created man in His image, He breathed His spirit into him, and He endowed him with the gift of reason. Why then should that highly gifted being called man be satisfied with the life of an animal, merely enjoying himself and procreating? Was it in vain that God told him that he was created in His image? God wanted him to aspire to spiritual growth so that he would do what was just and right.

"God has set us Jews apart from all the other nations of the world. He calls us His children, as it says, 'You are children to God, the Eternal.' And in order for us to prove ourselves worthy of being His children, He has given us the Torah, our precious gem, with which He created the world. Before a structure is actually built, an architect develops a building design in which he determines how his building will be constructed, and what it will look like — where the assembly halls, the staircases, the storage rooms, the bedrooms, and the hallways will be. And as he goes along with the execution of his project, he refers to his plan all the time, giving his orders accordingly as to how to construct the foundations of all the different parts of the building. And likewise, before God created the world, He created the Torah as His blueprint. All spiritual meaning and purpose of this world is contained within the Torah! And that is the precious jewel that God gave us, as it says: 'For I gave you good guidance, do not forsake My Torah!'

"And you, my brothers, have forgotten this Torah! You don't study it, and you don't raise your children on it. It just lies in a corner, without anyone taking any interest in it. You are depriving yourselves of all of its wonderful teachings, which provide understanding of this world and which allow you to earn eternal life for yourselves in the Next. Instead, you waste your time reading those corrupting Greek tales. You learn their drinking songs by heart, which you then sing at the feasts that you host, and you think you have reached your goal in life if you can cheer and laugh like all the rest of them. Such frivolous behavior often leads you to the worst kinds of sin, and many of you have lost the family purity which was always Israel's noble pride. Do you think that God's eyes do not see you? There is nothing in the world that God does not see! But He has given us free will, so that we can do good and reject the bad on our own volition.

"My brothers and friends, look how greatly you have abused that free will. Please, don't push my warnings aside coldheartedly! God is forgiving and compassionate. He doesn't want the sinner to die. He would much rather have him turn away from his evil ways and live! There was once an evil Jewish king by the name of Achav ben Omri. He was an idolater, a thief, and a murderer. But when the Prophet Eliyahu came to him and rebuked him for all his wrongdoings, he regretted his deeds and repented, and God forgave him. For God's right hand is always stretched out to accept the sinners that repent. There was once another evil king, Menasheh, who ruled in Judea. He set up idols in the Holy Temple, and he shed much innocent blood. But once when he was in difficulty, he turned away from all the powerless gods and prayed to the One and Only God, the Master of heaven and earth. And God accepted his prayer and rescued him from danger.

"My brothers and friends! You too are in great danger! I am not a prophet, nor am I the disciple of a prophet. But whoever has eyes to see will recognize that the earth is shaking beneath your feet. Do you think you can resist the might of Rome and defeat the legions? You are counting on your wealth, on the armies that you are capable of supplying, and on the fact that you are so numerous. These are the things you lean on, instead of relying on the only One that can really help you! It is not through wealth or a powerful army that one wins a victory, for it is God's will alone that determines who succeeds in war and who doesn't. As long as He hasn't sent us the Mashiach, any attempt to fight against the Romans is useless and can harm us greatly.

"There is only one thing that can help you, and that is to return to God with all your heart and soul, and to truly regret your sins. You must avoid all non-kosher foods, you must keep the holidays that God ordained, and you must raise your children with the Torah and for the Torah! When Jews turn away from the path of Torah, their lives lose purpose and God leaves them to their enemies and pursuers. Return to God, turn away from your evil ways, so that He will have mercy on you and save you from death!"

When Rabbi Akiva finished speaking, the people were crying.

"Stay with us, holy rabbi," many cried, "and teach us the proper path that we should follow!"

The heads of the community, however, disapproved of Rabbi Akiva's speech. They wanted to enjoy their great wealth, and they had absolutely no intention of changing their ways. They had the most beautiful horses, their sons won all the horse races with them; their daughters were celebrated beauties in Alexandria, and all the Greek and Roman aristocrats courted them. The most famous artists, poets, and philosophers assembled in their homes. Rabbi Akiva's heartfelt words did not move them, and they just smiled at his "old-fashioned" views. In their opinion, Greek philosophy was far superior to those views.

They met together for a quick consultation, and then the leader of the community approached Rabbi Akiva. "Stranger," he said, "Alexandria is not fertile ground for your teachings! We, the heads of the community, demand that you leave our city! Go back to Judea! And if you refuse to leave, we have all the means to force you to do so!"

Rabbi Akiva wanted to answer him, but the man turned his back on him and walked off arrogantly. "When God wants to destroy someone, He smites him with blindness!" Rabbi Akiva said to himself.

Chapter 31

Rabbi Akiva began to prepare for his trip home. He went to Alexandria's port, in order to book passage on a ship. Alexandria was the foremost city of trade in the ancient world. Thus it was from here that big ships, loaded with cargoes of grain, were sent to Rome, in order to supply the capital with foodstuffs. These ships were unusually big, and warships were assigned to escort them. The ships of grain were by far not the most prestigious aspect of Alexandria's commerce, though. Manufactured produce from India was brought to Egypt from the mouth of the Indus and the coast of Malabar, and from there it was sent all over the world. Ivory, tortoiseshell, and silks and cotton fabrics, which were still very rare and costly at the time, as well as pearls, diamonds, and spices, were sent from Alexandria to all the coasts of the Mediterranean Sea. Pliny tells us that the yearly profit they made on these goods was estimated at one hundred million sestertii, which was an enormous sum at the time. One of the main Egyptian products was known as "papyrus," which grew on the banks of the Nile. It was the finest material for writing on, and the word "paper" is derived from it.

Rabbi Akiva had to search for a while until he found a ship going to Jaffa. Most of the ships were bound for Rome, carrying grain, wine, oil, wool, spices, precious metals, and other luxury items. Finally he found a ship loaded with papyrus that was going to Asia Minor, and he arranged his passage on it.

As the ship pulled out of the harbor, Rabbi Akiva stood on deck, full of sorrow, looking at the beautiful, wealthy city.

"There is no one in our times who really knows how to rebuke people!" he told himself. "Yonah the Prophet was sent to heathens in Ninveh, and he succeeded in inspiring them to repent — and I could not even succeed in conveying my message to my own brothers in Alexandria!"

The weather was beautiful, and the blue sea was calm. The wind blew against the sails and the rowers worked relentlessly, and thus the ship sailed away smoothly and rapidly. In olden days, when it was a mild season and the wind was brisk, the ship was propelled by sails and rowers. The rowers could propel their ships much faster than modern ships! On a good day, a ship was capable of covering over 100 miles in twenty-four hours.

Rabbi Akiva rejoiced when the Asian coast came into sight. His heart leapt as he thought that finally, after such a long absence, he was returning to Eretz Yisrael, to his beloved wife and children, and to his friends and his students.

Rabbi Akiva saw dolphins following the ship, and he noticed all kinds of other strange sea creatures of the sea:

"How wondrous are your works, oh Master!" he exclaimed. "You created all of them with wisdom, the earth is full of Your works. These large creatures living in the sea would die immediately if they were on dry land, and the large creatures living on dry land would perish immediately in the depths of the sea. How many are your works, oh Master, and all of them You created with wisdom."

Rabbi Akiva looked up at the sky and saw, in the west, a small dark cloud the size of a human hand. He hurried over to the captain. "Look there," he said, "do you see that small cloud? There is bad weather coming! You must hurry so that we reach a port quickly."

But the captain just laughed at his warning. "There is no reason for worry, Judean! That little cloud will do us no harm! Although I could change our route and stop at a port close by, it would just prolong the trip unnecessarily. In less than twelve hours we will be arriving safely at the port of Jaffa."

"Do as you wish," Rabbi Akiva replied, "but you are going to be digging your own grave, with your lack of caution!"

Shortly afterwards, the whole sky was shrouded with somber clouds. A terrible storm arose and the mounting waves tossed the ship around like a child's toy. The sails ripped, the mast was bent out of shape, and the rowers were powerless.

"Dear God," Rabbi Akiva said, "is it my destiny to die here, in the waves of the sea, and become the prey of hungry sea monsters? Am I being punished for not having fulfilled my duty properly in Alexandria, for having left without once more trying to inspire my misguided brothers to repent? Oh, God, whatever Your will may be, let it happen! Everything God does is for the good!"

In the meantime the crew had thrown the cargo overboard in order to make the ship lighter. The storm was driving the ship off its course, further and further away from its destination. After a few hours an unidentified port came into sight. The rowers started to row again, using all their energy to reach the shore as soon as possible. Suddenly there was a terrible noise. The ship had crashed into a coral reef and was broken apart in the middle! The waves swallowed the crew and the passengers.

In Eretz Yisrael everyone was anxiously awaiting Rabbi Akiva's return. He had written a letter to his wife from Alexandria, telling her that he would soon be home. (The Emperor Augustus had initiated a postal service for his own official needs, and later Emperors permitted private people to use this royal service for their own mail as well.) The letter had found its way to Rachel safely, but her husband, whom she was desperately waiting for, still had not arrived. Then came the tragic news that Rabbi Akiva had boarded a ship in Alexandria, loaded with papyrus, which was said to have had a serious accident on the way. Rabban Gamliel, who was coming back from a journey, saw its debris floating in the sea.

In the *beis midrash* in Yavneh the Sages and Torah scholars had assembled, as Rabban Gamliel was going to give a lecture. He began to speak: "I am deeply distressed about our brother Akiva. I myself saw the debris of the ship that was meant to bring him home. Alas, that such a great scholar, someone with such vast knowledge of the Torah, should end up like this, in the waves of the sea! Alas, that such a pure and holy body should become prey for all the gluttonous fish and wild creatures of the sea!"

All the men in the *beis midrash* began to cry and their wailing became so loud that the walls shook and the floor became drenched with their tears. The great Sages were overwhelmed with pain and sorrow. They considered the loss to be as tragic for all of Israel as the destruction of the Temple!

At that moment the door of the *beis midrash* opened, and a tall, impressive-looking man made his way through the mourning crowd. The mourners stared at him in great astonishment. To their indescribable joy, they realized that before them stood their long-lost friend and teacher, Rabbi Akiva!

Rabban Gamliel stood up from his prominent seat and came rushing towards him with open arms. "Akiva," he cried, "my friend, my brother, my son, God's beloved one and the beloved of my soul — have you risen from the dead?"

They embraced and kissed each other. And Rabbi Yehoshua pushed his way through, and Rabbi Elazar ben Azaryah, Rabbi Tarfon, Rabbi Yishmael, Rabbi Yosei HaGalili, Rabbi Tzadok, Rabbi Chananyah ben Teradyon, Rabbi Chalafta, Rabbi Chutzpis, Rabbi Elazar Chisma, Rabbi Yehudah ben Beseira, Rabbi Ilai, Rabbi Elazar HaModa'i, and all the others, came to kiss and hug their dear friend.

Among those who rejoiced in the *beis midrash* were Rabbi Akiva's sons, Rabbi Yehoshua and Rabbi Shimon, both of whom had also become great teachers of Israel, and Rabbi Akiva's brother-in-law Rabbi Yochanan. (Rabbi Akiva had convinced his father-in-law, Kalba Savua, to remarry in his old age, and

God had given him a son, who became Rabbi Akiva's disciple and was now also a teacher of Israel.)

There was no end to the joy and excitement in the room. Finally, Rabban Gamliel demanded silence and he asked Rabbi Akiva to tell them the story of how he was saved.

And Rabbi Akiva spoke:

"The ship on which I was sailing from Alexandria crashed into a coral reef because of the storm, and it was ripped apart. I entrusted my soul to God, and I called out, 'Everything the merciful God does is for the good!' I found myself in the sea holding on to a plank of the shattered ship, and fortunately the waves did not pull me down, but carried me safely to shore. At that point I lost consciousness. When I came to, I found myself in a desolate place. So I started to walk inland and there I found a small town where Jews lived, and they supplied me with food and drink, clothing, and money, so that I could continue my strenuous journey home. Already from afar I found out that my death was being mourned at home. That is why I hurried to the *beis midrash*, to stop my teachers and friends from needlessly mourning and interrupting their Torah study."

"Bless you, Akiva," Rabban Gamliel said. "Even the misfortunes that happen to you help us to clarify and resolve the Halachah! We are just in the midst of analyzing whether someone who is assumed to have died at sea should be considered dead, thus rendering it permissible for his wife to remarry. Your miraculous rescue shows us that one can never establish that someone has died unless the dead body was found and identified.

"How great are the words of the Sages! All of their teachings come from God, Who revealed them to Moshe on Sinai!"

Chapter 32

The revolt that everyone had feared for so long broke out. The Jews of Mesopotamia, Egypt, Cyrenaica, and on the island of Cyprus initiated the uprising almost simultaneously. At first they were successful, and they managed to cause Lupus, the Roman general, to flee. Then the Emperor sent out his best general, Martius Turbo, against them. His first assignment was to fight the Jews in Egypt and Cyrenaica. A shrewd tactician, he avoided confronting them in open battle; instead he tried to harass and demoralize them through minor attacks here and there. Slowly but surely, though meeting great resistance in the beginning, he succeeded in wearing them down.

Trajan had ordered his general to destroy all the Jews who were living in the districts where the revolt had erupted, and Martius Turbo fulfilled this cruel command to the letter. Entire regions which the Jews had cultivated became desolate, and the bloodshed was enormous. Even women and children were not spared.

At this time the Jews of Alexandria also received their punishment. Their glorious synagogue was destroyed and razed to the ground. It was said that the blood of the slain flowed into the sea and colored it red.

Equally harsh was the general Lucius Quietus, the Emperor's favorite, who was waging a savage war against the Jews of Mesopotamia and the adjoining countries who had taken part in the revolt. Lucius was a Moor by birth and he had entered the military service with a group of his fellow countrymen. He knew how to win the Emperor's favor so well that the latter was planning to adopt him as his son and nominate him as his successor.

After Lucius defeated the Babylonian Jews, the Emperor appointed him governor over Eretz Yisrael. He abused this position to oppress the Jews and bring terrible suffering upon them. When he tried to force them to worship statues of the Emperor, and to offer sacrifices to them, Jews in the Holy Land also decided to rebel. Two courageous men, Pappus and Julianus, led the uprising. Their equipment and arms were poor, however, and they had no training in war, so they were no match for the Roman army.

Lucius Quietus defeated them and traveled throughout the country celebrating his victory by burning down entire villages and towns. Yavneh was destroyed as well, and the Sanhedrin moved north, to Usha in Galilee. Rabban Gamliel, the *Nasi*, would have been taken captive and led to his death if a noble Roman had not saved him by sacrificing his own life for him. The group of fighting men who had joined Pappus and Julianus fled, and the two leaders were taken captive.

The victorious Roman general then had them brought before him. "You filthy rebels," he shouted, "how did you dare rise up against your Emperor?"

"The cruelties that you subjected us to in the name of the Emperor were more than we could bear," Papus replied. "You wanted to force us to bow down before images and to worship them, but we Jews serve only the One and Only God, the Almighty, the Creator of heaven and earth."

"If your God is so mighty," the Roman general scoffed, "then why doesn't he save you from me?"

"We must deserve death," Julianus answered. "We are sinners. If God wants us to die, then He will do it. If not by you, then He would have many other ways and means to punish us. You, however, are not worthy of seeing a miracle with your own eyes!"

Lucius Quietus struck back. "You Jews must be insane to think that you can mock me like this even in the face of death! Listen to my words carefully: You are going to die now, but not only will you die — all your fellow Jews will die as well. I will go throughout all of Judea now, and I will destroy everything and everyone that is Jewish! And I will spare no one — neither men nor women, neither the young nor the old! And one day, when I become Emperor, my goal in life will be to annihilate all traces of Judaism from this earth! Perhaps this promise of mine will sweeten your death!"

"You can plan as you wish, but your plans will fail; say what you like, but it won't come to fruition, for God is with us and He decides!"

"Lead them to their deaths!" Lucius Quietus ordered.

At that moment something wondrous and unexpected happened. Two horsemen came speeding up to them and called out: "The Emperor Trajan is dead! Hadrian is the new Emperor! Lucius Quietus is dismissed from his office! Soldiers, seize him and tie him up! He is accused of high treason and he will be taken to Rome for trial! These are the orders of the Emperor Publius Aelius Hadrianus!"

Lucius Quietus' own soldiers seized him and took him captive. Pappus and Julianus were saved.

Trajan had fallen ill with dropsy in Antioch. While on his way back to Rome, he suddenly died in Selinus, Cilicia, without having been able to implement his plan to appoint his favorite general, Lucius Quietus, as his successor. His wife, Plotina, however, succeeded in arranging for her favorite, Publius Aelius Hadrianus, to become Emperor. This is how she did it: When Trajan died, she kept his death a secret, and had his body removed secretly from his chamber. Then she told one of her loyal servants to lie down on the Emperor's empty bed, and she closed the curtains around it. She called witnesses into the room, and they heard a weak, groaning voice similar to that of her dead husband saying that he was adopting his loyal and most beloved cousin Publius Aelius Hadrianus and nominating him as his successor. The witnesses documented the "Emperor's last wish" and the Empress signed it in his name as instructed by the groaning voice.

Two days later, Hadrian heard the news that the Emperor had adopted him and had died immediately afterwards. The legions acclaimed him, and he gave them lavish gifts. Then he convened the Senate, requesting that they confirm the Emperor's last will and examine the requirements of the legions. Most importantly, however, he tried to remove his most dangerous rival Lucius Quietus, which he succeeded in doing perfectly. Quietus was brought to Rome in chains and sentenced to death by the Senate. He was beheaded with a sword.

Quietus' death was a great relief for the Jews. The Sages of Israel instituted a special holiday called "Trajan's Day" to commemorate this miraculous redemption. But later on, when they suffered new tribulations, they annulled the holiday.

At the beginning of his reign, the new Emperor was quite favorable towards the Jews. He held Rabbi Yehoshua and Rabbi Akiva in the highest regard, and in his great thirst for knowledge he would come seeking wisdom from them.

Publius Aelius Hadrianus was born in Spain, just like Trajan. His family originally came from a small town called Adria or Hadria which gave its name to the Adriatic sea. They had gone to Spain with Scipio's army three hundred years before, and had settled in Italica, a Roman colony there. It was in remembrance of their old homeland that they added the name Hadrianus to their family name, Aelius. Hadrian had been brought up in Rome. When he lost his parents at the age of ten, Trajan, who was a cousin of Hadrian's father, was entrusted with his care. Trajan sent him to Athens for five years, where he was taught by the most outstanding teachers of that time. He started to live and breathe that city's spirit and culture. Not only did he master the language, but he was also able to compete with the Athenians in all their specialties: singing, athletics, mathematics, medicine, painting, and sculpture. His memory was extraordinary, and he was very hard-working. He had many interests and enjoyed a variety of things. His temper was fierce however, and he had a sharp tongue. He excelled in his physical pursuits as in his mental ones. Aside from the standard exercises in gymnastics and the martial arts, he also took an ardent interest in hunting. Since the death of Julius Caesar, Rome had not seen such broad mental capabilities in a ruler. And in addition, he had an impressive personality and a graceful manner. But despite all these shining attributes, he lacked the firm base of a refined, good character. All of Hadrian's deeds were ruled by his whims and moods, and in time he would make countless mistakes.

Chapter 33

We mentioned earlier that a close relative of the Emperor by the name of Aquila (which is Akylas in Greek, and Onkelos in Aramaic), had come to learn with Rabbi Eliezer and Rabbi Yehoshua.

Aquila was Hadrian's nephew, his sister's son. His father, Kalonikos (also called Kalonymos), was a wealthy man who lived on the island of Pontus. Aquila had learned Hebrew in his childhood with a Jewish teacher whom his father had bought at the slave market after the Roman war against the Jews. Later on, when his uncle became the Prefect of Syria, Aquila accompanied him on his travels and took advantage of the opportunity to meet the Sages and to learn from them.

"My dear uncle," he said to Hadrian one day, "allow me to travel around the region so that I can make some contacts for trade."

"Are you looking to make money? I have plenty of wealth, and I can provide you with as much of it as you want!"

Hadrian was married to Sabina, who was the daughter of Trajan's sister. They were not happily married, however, and they had no children. Sabina despised her husband, and he tried to avoid her as much as possible because of her evil ways and her ill temper. Thus he loved his sister's son dearly, for he was his closest relative. Since Hadrian was a blood relative of Trajan and had married his only niece, and since the Empress Plotina was also very fond of him, he had for some time pinned his hopes on becoming the next Emperor. Hadrian in turn was expecting to nominate his closest relative, Aquila, as his successor. It was therefore no wonder that he was willing to grant him a great part of his wealth.

"Thank you, Uncle, for your generosity!" Aquila answered. "It's not the wealth that I am interested in, however. It's the challenge of earning my own money that gives me joy. I am sure that you, the wisest of all men, can advise me how to buy and sell in the most successful way."

Hadrian was quite flattered. "Of course I will be pleased to advise you, dear nephew. Whenever you find a product which is of good quality but has gone out of style, and no one in the world is interested in it — buy it! You will be able to get it cheaply, and all you will have to do is wait until it goes up in price again. That is how you will do well!"

"Your advice is wonderful!" Aquila replied. "And that is no wonder, coming from a man like you, who is by far the best in all the sciences, in mathematics, in medicine, philosophy, rhetoric, and in all the arts as well."

Hadrian smiled. To him his nephew's generous praises seemed right on target.

Aquila went to Yavneh, where Rabbi Eliezer turned him away and Rabbi Yehoshua welcomed and encouraged him. Rabban Gamliel and Rabbi Akiva also taught him in a loving and friendly manner. Aquila converted to Judaism and he circumcised himself. Then he began to study Torah day and night, and he translated the Scriptures into Greek. Even Rabbi Eliezer took an interest in him then, when he saw how serious he was, and he shared some of his vast knowledge with him. When Aquila had finished his translation, he read it to his teachers Rabbi Eliezer and Rabbi Yehoshua, and both of them praised it greatly. They applied the following verse to him: "You are the most beautiful among all children of man, grace is poured upon your lips, God has blessed you forever."

Only very few fragments remain from this translation, and these are found in the *Hexapla* of Origen. Rabbi Azaryah de

Rossi tells us quite a bit about it in his work *Me'or Einayim*, *Imrei Binah*, chap. 45. We see from there that Aquila's main intention was to translate literally, word for word. Although this method is very exact, it can often obscure the meaning behind the words and violate the spirit of the language. That is why Aquila decided to write another translation of the Torah, this time into the Aramaic language that the Jews generally spoke at the time. With this work, he used the traditional interpretations of his teachers Rabbi Eliezer and Rabbi Yehoshua in translating the meaning of the words. It was this translation that was to become the famous commentary *Targum Onkelos*. It has remained intact, and every devout Jew reads it weekly along with the weekly portion of the Torah.

Aquila's appearance suffered from his diligent study and labors; his face had become pale and gaunt. Thus when he traveled to Antioch to congratulate his uncle Hadrian upon becoming Emperor, his uncle was alarmed.

"Aquila," he cried, "how awful you look! Your face is pale, your cheeks are sunken, and you're all stooped over! You must have done very poorly in your business."

"On the contrary, my dear uncle," Aquila smiled. "I have done very well!"

"Yes? And what kind of goods did you purchase?"

"The most precious goods there are, which you cannot buy with the greatest treasures in the world."

"So what price did you pay?"

"Just a piece of foreskin."

"You are talking in riddles!" exclaimed Hadrian.

"I have converted to Judaism, Uncle. So I circumcised myself."

"Oh, you poor creature! How did you come to do such a thing? You, who are my closest relative, should have consulted with me before making such a drastic move!"

"I did consult with you, my dear uncle, and you yourself gave me the advice!"

"How can that be? I have a very good memory, but I don't remember such a thing!"

"You advised me to look out for quality goods that have gone out of style, and that the world is not interested in, but will go up in price in the course of time. So with that in mind I looked at all the religions and the nations of this world, and I didn't find one that the world despises more than the Jews. And yet they will one day assume their lofty and rightful place in the eyes of the world, as Yeshayahu the Prophet has foretold in the name of the One and Only God: 'Thus God, the Redeemer of Israel, his Holy One, spoke... there will be a time, in which kings will see them and stand up for them... the One Who chose you.'"

A freed slave by the name of Alexander, whom the Emperor liked very much, was present during this conversation.

"Great and mighty Caesar!" he exclaimed. "One who dares to speak to you with such brazenness deserves to be killed! Are you, the ruler of the world, supposed to bow down to the Jews?"

The Emperor became very angry with the freed slave. He hit him in the face, causing him to fall backwards. "You are trying to incite me to kill my sister's son?" he cried "Even a simple legionnaire can rise to the top if the gods favor him. That does not mean that I have to bow down to him, for he is just a simple legionnaire. Know that although now, the Jews are a lowly and despised people, that is not to say that they won't reach great heights in the future."

The freedman was devastated by the Emperor's behavior towards him. He left the chamber and committed suicide.

The Emperor continued speaking to Aquila. "Tell me, my dear nephew, why you decided to convert to Judaism."

"I wanted to learn the teachings that God the Almighty taught the Jews, which are more valuable than all the riches of this world."

"But you could have learned these teachings without converting and without circumcising yourself."

"Oh, no, dear Uncle, that is not possible. It says in the Holy

Torah: 'He has proclaimed His words to Ya'akov and His laws to Israel.' Only those that join the nation of Ya'akov, only those that become one with Israel, can fully absorb God's word and His Oral Law. You cannot possibly do that as an outsider. You can only truly penetrate the depths of Torah wisdom if you learn with the intention of living by what you learn, and teaching others, for to others it remains hidden. Would you, dear Emperor, reward a soldier who didn't fight for your side? Circumcision is the only entryway to the palace of Torah."

"But tell me, what is so great about these teachings?"

"Mighty Caesar, not only are you a powerful ruler, but with your impressive mind you have also explored all the sciences. You are well aware of how hard the Greek men of learning tried to find the truth. Pythagoras, the Eleatics, Heracles, and Socrates were always searching for the truth, and Plato and Aristotle built massive philosophical structures, but none of them ever found it. But know that every Jewish child who starts reading the Torah is discovering the truth! The child learns that there is only One God, and He created heaven, the sun, the moon, and the stars, and made the earth with all its inhabitants. Furthermore, he learns that He set the borders for the oceans, so that the water should not inundate the shores, and He is the One Who rules and directs the whole universe, and without His will nothing can happen, not in heaven nor on earth."

"You are stimulating my curiosity, Aquila. Introduce me to one of the Sages of Israel so that I can learn more about these wonderful teachings. I would like to find the answers to the questions I have been pondering for years."

Chapter 34

When Aquila returned to his teachers and fellow students at Usha, Rabban Gamliel was busy preparing for his son's wedding. Rabban Gamliel, Rabbi Yehoshua, and Rabbi Akiva had gone to Emmaus to take care of some shopping for the wedding. But even while they were making their purchases, they didn't cease to learn Torah. It was for the most part Rabbi Akiva who, by continuously asking questions, influenced the Sages to discuss some of the most pertinent issues there. And that is how we have several halachos today that were resolved at the market of Emmaus!

The wedding was a grand and lavish celebration. All the Sages of Israel were invited. They sat at their tables and Rabban Gamliel himself served them. When they protested, Rabbi Yehoshua said, "In the Torah, we find that someone even greater served his guests personally! Avraham Avinu was the greatest man of his time, and when the angels came to his dwelling he thought they were Arab merchants who worship the dust beneath their feet. That is why he told them to wash their feet before they entered his dwelling. And yet he still served them, as it says, 'And he put it down before them, and he stood at their side [to serve them!] and they ate.'

"And with regard to Moshe Rabbeinu," he continued, "we find something similar, as it says, 'And Aharon and all the Elders of Israel came to Moshe's father-in-law to eat before God.' Where had Moshe gone? Could it be that he was not present at the meal? Surely he was there, but he wasn't sitting at the table

— he was on his feet, serving the guests. So why should we protest when our great Rabban Gamliel serves us?"

Then Rabbi Tzadok said, "For how long do you want to continue to glorify man and neglect the honor of God? God serves the entire world! He makes the wind blow, He makes the clouds ascend so that there can be rain, He sees to it that the grain grows and that everyone has their sustenance. And He provides not only for the learned, but for the ignorant too; not only for the pious, but also the evildoers; and not only for the God-fearing, but for the idolaters too! So surely you can accept that Rabban Gamliel is allowed to serve the wisest men of Israel?"

Shortly after his son's wedding, Rabban Gamliel fell ill. In those days it was the custom to clothe the dead in the most extravagant garments, for burial, and people spent a lot of money on this. As a result, everyone felt pressured to outdo his neighbors, and burying the dead became such a great financial burden, that some even tried to avoid this holy task. As Rabban Gamliel's condition worsened, he requested that when the time came, they bury him in a simple, white cotton shroud. And that has remained the custom to this day. From the wealthiest and most prominent to the neediest beggar, all Jews are buried in the same plain, white garments.

Everyone was deeply distressed about Rabban Gamliel's death. When the shofar was sounded to signal to all that he had died, the news spread all over, and people streamed in from far and wide to pay their last respects to him.

Rabban Gamliel was indeed buried in simple clothing, just as he had requested, but Aquila saw to it that the burial ceremony was conducted in the most impressive manner. It was the custom to burn some valuable clothing of a king or a prince, aside from other things. (We find this custom mentioned in Scripture (*Yirmeyahu* 34:5).) Aquila spent a small fortune on the burial.

Then Rabbi Eliezer fell ill as well. When Rabbi Tarfon, Rabbi Yehoshua, Rabbi Elazar ben Azaryah and Rabbi Akiva found out about this, they hurried over to his home to visit him. Rabbi Eliezer was in great pain, and when he saw the Sages, he said to them, "God is very angry with us."

Hearing that, they started to cry. Only Rabbi Akiva had a smile on his face. In astonishment they asked him, "Why are you laughing?"

And he asked them, "Why are you crying?"

"How can we not cry," they replied, "when we see a man who has absorbed the entire Torah suffer so terribly?"

And Rabbi Akiva answered, "That is exactly why I am rejoicing! All these years our great teacher lived in prosperity and enjoyed only good fortune. He succeeded in everything he undertook, and his wealth increased continuously. So I thought to myself, 'Perhaps my teacher has already received his full reward for his pious deeds and accomplishments — in this world! But now that I see that he too is suffering, I know that whatever he may have been deficient in here, in this world, he is atoning for now, and in the World-to-Come he will enjoy his lot of eternal life.' That is why I am happy!"

Then Rabbi Tarfon spoke: "Blessed are you, Rabbi Eliezer, for you have done a greater service for Israel than the rain which irrigates the ground! For the rain merely supplies the means for life in the mundane world, but you have taught people how to achieve life in the world of eternity! When the Holy Temple was destroyed, a great drought threatened to overcome Israel and smother all signs of life. You, however, made sure to let the Torah pour forth its treasures, and just as the rain comes down from heaven, bringing sustenance and life to the earth, you likewise revived Israel and showed them how to live in this world and how to attain life in the World-to-Come!"

And then Rabbi Yehoshua spoke: "Blessed are you, Rabbi Eliezer, for your deeds and accomplishments benefited Israel more than the sun! When the Holy Temple was destroyed, our nation was orphaned, as Yirmeyahu the Prophet has said, 'We have become like orphans, who must do without their father.'

Then you appeared, as a father of our people! With fatherly love and motherly care you saved and maintained the great treasures of Torah for your children, and distributed them generously. A man owes his parents gratitude for his existence in this world, but you deserve much greater gratitude from us, for you have taught us how to live in this world so that we may achieve life in the World-to-Come!"

And Rabbi Akiva said, "Suffering is commendable!"

Then Rabbi Eliezer called out to those sitting near him, "Help me sit up, so that I will be able to hear the words of my disciple, who said that suffering is commendable!"

And Rabbi Akiva said, "I learned this from the Torah. King Chizkiyahu brought up his son Menasheh in the most diligent manner, and yet he strayed from God's ways. And even when God's prophet came to inform Menasheh of God's words of rebuke, it was to no avail. Then God made him suffer greatly. The king of Assyria chained him, took him into captivity and mistreated him terribly. Only then did he finally do some soul-searching, and he humbled himself and prayed to God. God heard his prayers and brought him back to Jerusalem to his throne, and Menasheh recognized that the Almighty is the One and Only God. From here we learn how valuable and effective suffering is!"

"Are you trying to say that I have done something which I have to atone for?" Rabbi Eliezer asked.

Rabbi Akiva replied with a question of his own. "Rabbi, have you not taught me that there isn't a man in this world, no matter how pious he is, who has never sinned?"

A few days later the Sages heard that Rabbi Eliezer was dying. It was on a Friday. The Sages sat down at a distance from his bed, since the ban had not been removed yet. As the day was coming to an end, Rabbi Eliezer's son Hurkanos came to take off his father's tefillin before Shabbos, but Rabbi Eliezer didn't allow him to do this.

"It seems that my father has lost his senses already,"

Hurkanos said to the Sages.

Rabbi Eliezer heard him and raised his voice. "You have lost your senses — you and your mother — worrying about my tefillin before the Shabbos candles have been lit! Are you going to wait until Shabbos has come and you find that you have committed a sin worthy of the death penalty?"

When the Sages saw that he was still in complete possession of his faculties, they greeted him. When he saw them, he asked them, "Why have you come?"

"To learn Torah," they answered.

"And why haven't you come until now?"

"We didn't have time."

Then Rabbi Eliezer said, "You have sinned by not coming to learn from me! One day you will have to suffer a very gruesome death to atone for your sin!"

"And I?" Rabbi Akiva asked.

"Your death will be more cruel than theirs, for your heart is as big as the entrance hall in the Holy Temple, and you could have learned a great deal from me."

Rabbi Eliezer then placed his two arms over his heart, and cried, "Woe unto you, my two arms, you are like closed Torah scrolls that no one reads. I have learned much Torah and I have taught much Torah. I have learned much Torah, and I hardly received as much from my teacher as the amount of water a dog can drink from the sea! I have taught much Torah, and my disciples didn't receive more from me than the amount of paint a paintbrush absorbs when it is dipped into box of paint! I know three hundred halachos concerning leprosy spots, and no one has ever asked me about them! I also know three thousand laws concerning mysticism, and no one ever asked me about them except for Akiva ben Yosef!"

The Sages asked the sick man difficult questions, and he answered them all. The last answer he gave, before his soul departed, ended with the word "pure."

Then Rabbi Yehoshua cried out, "His soul has departed in

purity — the ban is removed! The ban is removed!"

Rabbi Eliezer died in Caesarea. After Shabbos was over, they carried his body to Lod for burial. Rabbi Akiva followed the funeral litter, and in a loud, wailing voice he called out, just as the Prophet Elisha had when Eliyahu was taken from him, "My father, my father, Israel's fighting chariot and military force! You fought and wrestled for us, and your prayers protected us more than mighty armies of war. Oh, I have so much to ask, but the one that could answer me is gone forever more!"

Chapter 35

Over fifty years had passed since Rabbi Akiva and Rachel had first met. Rabbi Akiva was still strong and vigorous in his old age, but his beloved wife Rachel had become ill.

As Rachel became weaker and weaker, she felt that her days were coming to an end. She parted from her loved ones and passed away peacefully.

Rabbi Akiva and his children, together with all Israel, grieved and mourned for her. Delivering a eulogy at her funeral, he praised her as a "woman of valor" with words of Scripture:

"Strength and dignity were her attire, and she joyously faced the last day. She opened her mouth with wisdom, and the teaching of kindness was on her tongue. She oversaw the ways of her household, and did not eat the bread of idleness. Her children rise up and praise her; her husband also, and he extolls her: Many daughters have done valiantly, but you have surpassed them all. Grace is deceitful, and beauty is vain. But a woman who fears God shall be praised. Give her of the fruit of her hands, so that her deeds may praise her in the gates."

Rabbi Akiva had hardly recovered from the great loss of his wife when he was faced with yet another tragedy. His second son, Rabbi Shimon, who was a great teacher of Israel, fell ill. Slowly but surely the deadly illness overtook his body, but his mind remained firm and untouched. And Rabbi Shimon never ceased to learn and teach, to his last breath. When he died, all of Israel came to console Rabbi Akiva.

"My friends," Rabbi Akiva said to them, "you have come from near and far, from all parts of our land and from other provinces as well, to comfort me in my sorrow. The farmers have left their fields, the artisans have left their workshops, and the scholars have left the *beis midrash* to honor my dear son and me. Who am I to deserve such honor? Surely this great honor is not intended for me, but for our holy Torah, which I have been privileged to represent. So now, go back to your homes!"

It is hard to describe how much people loved and respected Rabbi Akiva. Once, some of his students were robbed on the road; when the thieves found out that they were followers of Rabbi Akiva, however, they said, "Far be it from us to harm the students of that great and holy man!" They immediately returned everything they had stolen, and accompanied the students to their destination in order to protect them from further harm on their journey!

Hadrian had taken up residence in Athens again, which was his favorite city. He sent a messenger to Judea commanding his nephew Aquila to come to Athens and to bring along with him one of the great teachers of Israel. So Rabbi Yehoshua and Aquila set out for Athens, to meet with the ruler of the world's greatest Empire.

Hadrian was involved with the study of natural science in those days. When Aquila introduced Rabbi Yehoshua to him as the greatest teacher of Israel, the Emperor asked him, "What particular science do you specialize in?"

"Our holy Torah deals with anything and everything that is worth knowing about in the world," Rabbi Yehoshua replied.

"Tell me — how long does it take a hen to hatch her egg?" his host asked him.

"Twenty-one days, the time that it takes for the blossom of a hazel tree to ripen."

"And how long is the period of gestation for a dog?"

"Fifty days, the time it takes for a fig to ripen."

"And a cat?"

"Fifty-two days, the time it takes for a mulberry to ripen."

"And a pig?"

"Sixty days, the time it takes an apple."

"And a fox?"

"Six months, just like grain."

"A goat and a lamb?"

"Five months, like a grape vine."

"A horse, a camel, a donkey?"

"An entire year, like the date palm."

"And a cow?"

"Nine months, like the olive."

"And wild animals?"

"The wolf, the lioness, the bear, the panther, the leopard, and the giraffe need three years, like white figs. The basilisk takes seventy years, just like the carob tree..."

"And the snake?"

"God cursed the snake, and that is why it is the only creature that has a gestation period of seven years."

"But the sages of Athens claim that it's only three years."

"They are mistaken."

"But they discovered this through experimentation!"

"Nonetheless I say that they are mistaken."

"Do you think you are wiser than the sages of Athens, the wisest men of the world?" asked Hadrian.

"They acquire their knowledge merely through experiment and research, whereas our knowledge stems from God the Almighty, Who created heaven and earth. He revealed Himself to us and gave us His holy teachings, which contain the totality of wisdom."

"And it was revealed to you how long the snake's period of gestation is?"

"This too can be found in the Torah," said Rabbi Yehoshua. "It says in the holy Torah that God the Almighty said to the snake, 'Because you did this you shall be cursed from among all the animals and from among all the wild beasts of the field.' Therefore, just as from one kind of animal to the next, namely from the cat, which has a period of 52 days of gestation, to the donkey, which takes a year, there is a sevenfold difference, so too from the animals to the beasts of the field —from the donkey to the snake — there is a sevenfold difference. Thus a snake takes seven years."

"If you are wiser than the sages of Athens," said Hadrian, "then you may go and argue with them and defeat them. But you should know that if you are unable to answer even one of their questions, that will mean your death!"

The sages of Athens were for the most part Sophists; they asked Rabbi Yehoshua all kinds of deceptive questions. Rabbi Yehoshua was able to answer them all.

"When a man asks a woman to marry him and she refuses, would it make sense for him to try his luck with a woman of higher social standing?"

Rabbi Yehoshua took a nail and tried to push it into the bottom of a wall, but it wouldn't go in. Then he reached higher up, and found a place where he was able to push it in. "That is how the man will search for and find the woman he is destined to marry."

The Sophists' question was an allusion to Israel's relationship with God. It says in the holy Torah, "The Lord came from Sinai, shone to them from Seir, and appeared at Mount Paran." We have learned that God first offered the Torah to the other nations before He revealed Himself to Israel, and they all declined it. Does that not prove, the Sophists were asking, that Israel occupies a lower status and is less significant than the other nations? For a man who can't find a noble woman to marry will settle for one of lower rank. Rabbi Yehoshua, however, compared the Torah to a nail which serves to support everything. One cannot place it in the lower part of the wall; it only fits at a higher level.

The sages of Athens continued: "A man lent someone money, and he was only able to get it back from the borrower by prosecuting him. What would cause this man to lend money again?"

Rabbi Yehoshua replied, "A man went into the forest and he chopped a pile of wood. He couldn't find anyone to assist him with his heavy load, so he went on chopping wood because he didn't want a reduced load nor did he want to be idle. And then finally someone came and helped him."

The Sophists were presenting the age-old question, which we have been asked again and again. God gave us the Holy Land, and we were not able to keep it in our hands; He gave us the Torah, and we were not able to keep its laws. Can one assume that God would choose our nation once again, after it had not been able to fulfill His rightful demands? Rabbi Yehoshua's reply, however, was saying that the time will come, when the Mashiach will lift the heavy load onto our shoulders for us, and we will carry it with ease. Until then, we dedicate our lives to studying the Torah and trying to probe deeper and deeper into its essence.

"Tell us a joke!" the sages of Athens said to Rabbi Yehoshua.

"We had a mule and the mule gave birth. So the old mule put a sign around the neck of its young, saying that it has to raise a large sum of money for its father's house."

"Can a mule give birth?" the Athenian sages asked.

"It's a joke indeed," Rabbi Yehoshua answered.

The commentators on the Talmud found an allusion in this question and answer to a new religion which was gaining popularity at the time. The Greek philosophers regarded it as small and insignificant, and that is why they asked about it in the guise of a joke. Rabbi Yehoshua compared the new religion to a hybrid creature, because it adopted things from the heathens as well.

"How should one conserve salt which is threatening to

spoil?" the Athenian sages asked.

"With the mule's afterbirth," Rabbi Yehoshua answered.

"Does a mule have an afterbirth?"

"Can salt spoil?" Rabbi Yehoshua replied.

Israel is the salt of the world, and God made an eternal "covenant of salt" with them called *bris melach olam*. This covenant can never be annulled. The "old covenant" always remains new, and will never be replaced by a "new covenant." Salt does not spoil, and it therefore does not require another substance to keep it fresh.

The sages of Athens asked Rabbi Yehoshua many more questions, and he answered them all very well. Finally, they had to declare themselves defeated. Hadrian was delighted with Rabbi Yehoshua's wisdom, and he decided that he wanted to learn more about the essence of Judaism. But he couldn't comprehend the idea of One omnipotent and invisible God, and he demanded to see Him. Rabbi Yehoshua told him to look at the sun, adding, "If you cannot look at one of His many servants because it blinds your eyes, how do you expect to look at God Himself?"

Hadrian liked that answer, and he asked to become a servant of the One and Only omnipotent God.

Chapter 36

Judea was filled with joy and happiness. The Emperor had promised to come to Jerusalem and rebuild the Holy Temple. All of Israel, young and old alike, were deliriously excited. They compared Hadrian to the Persian King Cyrus, and dreamt of a wonderful new era for the Jewish state.

The Emperor came to Bithynia, and Rabbi Yehoshua and Aquila were among those who accompanied him. When they came to the town of Claudiopolis, all the people came running to see and praise the Emperor of the world.

But then something happened: As suddenly as Hadrian's enthusiasm for Judaism had risen, it fell. Unwilling to abandon his pagan ways for the commandments of the Torah, he rejected Judaism and became an enemy of the Jews. From then on Hadrian became the worst enemy of the Jews. He appointed a new Governor, of Judea, Tineius Rufus, who ordered that the Temple Mount be razed to the ground and that a temple for idol worship be erected on it in place of the Beis HaMikdash. The name Jerusalem was changed to Aelia Capitolina, in honor of the Emperor's family.

It was on Tishah b'Av that Tineius Rufus carried out the Emperor's orders. The Jews were filled with despair. From the heights of euphoria and anticipation they were plunged into deep sorrow and despair. So great was their anguish that many contemplated suicide. Then Rabbi Yehoshua came to console them, like a comforting angel.

He told them a parable: "The lion, who is king of the animals, once swallowed a bone which got stuck in his throat. Then a crane came by and stuck his head into the lion's mouth; with his long beak, he pulled out the bone. Now that the crane had saved the lion from choking to death, he demanded a reward. So the lion said to him, 'You put your head into the lion's throat and you came away safely — and now you ask for a reward? What more reward can you ask for than that?'

"We too were forced to put our heads into the lion's mouth. Imagine what would have happened to us and to our religion if Hadrian had converted to Judaism! He would have violated it and arbitrarily refashioned it until there was nothing left. Let us thank God that we have escaped from the jaws of the lion safely!"

In his great rage the Emperor didn't even spare his own nephew Aquila; on the contrary. Tineius Rufus' soldiers surrounded Aquila's house at night, burst in and pulled him out of bed, and arrested him.

He did not try to resist. As he walked along with the Roman soldiers in the tranquil darkness of night, he said to them, "Look, my friends, it is the world's custom that at nighttime it will always be the person of inferior status who will carry the lantern or torch for the man of superior status. Thus, a legionnaire will do so for the Magister Equitum, who in turn will do so for the Imperator Legionis, and so forth. Have you ever heard that a king should carry the torch for his subjects, leading the way for them in the darkness of the night?"

The legionnaires stood still, fascinated by Aquila's words.

"No, I have never heard of such a thing before," their leader replied.

"So then listen now, my friends. Once there was a nation living in Egypt, and the Egyptians enslaved and oppressed them. Then God the Almighty freed that nation by bringing terrible plagues upon the Egyptians, and the enslaved nation went out of their country of slavery — to freedom. And God the Almighty, Lord of the universe, led the way for them with a pillar of cloud by day and a pillar of fire by night.

"That nation is the Jewish people, which I have joined! And because I have joined them, my uncle, the Emperor, wants to punish me with death! Just as the Almighty once lit the way for the Jews by night, so does He still light the way for them every night! He has revealed Himself to this nation, He has given them His holy teachings, and He shows them the path which they are meant to follow by day and by night. For a Jew, you see, death is not the end of his existence. God has promised us a better, more beautiful life in the World-to-Come! There we will enter His holy palace of eternal light and bliss!"

"Ah," sighed the leader, "if only we too could have a share in that eternal bliss!"

"You could," Aquila said, "if you convert to Judaism like I did! Come back with me to Usha! You can stay with me and I will instruct you in God's teachings!"

And so they returned to Usha with him and Aquila taught them, and they all circumcised themselves and became religious, zealous Jews.

Aquila's friends advised him to escape and go into hiding, since the Emperor would presumably continue to pursue him. But Aquila said, "God can protect me here just as well as anywhere else! If it's God's will that the Emperor kill me, then his soldiers will find me even in the most secure of hiding places. And if God wants to protect me, then I am as safe in my home as I am in the most inaccessible mountain cleft!"

When Hadrian found out that his orders had been disobeyed and that the soldiers who had been sent to arrest Aquila had converted to Judaism, his rage knew no bounds. He ordered that soldiers be sent once again, threatening to kill them if they engaged in conversation with Aquila.

Tineius Rufus sent out a troop of soldiers under the command of one of his most trusted officers, and commanded them to follow the Emperor's orders diligently. They too went to Aquila at night. They too surrounded his house, burst in, woke him, and ordered him to get dressed and come with them. Aquila did as he was told. As he was leaving his house, he put his hand on the mezuzah on the doorpost and kissed it.

"What are you doing?" the officer asked him.

"I am kissing the mezuzah."

"What does that mean?"

Aquila began to explain. "Every king resides in the innermost part of his palace, while his guards stand in the entranceway, holding swords in their hands to protect him. But our King, the King of all kings, Israel's eternal God, is different! His servants remain at home, and when they are tired they sleep peacefully in their beds so that they can regain their strength. It is He Who doesn't sleep, for He is Israel's guardian. He commanded us to write His Name and place it on the doorposts of our homes, and He promised to protect us and take care of us if we do this faithfully."

"And is God's Name all that there is in this capsule?"

"It is also written there that we should love our God with all our heart, all our soul, and with all our might, and that we should heed His teachings by day and by night."

"And how does your God reward you for that?"

"He grants us His special protection for as long as we live in this world, and after death He leads our immortal souls into the next world, a haven of eternal bliss."

The soldiers were fascinated by Aquila's words. "Please — we want you to teach us and guide us," the officer said, "so that we too can one day have a share in the eternal life which God has promised to those who obey His commandments!"

And so it was. The officer and all of his soldiers circumcised themselves and converted to Judaism. Hadrian gave up, and from then on Aquila was left in peace.

Chapter 37

Rabbi Yehoshua ben Chananyah had passed away. All of Israel was still in deep mourning for him when they were confronted with further tragic news: Rabbi Elazar ben Azaryah had died as well.

Now Rabbi Akiva was the greatest and most distinguished man of Israel. He was indeed a prince of his nation, though he didn't accept the official title of *Nasi*, which was kept for Rabban Gamliel's son, Rabbi Shimon ben Gamliel, who was still very young at the time. He was at school in Beitar, which had blossomed as a new center of Torah study since Jerusalem had fallen.

In the meantime Tineius Rufus raged against everything and anything Jewish. He demanded that all Jewish men and women worship the statues of the Emperor, and whoever refused to do so was put to death in gruesome ways. Two great men of that time, Rabbi Shimon ben Nesanel and Rabbi Yishmael, were among those who were killed.

As the two of them were being led to their death, Rabbi Yishmael wept bitterly. Rabbi Shimon turned to him. "Great and noble man that you are, Israel's father and leader," he said, "you are only two steps away from the Hereafter, where you will join all of God's pious ones. Why are you crying?"

"I am not crying because of my approaching death," he replied. "I am crying because of the sins that I must have committed in order to deserve this punishment. For all God's deeds are perfect and all His ways are just, and if He is subjecting me to such a violent death there must be a reason for it! Have I transgressed Shabbos, or have I killed a fellow Jew, to warrant the death penalty?"

"Rabbi," Rabbi Shimon told him, "you know that God judges the pious very strictly! Who knows — perhaps once some people came to ask you a question about a religious matter, and you were either eating your meal or you were sleeping, and your servant sent them away. And then, because they were weary of asking, they decided to follow the more stringent ruling. And now you are atoning for this seemingly insignificant transgression with death, so you can have your full share of eternal bliss!"

Rabbi Yishmael was now able to wipe his tears away, and both of the pious men went happily towards their death.

Rabbi Akiva and Rabbi Yehudah ben Bava were teaching outdoors, in the fields, surrounded by thousands of students, when they heard the tragic news. Many tore their clothing in mourning and started to cry bitterly.

Rabbi Akiva said, "My friends and brothers, you should indeed cry, but not because of our great loss — rather, because of all the horror and evil that awaits us! For if there were good things in store for us, Rabbi Shimon and Rabbi Yishmael would not have been taken from us; they would have remained alive to enjoy those good things. Terrible things are coming in the near future! And that is why these pious men have died, for God has spared them from having to witness all the suffering! Brothers, let us take the death of these noble men to heart! We must examine our ways and return to God, so that the words of Scripture should not apply to us: 'The righteous is gone and no one takes it to heart.' Oh, my students, my sons! It is true that you are devout and good, that you devote day and night to Torah study — but many of you are proud of the knowledge you have acquired and you act haughtily toward your friends! You don't honor each other enough. Take this to heart, my children, and uproot your pride and arrogance! If you will truly do some soul-searching and follow the ways of those modest and noble leaders of Israel, Rabbi Shimon and Rabbi Yishmael, they will be your saviors from the misfortunes that await us. And then the words of prophesy, 'Peace will come when they will rest on their graves,' will be fulfilled."

Rabbi Akiva's warning went unheeded. A terrible epidemic broke out, and thousands of his students, who were Israel's pride and hope, succumbed. In great dismay and deep sorrow, the nation witnessed the elite of their youth wither away and die. The synagogues were constantly filled with people pouring out their hearts in prayer.

It was the time of the Omer, between Pesach and Shavuos. As the counting of the Omer advanced, the dreaded epidemic continued to spread, claiming the finest young men of Israel. The nation was in mourning. No public entertainment and no weddings took place, until finally, on the thirty-third day of the Omer, God accepted his people's prayers and the epidemic abated.

Since then, the time of the Omer has remained a time of mourning for us, and the 18th of Iyar, the thirty-third day of the Omer — *Lag baOmer* — has been instituted as a day of rejoicing.

Rabbi Akiva was not just a teacher to his students; he was also a father. Now that so many of his young students had passed away, he dedicated himself to the welfare of the widows and orphans they had left behind. But it was not easy to find the means to do so. All of Judea was impoverished under the Roman plundering, and it was therefore impossible to institute taxes. But the misery was so great that something had to be done urgently. Rabbi Akiva used a great part of his own money for this undertaking but even so it did not suffice.

On the seacoast, not far from Jaffa, an aristocratic Roman matron by the name of Paula Veturia lived in a lavish mansion. She had once met the Sages of Israel in Rome, and she consequently took a great interest in Torah, which she studied diligently. When her husband died, she came to Eretz Yisrael so that she could live closer to the Jewish teachers. There she built a palatial home on the shore of the sea, and she lived there with her many servants and maids. Paula Veturia was extremely wealthy, and Rabbi Akiva decided to approach her and ask her for a loan of 100,000 gold dinars.

Paula Veturia received Rabbi Akiva with great joy. "Welcome to you, Rabbi," she said. "I am so happy to see you again!"

"Don't be happy so fast, noble woman," Rabbi Akiva replied, "for I have come to ask you for something which requires you to put a great deal of trust in me. You have probably heard that most of my students died from a terrible epidemic. They have left behind thousands of widows and orphans who are unable to support themselves. Soon they will be dying of hunger if we don't intervene somehow! All our provisions are depleted. In order to save them we must raise 100,000 gold dinars."

"So you are collecting money for this, Rabbi? Of course I will give you a donation."

"Oh, no, noble woman, I'm afraid that a donation won't help us! I have come to you to ask you for a loan of the entire sum. God will provide me with the means to reimburse you within a year's time!"

"The whole sum! You are asking for a lot, Rabbi! One hundred thousand gold dinars is enough to impoverish *me* if I lose it!"

"You will earn a lot of interest on the money: Eternal life for having saved so many lives! Please do not reject my request. I have no one else to turn to!"

"And what will you give me as a surety?" asked Paula Veturia.

"All that I own," declared Rabbi Akiva, "and if you want, I can bring you ten other wealthy guarantors!"

"Even that is not enough for such a large sum. Look, Rabbi, do you see the sea out there? Can you count the waves? And yet there are certainly much less than 100,000. No, against that amount of money you must give me other sureties. May I suggest the following to you: Promise me that God and the sea will be your guarantors, and I will lend you the money!"

"Indeed, it shall be just as you have said: God and the sea will be my guarantors that I will pay you back all of the money within a year."

Rabbi Akiva took the money and used it to help the widows and orphans. He saved many from starving to death. He used part of the money to give loans as well, and the borrowers paid him back within a few months. He also asked all the wealthy Jews to contribute, and soon, even before the date of repayment had arrived, he was ready to return all the money. As he prepared to go and return his loan, he suddenly fell ill. As he lay in his bed wracked with fever, he lost consciousness.

When the day of repayment arrived, Paula Veturia waited impatiently for Rabbi Akiva. By noontime the Sage had not yet come. When the sun began to set, still there was no sign of Rabbi Akiva. Paula Veturia left her house and in her great despair she began to run back and forth along the seashore.

"Almighty God," she cried, "I trusted in Your guarantee! Am I going to lose my trust in You? Give Your command to the sea that it give forth its treasures and pay me back for what I have lost!"

And as she spoke, she gazed at the blue waves of the Mediterranean. What was that? A magnificent chest, decorated with gold and precious stones, appeared to be floating in the sea! Within a few minutes the waves had carried it ashore, and it landed right at Paula Veturia's feet! She tried to lift it, but it was too heavy, and she had to call her servants to carry it into her house.

With great effort they were able to open the tightly locked chest. And lo and behold, there were 100,000 gold dinars in it!

"God has performed a miracle!" Paula Veturia cried. "May His Name be praised forever and ever!"

Where had this chest come from? That we shall learn about in the coming chapter.

Chapter 38

It was December in the year 129 of the Common Era. The Emperor Hadrian set out for Alexandria with his whole court. His wife Sabina had preceded him, and she had taken up residence in the Caesareum, the magnificent palace of the capital. The chambers for the Emperor were already prepared as well, and he was expected to arrive any day.

Sabina was sitting on a couch surrounded by cushions, her feet deeply buried in buffalo skins. She held her head high and proudly. This was no small feat with all the heavy gems and pearls braided into her thick curls of hair. In fact her small face seemed dwarfed by all the jewelry she adorned herself with.

Hadrian had never cared for his wife. He had married her because she was Trajan's niece — because his patroness Plotina had wanted it, and because he had hoped thereby to secure the crown for himself. Over the years, his marriage had deteriorated. Hadrian and Sabina had no children. Hadrian was fond of a young boy, Antinous, whom he wanted to adopt as his own son. And all of Sabina's love went to her nephew, the Praetor Lucius Aelius Verus. She had her mind set on seeing him become Hadrian's successor, and she was inspired by what Plotina had done for Hadrian. Verus was a very good-hearted and knowledgeable man, but those who knew him predicted a short life for him.

The servants announced that Titanius, the Prefect of Egypt, was waiting to see the Empress, and ushered him in.

Titanius bowed deeply as he entered the chamber, but the

Empress received him coldly. "What brings you here?"

"A messenger on horseback brought me a letter from the Emperor saying that the Emperor has decided to take up residence in the old palace of Lochias instead of here in the palace of Caesarium."

The Empress frowned and stared down into her lap. "Because I am here!" she hissed to herself.

Lochias was a palace which one of the Ptolemaic kings had built on the seashore. "Please tell Verus — the Praetor Lucius Aelius Verus — to come to me!" Sabina said.

The Prefect left and carried out his mission.

Presently Verus appeared before the Empress. She was in the midst of drinking a cup of fruit juice, which her servant had prepared for her. As soon as she finished Verus took the cup from her and handed it back to the servant. He treated the Empress in such a caring and solicitous manner that one might have thought he was a devoted son looking after his mother.

The Empress acknowledged him in gratitude and commanded her servant to leave the room. "My dear Lucius, I have some very important matters to discuss with you! Hadrian has chosen to stay in the old and run-down Lochias palace instead of coming here — just because I am here! You know how much I care for you and you know what great plans I have for you. You are the only person who is concerned about my well-being!"

"You are like a second mother to me," he murmured. "And you always have been so, since my childhood."

"My dear son, listen to me — our plans are in great jeopardy. I am afraid that Hadrian is going to adopt that Antinous and nominate him as his successor!"

"Impossible!" Verus cried out.

"Is there anything a Roman Emperor cannot do?"

"He wouldn't dare slap the face of the Senate and his people by promoting his Antinous to such a high position!"

"Hadrian does whatever he pleases! That is why I am telling you: We must get that boy out of the way!"

Verus went pale. "Imagine the Emperor's rage if he knew what we were discussing! He would crush anyone he ever slightly suspected!"

"We must do it cleverly then. You are a man with initiative. Think of something. Now leave me — all this talking tires me out! Send my servant in again!"

Verus left. Sabina's news astonished him, and he started to ponder how Antinous might be removed. He would have to find a way to do it without any violence, without any murder involved. First, he decided, he would have to get to know the boy a little, and find out his weak points.

Hadrian had arrived in Alexandria with his entourage and settled in at the palace of Lochias. Verus hurried to the palace to greet the Emperor, and Hadrian received him in the friendliest manner.

"You have come at exactly the right time, my dear Lucius! I have a mission for you. Antinous has been suffering from melancholy for a while now. It's no wonder that a young boy is not happy with an old man like me as his only companion! Please try to cheer him up a bit! No one knows how to enjoy life better than you do!"

The Praetor was overjoyed. Now, through the Emperor's own orders, he would have the opportunity to render Antinous harmless! "I will do what I can," he replied.

Hadrian called in Antinous, and he said to him, "My dear Antinous, I have some affairs of state to look after in Alexandria, and these will be taking up a lot of my time during our stay. You will not have to be idle, however, for my relative, the Praetor Lucius Aelius Verus, will be very happy to show you around this beautiful city. He will take you to its palaces and temples and places of amusement, so that we can drive away the sad look on your face!"

The Emperor left, and Verus and Antinous were alone.

"My dear Antinous," the Praetor said to the boy, "I will be happy to do some sightseeing with you. Although I don't know you very well, we do have something special in common: we both love the Emperor!"

"I certainly love him," Antinous replied. "He has treated me like a son."

"Very well, then!" exclaimed Verus. "Then it will be in your interest as much as it is in mine to maintain the Emperor's good spirits and tranquility so that he will be able to bear his heavy burdens more easily! The Emperor loves you dearly, and you must honor him with a happy face. Naturally you can do so only if you are truly happy, and this you will achieve through enjoying the pleasures of life. I am a disciple of Epicurus, who teaches us how to live in the joy of the moment! Follow me, and I will teach you how to be happy in a circle of happy friends!"

And Antinous followed him. Under Verus's guidance he learned how to drink good wine, and how to experience various mundane pleasures of this world. They made the acquaintance of the entertainments and amusements of Alexandria, but this did not seem to help the boy's melancholy.

Hadrian saw this when he returned, and tried a new way of cheering him up. "Are you ambitious, my dear boy?"

"No, my lord."

"Tell me, by whom does a man like to be called Father?"

"By someone that he loves very dearly."

"Most certainly," said the Emperor, "and you, my dear, are the closest person to my heart, and I will bless the day that I will grant you permission before the whole world to call me Father. No, don't interrupt me, my dear boy! If you focus your mind and your spirit, and you observe the people around you very carefully, if you try to sharpen your intelligence and absorb what I teach you, then it might happen, one day, that you will become Emperor in my place!"

The young boy felt dizzy. The Emperor's grand offer didn't excite him in the least. On the contrary, he felt worse. But all he said was, "May the gods grant you such a long life, oh Caesar, that you part from this world long after me!"

"I am a human being like all others," the Emperor replied, "and it is the course of nature that older people die before younger ones do. Knowing that the person I love most in the world will inherit all my power, honor, and wealth will surely sweeten the moment of death for me!"

Chapter 39

Antinous had received the Emperor's permission and blessing to tour some parts the country. Verus, the Praetor, and several servants and slaves came along as an escort. Among them was the Emperor's most loyal slave, Mastor, who usually served as Hadrian's personal bodyguard. He was well-suited for the job, for he was as strong as Hercules. Hadrian had given him special instructions on this occasion to protect his beloved Antinous very carefully.

The destination of their journey was Besa, a city on the Nile.

As Antinous and Verus rode along on their mules at the head of the group, they chatted. "My dear Verus," Antinous said suddenly, "would you care to enlighten me a little? I am an ignorant boy from a simple background. There are so many things that I do not understand."

"Speak!" Verus said. "I will be happy to be of service to you with whatever I know."

"Very well. You told me recently that it was my duty to show the Emperor a happy face in order to ease the heavy burden of rulership he carries on his shoulders. Tell me please, is it really so difficult to be the Emperor?"

Verus looked at him with piercing eyes. "Is that what you want me to teach you about? Why don't you ask Hadrian? Surely he will be able to tell you more about it than I can!"

"I want to tell you a secret," said Antinous quietly. "The Emperor has told me that he plans on adopting me and appointing me as the next Emperor!"

Sabina had been right! Well-trained in diplomacy as Verus was, he managed to mask his feelings of bitterness in a masterly way. In a friendly tone he replied: "In that case I must congratulate you, Antinous! Are you overjoyed?"

"That is exactly what I wanted to ask you about: Should I be overjoyed? Is it such a great privilege to be the Emperor?"

"Is it a privilege?" Verus laughed. "For those who are ambitious there is no greater privilege than that: to be the highest authority, to be a god on this earth, to have the entire world at your feet! But of course not everyone is cut out for this grand task. For smaller intellects it could be a miserable job."

"Explain that to me," said Antinous.

"An Emperor must primarily be a warrior, a hero. He must know how to lead his army in war, how to defeat the enemies and subjugate them, in order to increase his glory and splendor. If he is incapable of doing this, then his reputation and prestige go down. And then the ambitious legionnaires make sure to win the soldiers' hearts for themselves, and they persuade them to overthrow the Emperor! Would you know how to lead an army into the battlefield, Antinous?"

"Certainly not!"

"Would you know how to devise the right strategies in war? Would you be able to figure out what the plans of the enemy were, and combat them?"

"Never!"

"An Emperor also has to be a very good judge of people," Verus went on. "He must be able to see through the hearts of those that surround him. He must have the ability to discern whether they are loyal to him or not; he must know how to distinguish between sincerity and falseness, and between love and flattery. And he must make sure to keep the traitors far away from himself. Are you a good judge of character, Antinous?"

"I trust everyone!"

"A ruler of a great Empire," Verus continued, "which consists of many countries and nationalities, must know all the branches of administration very well, so that he gives the various posts to the right people. If he is incapable of doing so, he can cause the whole Empire to crumble, and the provinces will rebel. And he himself becomes the tool of all the unscrupulous men who try to push him into committing evil deeds and atrocities. Then people start hating him for his crimes and they seek revenge, and he fears for his life constantly. Indeed, that is how Caligula was killed, that is how Nero was killed, and the same thing happened to Domitian. And before they were killed, they spent their days and nights in fear of death! Can you imagine anything worse than to live a life of constant dread, a life in which all joy and happiness have vanished, because you are afraid of being murdered all the time?"

"No, no! I don't want to be Emperor! I will ask Hadrian to abandon his plan!"

"Silly boy! Have you ever heard of anyone who was able to convince Hadrian to change his mind about something he had decided on?"

Antinous was silent. He knew that the Praetor was right.

They continued to ride side by side in silence, until Antinous spoke. "Give me advice, my dear Verus. How can I escape this terrible fate?"

Verus chose his words very carefully and spoke softly. "If you are afraid of becoming a god on this earth, Antinous, then you should take advantage of the special privilege we human beings have, which the gods do not have."

"I don't understand you. What do you mean?"

"Every man has the right to step out of the ranks of the living when his existence in this world seems more unbearable to him than death. The gods cannot die, and in that sense we are superior to them."

"Verus! Are you advising me..."

"I am not advising you. I have just answered your questions."

They rode on in silence, Antinous absorbed in his thoughts.

Soon they arrived in Besa, where they spent the night. The next morning a messenger of the Emperor came to call Verus back — Sabina had asked to see him.

Antinous bid him farewell. The boy had not slept all night. His mind was filled with frightening images and fantasies. He had envisioned a murderer thrusting his sword at him, and he saw all the misery and evil which Verus had described to him so vividly. After breakfast, taking Mastor with him, Antinous went for a walk on the banks of the Nile, which is three miles wide at Besa. The waters sparkled in the morning sunlight.

"Oh," Antinous cried to himself, "how wonderful it would be to put an end to all my suffering and misery here in the river!"

There were boats at the shore. Suddenly Antinous bent down, pushed it into the water, and jumped aboard. Mastor called out to him, "My lord, what are you doing?"

"Give my greetings to the Emperor!" shouted Antinous rowing furiously. "He will never see me again!"

"Stop, poor boy, come back!" the servant called out to him, and he too jumped into a boat to follow him. But Antinous was rowing with all his might, and his boat moved faster and faster. Mastor tried with all the strength in his strong arms to catch up with the boy, but to no avail. In a wild race, Antinous finally reached the middle of the river. Mastor stared horrified, as Antinous flew through the air. Antinous had dived into the water and disappeared.

At the same time that this was happening in Besa, a delegation of Egyptian priests had come to pay tribute to the Emperor. They brought him a chest containing 100,000 gold pieces as their gift to him.

Hadrian received them in majestic purple robes, and his entire court was present. All the prophets and higher clerics of the various temples in the Nile Valley had come to worship him as the son of the sun god. Hadrian in turn had to assure them of his benevolence and compassion, in accordance with custom.

They asked him to sanctify their temples by coming to visit, and he agreed.

Then the high priest from Memphis handed him the beautiful chest, decorated with precious stones and gold. Hadrian accepted it graciously, delighted with the generous gift.

It was at that very moment that Mastor came running into the royal hall, his hair unkempt and his face filled with fear and horror.

"Caesar!" he called out. "Your Antinous —"

"What is it, what is it?" The Emperor turned pale.

"He has killed himself!"

The Emperor leapt up from his throne, he tore his majestic robe into pieces, and started to race back and forth like a madman. Then he took the chest into his hands, and with superhuman power he hurled it out of the window into the waters of the sea. A terrible storm came up, and the wild waves carried the chest to the shores of Jaffa, where Paula Veturia stood, appealing to the Almighty.

A whole night and half a day had passed since the death of Antinous. Ships and boats from all over the country had assembled in Besa to search for the body; the banks of the river were filled with people, and there were torches set up everywhere to enable the search to go on at night. And yet they still had not found the boy.

The Emperor couldn't eat or drink. He forbade anyone to approach him, including his wife. So great was his despair that it clouded his thinking, and he was in such great distress that just hearing a familiar voice made him uneasy, and every so often he would lash out in fury. As he sat staring at nothing, he mumbled under his breath, "All of humanity shall mourn with me!"

Finally he rose and declared with authority: "I will reach out my hand, and send a message to the gods: Every city throughout the Empire must build an altar for Antinous. My beloved friend, whom you have taken from me, will become one of you now! Treat him well, immortal rulers of the world! Who among you could ever be as loyal and kind to me as he was?"

Hadrian's vow seemed to have comforted him. He sent for Heliodor, his private secretary, and dictated to him an announcement to the public.

What Hadrian demanded was no less than an order that the whole Empire worship Antinous as a new god. And that is exactly what happened. The renowned sculptors of the Empire competed with each other in their depictions of Antinous, and these statues were erected in new Antinous temples.

A few weeks after these events had taken place, Rabbi Akiva recovered from his serious illness. He rushed to Paula Veturia immediately to pay her the money he owed her. "Forgive me for not having come on time, but I have been very ill," he explained. While Rabbi Akiva was speaking, two of his students handed the money to her.

She declined it, however. "This money belongs to you, Rabbi Akiva. Your guarantor has paid your debt already!" And then she told him the whole story.

Chapter 40

After the death of Antinous, Hadrian gave in to his wife's pleas that he adopt the Praetor Lucius Aelius Verus as his son. (As it turned out, though, Verus himself did not rule, but his son Marcus Aurelius, surnamed Antoninus, who was born many years later, was to become an Emperor, and one who would affect Jewish history greatly.)

In his mourning, the Emperor found Egypt unappealing, and he decided to move on to Antioch. Tineius Rufus, Governor of Judea, came to greet him there. A Jewish delegation, headed by Rabbi Akiva, arrived there at the same time. They had come to complain to the Emperor about the unbearable oppression and persecutions that Tineius Rufus was subjecting them to. The Emperor received Rabbi Akiva cordially, and heard his complaints. There were three points that Rabbi Akiva brought to Hadrian's attention: Tineius Rufus had forbidden the Jews to circumcise themselves; they were not allowed to observe the Sabbath; and the Governor forced them to worship idols or face death.

The Emperor called in Tineius Rufus and asked him to defend these measures.

"Tell me, Jew," Tineius Rufus said, turning to Rabbi Akiva. "You honor your Only God, Creator of heaven and earth; you call Him the Omnipotent, and you praise Him as the greatest of all artists and architects in the world. So tell me then, whose works are more beautiful, the works of the Almighty or the works of human beings?"

Without pausing to think, Rabbi Akiva replied, "The works of human beings."

"Do you, my dear Jew, really know what you are saying?" asked Tineius Rufus. "Can man possibly beautify the heavens with the splendid sun and the lovely moon, and can he direct the course of all the stars? Can man create a world like ours, erect the mountains, and make the springs flow so that they become mighty rivers? Is man able to create the ocean with all its wonders?"

Rabbi Akiva replied, "You asked me whose works are more beautiful, and I answered that man's works are more beautiful. I was not saying, however, that man could create things which are beyond his capabilities. But within the realm of human potentialities, man's works are more beautiful. Allow me, oh Emperor, to demonstrate this with an example."

Hadrian gave his consent. Rabbi Akiva left and came back shortly with a servant, who was holding a bundle of grain and a beautiful cake baked by a master baker.

"Look, my lord," the Rabbi said. "These ears of grain are the works of God. That is how God let them grow. But from that grain human beings have succeeded in making this wonderful cake. The cake is man's creation. Am I not correct, then, when I say that man's works are more beautiful than God's?"

"Why do you circumcise yourself?" Tineius Rufus asked. "Are you trying to improve on God's work?"

"I knew you were driving at that, and that is why I answered the way I did. When God Almighty created the world, He rested from all the works He had created, as it says in the Torah. Now look — man is also God's work, and the special spirit he was imbued with is a gift from God. Whatever man creates with his skillful hands is inspired by his mind, and thus it is God's work as well. God granted him the ability to use the raw materials of the world to create new things from them. Thus, marble in itself is beautiful, but a sculpture crafted by a gifted sculptor is far more beautiful than that!

"Likewise, an artist uses the simple pigments of color found in the earth or in plants, and he creates paintings which are a delight to everyone's eyes. The architect uses stone and marble to build magnificent palaces, which kings and emperors can live in luxuriously. Sheep's wool and flax would never be wearable if man didn't make clothing out of them with his efficient hands. And that clothing not only covers our bodies and protects us against the elements; it also serves to enhance man's beauty and give special honor to kings and emperors. Meat from animals, and fruit and vegetables from the fields, would be useless to us if it were not for man's skill in preparing and cooking them, making them edible and delicious at the same time. Thus God granted us the ability to improve and develop His creation.

"Another aspect of God is that He revealed Himself to the Jews, and He gave us laws and commandments which enable us to purify our souls and to prepare our bodies for His service, as it says in the Torah, 'God's word is pure; He is a shield to all those that trust in him.' The first rung of the ladder in our service to God, which starts here on earth and reaches into Heaven, is circumcision. It is a sign of the covenant that God made with our forefathers. On the eighth day of his life, a male must enter this covenant, and he receives an indestructible sign on his body reminding him that a Jew's duty in life is to serve God and to sanctify His Name in the world.

"God didn't intend to destroy our natural human desires with His commandments, but rather He wanted to set the ideal boundaries for our emotional and physical well-being. That is the purpose and goal of the covenant that God made with our forefathers. And that is why we circumcise ourselves — to perfect God's creation by actualizing our great potential. So when you ask whether we are trying to improve on God's creation, Rufus, the answer is yes, we certainly are. But we are doing so with God the Almighty's own guidance!"

"Well put!" exclaimed Hadrian. "I had understood your custom to be superstitious and stupid, but you have explained it very well! Circumcision will be permitted once again."

"Thank you, Emperor!" Rabbi Akiva said. "Will you be so kind in your great compassion as to allow us to keep the Sabbath as well?"

Upon hearing this, Tineius Rufus continued to probe. "Why do you celebrate the seventh day in particular? Couldn't you just as well celebrate any other day of the week?"

"Why did the Emperor appoint Tineius Rufus as Judea's governor?" asked Rabbi Akiva. "Could he not have chosen anyone else just as well?"

"He wanted to honor me over all other people."

"So too God, the King of all kings; He wanted to honor the seventh day over all other days!"

"If God really wanted to honor the seventh day," said Tineius Rufus, "He should have made it different from all other days. Rain falls on the seventh day just like on all other days, and the wind blows just the same. And people are born and people die on that day, just like they do on any other day."

Rabbi Akiva explained: "When God redeemed our forefathers from Egyptian slavery, He took them through the desert for forty years in order to shape them as a holy Jewish nation. During that time He provided them with food and drink. On six days of the week, He would let manna rain down from the skies, and on the sixth day God gave them manna for *two* days — that is how He distinguished between Shabbos and all other days, for they didn't have to gather manna on Shabbos."

"What do I care about stories that happened many hundreds of years ago!" said Tineius Rufus. "And how could you prove it to me anyhow? Could you bring me trustworthy witnesses who saw these events? Don't bother telling me about things that took place ages ago. Give me proofs from today that I myself can examine!"

"In India," Rabbi Akiva answered, "there is a river by the name of Sambatyon. For six days the water in the Sambatyon gushes forth wildly, and big rocks fly all over the place. On the seventh day, however, the river rests, and the water is completely still. That river is God's sign to us that the seventh day is a day of rest!"

"Rabbi Akiva, you are shrewd for choosing a proof that is far away! Are you suggesting that we all go to India now to look for the Sambatyon River? If you can't bring us a proof close by, then we will have to declare the Sabbath as a superstitious custom! And moreover, it prevents people from working, encouraging them to become lazy!"

At that moment Rabbi Akiva prayed to God in his heart: "Almighty God, You have performed so many miracles for the pious. Please demonstrate Your power to us as well, so that we can put this wicked man to shame!"

And then he said, "Very well then, Rufus. I know that your father's grave is here in Antioch. He is presently being punished for all the evil deeds he committed in his life. During the six ordinary days of the week sinners in the Hereafter suffer the tortures of hell, but on the seventh day they are granted rest. Send someone to your father's grave to observe it! For six days smoke rises from it, but on the seventh day even your father is granted rest, and no smoke is visible then."

A servant was dispatched to the grave, and all that Rabbi Akiva had described took place. Then Hadrian gave the Jews permission to observe the Sabbath again, and Tineius Rufus was put to shame.

Chapter 41

Once again Rabbi Akiva and Tineius Rufus appeared together before the Emperor. "There is no other nation in the world," Tineius Rufus said, "which is as intolerant as the Jews! Every nation worships its own gods and laughs at other religions. The Jews, however, *hate* the other gods, and they teach that their God hates all idol-worship! The God of the Jews hates the Romans, the Greeks, the Egyptians, and all the other nations of the world, since they worship other gods and not Him!"

"How do you defend yourself against such a weighty accusation?" the Emperor asked Rabbi Akiva.

"Allow me to tell you a dream I had recently," replied the Sage. "In my dream a friend of mine gave me a gift — a pair of dogs. I called the male Rufus and the female Rufina."

Tineius Rufus turned red as a beet, while Hadrian laughed unabashedly.

"You deserve to be beaten to death!" Tineius screamed. "Even your dreams show how evil and rebellious you are! How dare you call your dogs by my name and the name of my wife!"

"Why should that upset you so greatly?" asked Rabbi Akiva calmly. "Is there such a great difference between you and a dog? You eat and drink, and the dog eats and drinks; you sleep, and the dog sleeps; you will die, and the dog will die. But nevertheless you are angry, because I have given a dog your name in my dream! Then what about the Almighty, Who created heaven and earth? Should He not become angry when foolish people take wood or stone and call it by His Name?"

Hadrian acknowledged that Rabbi Akiva had won the argument again. The decree that the Jews worship the statues of the Emperor and of Antinous was abolished.

Tineius Rufus returned to his home utterly crushed. When his wife Rufina saw him, she became alarmed. “Rufus, my dear! What happened? Have you lost the Emperor’s favor? Has he condemned you to death? You look terrible! Tell me, dear husband, what is the matter?”

“That Jew, that Akiva, annoys me to death! Whatever I say, he refutes it, and the Emperor always agrees with him! I could kill myself! There is not a day that passes that he doesn’t put me to shame!”

“I will free you of him!” Rufina said.

“You?” her husband asked in surprise. “How will you do that?”

“You will see. I will find a way.”

Rufina dressed in exquisite clothes and her finest jewelry, and went to visit Rabbi Akiva. When Rabbi Akiva saw her, he became very sad. Tears streamed down his cheeks.

Rufina was taken aback. “Are you the great rabbi of the Jews?” she asked. “Why are you crying?”

“I am crying for your beauty which is destined to be consumed by worms in the ground. Your immortal soul will descend into the depths of hell and suffer tortures forever, for there is nothing that you do in your life to grow spiritually, to become a better and wiser person! There is nothing that you do to contribute to the purpose of Creation!”

Rufina was spellbound. She had never heard such words! The pained look on Rabbi Akiva’s saintly face, and his soft way of speaking, moved her deeply. All her plans to humiliate him were forgotten, and she began to cry. “Rabbi, is it still possible for me to change?” she sobbed.

“Yes, certainly it is,” Rabbi Akiva said reassuringly. “God the Almighty is merciful. And He is full of compassion for sinners who repent!”

"Rabbi, can I, or may I, convert to Judaism?"

"You can and you may. Study the Torah, my daughter, and seek your eternal salvation! But you will have to give up all the idols and all the immorality of the Romans! Be sure to make your decision very carefully, for it is very hard to keep all the commandments and laws of the Torah — the Sabbath, the dietary laws, the laws of purity and impurity, and more."

"Rabbi, I came to you in order to shame you. I wanted my husband to triumph over you, since you have put *him* to shame so many times! And now — now you have disarmed me with your wise and convincing words! I abandoned all my foolish plans immediately, and now I wish to set out on a new path. I must do a lot of soul-searching, and learn to imbue my life with meaning and content. And, Rabbi Akiva — I will drink with great thirst from the fountains of wisdom and truth!"

"And your husband?"

"I will try to convince Rufus to join me on my new path. In his heart he too despises the gods, and he just pretends to honor them."

"It is true that whoever renounces what is false is already close to embracing the truth. Nonetheles it is still highly unlikely that a man who is used to such a sinful way of life would leave everything at once. And we cannot forget that his hands have shed much innocent blood — of noble men, women, and young girls and boys! And yet… there is no sin so great that it cannot be atoned for with sincere regret and repentance!"

"I will try," said Rufina "I have seen the truth and will try to show Rufus the truth. I will plead with him, and beg him, and then perhaps I will soften his heart!"

"And if he refuses?"

"Then I will have to divorce him! Farewell, Rabbi. You will hear from me!"

Chapter 42

The Emperor returned to Rome and Tineius Rufus went back to his home in Caesarea. Rabbi Akiva went to Usha. There was a new excitement in the air. Everyone was talking about the joyous event that had taken place: the long-awaited Mashiach had appeared!

Eighteen years earlier, a man named Reuven had encountered an Arab on Tishah b'Av, who said to him, "Rejoice, Judean, for at this moment the Messiah has been born!"

"In which city?" Reuven asked.

"In Beis Lechem."

"What is his name?"

"Menachem."

"And what is his father's name?"

"Chizkiyahu."

So Reuven sold his cow, which was the only thing of any value that he owned, and bought all kinds of small items for young children, and went off to Beis Lechem to get acquainted with the Mashiach.

When he arrived in town, he began to sell the childrens' accessories to young mothers, and they bought a number of items from him. Then one of the women called out to a young mother and her little boy who were passing by, "Don't you want to buy something for your Menachem?"

"No," she replied. "He was born on the day that the Temple was destroyed. How can I buy him presents?!"

"Just take something," Reuven interjected, "and perhaps

the Holy Temple will be rebuilt through his merit!"

"I don't have any money," the mother said.

"You can pay me the next time I come to Beis Lechem."

And he gave her all the goods that were left, and he hung a chain with a coin attached to it around her son's neck. The coin was from Hasmonean times; there was a palm tree imprinted on one side of it and a grapevine on the other.

One year later Reuven returned to Beis Lechem to see how Menachem was doing. This time the mother approached him in tears. "Just a few days after you saw my Menachem last year, there was a terrible storm and I lost him in the woods!"

This is what happened: Menachem's father, Chizkiyahu (who was a descendant of King David), was very poor. His wife went into the woods to collect twigs and branches for firewood. She took the child along and put him down under a tree. While she was gathering the wood nearby, the sky became dark with clouds and a sudden storm arose. There was thunder and lightning; heavy winds and strong rain made it hard to maintain a sense of direction. Menachem's mother searched for her little boy desperately, but she couldn't find him anywhere. When the sudden storm passed, she rushed to the place where she had put him down, her heart was pounding with fear. Was he still alive? Had he been struck by the lightning? Had he drowned in the heavy rains? When she got there, she found that the child had disappeared without trace! Crying and moaning, the mother searched for him throughout the woods. Then she rushed home, and soon Chizkiyahu and all the inhabitants of Beis Lechem began to search for Menachem, but to no avail.

What had happened? The rainstorm had swept the little boy down the slope of the mountain, and deposited him in a pool of water. At that very moment a man named Levi had passed by. He was from Keziv, which is where our forefather Yehudah was when his wife gave birth to Shelah. Imagine his surprise when he saw the child, alone in the forest in the midst of a violent storm, and who was in danger of drowning! He rescued him and brought him home to Keziv.

Levi raised the child as though he were his own. He called him Shimon, since he didn't know his original name. The young boy developed beautifully. He grew to be exceptionally strong, tall, and good-looking. And he stood out for his intelligence as well. He surpassed all his peers in his studies, and he was the pride and joy of all his teachers. So it was that everyone loved and respected him. Sometimes his classmates would tease him, calling him *asufi* — a foundling, whose origins are not known. But Shimon knew how to defend himself and always fought back well, even when his assailants were older than he was.

Shimon suffered from the fact that he didn't know anything about his true origins. Who was he, who were his parents, and why had they abandoned him? Was he perhaps a child born in sin, who was thus forbidden to marry a Jewess?

His adoptive father consoled him: "Just study Torah and learn well, and one day, when you will become learned in Torah, you will surpass the Kohen haGadol in greatness!"

And Shimon learned zealously. With his great clarity of mind he succeeded in covering all of the Torah even at a very young age. And his great success awakened within him the noble ambition of redeeming his people from all their suffering.

"Oh, if only I could free my people from the terrible yoke of our enemies! If I were to lead them in war against the oppressors, and the trumpets would call us to battle, I would either win like David or fall like Shaul! But then again, who am I? A man without a name, an outcast! How can I dare dream of fighting for my nation? And yet, why would I have to be the leader? If only I could swing my sword against those enemies, I would do it gladly even as the most insignificant warrior in battle! Almighty God, if we are worthy, send us the Mashiach soon, for Israel needs him more than ever! Have we ever been more despised, more oppressed, and more miserable than now? The enemy commands us to worship idols, to work on Shabbos, and to give up circumcision! How I would love to inspire all Jews to unite, to gather courage and strength in order to free ourselves from our bondage. But who would listen to someone like me, an outcast, a foundling?"

One day Shimon came to his adoptive father with a distressed look on his face.

"What is troubling you, my son?" Levi asked.

"I had a dream," the boy answered. "May I tell it to you?"

"Tell me everything, my son!"

"The dream went like this: I was standing on a high mountain gazing at the stars. Suddenly I heard the sound of a trumpet. The sound pierced my soul, and I can still hear it vividly! I have never heard such glorious, sublime sounds in my life! Then a sea of flames spread across the sky and the stars vanished; the sea of flames split, and a huge, powerful army stepped forward. Never has a human being set eyes on such a glorious army! Chariots and horsemen, long columns of warriors armed with glittering weapons, countless banners with the emblems of Israel's Twelve Tribes on them, and Levites with golden harps singing of Israel's golden future! 'What a delight for Israel,' they sang, 'for he's coming, the long-awaited Mashiach is coming!' And then, lo and behold, there was an enormous wagon, pulled by wondrous-looking oxen, which emerged from the flames, and in the wagon stood a warrior, proud and erect. When I looked into his face, I recognized my own features! I fell back in shock, and I woke up from my dream. The vision had disappeared. I looked outside and all that I could see in the sky was the moon. So I sighed and said to myself, 'Woe unto me, that I, the insignificant *asufi*, am dreaming such dreams!'"

Levi replied to him, "Do not be upset, my son... it is indeed a dream to recount. Perhaps we can still clear up the mystery of your background! When I found you, you had a chain hanging around your neck with a Hasmonean coin on it. I will show you."

He went to one of his cupboards and brought Shimon the

coin. At that moment the door opened, and a man entered the room. Levi ran towards him and called out in great joy, "Reuven, my friend! You haven't been to Keziv for many years!"

Reuven did not shake Levi's hand, though. He stood absolutely still and stared at the coin in Levi's hand.

"Levi, where did you get this?"

"It was hanging around the neck of a little boy who had been abandoned in the forest. I saved him from drowning in a pool in the midst of a rainstorm!"

"Where did you find the child? Tell me, Levi, where?"

"Near Beis Lechem."

"And what has become of him?"

"He is a wonderful young boy, pious, good-hearted, refined, and quite outstanding both physically and mentally. Here he is!" Levi pointed proudly to Shimon.

Reuven looked at the young boy, amazed. "Truly," he cried, "Shlomo HaMelech in his youth could not have been more impressive! May God's Name be blessed forever and ever!" He addressed the boy. "Menachem, I am now greeting you as God's anointed one, the savior and redeemer of our people!"

Shimon turned pale. "Me-na-chem?" he stammered. "My name is Shimon."

"No, your name is Menachem," said Reuven. "You are a consoler. ["Menachem" means "consoler"] Your father's name was Chizkiyahu, and he was a descendant of King David's family. I myself put this chain around your neck about 17 years ago. This side of the coin has a palm tree on it; the other should have a grapevine on it. Not long after I last saw you there was a terrible storm and your mother lost you in the forest." Reuven went on to relate everything he knew about Menachem's background and also about the prophecy he had heard about him. Levi and Menachem listened to him, stunned.

All three of them then set out for Beis Lechem. Chizkiyahu and his wife were no longer alive, but many people in Beis

Lechem remembered the whole incident. And soon the word had spread all over that the Mashiach had come. People flocked to Beis Lechem to have a look at the redeemer, but not all of them were swept off their feet.

"Let us hear what Rabbi Akiva in Usha has to say about this!" they said. "He shall decide whether the moment of redemption has indeed arrived or whether this Bar Koziva is a liar!"*

The new Mashiach traveled to Usha with his adoptive father, Reuven, and a large group of followers. When they arrived there, Rabbi Akiva had not yet returned from a visit to Antioch. People were flocking from all parts of the country to see the Mashiach, and to make their own judgments about him. The town of Usha was filled to capacity. People had to camp out in the fields because there wasn't enough room in town to accommodate them. The excitement in the air grew day by day.

---

* This is a play on words, "Bar Koziva" meaning both "a man from Keziv" and "a liar."

Chapter 43

One of the men in the crowd was Rabbi Elazar HaModa'i, who was Menachem's uncle — his mother's brother.

"Indeed," he declared, when he saw him, "you are the Menachem that was lost! You resemble your father in the way that only a son can resemble his father!"

Finally Rabbi Akiva returned and all the Sages assembled around him. This was a crucial moment. If the Sages were to reject the Mashiach, then civil war would erupt in Eretz Yisrael — for the new Mashiach already had thousands of followers who were ready to anoint him as their king, to fight for him, and even to die for him. At the same time, for the Sages to declare him Mashiach would lead to war against the world's capital, Rome, for life or death! But how could they know whether he was indeed the Mashiach or not?

First they would try to clarify what had happened. Reuven stood up at the head of the assembly and spoke about all the wondrous things that had happened to Menachem. Then Levi came and related the story of Menachem's youth. He told them how he found him, and described the way his youth had unfolded — his precocious mental abilities, his exceptional talents and physical strength, his enormous willpower and determination, and his high aspirations and lofty dreams. Rabbi Elazar HaModa'i confirmed his family lineage.

Rabbi Akiva was very excited when he heard all these reports, and almost all of the Sages of the time felt that their greatest dreams and hopes would shortly be fulfilled. Not all the Sages agreed on this matter, however.

Rabbi Yosei ben Kisma argued, "How can we rebel against the huge and powerful Empire of Rome? God has allowed them to destroy His Holy Temple, and we attempt to go to war with them?" Rabbi Yosei ben Kisma was one of the most revered teachers of Israel and the Romans also respected him greatly. They had offered him a highly prestigious position in government affairs, but he had declined because he wanted to dedicate his life to the study of Torah. That is why his opinion carried a lot of weight.

Rabbi Yochanan ben Torta agreed with him. "The time is not ripe for us to expect the coming of the redeemer! Our generation is not ready for it! Grass will have grown over your grave, Rabbi Akiva, and the Mashiach will not have come yet!"

At that moment the door opened and Bar Koziva entered. His impressive appearance was overwhelming. With his imposing height, his noble face, the fire in his eyes, and his aristocratic grace, he captured the hearts of everyone immediately.

"Here is the Mashiach, the King!" Rabbi Akiva cried out in joy. He stood up and walked towards the youth, quoting the verse, "*A star has come forth from Ya'akov, a scepter from Israel*. Edom will be beaten, and Israel will be the victorious hero!"

The youth leapt towards Rabbi Akiva and embraced and kissed him. And the whole crowd of people repeated Rabbi Akiva's words loudly: "*A star has come forth from Ya'akov*!"

From that moment on everyone called the new Mashiach "Bar Kochva" — "the star."

Now that Rabbi Akiva and the Sages had confirmed that Bar Kochva was the Mashiach, Jewish warriors came streaming in from many different countries. Bar Kochva, however, did not accept everyone in his army. Only those who could prove themselves willing to undergo sacrifice, and to be courageous and resilient, were allowed to become God's warriors in the Mashiach's army.

When the news spread of the rebellion in Caesarea, Tineius Rufus, who had acted so cruelly towards the weak and subjugated Jews, made sure to escape immediately. He had divorced his wife, Rufina, long before then.

One day an aristocratic Roman woman with a great entourage arrived in the camp where Rabbi Akiva and Bar Kochva were staying.

"Show me the way to the great teacher of Israel!" she said to the guards.

The guards brought her to Rabbi Akiva. She entered his tent and threw herself at his feet, crying, "Wise and noble man that you are, let me serve you like a humble maid! Let me stay with you! Oh, please don't reject me!"

"Stand up, Rufina. You cannot stay here. You are married to someone else!" said Rabbi Akiva.

"I am no longer married to Rufus! When I told him that I had decided to convert to Judaism, he became very angry and he divorced me. But once I was freed, I immediately carried out my plan. I did as I said I would. I repented and I studied. Rabbi Yehudah ben Bava converted me, and now I am a Jewess. I have come to you, Rabbi Akiva, because there is no one I respect more then you! Please don't turn me away!"

She remained, and Rabbi Akiva married her. All the wealth that she had brought with her they donated to the people of Israel.

Bar Kochva was unusually successful in his first battles; the Judean army seemed to be invincible. They drove the Romans away from all the fortresses in Judea, and they captured Galilee as well.

Bar Kochva had chosen the city of Beitar as his place of residence. Beitar had been a prominent city even before the fall of Jerusalem, but afterwards it gained considerably in status.

When the Emperor Hadrian found out about the uprising in Judea, he was sure he could suppress it with a small army. But after the Jews had succeeded in defeating the Romans in a number of battles, Hadrian decided to appoint one of his best generals, Paulus Martius, for the task.

Bar Kochva stood inspecting his army, two hundred thousand heavily armed infantry, thirty thousand bowmen and light troops, and twenty thousand horsemen. In their midst, a man of gigantic size by the name of Barak carried a banner with the words "A star has come forth from Ya'akov" in gold lettering.

Bar Kochva sat on a throne, with Rabbi Akiva at his side as the entire army marched by, lowering their weapons in respect when they passed in front of the glorious throne.

In the valley of Sharon the enemy was ready for battle. The Jewish army marched out to position themselves for combat, setting up their camp at a distance from the enemy. One could easily tell which of the fires belonged to which side. Every now and then there would be the sound of trumpets warning the warriors of the impending battle. The coming day might determine the fate of the Jews for centuries to come.

At the time of the second shift of the night guards, Bar Kochva left his bed. He went out in front of his tent and glanced with satisfaction at his enormous army. Here they were, thousands of warriors, ready to fight for him.

"Oh, how impressive they look! And I have put this mighty army together! All across the valley, as far as my eyes can see, there are white tents covering the ground! And all those soldiers are willing and eager to go to war for me!"

The day had begun. Bar Kochva sounded the trumpets, giving the signal to attack. With the core of his army he crashed into the center of the Roman camp, creating great confusion among them. The Romans were forced to retreat, and Bar Kochva killed the Roman general with his own hands.

Bar Kochva was already certain of victory. The left wing of his army, though, was not quite as successful. Sulpicius, second in command to Paulus Martius, not only launched a retaliatory attack, but also caused the Jews to scatter in confusion.

Sulpicius was so engrossed in his efforts, however, that he didn't notice how badly the center of the Roman camp had been hit. If Sulpicius had attacked Bar Kochva from the rear after he defeated the left wing, he would have surely defeated the Jews. Now, however, Bar Kochva's keen eye discovered the negligence, and he regained the advantage immediately. He left the Roman center and rushed over to help the left wing. With his own hands he killed Sulpicius and put his legions to flight.

The battlefield was covered with thirty thousand Roman dead. The remaining Romans fled. Some of these were taken captive by the Jews while they were escaping, and some were killed. It was a complete victory for Bar Kochva; his army had suffered only few losses.

Rabbi Akiva embraced Bar Kochva. "May God the Almighty be praised!" he said. "Today He has fulfilled what He promised us through His Prophet Chaggai: 'Just a little more, and I will shake heaven and earth, and I will overthrow the throne of the rich and destroy the power of the heathens!'"

When Hadrian found out about the defeat his army had suffered and about his general's death, he was stricken with worry and fear. At the rate it was going, the Jewish rebellion was threatening to shake the Roman Empire to its core. All the subjugated nations throughout the Empire were longing for freedom and independence, and if they saw that the Jews were succeeding in defeating the Romans, then they too would do everything in their power to overthrow them as well.

Thus Hadrian decided to entrust his best general with the success of this important mission — Julius Severus. At the time he was involved in suppressing the Britons, who were also desperately longing for freedom. Bar Kochva, in the meantime, fortified his territories and readied all his fortresses. The towns of Kabul, Sichin, and Magdala stood out most among all of them. Tur Shimon was also an important locality. It lay in the mountains of Tur Malka, and every Friday three hundred baskets of bread were distributed to the poor there. Bar Kochva fortified this place too, and he assigned one of his generals by the name of Bar Dorma as its commander in chief.

After all these victories, the Jews believed in Bar Kochva more than ever. They were convinced that he was their Heaven-sent Mashiach, and that no one could hold them back anymore from achieving their independence. At the same time Julius Severus was approaching Eretz Yisrael with a mighty Roman army.

Chapter 44

Bar Kochva had conquered over 900 towns and 50 fortresses; Jerusalem, however, was still in Roman hands. As we mentioned earlier, Tineius Rufus had razed the area of the Temple Mount to the ground and had built a temple of idol worship in place of the Holy Temple. Even the name Jerusalem had been changed to Aelia Capitolina, in the Romans' desire to obliterate it from memory.

Bar Kochva had saved the conquest of Jerusalem for the end. He approached the city with his huge army and climbed the city wall with a thousand warriors. They jumped into the city, fought off all opposition, and opened the city gate. The entire Jewish army entered, some of the Roman occupation forces were killed, and others were taken captive. Once again the Jews were in possession of their Holy City.

From all ends of the world Jews came to help rebuild the City of God, to erect new, strong walls around it, and most of all to construct a new Holy Temple. Songs of praise and joy could be heard throughout the city, and the streets that had been desolate were now filled with people. Everyone was busy, bringing stone and marble, cedar wood, acacia wood, clay and mortar, iron and copper, silver and gold — everything that was needed to build the palace for the King of all kings. Men and women, old and young, and girls and boys vied in their efforts to supply the materials. The Kohanim came together to discuss the election of a new Kohen haGadol and to review the laws of the sacrifices. The Levites rehearsed the singing of the psalms and the playing of their instruments for the Divine Service.

The Sages met to discuss their plans of instituting a proper Sanhedrin in the Temple and smaller bodies of this kind in all the cities of Israel. One thing they all agreed upon: Rabbi Akiva would head the Sanhedrin, as the prince of all the teachers of Israel, just like Shimon HaTzaddik, Yehoshua ben Perachyah, and Hillel HaZaken had been in their times.

The temple of idol worship with its pagan images had been destroyed, and the time had finally come for Bar Kochva to lay the foundation stone for the rebuilding of the House of God. The preparations had been made; the whole Temple Mount and all its neighboring streets and squares, were packed with people, and joy and excitement filled the air. Then Rabbi Akiva went up to the podium to speak, and in an instant the whole crowd was utterly silent.

"My brothers!" Rabbi Akiva spoke loudly and clearly. "This is a day of joy and happiness for the House of Israel! Mount Moriah is the holiest place on earth. It was from the dust thereof that God created man. Adam brought his first sacrifice here — the bull that had only one horn on its forehead, and Kayin and Hevel brought their sacrifices here as well, and fire came down from Heaven to consume Hevel's sacrifice. It was here that Avraham Avinu prepared the altar for the sacrifice of his only son, Yitzchak, in obedience to God's commandment. And it was here that God revealed Himself to Ya'akov, and Ya'akov had a vision of a ladder which stood on the ground and reached Heaven, and he could see God's glory on it.

"But the special nature of this place remained hidden from the nations of the world and even from Israel until King David bought the threshing floor of Aravnah and dedicated it to its holy purpose. After King David's death, his son Shlomo, the wisest of all kings, built the Holy Temple. Tyre was the most famous city for crafts at the time. King Shlomo made an agreement with Chiram, King of Tyre, and ordered large, costly stones to be brought to Eretz Yisrael for the foundation of the

Temple. For seven years the most efficient builders and craftsmen, many hired from Tyre, worked at the task with the help of 80,000 woodcutters and 70,000 carriers. And the wisest king of all was also the richest king of all; he imported the most exquisite treasures from all over the world for the Holy Temple. And God Himself blessed the building, so that it became the most magnificent work of architecture on earth. But because of our forefathers' sins, Nevuchadnetzar, the king of Babylonia, destroyed our Holy Temple, and the Jews were taken into exile. Seventy years later God had mercy on us. He commanded Cyrus, the king of Persia, who ruled the Babylonian Empire at the time, to grant the Jews permission to return to their homeland and rebuild the Temple.

"My brothers, that Temple was beautiful as well! I saw it with my own eyes, when I was a young boy, and it was an unforgettable sight to behold! As you know, the Roman Emperors Vespasian and Titus destroyed the Second Temple. Now God in His compassion has sent us His Mashiach so that we shall build the Third Temple, more beautiful and glorious than ever! Peace and truth will reign there, and it will carry the name of God in it; all the nations will come here to say their prayers to the One and Only God of truth! And if we succeed in the final battles that still await us, then the teachings of the Torah will go forth from Zion, and the word of God from Jerusalem! And then we will enter a new era that will bring the blessings of peace and happiness to all the nations of the world! And they will all transform their weapons into benevolent tools of work, and they will no longer have the desire to kill and eliminate each other! Sin will vanish from the earth, and all the nations will recognize that the One and Only God has created the world, that He is the Father of all nations, and that all people are therefore brothers and shall treat each other accordingly.

"This wonderful future I am talking about is something I have always waited for, and I have never given up hope that it would come true. I once came here with my teachers Rabban

Gamliel, Rabbi Yehoshua, and Rabbi Elazar ben Azaryah to pray for Israel in times of terrible danger and persecution. At that moment we saw a fox coming out of the place where the Holy of Holies had been. My teachers cried, but I laughed. They cried because of the destruction of the Temple, and I laughed and rejoiced because I was looking forward to the time when God would fulfill His promise to us. I was happy, for I was anticipating the inspiring and exciting times that we are experiencing now! 'Just as all God's warnings have come true,' I told my teachers, 'so too all the good things He has promised us through the Prophets will surely come true! He will send us His holy redeemer; He will bring us eternal peace; He will rebuild the cities of Judea and the Holy Temple; and His people will thrive on mercy and justice.'

"My brothers, the time of consolation and happiness has arrived! God has sent us the long-awaited Mashiach! *A star has come forth from Ya'akov*, and He is holding high the scepter of Israel which has freed us from the power of Edom. Their armies have scattered, their leaders have fled, and Hadrian is shaken. Edom will continue to fall. All the nations will rise up against them and free themselves of the Roman yoke, until the mighty Roman Empire will crumble!

"And now God's anointed one shall come forth and lay the foundation stone of the Holy Temple! Let us sing to God, let us praise Him and thank Him for answering our prayers and for letting us live to experience this day. Let us cheer loudly, so that the Prophet Zecharyah's words will now come true: 'Thus said Hashem: "I have returned to Zion and I will dwell in Jerusalem."'"

They cheered so loudly, in fact, that the earth shook beneath them and the Temple Mount seemed to tremble. And in time with the music that the Levites played and the songs they sang, the builders walked up to the front of the site to bring the foundation stone to Bar Kochva. It was a stone of enormous weight. Bar Kochva took it in both hands and lifted it high above his head. Everyone was stunned. “This is God’s Mashiach indeed!” they said to one another. “No one else could have lifted that stone!”

Bar Kochva put the stone in the place that the builders had assigned. Rabbi Akiva placed a golden crown, sparkling with diamonds, on Bar Kochva’s head. “Long live the king!” he called out.

And the crowd responded: “Long live the Mashiach, the King, forever and ever!”

Chapter 45

The Jews were in the midst of constructing the Temple, when a delegation of Kutim, Samaritans, came to Bar Kochva. They offered the Jews an alliance with them and asked permission to take part in the building of the Temple.

The Kutim were a heathen nation but they had adopted some Jewish customs. When Shalmaneser, King of Assyria, destroyed Israel, he took the Ten Tribes into exile and brought them to Chalach and Chabor and to the River of Gosen and the cities of Medien. At the same time, he sent tribes from Babylonia, Kutha, Awa, Chamath, and Sepharvayim to Eretz Yisrael, to live there. And so they settled in the capital city Shomron, also called Samaria, and in other cities as well, and therefore they were called Samaritans or Kutim, names which referred to their origins. Since the pagan nations didn't fear God however, God sent out lions against them and the lions killed some of them. Then the King of Assyria was told that the nations he had sent to live in Israel were not living according to the ways of Israel's God, and that God was therefore punishing them. So the King of Assyria commanded the following to his people: "Bring some of the priests that you have driven away from there and send them back to live there and to teach the nations the ways of their God!"

Thus one of the priests who had been driven away from Samaria came back to settle in Beis El to teach them the ways of God. From then on these heathen nations started to honor God, without, however, abandoning all their heathen customs.

The Kingdom of Judea outlasted the Kingdom of Israel by 130 years. Then Nevuchadnetzar, King of Babylonia, captured Jerusalem, destroyed the Holy Temple, and exiled the Jews to Babylonia. Seventy years later God had mercy on the Jews, and under the leadership of Zerubavel, the son of She'altiel, and of the Kohen haGadol Yehoshua, the son of Yehotzadak they returned to Eretz Yisrael to rebuild Jerusalem and the Holy Temple.

And it was two years and two months after they had returned that they laid the foundation of the Holy Temple. It was a very joyous occasion indeed, and the crowd cheered while the sound of trumpets and horns reverberated. When the Kutim found out that the Jews had returned and that they were rebuilding the Temple, they sent a delegation to Zerubavel and other leaders of the nation, saying: "We want to build the Temple with you, for we too have been serving your God and bringing Him sacrifices from the time that the king of Assyria sent us here!"

And Zerubavel and Yehoshua and the other leaders of the nation answered them: "It is not proper for us to build the House of God together with you. We want to build it alone for the Almighty God of Israel."

From that moment the Kutim became the worst enemies of the Jews. They tried to harm them in every possible way: they misled them, complained about them to the Emperor, attacked them, disturbed them while they were building the Temple, and burnt down the new cities and villages. It was only when Ezra and Nechemyah came with a new colony from Babylonia that conditions improved. Nechemyah and Ezra succeeded in bringing the Temple to its completion and in rebuilding the country, and they were able to keep the Kutim under control. This is not to say, however, that the Kutim ceased to hate the Jews; in fact, they continued to look for every opportunity to harm them. When Alexander the Great destroyed the Persian Empire, they succeeded in kindling his anger against the Jews to the point that he wanted to destroy them. Shimon HaTzaddik, who was the Kohen haGadol at the time, made peace with the Emperor, however, and thus he saved his people from ruin.

Alexander had besieged Tyre, and had demanded from the Jews that they come to his aid. But as loyal subjects of the last Persian King Darius Codomanus, who was still alive at the time, they refused to help out their Emperor's enemy. Later on, when Tyre had fallen, and Darius, who was now dying, nominated the King of Macedonia as his successor, the Kutim came to Alexander and persuaded him to march against Israel, conquer Jerusalem, destroy the Holy Temple, and annihilate the Jews.

When the High Priest Shimon HaTzaddik heard about this, he put on the white garments of the priesthood of his office and mounted a white horse. He told his fellow Kohanim to do the same, and together they set out for Alexander's camp.

When Alexander saw the tall and noble figure of the pious Kohen HaGadol arriving, he threw himself to the ground in humility. Startled, his generals said to him: "Conqueror of the world, exalted son of the gods, why do you humiliate yourself in front of that Jew?!"

Alexander replied, "Every time I was about to go into battle, this venerable old man appeared to me in a dream, and I knew that I would be victorious!"

And so Alexander was very good to Shimon and his people, and he gave them free reign over the Kutim. He visited Jerusalem and the Holy Temple and he exempted the Jews from worshipping him as a god. The Jews were very grateful to him, and that year all the Kohanim who had newborn sons named them "Alexander." That is why the Greek name Alexander is considered a Jewish name to this day, and every Jew named Alexander can be called to the Torah by that name.

Needless to say, this did not improve the relationship between the Jews and the Samaritans in the slightest; they remained archenemies. But now that Bar Kochva had won so many victories, they wanted to make peace with the Jews and join them in their uprising against the Romans. The head of their delegation was one of their most aristocratic leaders, a man by the name of Menashe.

Bar Kochva called together his Council to present the proposal of the Kutim. "My friends, I have an important issue to discuss with you," he said. "When God favors a man's ways, He turns his enemies into his friends. For nearly five hundred years the Kutim have been pursuing us — and now they want to make peace. They want to be our brothers, they want to help us defeat the Romans, and they want to rebuild our Temple with us. I believe that we should joyously accept the hand of friendship they offer, for their proposal is a double gain: it reduces the amount of opposition to us and it strengthens our army!"

"King of Israel, your words are puzzling!" Rabbi Akiva exclaimed. "You must be saying this just to test us, to see whether we are fully convinced of your Divine mission, and whether we fully trust in you! Why should we need human assistance if God is with us? Are you suggesting by any chance that the Almighty's Hand is (God forbid) 'too short' to help us, whether we are few or many? Had we been interested in being friends with the Kutim, then we would have made an alliance with them five hundred years ago, when they first approached us! At that time they asked to join us and build the Temple with us as well, and Zerubavel and Yehoshua rightfully rejected them! Our nation must remain pure! We do not want foreign influences."

"But the Kutim have changed since then!" Bar Kochva argued. "They no longer worship idols and they keep some of the Jewish laws even more strictly than the Jews!"

"They do worship idols, just as their forefathers did!" replied Rabbi Akiva. "They bring their sacrifices on Mount Gerizim, even though it is forbidden to bring sacrifices anywhere other than on the Temple Mount in Jerusalem! I have heard that they worship an idol in the shape of a dove. They don't believe in the Oral Law, and they would corrupt and mislead our people if they were to join us! King of Israel, why do you wish to rely on human aid when God, the Almighty, is with us and is overthrowing one enemy after the other for us? We don't need the Kutim! We don't need them and we don't need their help! I therefore advise you to deal with them in the same way that Zerubavel and Yehoshua dealt with them!"

To this, Bar Kochva answered, "Must we voluntarily increase the number of enemies we have? I have just heard that Julius Severus, the greatest Roman general, is on his way here with a mighty army, and we are going to need all our strength to fight him. So now we should force the Samaritans to become our enemies? They live in this country just like we do, and they too know all the mountains and valleys, all the ravines and passes — and they can show the Romans all the secret pathways that lead to our fortresses!"

"Shimon bar Kochva," Rabbi Akiva said in great distress, "are you focusing only on war strategy and diplomacy? Don't you trust in God, in the assistance of the Almighty? Do you think that it is your powerful hand and your strong armies that will bring you success? Didn't Gidon manage to defeat hundreds of thousands of Midianites with an army of only three hundred men? Only God can help us! It is His power that I trust in!"

"Your words are well-founded, Rabbi Akiva!" said Rabbi Elazar. "What you say is true! How can we possibly hope to defeat the enemy if we rely only on our own strength? The Roman Empire is enormous and powerful! Their soldiers are as innumerable as grains of sand at the seashore, and no one is as skilled at war as they! Not one nation in the world has been able to withstand them, and their Empire reaches from one end of the world to the other. How could our own small Judea possibly overcome them?

"In the eyes of God all the nations are as little drops of water on the rim of a bucket, like specks of dust on the scales. It is He, with His bare hand, Who gives size and form to all the bodies of water on earth. And it is He Who holds up the heavens above us and weighs the mountains and hills on His fingers. All the nations are like nothingness before Him. It was only through His help that we have won victories until now, and it is only with His help that we will win in the future! Let the Kutim join our enemies! We don't need their assistance!"

Bar Kochva rose. "I am closing this meeting of the Council," he declared, "and we shall continue to discuss the matter tomorrow."

Chapter 46

One of Bar Kochva's bodyguards by the name of Barak was standing in front of Bar Kochva's chamber with a drawn sword. In the middle of the night Rabbi Akiva approached him and said, "I must speak to the king!"

"I cannot allow it. The king does not want to be disturbed."

"Do you know who I am?" asked Rabbi Akiva.

"You are the man that all Israel looks up to and admires as their teacher and father."

"So then let me enter!"

"I cannot!"

At that moment the door opened and Bar Kochva, in full armor, came out. "Rabbi, it must be something very important that brings you to me at such an hour. Come in!" Bar Kochva sat down and motioned to Rabbi Akiva to do the same.

"Is Israel in danger?" asked Bar Kochva.

"Yes, Israel is in danger!" declared Rabbi Akiva. "Israel is never threatened as long as God, Who never forgets His loyal and beloved children, watches over them. Oh, Bar Kochva, descendant of King David, you were chosen to help your nation! My heart is full of sorrow and worry. You are trying to forgo God's help by turning away from Him and by seeking to play politics and diplomacy!"

Bar Kochva stood up and Rabbi Akiva did the same.

"Beware," Rabbi Akiva said, "that you do not turn away from God's path, neither to the right nor to the left! God has appointed you, but you will be able to fulfill your mission of redemption only if you behave like a man after God's heart — like King David!"

The light of the full moon shone on Rabbi Akiva's imposing stature.

Bar Kochva stood across from him and looked at him intensely. "What do you want, Rabbi?" he asked. "Do I not do everything possible for the sake of my people? You see that I am in full armor — I don't even allow myself to sleep at night!"

"Israel's Guardian neither sleeps nor slumbers," said Rabbi Akiva, quoting words of Scripture. "If God is not building the Temple then the builders will work to no avail, and if God does not watch over the city, then the guards will be of no help. God protects those who love Him, and He gives them in their sleep what others will never acquire even with the greatest effort and concentration."

"What are you asking for, Rabbi?"

"What I am asking for is that our people should be a Godly people, relying on God alone and trusting in His boundless power."

"And should we sit idly, waiting for God to do everything for us?"

"Of course not! We must do our part too, but only that which is right and good in God's eyes. Look, Israel is a nation that must live on its own; we are not supposed to join other nations. Don't misunderstand me — Israel doesn't regard the other nations negatively. Far be it from God's true servants! All people are brothers, for they are all the children of God. And God commanded that one must love his fellowman like he loves himself — not just his brother of the same nationality and religion, but all his fellowmen as well. And this is the most important principle in the Torah.

"We Jews are, however, the chosen people, chosen to be entrusted with a special, exalted mission in our worship of God. That is why we have the Written Torah and the Oral Law, and we must preserve complete purity! But we can only do so if we remain distinct and separate from all the nations. We therefore cannot make a pact with the Kutim. And because they, among all the nations, are closest to us in their thinking and in their beliefs, they are even *more* threatening to us than all the rest, and we must be firm with them!"

"My friend and teacher," responded Bar Kochva, "I am very grateful to you for all that you have done for me. It was your consent that made the people recognize me as their redeemer. I am sorry that we have different views concerning the Kutim, but I must accept their offer! I cannot allow them to turn into our enemies! Look, the mighty Roman Empire is like a tower — once it suffers a blow in the right place, it is bound to collapse. I have shaken its foundations, and soon all the subjugated nations in all corners of the world will rise up against the Romans and overthrow them. Thus every nation that longs for peace is my natural ally. How could I possibly drive the Kutim into the arms of the Romans? They would become our bitterest enemies!"

Rabbi Akiva continued to press Bar Kochva. "You are forgetting that you must view these matters differently from all the other kings in the world! You are a descendant of King David, you are God's Mashiach! God will join with us in war, and with the breath of His mouth He will destroy all our enemies! He will send us His countless angels and they will paralyze the hands of the enemy and render their weapons harmless!"

Bar Kochva smiled. "I don't rely on miracles, my friend. I have faith in my large and powerful army. As long as God doesn't help the enemy, I will be able to defeat the Romans — even without His assistance!"

When Rabbi Akiva heard these words of blasphemy, he tore his clothing in a gesture of grief and cried out. "Bar Koziva, you are not God's Mashiach after all! You are not the long-awaited redeemer whose sole desire is to serve God faithfully! You have just proven to me with your words of heresy that I was living in an illusion. My vision was clouded at the time, but now I see clearly that I was mistaken."

Bar Kochva drew his sword and jumped at Rabbi Akiva, "You are a rebel, Akiva!" he cried out. "I must kill you!"

"Kill me then! I prefer to die than to live with this bitter disappointment!"

Bar Kochva lowered his sword. "No, I won't kill you, because if I did, all your friends would rise up against me and soon the whole nation would follow. So go and tell everyone that I am not the Mashiach! Tell them to abandon me and deliver me to the Romans! And then you can subjugate yourselves to the Romans once again, and they will come and butcher all the defenseless people, without sparing anyone, neither the old nor the young, and not even the baby in its mother's womb!"

"This is a terrible quandary," said Rabbi Akiva. "I don't see any way out! After those words that you uttered I cannot possibly continue to stand at your side! But I am not going to oppose you in public; I will not tell the people to leave you. All the signs that misled me would not have happened if God had not allowed it. And it was He Who gave you superhuman strength, and He will continue to direct the future of our people according to His Holy Will. All those who erred regarding you will have to suffer the bitter consequences! And that includes me as well! But far be it from me to intervene once again and announce publicly that I have changed my views about you! Now I must depart from you, and I will make sure to distance myself from your circles of influence!"

"Rabbi, don't leave me!" Bar Kochva cried out. "Forget the foolish words I said! As you can see, I am still very young. Come and be my guide, for you are older and far more wiser and experienced than I am."

"Very well then," said Rabbi Akiva. "I will forget what you said, although it is hardly believable that such words could have come from the mouth of God's Mashiach. May God forgive you. *I* will forgive you gladly."

Bar Kochva shook Rabbi Akiva's hand and said, "Thank

you, Rabbi. As long as you guide me in your wisdom, I will not succumb!"

"My wisdom can only be of help to you, if you follow my advice! So do as I tell you — and send the Kutim away!"

"Oh no, I can't do that! It goes against all logical reasoning!"

"Logical reasoning is not the deciding factor here!" exclaimed Rabbi Akiva. "The only thing that really holds weight is what our holy Torah commands us concerning the greatest spiritual benefit to our nation! We are not striving for authority and power. All we long for is that the light of truth reign in this world. For us to become allies with the Kutim, even if it means achieving independence, is a greater danger than the Roman yoke of servitude! According recognition to the principles of the Kutim would be like laying an axe to the tree of Judaism!

"God planted the Tree of Life in the middle of Gan Eden, and twelve branches grew out of it, which were to provide shade and shelter for all of humanity. That tree symbolizes Ya'akov our Forefather, and the twelve branches are his sons, the tribes of Israel. And the birds in the sky came and consumed the blossoms and the fruits, and then the caterpillars and beetles came and devoured the leaves, and a horde of monkeys came by and broke off the branches, and a wild man came with an axe and chopped through the trunk. But the roots remained, and the tree was able to grow back and blossom in its full beauty again.

"But if, God forbid, worms undermined the roots of the tree, the tree would surely die! The nations of the world have done a lot of harm to Israel. They have devoured the blossoms and fruits of our tree, they have taken all the leaves from it, they have broken the branches, and Nevuchadnetzar and Titus have chopped through the trunk — but the roots have always remained and we have always been able to flourish again. We must make sure that the roots remain strong and healthy!

"There is no outside force that can destroy Israel. But that requires that the purity of our faith be maintained! If in spite of everything you decide to join the Kutim, then I will have to leave you!"

Bar Kochva answered defiantly, "So go then! It's not the Rabbis that I depend upon in war anyhow! It is with the help of my courageous army that I will defeat the enemy. And I am tired of being led by you and your friends like a child who is tied to its mother's apron strings!"

"You are mistaken," Rabbi Akiva replied softly, "if you think that I am trying to impose my views on you because I want authority and power. Such lowly desires are foreign to me. I have lived over a hundred years already and I have experienced many things. I have always observed and studied everything carefully and attentively, and my sole desire and longing in life has been to sanctify God's Name! I thought that God sent you to sanctify His Name in the world and to fulfill the prophecy, 'And it will be on that day that God will be One and His Name will be One!' It was a fateful error that seized me in its grasp. And now I am leaving you, and I am compelled to do so because of my duty to once again sanctify God! May God have mercy on you and on our nation!"

Chapter 47

The next morning Rabbi Akiva left the city accompanied by his student Peretz. Who was Peretz? A perfect example of the great love Rabbi Akiva had for his people. Peretz's father had been an evil man who spent his life pursuing the vices of this world. Peretz had never known his father, who died before he was born, but nevertheless he appeared to have inherited his sinful nature. Even at a young age he tormented the people of his town, and they dreaded the future, when Peretz would probably do even more harm than his father had done! Then one day Rabbi Akiva came to the town, and he heard all about the notorious boy. He went to see Peretz's mother and asked her if he could take the child with him, to raise and educate him.

"By all means — take him!" she exclaimed. "You will be releasing me and the entire city from the trouble he has been causing us!"

Rabbi Akiva took the boy with him and tried to teach him Torah. Peretz was defiant, however, and seemed to have no interest in learning at all. Rabbi Akiva persisted, and was extremely patient with him. He prayed to God from the depths of his heart that he succeed in reaching out to the boy and opening his heart to Torah. After all his efforts had failed, however, Rabbi Akiva took it upon himself to fast for forty days.

Finally, Rabbi Akiva's tenderness and his boundless love and concern for Peretz won the boy's heart. He started to learn and soon he was able to understand a few *mishnayos*. Then for the first time he said Kaddish for his father in the synagogue.

The Kaddish prayer does not entail any requests concerning the well-being of the soul; it is purely a sanctification of God's Name. We are brought into this world in order to sanctify God's Name; that is the purpose and goal of our lives. Thus when a son says Kaddish for his deceased parents, he gives their souls endless joy.

After Peretz said Kaddish for the first time, Rabbi Akiva heard a voice in one of his dreams: "I am the soul of Peretz's father. Thank you for all the love and care that you give my son. I too am benefiting from it. After my son said Kaddish, I was given a reprieve from the terrible tortures of Gehinom that I was suffering as atonement for all the grave sins I committed. May God reward you generously for your noble and pious pursuits!"

Peretz became devoted to his teacher, and he was overjoyed whenever he could do anything for him.

Now they left Jerusalem together and journeyed to the south of the country. Rabbi Akiva took a donkey with him to carry his belongings and a rooster to wake him in the mornings. They traveled all day long, and when the sun had set they decided to go to the city of Sekonia to find a place to sleep. When they arrived, the guards of the city refused to grant them entry.

"We are not allowed to let anyone in," they were told. "The Romans are approaching, and a traitor could easily dress up as a harmless traveler and try to make his way into the city!"

"Are you telling me," Peretz asked, "that my elderly teacher must spend the night outside, exposed to all the dangers of the night?"

"There is nothing we can do for you."

"But do you know who is asking for entry? He is none other than the great and famous teacher of Israel, Rabbi Akiva!"

"Now it is clear that you are liars!" declared the guard. "Everyone knows that Rabbi Akiva is with Bar Kochva, the King of Israel! He is not wandering around the country!"

The gate was locked, and they stood there all alone.

"Don't be upset, Peretz!" Rabbi Akiva said to his pupil. "Everything that God does is for the good! Let us go into the woods and take shelter under the trees."

They went to the woods nearby to look for a suitable spot. Peretz kindled a fire and lit a lantern which they had brought. Now they had light.

"This is good," Rabbi Akiva said. "Now the wild animals in the woods and the birds of prey will see us and fear us, as it is written, 'And the awe of you and the fear of you will be on all the wild beasts of the earth and on all the birds in the sky.'"

Rabbi Akiva had barely finished his sentence when a sudden rainstorm broke out and extinguished the lantern.

"What should we do now?" Peretz asked in despair.

"We will have to get along without light! Everything that God does is for the good!"

The storm abated, and the donkey and the rooster fell asleep. Rabbi Akiva and Peretz lay down on the bare ground. Suddenly there was a violent roar.

"What is that, Rabbi?" Peretz asked in a trembling voice.

"Be quiet, my son — it's a lion! When the lion roars, who is not afraid?"

The great lion sprang on the donkey and devoured it. After he satisfied his hunger, he went off.

"Our wonderful donkey! Who is going to carry our load now?" cried Peretz.

"Everything God does is for the good!" said Rabbi Akiva. "Let us rejoice that the lion spared us! And now we should go to sleep, so that we can regain our strength to continue our journey tomorrow. Israel's guardian neither sleeps nor slumbers! He will protect us!"

The two of them had barely fallen asleep when a terrible cry awakened them. A huge eagle had come down from the sky, killed the rooster, and carried him away.

"When will the perils of this night come to an end?" Peretz lamented.

"Everything God does He does for the good. May His Holy Name be praised!" Rabbi Akiva said.

It was quiet once again and both of them fell asleep once more. Suddenly they were awakened by the sound of marching. They jumped up and saw soldiers approaching the city of Sekonia with burning torches in their hands.

"Be quiet," Rabbi Akiva whispered. "We must remain utterly silent. The Roman army is on its way to attack the city!"

The Romans used powerful battering rams against the gate of the town. The defenders on the wall shot their arrows down at them and hit many Romans. But the attack went on, and the gate was breached. The Roman warriors broke into the town and plundered and killed. Then they set fire to the town, and withdrew.

Rabbi Akiva said to his student, "Now you can see how God saved us in His great mercy! If the guard had let us enter the city, we would have suffered the same fate as all of the inhabitants! But even the light of our lantern and the sound of the donkey or the rooster would have given us away to the Romans, and they would have killed us! You see, that is why God hardened the heart of that guard — so that he wouldn't have compassion for us, and that is why the storm extinguished our light, and why our animals were killed — to save us from death! Everything God does is for the good! May His Holy Name be praised forever and ever!"

Rabbi Akiva and Peretz continued on their journey, making their way to the south of Eretz Yisrael, where Rabbi Akiva wanted to visit some of his students who, far removed from the turmoil of war, were studying Torah diligently. Maintaining the study of Torah among the people of Israel was his sole concern, and at that time there was a danger of Torah being neglected and forgotten. Of the thousands of disciples that Rabbi Akiva and the other teachers had educated, many had died from the plague, many had been killed by the Romans, and many had joined Bar Kochva's army.

"It says in *Koheles*, 'In the morning sow your seed, and in the evening you shall not let your hand rest,'" Rabbi Akiva said to Peretz. "If you have taught during your youth, then you should make sure to continue in your old age as well, for you never know what will be more productive. I had thousands of students, but only a few of them will be capable of maintaining their Torah study and transmitting it to the coming generations. My high hopes for Israel's future are encouraged by four young men in the south.

"One of them is Meir, who comes from an aristocratic heathen family similar to mine. He once came to join one of my classes, but he was too young at the time and he couldn't follow my lectures. Since then he has learned from Elisha ben Avuyah, who is also known as Acher — 'other' — for his unacceptable views. Meir doesn't allow himself to be misguided by him, however. He is a very learned man, and Meir 'consumes the kernel and discards the husk.'

"The second one is Yosei, the son of one of my former colleagues, Rabbi Chalafta. The third one, Yehudah, is also the son of an old friend of mine, Rabbi Ilai. The fourth one, Nechemyah, is a descendant of the famous Nechemyah who rebuilt the country with Ezra after they returned from the Babylonian exile. May God grant me success in teaching and influencing them, so that they become great Torah scholars so Israel will not be left orphaned!"

When Rabbi Akiva reached the destination of his journey, he found the four young men he had talked about, and they felt very privileged to sit at the feet of the great teacher of Israel. There was a fifth young man among them by the name of Shimon ben Yochai.

Rabbi Akiva addressed him. "Are you not the pupil who once complained to Rabban Gamliel about Rabbi Yehoshua? You will have to leave — I cannot accept you as my student!"

"Please, Rabbi, I cannot and I will not give up the opportunity of being taught by you! Just as a thirsty deer longs for a flowing spring, so does my soul long for Torah!"

"My son," Rabbi Akiva said with a smile, "I cannot combat such vehemence! It is said, you know, that more than the calf wants to suck, the cow wants to suckle it."

"Who is in danger, though, the calf or the cow?" Shimon responded. "Is the calf not in danger of dying of hunger? Save me, Rabbi, from the danger and open your fountains of wisdom to me!"

"First I must ask you a question," Rabbi Akiva replied. "It says in the Torah, 'You shall not tie the mouth of an ox when it is threshing.' Are you allowed, then, to tie its mouth and then lead it to the threshing floor?"

Shimon answered with a different verse: "'Wine and intoxicating drinks you and your sons shall not drink, when you come to the Tent of Meeting.' Would the Kohen be allowed to drink *beforehand* and enter the Sanctuary in a drunken state? Of course not! And likewise it is forbidden to take the ox to the threshing floor with its mouth tied."

"God bless you, my son. I won't hold you back any longer from becoming my student! God has destined you for great things!"

Chapter 48

Bar Kochva concluded the pact with the leader of the Samaritans.

"My nation shall be your nation, my army shall be your army, and we shall fight together against our mutual enemy!" Menasheh said.

"Any harm that is done to your people I will be sure to revenge," Bar Kochva replied. "All the fighting between the Jews and the Samaritans shall be forgotten; all the hatred shall be eradicated! We shall love each other like brothers and become one nation and remain one nation forever!"

There was hardly time for anyone to notice that Rabbi Akiva had left the supposed Mashiach, because very soon after his departure the news came that Julius Severus was approaching Jerusalem with a huge army. He was burning down all the unfortified cities and villages on the way, killing their inhabitants and destroying fields and vineyards. The builders immediately interrupted their work on the Holy Temple; the Levites and the Kohanim ceased their preparations; and the scholars stopped learning. They all hurried to Bar Kochva, eager and willing to fight for their homeland. But the army's morale and idealism were not what they had been. After Bar Kochva made an alliance with the Kutim, and Rabbi Akiva left, the Divine spirit that had rested on Bar Kochva seemed to have vanished.

Bar Kochva was now just a courageous general. He no longer saw himself as God's anointed one who was meant to bring peace and happiness to his people and rebuild the Divine character of the Jewish nation. All of his soldiers had been inspired by his ideals, and this had enabled them to perform miraculously. And now they felt the difference. The warriors knew very well that God didn't need the assistance of the Kutim to rebuild His land and His nation. The uprising had lost its spiritual significance. Now its sole aim was to overthrow the Romans. This in itself, of course, was still a good enough incentive to motivate the fighters and inspire them to great acts of heroism.

Bar Kochva left Jerusalem with his army and they marched out against the enemy. Ten thousand Kutim had joined him under the leadership of Menasheh. The two generals embraced each other in front of their armies and everyone cheered.

Just then a messenger arrived in torn clothing, covered with dust. He threw himself to the ground in front of Bar Kochva and cried out, "I have terrible news, Master! The Romans attacked Sekonia in the middle of the night! They killed the people, stole whatever they could find, and set fire to the city. Only I have escaped to tell the tale!"

The man had barely finished his last sentence when another messenger arrived in similar condition and with a similar report from a different city. And then more messengers followed one another, and they all brought word of terrible calamities. When the soldiers heard this they began to weep bitterly.

Then crowds of refugees began to arrive, who were fleeing from the Romans. They told terrible stories of the Roman massacres and the size and strength of the Roman army, comparing it to a plague of locusts that spread over the land.

"King of Israel, we dare not march out against the Romans and risk a battle against them on open ground," said Menasheh, the leader of the Kutim, to Bar Kochva. "We would have no chance of victory! Our soldiers are inexperienced, while Severus' men have fought hundreds of battles before! But if we just give it some time, we can exploit the fact that their army is so large. They will soon become hungry, sick, and discouraged

— and then we will be able to fight against them successfully! Let us place our forces in Beitar, for it is a large city and it is well-protected. We have huge supplies there, which will suffice not only to sustain our warriors and ourselves, but also those that come to take refuge there. And the Romans can do whatever they please, but they will have no way of passing through the thick walls of Beitar!"

"I like your advice. Let us go to Beitar!" Bar Kochva replied.

Jerusalem was overrun once again, and the Romans destroyed the recently built walls of the Holy Temple. All the walled cities that the Jews had conquered now fell into Roman hands, and the Romans killed their inhabitants; only a few managed to escape. Some of them fled to the mountains and hid in caves, and some of them went to Beitar to join Bar Kochva. There they were received warmly; the spirit in Beitar was one of confidence and hope. Everyone had faith in Bar Kochva's competence and courage. And Bar Kochva was everywhere, directing and organizing everything. People worked day and night to strengthen the walls and fortify the ramparts. Full of trust in their leader, they obediently followed all his commands.

The walls of Beitar were so high they appeared insurmountable; and they were so strong that no Roman battering rams or other device would be able to smash them. And if the enemy tried to scale the walls with ladders, Bar Kochva's men would immediately shoot arrows at them from above, and whoever dared come too close was killed.

Even the children in Beitar were excited and enthusiastic. One day Bar Kochva was riding by on his horse when the school day ended, and thousands of children crowded around him, calling out, "Long live the King of Israel!" And one young boy pushed his way through to Bar Kochva and said, "Lead us into battle against the heathens, oh King of Israel! We will pierce those idol-worshippers with our writing implements!"

Bar Kochva lifted the child onto his horse and kissed him. "What is your name, my child?"

"My name is Shimon, and I am the son of the deceased *Nasi*, Rabban Gamliel."

"You are a worthy descendant of great ancestors! God bless you, my child!"

Shimon had been born when Rabban Gamliel was advancing in years, not too long before he died. He was a child of Rabban Gamliel's second marriage. When Rabban Gamliel died, the boy was brought to his relatives in Beitar to study Torah there. (Rabban Gamliel also had an older son from his first marriage, whose wedding we mentioned above.)

The siege of Beitar had continued for two years already. The Jews remained firm and confident; not so the Kutim, however. They now regretted their pact with the Jews, for they had dreamed of glory, power, and wealth, and they had expected Bar Kochva to guide them to independence. Now none of their expectations had materialized.

"How much longer must we endure this siege?" the servant Efraim asked his master, Menasheh. "Why should we tolerate this misery?"

"I would be happy to make peace with the Romans and subjugate myself to them," replied Menasheh, "but Bar Kochva won't hear of it! Yesterday, in the meeting of the Council, the king's uncle, Elazar HaModa'i, also suggested it very strongly. But the king became angry with him, saying, 'You scholars are all the same! Rabban Yochanan ben Zakkai also had himself secretly brought out of Jerusalem during the time of the Roman occupation, in order to speak to them! Absolutely not! Whoever speaks to me about peace and subjugation shall be put to death!' When I heard that, I was too afraid to admit that I generally agreed with the Jewish scholars! I didn't dare say a word about it!"

"Master, if we could contact the Romans secretly and offer them our help, then we would surely be able to negotiate peace conditions to our advantage!"

"There is nothing I desire more than that," replied

Menasheh, "but how would we go about it? The Jews are suspicious of us anyway; they watch us like hawks. How could we possibly send the Romans a message?"

"Master, I was born in Beitar and I know the city very well! The Romans built it a long time ago, and you know that they always construct secret underground passages. I was once playing in one of the cellars in Beitar with some friends of mine when we found a trap door. We opened it and went down some steps that led into a long passage. At the end of the passage there was a small metal door. When we it pushed it open, we emerged into daylight — far away from the city! After that we closed up the passageway again and went back to the basement. We must have caught a cold in the damp cold underground room, because we all got sick after that, and my three friends died. Therefore I am the only one who knows about that underground passage. If you so desire, I shall follow that passage and go to the Romans to deliver your message to them!"

"Indeed, that sounds like a very promising plan! But first of all you must show me the underground passage, so that in case something happens to you we will know where it is."

The house which Efraim was talking about belonged to one of the Kutim, and therefore no one became suspicious when Menasheh moved his quarters there. He went down into the basement with his servant and he found everything just as Efraim had described it. Then he wrote a letter to the Romans promising to deliver the entire city to them if Julius Severus would set him and all his people free. He gave Efraim the letter and sent him off on his mission.

Julius Severus had grown weary of the siege of Beitar. Since the Romans had devastated the entire country, they had to bring in supplies from abroad in order to sustain their enormous army. It was not unusual therefore that they often lacked the most basic items. His soldiers' health suffered; epidemics broke out and many had succumbed. And so Julius Severus sent a delegation to Rome asking the Emperor for permission to put an end to the siege, since it wasn't achieving its purpose and it was costing the army heavy losses.

Instead of sending him a reply, however, the Emperor Hadrian himself came to Judea to take charge of the siege, hoping to be more successful. But it didn't take very long for him to realize that Julius Severus had been right — that Beitar simply could not be conquered. He had already made the decision to give up on the impossible task and retreat from Beitar when his soldiers brought in a captive who was carrying a message from Beitar. And who was that captive? None other than Efraim the Samaritan!

Chapter 49

Efraim returned to Beitar. He went to look for his master, but he wasn't at home. Lately Menasheh had been pretending to take a great interest in Judaism, in order to dispel any suspicions of disloyalty about himself. Thus he had started attending the great synagogue of Beitar three times a day for prayers. That is where Efraim looked for him next, but the services were over already and the synagogue was empty. Only one man was there, and he was praying with great fervor: Rabbi Elazar HaModa'i! He was beseeching God to save Beitar from destruction.

"That old fool," Efraim murmured to himself. "He is so lost in his thoughts that if the Romans conquered the city he wouldn't even realize it! I will try to get through to him and capture his attention!"

He went up close to Rabbi Elazar and whispered in his ear, "Old fool that you are, what are you trying to do? Your prayers won't redeem the city! The Romans are going to invade it and rivers of blood will flow!"

Efraim was right — Rabbi Elazar didn't even hear him. In the meantime the caretaker of the synagogue had come to lock up the house of worship. He was under the impression that Efraim and Rabbi Elazar were engrossed in a deep conversation, so he waited patiently. Then Efraim left the synagogue and went back to his master's house to look for him again — and this time he was there.

"Oh, Efraim!" Menasheh called out. "I see you have arrived

safely — tell me, what have you accomplished?"

"I have wonderful news! The Emperor Hadrian himself is in the Roman camp."

"And you spoke to him?"

"They brought me to him and he received me cordially. He agreed to everything we asked for. Three days from now Romans will enter the city through the secret passage. They said that we should wear white armbands so that they'll be able to recognize us. Then we should all assemble and open the gates to the Roman army. They will reward us by protecting us from all harm, by granting us full pardon, and by giving us special privileges in the future. The Emperor sends you warm regards; he wants to appoint you to a prestigious position and honor you with glorious awards!"

"You are the bearer of wonderful news, Efraim! Here, take this purse of gold coins as your reward for now — I hope to give you a lot more in the near future!"

Efraim kissed his master's hand gratefully. Then he went to the wine shop to treat himself to a drink as partial compensation for the hardships he had undergone in carrying out his mission. There he found a lot of people, Kutim and Jews alike, discussing the political situation.

"The Romans are in a bad state," a Jewish general by the name of Achiah agreed. "I was standing guard at the wall and we saw the Romans burying a great number of dead!"

"They won't be able to last much longer!" a Jewish officer named Avner agreed. "Hopefully they will soon retreat and leave us alone."

A Jew named Azriel added, "If they retreat, then we will pursue them and kill them! Then they will have to run for their lives, and we will destroy them just like Gidon killed the Midianites in his time! And then their leaders will fall into our hands like Orev and Ze'ev, like Zevach and Tzalmuna!"

In the meantime, Efraim had been gulping down one glass of wine after another. The heavy wine, which he usually diluted, was starting to have an effect on him. Now he jumped up and spoke. "What foolish talk! Just wait and see — very soon the Romans will be entering the city and they will destroy it completely. They will feed your dead bodies to the wild beasts of the field and to the birds in the sky!"

All the people rose and fixed their eyes on Efraim.

"Cursed Samaritan, you are a traitor!" Achiah called out. "I will kill you!"

The other Kutim came rushing over to protect him. "Leave him alone, Achiah!" cried Avimelech, a Samaritan general. "I know this man! He is one of Menasheh's servants. If you dare touch him, you shall die by my sword!"

"Quiet, quiet!" Avner said, as he stepped in between the two sides. "Do we want to start a war between the Jews and the Samaritans? Should we kill each other off and save the Romans the effort?"

"And are we to tolerate a traitor in our midst?" Azriel cried out in rage.

"Very well then," said Avner, "let us bring him to the king! He shall judge the case. If he deserves to be killed, then the king will sentence him to death!"

Everyone agreed with Avner's suggestion, both the Jews and the Kutim.

They seized Efraim and brought him before Bar Kochva. "Master, this Samaritan said with great certainty that the Romans will be entering the city in a few days," Achiah said. "The wine he drank loosened his tongue — as the saying goes, 'When wine goes in, secrets go out.' The man seems to be a traitor! Only you in your Divine wisdom will be able to get to the bottom of this!"

Efraim had become sober again, and in a trembling voice he said, "It's true that it was the wine that made me talk like that, but I am not a traitor. I am a loyal servant of your friend Menasheh."

"Tell me the whole truth!" Bar Kochva said harshly.

"I don't know anything, I don't know anything," Efraim whined.

"Speak — and do so on your own volition, for otherwise I will have to use other ways to make you speak!"

At that moment Efraim thought of an evil plan. He had heard that Rabbi Elazar HaModa'i had promoted the idea of peace with the Romans, in the Council meeting. Now he decided to take advantage of that piece of information. He would make up a convincing story for Bar Kochva, and thereby save himself from death.

"Master, I shall die no matter what I say! You will kill me if I speak and you will kill me if I keep silent!"

"Tell the truth," Bar Kochva said, "and I will let you live!"

"Thank you for your promise, my king!" Efraim said, overjoyed. "In that case I shall not keep anything from you. I will tell you the whole story. An old rabbi by the name of Rabbi Elazar HaModa'i asked me to help him work out a plan that would enable us to deliver the city into Roman hands. This afternoon I spoke to him in the great synagogue. 'The city is lost,' he said. 'Let us try to save whatever we can, just as Rabban Yochanan ben Zakkai did during the siege of Jerusalem. Let us follow the example of the wise woman in Avel Beis-Ma'achah, who threw the head of Sheva ben Bichri over the wall, which satisfied Yoav and induced him to withdraw — thus saving her city.'"

"What? Is my own uncle plotting to kill me?" Bar Kochva cried.

"Yes, indeed! He ordered me to kill you, and he gave me this purse filled with gold coins as a reward in advance. It was because of these coins that I was tempted to go to the wine shop. Here is the gold that Rabbi Elazar HaModa'i gave me!"

He showed Bar Kochva the gold coins that Menasheh had given him.

"I can't believe it, I can't believe it! Bring my uncle to me!"

A few of the servants quickly went to bring Rabbi Elazar.

"Traitor, what have I done to you to make you want to murder me?" Bar Kochva said to Efraim, who was trembling.

"Oh master, you can't imagine how persuasive the old man was! He convinced me that it was a noble, godly act to kill one man in order to save hundreds of thousands of innocent people!"

Bar Kochva was pacing back and forth. "That's how they are, those fanatics, those pious scholars! When they have their principles that they believe in, their own relatives don't mean a thing to them anymore!"

"'He is not God's anointed one,' he said to me," Efraim continued, "'for otherwise he would have killed the Romans with the breath of his mouth. And also Akiva would not have left him.'"

"Ha! Akiva! He's the cause of all the trouble — now I can believe you. They are after me!"

Rabbi Elazar HaModa'i was brought to Bar Kochva.

"What does my king desire?" he asked.

"'My king'? Do you still consider me your king?"

"Why should I not?"

"Well, we shall see if you have remained loyal to me or not! Look at this man!" He pointed at Efraim.

Rabbi Elazar looked at him in surprise. "What about him? I don't know him!"

"You don't know him, eh? Didn't you hire him to kill me so that with my head you could beg the Romans for peace and compassion?"

"How can you believe such a thing of me, my king? I don't know this man, and as far as I know I have never seen him or said a word to him!"

"That's a lie!" Efraim called out. "The synagogue caretaker was there to witness it!"

"Bring in the synagogue caretaker!" Bar Kochva commanded. The servants followed his orders.

Rabbi Elazar was angry, "That man is either insane or a liar! I repeat: I don't know him and I have never spoken to him in my life! It is true that I consider the situation to be hopeless, but all I can do is pray to God that He saves us!"

The synagogue caretaker was brought before Bar Kochva.

"Do you know this man?" Bar Kochva asked him.

"Certainly — who doesn't know Rabbi Elazar HaModa'i?"

"And do you know *this* man?" Bar Kochva pointed to Efraim.

"I don't know him personally, but I have seen him. This afternoon, after the prayers were over, he came to the synagogue. It was empty, and no one was there except for Rabbi Elazar HaModa'i, who always remains to pray for a long time after everyone leaves. Over an hour had gone by since the services ended, and I came to close the synagogue. When I entered, I found these two men in a conversation."

Bar Kochva was enraged. He leaped at his uncle. "Traitor! Do you still want to deny that you have been plotting against me? You are trying to murder me! Now I shall pay you back!"

He lifted his foot and thrust it against the elderly Rabbi with all his might. Rabbi Elazar HaModa'i fell to the floor.

"Look what you have done!" gasped the dying Rabbi. "You have killed your most loyal friend! Dear God, don't punish him for it, be compassionate with him and with my people!"

These were the last words of Rabbi Elazar HaModa'i.

Chapter 50

It was Tishah b'Av, the Ninth of Av, a day of mourning in Jewish history. Nevuchadnetzar destroyed the First Temple on that day and Titus destroyed the Second Temple hundreds of years later on the very same day. The people of Beitar approached the date with a feeling of dread. From the time that Bar Kochva had killed his uncle, his unique spirit had left him completely and he was dominated by sadness and despair. Even his brave soldiers seemed to have lost their faith in him. The siege had lasted for two-and-a-half years already, although supplies had not run out yet and they had everything they needed. The Romans, however, were not showing any signs of retreat. In fact, they seemed to have gained in resolve lately, for they were attacking more frequently and more aggressively than ever. And the Jews were not aware that Hadrian was behind it all.

Suddenly a cry arose in the streets — "*Treason!*" — that could be heard throughout the city. Armed Roman soldiers seemed to be coming out of the ground. Bar Kochva immediately raced to the place where this was happening and commanded his people to occupy the house where the Romans were coming from. But the Samaritans protected the house and more and more Romans streamed out by the minute.

"Menasheh!" Bar Kochva called out. "Are you a traitor?"

"I am not a traitor! I wanted to assist the Mashiach, but you are not God's Mashiach!"

Bar Kochva cried out in despair, "Oh, Akiva! You warned

me against this lying brood! Why didn't I listen to you?!"

A fierce battle raged, and the bloodshed was great. Bar Kochva fought miraculously, and many Samaritans and Romans fell under his sword. It was not too long before he captured the house and his men locked up the secret passage that the Romans had used to enter the city.

In the meantime a group of Samaritans was trying to open the city gates for the whole Roman army outside, but the Jews held them back by their firm resistance. Bar Kochva came to their assistance and soon the danger was averted. At the same time, however, the Roman general launched a heavy assault against the fortifications of the town. The Jews were reaching the end of their strength: They had to fight on two fronts — the Romans on the outside and the Samaritans and Romans on the inside. Then the Roman army succeeded in making a breach in the wall and the Romans poured in through it.

In Beitar everyone become a warrior. Men, women, and children alike took up positions to form a living wall to prevent the Roman's entry. It was a violent battle, and Bar Kochva stood at the head of his loyal people, fighting heroically.

"Ben Koziva!" Efraim called out to him. "Stop this useless fighting! Surrender to the Romans!"

"Traitor!" Bar Kochva screamed, and he hurled a boulder at his head with all his might. Efraim was struck and he fell to the ground.

As he was dying, he said, "Your uncle was innocent, and you are his murderer!"

Bar Kochva was deeply shaken. "Oh God, forgive me for my terrible sin! Let me not fall into the hands of my enemies!"

Bar Kochva leaned against a wall. Suddenly a huge snake came rushing at him from a hole in the wall and in an instant it coiled itself tightly around his neck. Bar Kochva died instantly.

The Romans and Kutim sounded a cry of triumph. One of the Kutim chopped off Bar Kochva's head to bring to Hadrian as a trophy.

The Jews refused to surrender. Although they knew that they had no chance of winning the battle, they were determined to continue fighting until death rather than be taken captive. Yes, they would die, but they would do so with pride. And they would make sure that many of their enemies died as well.

There were 580,000 Jews — men and women, children and old people — in Beitar and not one surrendered. They fought the Romans until the bitter end. All of them died a heroic death.

Among the thousands of children of Beitar, only two escaped. One of them was Rabban Shimon ben Gamliel's son. An old man had taken him by the hand and said to him, "You come from the home of a *Nasi*. I can't let you die!" He brought him into a hidden cellar, and later led him out of the city by night. In later years, whenever Rabban Shimon ben Gamliel would tell the story, he always quoted the verse in *Eichah*, "My eye cries more for me than for all my comrades." He explained that he would have preferred to die like them rather than witness what he had seen.

The Romans also suffered great losses, however, and when Hadrian reported the conquest of Beitar to Rome, he didn't conclude his letter with his usual phrase: "I and the army are doing well," but instead he only mentioned himself. His army was not well.

Hadrian was furious with the remaining Jews, and he appointed Tineius Rufus to execute judgment against them. And once again he destroyed the Temple, which had been partially rebuilt, and he erected the temple of Jupiter in its place. At the southern gates of the city they placed a pig's head in order to anger the Jews, and Jews were forbidden under penalty of death to enter the inner city. It was strictly forbidden to observe the mitzvos, such as of circumcision, the Sabbath, Sukkos, Torah study, and tefillin, and the Jews were punished severely for any violations of the Roman decrees. Roman spies watched the Jews all the time, and whenever they caught them performing the Jewish commandments, they would arrest them. Afterwards these Jews would be tortured to death.

Rabbi Akiva saw his people's suffering and he was filled with compassion and grief for them. Despite the great danger of being caught and sentenced to death by the Romans, he left his hiding place and came to Lod. There he took refuge in the home of a man named Nitzah. From there he sent out messengers to call together the surviving members of the Sanhedrin, who, sadly, were few in number. Most of Rabbi Akiva's colleagues had either died natural deaths or had been killed in the war, or they could not be found, since they were in hiding. Among those who came were Rabbi Tarfon and Rabbi Yosei HaGelili. The Sages held their secret council meetings in an attic.

"My friends," said Rabbi Akiva, "this is a time of great sorrow and distress for our people. However, we have not come together here to mourn and to lament, but rather to consult about how we can survive and go forward despite the destruction that threatens us. The Roman Emperor is executing Jews for keeping God's commandments, just like the Syrian king Antiochus Epiphanes did in his time. We must teach our children to recognize when they must sacrifice their lives for Torah and when they are allowed to transgress the Halachah to survive!"

"You know," Rabbi Tarfon said, "that our great teacher Rabbi Eliezer taught that when we are commanded to worship idols, we must give up our lives rather than transgress. And the same applies to the two other most severe transgressions — murder and illicit relations. These are the three sins which we must always avoid, even at the cost of our lives. One is allowed to transgress the other commandments in a life-threatening situation, as it says, 'And you shall keep My commandments and My laws, which a man should practice, so that he shall live by them' — but not that he shall die by them."

"But when the persecutor is wholly intent on turning us away from God," said Rabbi Yosei HaGelili, "then we are forbidden to transgress even the least of the commandments in order to save ourselves from death. We must therefore be sure to remind our sons and daughters to keep their religious practice as secret as possible, so that they won't come into conflict with the Romans. We must build our *sukkos* in the most inconspicuous manner, and we must try in every way to avoid being seen. Should it happen, however, that a Roman officer forces someone to publicly transgress a commandment, no matter how insignificant that commandment may seem, then that person is obligated to give up his life rather than transgress."

"That is correct, and we must teach all of Israel accordingly," Rabbi Akiva said. "But there is one more issue I would like to bring to your attention. If one commandment or another may be neglected now, then no doubt it will be kept all the more diligently as soon as these stormy times have passed.

"But there is one thing which we cannot tamper with in any way, even in times of greatest danger and sorrow, and that is the study of Torah. For if we try to set limitations to Torah study, then the roots of that endeavor, which will bring us new life in the future, will begin to dry up. Torah study is like a long chain which emanates from Mount Sinai and reaches out to all the future generations. Every generation is a link in that chain, connecting the past with the future. If, God forbid, one generation were to neglect the study of our spiritual heritage, then Torah would be lost for all the generations to come.

"We have been taught that in Judaism deeds are more important than learning and teaching. If someone learns and does not act according to what he learns, he is compared to a farmer who sows the land but does not reap. But in essence, learning is more important, because no one would know what to do without learning about it. That is why we cannot limit Torah study in any way, and we also should not keep it a secret, even if that means subjecting all the teachers to the danger of being killed by the evil Romans."

At that moment everyone rose and called out in unison: "Indeed, learning counts for more than doing, for it is through learning that we are able to do!"

Chapter 51

It was a time of terrible persecution in Judea. The Jews were at the complete mercy of the Roman soldiers. The penalty for killing a Jew was only a small fine. Hadrian pointed the way in his evil behavior towards Beitar's defeated Jews; he didn't even allow the dead to be buried. The Sages considered it a miracle that the corpses didn't decompose or contaminate the area with illness and plagues.

One day Hadrian was taking a walk with his entourage. A Jewish man happened to walk by and he greeted the Emperor respectfully.

"Dog!" the Emperor yelled at him. "How dare you greet me? Hang him!"

Hadrian's guards seized the poor man immediately and hanged him from the nearest tree.

A few days later another Jew was unfortunate enough to pass near the Emperor. He had heard what happened a few days earlier, so he flattened himself against a wall and desperately tried to hide from the Emperor.

"Look at that Jew!" cried Hadrian. "He has some nerve not greeting the Emperor! Hang him!"

Then one of Hadrian's people stepped forward and said, "Great and mighty Emperor, would you be so kind to reveal the wisdom of your judgments to your servants? A few days ago you condemned one of these Jews because he greeted you, and today you want to put another one of them to death because he didn't greet you."

"Yes," said Hadrian, "it's true indeed. You see, I don't care whether these Jews greet me or not — all I care about is hanging them from the trees!"

The Jewish rebellion had shaken the Roman Empire to its core. Suppressing the revolt had cost them heavy losses. None of the Roman generals had been successful, with the result that Julius Severus, whom Hadrian envied and hated, had to be called to the rescue from Britain. As soon as the campaign had come to an end, Hadrian made sure to quickly send the celebrated general back to the far west. The Senate had denied Hadrian the honors of an official triumph, since he had not himself won the victory. All this disturbed him greatly, and increased his hatred of the Jews.

Since Hadrian himself detested the Jews, it was only natural for his officials, headed by Tineius Rufus, to treat the Jews in the cruelest manner. Whoever was caught observing any religious commandments was executed or slowly tortured to death. Jewish informers and spies assisted the Romans in their pursuits. Acher, who himself was very learned, knew well how to put the Romans on the right track, and he spared no efforts. He chased the schoolchildren out of school and told them to learn a trade, and whenever the Jews violated Roman law even in the slightest way, he would immediately report this to the Romans. He thus caused his brethren immeasurable suffering.

In the meantime Rabbi Akiva was living in the south of the Holy Land and he was teaching as usual. Now that the Jews had suffered a defeat as never before, everything seemed to be lost. More than half a million dead lay unburied in Beitar. The remnant of Israel suffered from severe persecution and humiliation; the Romans murdered the finest and most distinguished among them.

Since the Jews had set such high hopes on Bar Kochva, their supposed Mashiach, coming to terms with the bitter reality that ensued was all the more painful. The firm spirit of Rabbi Akiva did not succumb to despair, however. After all the fruits of his lifelong efforts had vanished before his eyes, he still continued his work with the same hope and determination.

Our Sages teach that Moshe's face was like the sun, while Yehoshua's face was like the moon, for just like the moon receives its light from the sun, so was Moshe's light reflected in Yehoshua. Rabbi Akiva's face was also like the sun — but there were five moons surrounding him. Each of his five disciples developed a special field of expertise from what they had learned from Rabbi Akiva.

Rabbi Meir and Rabbi Nechemyah focused mainly on the Halachah as a strictly authoritative and independent entity. Rabbi Meir's halachos, which he had learned from Rabbi Akiva, were to become the foundation of the Mishnah, compiled by Rabbi Yehudah HaNasi and his students and colleagues. Rabbi Yehudah HaNasi was the son of Rabban Shimon ben Gamliel, one of the only two survivors of Beitar. On the other hand, the halachos which Rabbi Nechemyah received from Rabbi Akiva were to become the foundation of the Tosefta. The Tosefta is basically a companion to the Mishnah. It is written in a different form, however, at times more lengthy and at times more abbreviated then the Mishnah, so that it often sheds light on *mishnayos* that are difficult to understand.

Rabbi Yehudah ben Ilai adopted Rabbi Akiva's style of linking the Halachah directly to the written transmission. He was the one who authored the Torah commentaries *Sifra* and *Sifre*, on the third, fourth, and fifth books of the Torah.

The fourth of Rabbi Akiva's students was Rabbi Yosei ben Chalafta, of whom the Sages said that he penetrated the depths of mysticism. And aside from his focus on Halachah, he also took an interest in Jewish history, absorbing the wealth of knowledge his teacher had to offer. Thus, it was on the basis of the historical information which he received from Rabbi Akiva that he compiled the two works *Seder Olam Rabbah* and *Seder Olam Zuta*.

The fifth of Rabbi Akiva's students was Rabbi Shimon ben

Yochai. He too excelled in Halachah, but his main expertise was the field of mysticism — Kabbalah — which he learned from Rabbi Akiva, the master. Rabbi Shimon bar Yochai's understanding of mysticism was so profound that he came to be regarded as its founder. His contemporaries said of him, "Fortunate are the times in which Rabbi Shimon ben Yochai is counted among the living!" He was to become the teacher of Rabbi Yehudah HaNasi.

While Rabbi Akiva invested all his strength in his life's mission, his second wife, Rufina, stood at his side in selfless devotion and loyalty, easing and comforting his later years. In those days he would teach in an open field in the shade of a fig tree. The field belonged to Papus ben Yehudah, a grandson of the very Papus ben Yehudah who had come to Kalba Savua as a suitor of his daughter, Rachel. Now, every day he would come, during Rabbi Akiva's classes, to pick ripe figs from his tree. One day Rabbi Akiva remarked to his pupils, "Does this man perhaps suspect us of eating his figs?"

And so he chose a new place for his lectures. Then Papus came and said, "My teacher, why have you left the shade of my fig tree?"

"Since you came every day during my lectures to pick your figs, I thought perhaps you were concerned that we were eating your figs."

"Please, Rabbi, come back and give your lectures under my tree again!" Papus replied.

And so Rabbi Akiva renewed his teaching at that spot, and Papus no longer came to pick the figs off. But then the figs began to fall off the tree; they had ripened and not been picked in time. They became wormy and inedible. And Rabbi Akiva said to his pupils, "Look at this — the owner of this fig tree knew exactly when it was time to pick his figs! And likewise does God know exactly when to take man from this world!"

Rabbi Akiva was already 119 years old, but his eyesight had not dimmed nor had his mental capabilities or physical strength diminished in any way. He pursued his holy tasks with the same youthful vigor and boundless energy as always. One day it was very hot and humid outside and his students had a hard time concentrating. They were on the brink of dozing off when Rabbi Akiva asked them with a smile, "Who was the woman who gave birth to 600,000 children at once?"

The pupils immediately became attentive, but no one was able to answer the riddle. So Rabbi Akiva answered, "It was Yocheved, the daughter of Levi and the wife of Amram. She gave birth to Moshe Rabbeinu, who raised up all Israel and in his greatness was equal to the entire nation!"

On another hot summer day, when the students were beginning to doze once again, Rabbi Akiva asked them, "How did Queen Esther merit the great prestige of ruling over 127 countries?"

The students once again emerged from their drowsiness, but they couldn't find an answer to their teacher's riddle. Rabbi Akiva answered, "It was through the merit of Sarah Immenu, who lived for 127 years!"

Despite his age, Rabbi Akiva's mind was even sharper than that of his young students.

People kept warning Rabbi Akiva to stop teaching publicly, since it was so dangerous. Once Papus ben Yehudah said to him, "Don't you know, Rabbi, that the Romans have prohibited Torah study under penalty of death? Aren't you afraid of being taken captive and killed?"

"Let me tell you a parable, Papus!" Rabbi Akiva answered. "A fox was walking along a riverbank. He saw the fish swimming downstream in great haste, and he asked them, 'Are you running away from something?' They replied, 'We are running away from people who are trying to catch us in their fishing nets!' 'Then come to me on the riverbank here,' the fox said, 'and you will be able to hide in the woods!' And the fish said, 'Are you really a fox, which is known to be shrewd and clever? Don't you know that water is the source of our life, and if we are not safe here then how can we hope to find security on dry land, where we would die immediately?' So you see, Papus, Torah is the source of our lives, as it is written, 'For she is your life and the length of your days,' and if we were to give up Torah, Judea would die and its name would be erased from the face of this earth! The Torah will always remain the staff of our lives, and it is only within the bounds of Torah that we can hope to find happiness and security!"

Chapter 52

After the Romans had crushed the Jewish uprising and Tineius Rufus was restored to power, he began to miss his former wife, Rufina. He sent out his spies to find out what had happened to her, and they brought back the surprising news that she had married Rabbi Akiva. He immediately gave orders to have Rabbi Akiva and Rufina watched very closely and arrested at the first opportunity.

It was the fifth of Tishrei when Tineius Rufus' guards entered Rabbi Akiva's *beis midrash* and arrested him and Rufina. They threw Rabbi Akiva into prison in Caesarea and brought Rufina to her former husband.

Tineius Rufus smiled at her and said, "Come back to me, Rufina! Everything that ever divided us shall be forgotten and forgiven!"

"I am no longer your wife," Rufina answered. "I am married to someone else and I have converted to Judaism!"

"I know, I know, but that doesn't matter! That man is doomed anyway and after he is executed you will be free to remarry me. If you insist, I'll allow you to remain Jewish."

"Do you think that someone who was married to the noble, wise, and pious Rabbi Akiva could be married to a murderer like you?"

"You call me a murderer? I just obey the Emperor's commands! Rufina, you may ask me for anything you want and I will grant it to you! I will even spare Rabbi Akiva's life for your sake, if you agree to return to me."

"Rufus, I can never marry you again. If I could save Rabbi Akiva's life by giving up my own life, I would do it with the greatest pleasure, but what you are asking of me is too high a price to pay!"

"Rufina, I will give you time to think about it. If you agree with my proposal, then Rabbi Akiva shall be freed; and if not, he shall be tortured to death in the most gruesome manner possible!"

"Your threats are as useless as your pleas! Rabbi Akiva will gladly die for God and for His Holy Torah. Torah is the sole purpose of his existence. This is what he has toiled for all these years and this is what he has lived for throughout his long life!"

So Tineius Rufus sent his former wife to prison too.

Rabbi Akiva's students had followed him to Caesarea. One of them, Yehoshua from Gerasa, brought him water every day so that he could wash his hands before eating bread. One day the prison warden met him on his way and asked him, "What are you doing with all that water? Are you trying to drown the prison?" He grabbed the pitcher out of Yehoshua's hands and poured most of the water out.

Afterwards, when Rabbi Akiva was about to eat his slice of bread, he said to Yehoshua, "Please hand me the water so that I may wash my hands."

"Rabbi," Yehoshua answered, "the prison warden poured out most of the water. What is left is barely enough for drinking!"

"What can I do?" replied Rabbi Akiva. "The Sages prohibited us from eating bread without washing, and whoever transgresses the Sages' proscriptions deserves to be punished with death. I would rather die of hunger than commit a sin."

Yehoshua went to the warden and paid him a large sum of money; then he allowed Yehoshua to supply Rabbi Akiva with water. Rabbi Akiva was able to wash his hands and satisfy his hunger.

When the Torah scholars heard how scrupulous Rabbi

Akiva was in his observance of the mitzvos in spite of his old age and in spite of the fact that he was in prison, they were amazed. "Imagine how devout he must have been when he enjoyed youthful energy and freedom!" they said.

When Tineius Rufus saw that he had no success convincing Rufina to return to him, he decided to use a firmer hand against Rabbi Akiva: He forbade his students to visit him. At this time the Sages were struggling with a certain halachic question which no one felt confident enough to answer: According to Jewish law, a woman who is divorced and has remarried and then either divorces her second husband or he dies, is not allowed to remarry her first husband. The case under discussion here concerned a minor who had dissolved her second marriage with a letter of refusal — *Me'un*. Was she allowed to return to her first husband or not?

The Sages hired a special envoy who knew how to find his way into the prison and could place the issue before Rabbi Akiva. The answer that Rabbi Akiva sent back was that it was forbidden.

Not too long after that, another question concerning the laws of marriage was raised. A widow had carried out the *chalitzah* ceremony with her brother-in-law in a prison [releasing him from the obligation to marry her], for they were both incarcerated. Was this act valid, even though it was done without the supervision of a *beis din*? The Sages could not come to a definite conclusion on their own. And they couldn't find anyone who was willing to try to enter the prison in order to ask Rabbi Akiva, although they were offering a large sum of money to anyone who would try. Finally one of Rabbi Akiva's pupils, Rabbi Yochanan of Alexandria, disguised himself as a peddler and walked through the streets of the city carrying a load of cheap merchandise. When he came to the prison, he called out loudly: "Who wants to buy needles and who wants to buy thread, and how about *chalitzah* done by the brother-in-law and sister-in-law privately?"

Rabbi Akiva's voice was heard through the window of his cell as he called out, "It sounds very kosher!"

There was yet a third time that Rabbi Akiva ruled on a halachic question from his prison cell. The Jewish calendar is based on solar years and lunar months. No nation had a calendar system as carefully planned and accurate as the Jewish one. The calendar of the Christian nations is accurate regarding the years, but not regarding the months. They simply divide the 365 days into twelve months, which have no connection to the phases of the moon. The calendar of the Moslem nations is accurate with respect to the months, but not with respect to the years. They just add the twelve months together to create a year. Since the moon's revolution about the earth takes a little over 29½ days, the months have either 29 or 30 days and thus the year comes out with only 354 days: 11 days too short! Their months and religious holidays are therefore not bound to the seasons, so that they fall in spring, winter, autumn, summer, and then in the spring again. Over a period of 33 years the Moslem months and holidays will have covered the entire cycle of seasons.

The Jewish calendar is completely different; it is exact and accurate in every aspect. Our months are determined according to the phases of the moon, whereas the years are calculated according to the earth's path around the sun. This is achieved by instituting a leap year every so often, in which a whole month is inserted. In a cycle of nineteen years, there are seven leap years, which make up for the difference of 210 days.

The Sanhedrin instituted the leap years, but during Bar Kochva's revolt and for a long time during Hadrian's persecutions as well, the Sanhedrin had been unable to fix the leap years. Thus the Jewish calendar was in danger of falling into disarray. Pesach, for example, must always be celebrated in the spring, but since several leap years had been left out, it became necessary to make up for it. It was a firm principle, however, not to institute two leap years one after the other, and now there was an urgent need to institute even three of them consecutively.

Among all the Sages of Israel, Rabbi Akiva was the only one who was capable of solving the problem. He was the light of the nation, but he was in prison and the chances that he would ever be released were very slight. It was only with great effort and under highly dangerous circumstances that the Sages were able to get an answer from him. He instituted the three consecutive leap years, but he determined that the *beis din* would have to establish them and announce them each time.

Tineius Rufus had ordered that Rufina be brought before him daily. He pleaded with her to come back to him, but she remained firm. It was on the eve of Yom Kippur when Rufina stood before Rufus once again.

"I am asking you for the last time," he told her. " Will you re-marry me?"

"I have told you again and again that I will never do so!"

"Rufina, I will do anything that you ask of me — I will even convert to Judaism!"

"You could never become a pious and God-fearing Jew!" she replied. "You have committed too many crimes and there is no room in your impenitent heart for the love of God. But even if you were to become Jewish, I could never marry someone like you after having been married to the noblest and wisest of men! Look, it says in the Torah: 'There never arose a prophet like Moshe.' That, of course, is true for the prophets; but among the Sages there is one, and only one, person who can compare with Moshe Rabbeinu — and that is Rabbi Akiva, whom I am immensely fortunate to call my husband. So how could I possibly stoop so low?"

"My dear Rufina, you will see that I will find ways to get you back. I have run out of patience! And whatever I have not been able to accomplish with softness, I will certainly be able to achieve with harsher means!"

"You will never be able to force me, Rufus," Rufina said calmly. "I will remain Rabbi Akiva's wife in purity and holiness until the end of my days. And if I am separated from him in this world, then I will rejoin him in the world of eternal bliss!"

She then pulled out a dagger and thrust it into her heart. Rufus leapt up immediately — but it was too late.

Chapter 53

Tineius Rufus was furious. He decided that now he would have Rabbi Akiva tortured to death.

It was in the early morning of Yom Kippur that Rabbi Akiva was brought into the courtyard in front of the prison. A huge crowd had assembled there. Tineius Rufus sat on a high ornamental chair, waiting to witness Rabbi Akiva's suffering.

It was a sorrowful Yom Kippur. The great teacher and father of the nation was the sacrifice of atonement. He had always treated people with love and tenderness. He had reached the age of 120, but he was still strong, his eyes were undimmed, his mind was clear, and his spirit was unbroken.

Rabbi Akiva was tied to a stake. The Roman torturers took burning tongs and began to tear pieces of flesh from his body with them, but Rabbi Akiva did not utter a sound.

Day was breaking. The sun rose above the hills in the east. Rabbi Akiva put his hand over his eyes and called out loudly:

"*Shema Yisrael! Hear O Israel, our God, the Eternal is the Only One! Praised be the name of His kingdom forever and ever! And you shall love your Eternal God with all your heart, with all your soul, and with all your might!*"

"The man is a sorcerer!" Tineius Rufus called out. "He has clearly taken something to make himself immune to pain!"

His students came closer to him, and Rabbi Meir cried out, "Rabbi, Rabbi, our hearts bleed to see you suffer so greatly!"

"My dear children, do not mourn over me! I have attained what I wished for most, the sanctification of God's Name. For eighty years I have longed for the opportunity to sacrifice my life for the sanctification of God's Name, as we say, 'And you shall love your eternal God with all your heart, with all your soul, and with all of your might' — how could one possibly express that love better than to give up one's very soul, one's very life, for God's Name!"

And again he started to recite Shema Yisrael: "*Shema Yisrael, Hashem Elokeinu, Hashem Echad!*"

As he said the last word, *Echad* — "one" — Rabbi Akiva passed away. Tineius Rufus ordered that his body be brought back into the prison, put in a cell, and left there to rot and decay.

That night Rabbi Yehoshua was awakened from his sleep. He saw a man standing before him. "Wake up, Rabbi!" the man said, "and help me bury our great teacher! I am a Kohen and I need your help!"

Rabbi Yehoshua got up immediately and followed the stranger. When they arrived at the prison, they found its doors wide open. The warder and all the guards were fast asleep, and they were able to enter the cell without any hindrances. Rabbi Yehoshua placed Rabbi Akiva's body on a wooden plank that he had brought with him, but he was unable to carry it on his own. So the stranger took the plank too, and helped him carry it. "Didn't you tell me that you were a Kohen?" Rabbi Yehoshua asked him. "That means that you are forbidden to defile yourself by contact with a dead body."

"I assure you, Rabbi Yehoshua," the stranger replied, "that a Kohen is allowed to attend the body of a prince of Torah!"

They walked all night, until they came to Antipras. They went uphill and downhill, and at last they found a cave in the mountains, and there they buried Rabbi Akiva.

They closed up the mouth of the cave, and the stranger spoke: "Fortunate are you, Rabbi Akiva! Your pure soul has passed on to eternal life, and your holy body will rest here in peace until the day comes when God will open all the graves and bring the dead to life again!"

The news of Rabbi Akiva's death filled Israel with dismay and grief. It seemed that the light of Israel had been extinguished, and the springs of wisdom had dried up forever. Rabbi Tarfon, Rabbi Chananyah ben Toradyon, and Rabbi Chutzpis were all sentenced to death and executed, one after the other. Nearly all the old, established teachers were gone, and the young ones had yet not received ordination. (When Moshe appointed Yehoshua as his successor, he had placed his hands on Yehoshua's head, as God had commanded. In the same manner, all teachers grant ordination to their students, giving them in this way authorization to teach and to decide the law, that is *semichah*.)

In the times of the Hadrianic persecution, *semichah* was strictly forbidden. Teachers and students caught transgressing this law were sentenced to death; and even the city in which *semichah* was performed was destroyed. That is how it happened that Rabbi Akiva had not given *semichah* to his students.

Now Rabbi Yehudah ben Bava decided to risk his life and to give *semichah* to Rabbi Akiva's students, namely, Rabbi Meir, Rabbi Yehudah, Rabbi Shimon, Rabbi Yosei, Rabbi Nechemyah, and Rabbi Elazar ben Shammua. He chose a place between two large towns in the Galilee, Usha and Shefar'am, and he placed his hands on their heads. But someone had told the Romans about it: the procedure was barely over when Roman soldiers arrived on horseback.

"Hurry, my children!" Rabbi Yehudah ben Bava said, "Escape! Save yourselves from death!"

"And what about you, Rabbi?"

"Just save yourselves! You carry the future of Israel on your shoulders! I will try to ward off the enemies. While they are venting their anger on me, you can escape."

And thus the young men escaped, and their old master calmly awaited his fate. The Romans slashed him with their swords, and were satisfied. They did not pursue the others.

We read in *Koheles*, "The sun rises after it sets." On the very Yom Kippur that Rabbi Akiva's radiant light had been taken from this world, a baby boy was born who was to bring new light to the world.

Rabban Gamliel's little son, Shimon, who had escaped the massacre at Beitar, had grown up and married; the Sages appointed him *Nasi* of Israel. On the day that Rabbi Akiva died, a son was born to Rabban Shimon ben Gamliel, whom he named Yehudah. Since he circumcised his son in violation of the law, he was brought to court before the Roman governor.

In the meantime, the Emperor Hadrian had become seriously ill. He was tormented by such pain that he begged his servants to kill him either with the sword or by poison. He died on July 10, 138 of the Common Era.

At the time of Hadrian's illness, his adopted son Titus Aurelius Antonius ruled, and Tineius Rufus was afraid to sentence Rabban Shimon ben Gamliel to death; he had been told that the new Emperor was friendly to the Jews.

Rabban Shimon ben Gamliel was called to Rome to defend himself before the Emperor. By the time he arrived, Hadrian had died. Emperor Titus Aurelius Antonius had a mild and kindly nature. He was later on called "the Pious One." As it happened, the Emperor's daughter was ill at the time and Rabban Shimon ben Gamliel succeeded in curing her. Thus he won the Emperor's favor, and he was able to persuade him to abolish Hadrian's edicts against Jewish practices, and also to allow the dead of Beitar to be buried.

When Rabban Shimon ben Gamliel came home with this wonderful news, the Jews in Eretz Yisrael were greatly relieved. To commemorate the occasion, a fourth blessing was added to the *Birkas HaMazon*, the Grace after Meals.

Tineius Rufus was dismissed from his honorable office and he committed suicide.

The Emperor Antonius the Pious had no sons. He adopted Marcus Aurelius Verus (the son of Lucius Aurelius Verus, whom Hadrian had once appointed as his successor, but who had died before Hadrian). Marcus Aurelius Verus added his adoptive father's name, Antonius, to his own. It was he who later became close friends with Rabban Shimon ben Gamliel's son, Rabbi Yehudah HaNasi.

It was a time of peace for Israel, and Rabbi Yehudah made use of this period to put the Oral Law into writing. Rabbi Akiva's *mishnayos*, as transmitted by his disciple Rabbi Meir, became the foundation for Rabbi Yehudah HaNasi's Six Orders of the Mishnah.

Thus does Rabbi Akiva continue to live in our midst. We are all his pupils.